An Unchoreographed Life
JANE DAVIS

Copyright © 2014 Jane Davis

All rights reserved.

Second Edition

Printed and bound in Great Britain by Clays Ltd, St Ives plc. for Rossdale Print Productions

An Unchoreographed Life is a work of fiction. Names, characters, places and incidents are either the product of the author's imagination or are used fictitiously.

No part of this publication may be reproduced, stored in a retrieval system, or transmitted, in any form or by any means, electronic, mechanical, photocopying, recording or otherwise, without the prior permission of the copyright owner.

ISBN: 978-0-9932776-3-4

Cover design by Andrew Candy, based on original artwork by Nejron, Dragoneye, Pakhnyushchyy and Ti-to-tito @ Dreamstime.

FOR VIKKI

Braver than a barrel full of bears

"If I have learnt anything, it is that life forms no logical patterns. It is haphazard and full of beauties which I try to catch as they fly by, for who knows whether any of them will ever return?"
Margot Fonteyn (who referred to her tumultuous off-stage existence as her 'unchoreographed life').

PRAISE FOR THE AUTHOR

'Davis is a phenomenal writer, whose ability to create well rounded characters that are easy to relate to feels effortless.'

Compulsion Reads

'Jane Davis is an extraordinary writer, whose deft blend of polished prose and imaginative intelligence makes you feel in the safest of hands.'

J. J. Marsh, author and founder of Triskele Books

CHAPTER ONE

"I know you're in there, Belle." Although her mother's voice was teasing, it also had a prickly quality. At the first of three knuckle-sharp raps, the girl's head jolted, colliding with the shelf above her, more startling than painful. "It's time to come out of the cupboard and say goodbye to Uncle Sergei."

Curled horizontally, peering out through slanted wooden slats, Belinda could see the rippling silk hem of her mother's turquoise dressing gown. It was the one Mummy called a kimono. She had bought it from a Chinese market before she gave up travelling and made her home in a place called Worlds End, sandwiched, not on a cliff's edge with the roar of the ocean below, or next to the flag at the North Pole, but just beyond the snake in the King's Road where the bus service was excellent. Her mother had christened the estate 'The Land Architecture Forgot', but there weren't too many buildings you could learn about hexagons from, so that had to mean something.

Two pairs of shoes stood side by side: one towering, blister-forming; the other, sensible brown lace-ups. Hand-stitched, a little scuffed at the toes. The type Belinda would later recognise in the windows of old-fashioned men's outfitters and think, *He must have been nice.*

Having accumulated all the wisdom and secret worries that being six can afford, Belinda understood that by insisting she called her friend 'Uncle', Mummy was suggesting that he could be trusted. As opposed to, say, the undercover abductors she was warned lurked outside school gates, elbows poking out of drivers' windows, concealed cameras, a tempting selection of sweets spilling onto the dashboard (Fruity Frogs, Freaky Fish, and so on), ready to pounce the moment your mother's back was turned. For someone with so few known blood relatives, Belinda had acquired a number of uncles.

"Bye, Uncle Sergei," she murmured unenthusiastically, nestling deeper into the spare duvet (second-best, synthetic).

"She's locked herself in!" The door was rattled, tentatively at first.

Children and long-haired cats - strays especially - weren't supposed to lock themselves in the airing cupboard. Whether this rule had been dreamt up by their landlord, Mummy or the prime minister was unclear. No matter: at this moment neither cat nor child cared much for rules. "Don't want to," she muttered.

"Belinda!" Using her full name was intended to ruffle. At home, the girl was usually Belle, only ever Belinda (the name she preferred under friendlier circumstances) when offence had been caused. She wasn't fooled by the sing-song tone of her mother's, "You don't want Uncle Sergei to think you're rude, do you?"

It was a question there was no sensible answer to (at least none that could be made without crossing your fingers behind your back). As far as Belinda could work out - and that was as far as tellings-off suggested - despite everything adults told you, despite promises that you'd *never* be punished for telling the truth, *nothing* was more likely to get you into trouble.

Belinda had been avoiding men ever since Emily's mother's boyfriend had swooped down and kissed her. She had managed to resist the almost overwhelming urge to scrub the kiss off until he'd left the room. She could feel the detestable prickle of it clinging, even after two baby wipes.

"I *know!*" Emily had said, handing her another. "He does it to me *all* the time. And they're *always* doing it."

Few people kissed as reluctantly as Belinda, barely a brush, and then at the furthest point from a mouth that she could reach.

None of her mother's friends ever stayed for tea or sleepovers, thank goodness - not like Emily's mummy's horrible bristly boyfriend, who transformed breakfast into a circus of broken eggshell and tossed pancakes, leaving washing-up piled high in the sink after he had basked in applause.

The fact was, Belinda couldn't care less what impression she made on Mummy's friends. If they thought she was rude, well then, she thought most of them were fat, loud and full of themselves. They carried strange smells - concoctions of beer and aftershave - into the flat and *breathed* them as they bent towards her. Somehow she didn't think, "I don't want to come out, because your yucky friend might try to kiss me," was going to earn her many gold stars for her good behaviour chart.

"Come out of there, Belinda!"

She crossed the fingers of both hands, making a *d* and a *b*. "I can't."

"Are you stuck?" Rattle, rattle.

"No. I'm - I'm busy."

"Busy? Doing *what?*"

Her rumbling stomach betrayed her. In desperation, Belinda turned to consult the coiled cat, the co-conspirator she had christened Ink. Ink was old and not remotely pretty, the point of one ear shredded through too many back-alley encounters, and a permanent bald patch on one thigh owing to a scar. But he had caught her attention by mewing urgently, desperate to communicate something of great importance whenever she passed the garages.

"That one No Good Ca'," their downstairs neighbour, Mr Oo, had observed from the concrete step of his kitchen, tempura batter popping fiercely in the background. She liked Mr Oo, and not just for his name (which she used as often as possible). "You shoot be friends wi' him."

Perhaps Mr Oo had been right. A fat lot of good Ink's Buddha-like expression was now. Whatever wisdom he'd been blessed with he selfishly kept to himself. Belinda's nose wrinkled involuntarily, the way it always did when she was bending facts. "Thinking," she answered, feeling inspired - at least it had the advantage of sounding important.

"You can carry on thinking after Uncle Sergei has left."

"Really, it doesn't matter." His softly-lilting voice was tinged with sadness. "I enjoy a little thinking-time myself…"

The inside workings of the lock revolved. "Belinda, I'm going to count to three and I want you to come out: one, two -"

Her mother bent facts, too. So much for 'This is the *girls' house*. We *girls* have to stick together.' After her chest rose and fell, anger erupted from Belinda's throat. "He's not *my* friend: he's yours! I don't see why I have to -" Ambushed by her own outburst, one of Belinda's hands flew to her mouth. She clamped it in place with the other. Too late. She had broken her own rule: think whatever you like but don't *say* anything.

"*Don't* raise your voice, Belinda! I'm *so* sorry, Sergei," her mother gushed, always more apologetic on account of others than she ever was for herself. (Come to think of it, Belinda couldn't remember ever having heard her mother apologise.)

"I should leave. She'll come out after I've gone."

Startling in their proximity, fingertips alighted on a nearby slat, manicured square nails, unmistakably masculine. A pair of unseeing eyes widened with effort as they appeared directly opposite hers, peering into the semi-dark, with much the same success that Belinda experienced when she once tried looking inside a letter box.

"Goodbye, Belinda. Another time, maybe."

Quietly, she offered up an expression of misery, a half-moan, imagining he would probably be too deaf to hear her whimper, "I have a tummy ache."

"Try rubbing it," the voice whispered back. "That always works for me." The marble eyes blinked; the fingernails slipped away.

Her mother was crooning, "I'll see you out."

"One moment," she heard him reply, then his voice was warm and close by: "Psst. Don't tell anyone, but I have a dog who only speaks Russian."

Belinda heard her own sharp intake of breath. The possibility of a talking dog wasn't a stretch for her imagination, but *Russian?* Actual *Russian?* Like submarines and baddies? Meanwhile, the brown shoes pivoted away and the light was flicked off, plunging her hideaway into darkness. The kind where it made no difference if your eyes were open or shut.

Footsteps paused on the narrow staircase and there was her mother's breezy laughter, voices retreating.

"Your tie's crooked. Here, let me."

The soft low tone of his: "Oh, thank you. You know, I used to hate being paraded by my parents. They forced me to recite poetry for visitors."

The exaggerated enthusiasm of her mother's: "Poetry?"

Up on one elbow, eyes open but unseeing, Belinda hoped her mother wasn't getting any funny ideas. She had never seen the fact that they had so few books, and no space for bookcases, as an advantage. There was rarely even a made-up bedtime story now that Belinda could read and had her library books for practice. But her mother knew one poem off by heart. *Her* poem, the one she had been named after: *The Tale of Custard the Dragon*. She had been lulled to sleep by its rhythms, soothed by the cadences in her mother's voice. There was excitement, too, in the later verses. The prospect of adventure. Once a worrier, always a worrier: Belinda was afraid that, unlike Custard, she wouldn't be ready when bravery was required. And then, from watching *The Wizard of Oz*, she'd learned that the lion who thought he'd lost his courage discovered that all he had needed was a medal. There had never been any doubt that it was Belinda's destiny the poem described. And when they moved to a flat with quite so many stairs - stairs made for chasing lions down - Belinda was pleased by how neatly everything was falling into place. Soon there would be pirates. But, when pressed, her mother now claimed not to remember anything beyond the fifth verse. Perhaps Uncle Sergei, who had been forced to recite poetry, would know what it was the vile pirate gulped from his pocket flagon!

"- or play violin."

Not interested in violins, she settled back down in the dark and experimented with different methods of rubbing her stomach. Up and down, side to side, small circles. It certainly seemed to help.

"You didn't tell me you played an *instrument!*"

"*You didn't tell me you played an instrument!*" she mouthed, pulling faces, safe in the knowledge that there were no witnesses who might tell tales.

"Oh, not for a long, long time. And I was never terribly good."

"I bet you were."

"No, really. I wasn't."

"Well." During the pause, cold air wafted in. "Just say when!"

"Go upstairs and rescue your daughter."

"I'll probably end up having to take the cupboard door off its hinges!"

He laughed (it was a nice laugh).

Belinda listened to the slam of the door, the sound of the lock being drawn, the rush of her mother's footsteps, not stopping, but going all the way up to the top-floor landing. Mummy always showered and changed immediately after visitors left, even if she had only showered and changed half an hour before they arrived. She was very big on saving her nice clothes for best. Most of the time, Mummy wore jeans teamed with a white blouse and, when they went out, she added her pair of enormous sunglasses, which made people wonder if she was a film star.

Belinda waited for the heavy downpour of the shower before she risked unlatching the cupboard door. It swung outwards, allowing dusk to seep in.

Locating the cat's lazy flank with her feet, she flexed her legs. "We've got two minutes, Ink!" He dug his claws into the duvet. "Don't be such a stubborn so and so."

Humming mingled with the sound of running water, then both sounds stopped abruptly, as if the tap controlled dual functions.

"Budge!" Belle kicked the cat's dead weight off the shelf, heard a thump, then clambered down in pursuit - hands in the slats of the upper shelf, one socked foot reaching down, searching, until it came into contact with a lower shelf - to see what damage she'd done. Ink was a black shadow, apparently in one piece. Crouching like you had to when you were in goal, she was ready to shepherd him back on course if he made a dash for the kitchen. He trotted down the staircase, an old-fashioned slope-walking toy, then tucked his head low to tackle the plastic cat flap, the previous tenants' legacy, which Belinda had secretly unlocked.

No sooner had the plastic cat flap flapped its statutory three flaps, her mother's voice was behind her. "So, you've decided to come out, have you?"

Belinda spun, a gasp lodged in her throat. Adopting a pose of innocence, her eyes were especially wide and her smile wavered uncertainly. Her mother was coming down the stairs, fluffy-slippered once again. "And the Oscar for best actress goes to... Belinda Brabbage." Her mother, she knew, felt entitled to be cross. Even now, towel-drying the ends of her hair, Mummy crossed the landing with an elegance an uncoordinated six-year-old could only envy. Then Mummy froze as if they were in the middle of a game of statues. "What's that you've got all over your school uniform?"

Following the direction of her mother's gaze, Belinda scanned the zip of her grey pinafore dress. Telltale black fuzz stood out. Mouth gaping, she looked back up at her mother's make-up-free face as it was transformed.

"You haven't had that flea-ridden moggie indoors, have you?"

It was a mistake to glance towards the airing cupboard.

"Don't tell me..." The little girl winced as her mother turned to open the door. "You know how allergic I am!"

Mummy certainly didn't *like* cats, never stooped to scratch behind their ears, wasn't even that keen to circle around black ones to herd them across her path for luck. "I -" But if an allergy had ever been mentioned, it had slipped Belinda's mind.

"I don't believe it: you have!" Tugging at the spare duvet as if she were a bird and it was a worm she was trying to pull out from hard soil, her mother said, "Fetch me a bin liner, please. Quickly!"

Belinda returned from the kitchen flapping a white plastic bag at arm's length. Surrender was snatched from her, examined and discarded as hopelessly inadequate.

"How am I supposed to fit this great big thing in there? Fetch me one of the black sacks!"

"I don't know where they live," she whimpered.

"Of course you do. They're in the cupboard under the sink."

Hot tears sprung to Belinda's eyes.

The duvet was captured. Dispatching a series of perfectly pronounced sneezes that anyone might have been forgiven for thinking were fake, Mummy pushed the sack downstairs. Without even pausing to watch the avalanche, she began furiously casting pillowcases and sheets onto the floor behind her. The frantic activity was unsettling. Was anything safe? Backing towards the top of the staircase, Belinda watched as tea towels and a tablecloth she couldn't remember having seen before were strewn about.

"I can't wash your uniform. It'll never dry in time for school tomorrow."

Her mother cranked the dial of the washing machine to sixty degrees, ignoring the fact that they were supposed to be saving the planet. Only when the sound of gushing water filled the room did Mummy's hands find time to return to her hips. Head-scratching, she cast her eyes about for a solution - "You and your thinking!" - opening and closing drawers, extracting everything from plastic spatulas to paperclips.

"Sellotape!" she declared at last. "Right. Let's have you standing over here with your arms out."

Rotating the roll, an enquiring thumbnail located the invisible end and prised up a corner. Kneeling on the floor, accompanied by the sharp sound of ripping, Mummy bared her teeth to bite off a strip. For a moment Belinda, who had recently unearthed the Egyptians, wondered if she was going to be mummified. Instead, applying the sticky side to her tunic, her mother pulled the Sellotape away - press, pull away, press, pull away, press, pull away - surveying the bald patch on the material with satisfaction. Hair - human or cat - was quite acceptable while attached. Discarded, the matted strips of tape littering the kitchen floor seemed germy.

Downwards progress was made, towards the crease of the taken-down hem. After a while, her mother forced air out through her nose. "This dress is getting too short for you," she said.

Gazing solemnly, Belinda sensed something else she might be held accountable for. Among her many infuriating habits, growing - and the resultant expense she put her mother to - was her most consistent. Mummy had been furious when she caught Belinda eating an unauthorised bag of prawn crackers. Other people had front doors leading onto streets, but Belinda and her neighbours had only back doors leading to the garages and bin sheds. In the absence of gardens, people took pride in their back steps, decorating them with potted passion flowers trained up short runs of trellis, and concrete sculptures, mainly of the tortoise and frog variety. Wind chimes, strings of seashells and hanging baskets overflowing with pansies were suspended from stray nails. Finding Mummy's arrangement lacking, Belinda had contributed her plastic windmill and a helium balloon (rescued after its escape from a careless street-seller), its silver and pink foil now slack.

"Where did you get those?" her mother demanded.

Belinda had bent protectively over the paper bag nestling in her lap, so that the crater-like crackers couldn't be snatched away. "Mr Oo gave them to me."

The commotion brought Mr Oo scurrying to his back door, wearing a white hairnet, his face a grid through the wire in the glass. "Oh, Mrs Brabbage," he appealed, highly respectful as always. "Only broken bits. Mostly air."

"I'd rather you didn't feed my daughter. I don't want her eating between meals!"

To Belinda, it seemed that her mother rarely ate. At least not meals you could identify as breakfast, lunch or dinner. But she would watch over Belinda, making sure she finished every last pea. It wasn't like that at Emily's house, where you could leave your vegetables and still get a pot of chocolate mousse for afters.

"I understand. Las' time." Mr Oo's expression was genuinely sorrowful when he looked at Belinda before returning to his bubbling cauldron: *What can I do? If she says I can't, I can't.*

Now her mother was sighing. "You're getting so tall."

Experience had taught Belinda it was better not to respond. She had stuck to her mother's no-eating-between-meals rule, even though the constant smell of sweet and sour pork rumbled her tummy, and she'd still grown. In contrast, her mother's neat figure was unchanging. Mummy boasted that she owned dresses that were older than Belinda. She had seen them hanging in the wardrobe on one of the rare occasions she had been allowed in the 'grown-up bedroom', with its big bed and slippery sheets; where nothing was for touching and spare eyelashes were kept in white plastic boxes.

Now her mother cocked her head to one side, tearing a strip of Sellotape away: "This is a bit like waxing my legs."

The pile of discarded strips had grown into a nest. "Why would you want to wax your legs?"

"To keep them nice and smooth."

It hadn't occurred to the child that her own legs were anything other than smooth. "By polishing them?"

"No, silly. You pull the hairs out."

Thinking of the horrible tugging that occurred when a knot became trapped in the teeth of a comb, Belinda opened her mouth, but before she could ask any more questions her mother stole the conversation. "You know what my mummy would have said to me if I pulled a stunt like you did today?" Then she did a deep voice. *"Wait till your father gets home!"*

Belinda held her breath at the sound of the Forbidden Word.

"And my daddy would get home from work, exhausted and starving hungry, and be expected to deal with me before he was allowed to sit down to dinner. But he was never really up to the job, so he would frog-march me to my room and say, *'I take it your mother's already given you a good ticking off?'* and I'd say, 'Yes,' and he would sigh and say, *'Usual drill.'* Then he'd work himself up for five minutes or so, and every time he shouted, *'Do I make myself clear?'* I'd say, 'Yes Daddy.' Then he'd say, *'Right, let's go and eat - and, for God's sake, pretend to look sorry.'* One time, we had sat down at the table and my mummy complained, 'You didn't wait to hear what Alison did.' For a moment, Daddy looked as if he was the one who'd been caught misbehaving, then he trumped her. *'She upset you, love. That was good enough for me.'"*

This wasn't the cue for Belinda to ask about Mummy's parents. Once before, she had commented, "Your daddy sounds nice," only to have her mother snap, "Yes? Well, he wasn't!"

Having discarded her own family quite happily, Mummy seemed to think she could dispel the girl's curiosity with a swift, "Believe me, you don't want to know." But with gruesome secrets hinted at, it had been disappointing to learn that her grandparents were on the list of people who should never be mentioned. Too old to fall for all that sugar-and-spice nonsense, Belinda clung to the smallest nuggets of information, knowing they were vital parts of her flat-pack assembly kit, for which the instructions would arrive any day now, and then she could be complete.

Instead, wondering what her mother was building up to, she asked, "Are you going to shout at me?"

Her mother did the thing where she held both of Belinda's hands, pulled her closer and looked straight into her eyes. It was a position that seemed to have been designed to make it impossible to answer back. "I'm not sure I've got the energy. But, Belinda, you have to understand that Mummy was very worried. I didn't know where you were, and then, when I eventually found you, you'd locked yourself in the airing cupboard -" The sentence trailed off, as if the rest should have been obvious.

The cupboard in the hall was Belinda's nice safe cage. Somewhere warm, where she could be assured of being left alone. Since her mother hadn't asked a question, there was no need to give an answer. So far, she hadn't specifically been banned from the airing cupboard, only from locking herself inside it. The problem was that the door wouldn't stay closed unless you locked it and, without a door, it wasn't much of a cupboard at all. It was really more like shelves. And why would anyone want to lie on a shelf?

"Would you do something else for me?"

Belinda swallowed: a big question was coming. She tried to look willing. An outright ban from her nice safe cage would make things very difficult.

"Would you please *try* to be a little bit nicer to our visitors?" Relieved, Belinda allowed her nose to be tweaked, even though it was one of her least favourite things. Trying was something she could safely agree to. People felt sorry for you if you failed at something, but looked all sad and said, "But I tried *really* hard!"

"You want people to like you, don't you?"

"Yes?" she ventured, although it depended very much who those people were.

"We can't afford for you to behave quite so... so... eccentrically." Sitting back on her heels, her mother bit off another strip of tape.

A safe subject. "What's behaving eggs, eggsent, eggsentric -?"

"Eccentrically. Well, it's locking yourself in cupboards for starters!"

"There's a special word for that?"

"That's just an example. It's the way you're allowed to behave when you're very rich or very famous. Or perhaps very old. But definitely not when you're six years old and live above a bloody Chinese takeaway." Noticing her own slip-up, Mummy bit her bottom lip and looked almost ready to say she was sorry.

With so little idea of who she was, Belinda was unsure how she was supposed to behave. Seeing her mother so sad, she offered a snippet of hope. "I won't be able to fit in the cupboard much longer. I almost don't fit now."

A nod, eyes that glanced away, the twitch of a smile. "That's something to look forward to, then. Come here. I need a hug." Pulled close, damp hair tickled Belinda's nose. "What are you?"

She recited the answer she knew would please, although it was never very clear why. "I'm not perfect, but I'll do."

"Did I ever tell you about a man called John Christie?"

Belinda barely dared to move as she spoke over the top of her mother's shoulder, towards the churning washing machine. "I don't think so." She tried the name combined with hers: Belinda *Christie*. An improvement on Brabbage, but it didn't feel quite right as she rolled it around her mouth.

"He was sitting next to the Queen one evening at dinner" - a story, only a story, not her daddy - "when he took out his glass eye and polished it with his hanky. When he'd finished cleaning it, he popped it back, turned to the Queen and asked, 'Is it in straight, Ma'am?' *That's* what you call eccentric. Perhaps I should be grateful you only hide in airing cupboards!"

It was taken for granted that Belinda would know some people had glass eyes. As far as she was concerned, the most important aspect of the story was completely glossed over while the Queen stole centre stage. As it turned out, the children's librarian from their local library - the second most important person in Belinda's world - was able to supply details of a variety of ways in which eyes could be lost. A collector of useful facts, the girl wrote them down in her notebook, which said *Don't Forget* on the front. (She could do joined-up, especially 'g's and 'y's.) Previously, Belinda had never dreamed that she needed to worry about bottles of Coca Cola exploding, things called brain tumours and 'friendly fights'. (Not *that* friendly, she would think.)

"Sammy Davis Junior." The Librarian was impressed with one of the names that appeared on the list of ten famous people who had glass eyes. "I used to love him!"

"Were you married to him?"

"No!" She burst out laughing. "That really would have made me a child bride! He was a famous singer when I was a very little girl. He acted, too. I saw his films quite a while after they were made."

"How did he lose his eye?"

"Let's see. It says here that he lost it in a car accident."

Belinda had never seen *not* having a car as an advantage before. That was the good thing about facts. If you knew what you were up against, you could stay clear of danger.

While her mother stamped on the pedal of the bin and the lid clanged open, she chased the strips of Sellotape that had escaped.

"We could knit a whole new cat from that!"

"Mummy?"

Her "Mmmmm?" was perhaps intended to suggest that it was time for Belinda to say she was sorry.

"What sort of a name is Sergei?"

Mummy rearranged her narrow shoulders as if she'd been bitten by one of the fleas she imagined Ink was infested with, saying, "A scratchy name."

"He talks funny."

"That's because he's Russian. Now, run upstairs and put your jim-jams on. It's nearly bedtime."

Finding her brow had wrinkled, she rewound the conversation. "He called you Alicia."

"Wasn't that silly of him?" Her mother had extracted a screwdriver from another kitchen drawer.

"Why would he do that? Your name's Alison." Even though she didn't like men, Belinda rather hoped Mummy would get married before long. Not for the dress that would be bought without thought of expense (Emily Ambrose had worn a really pretty bridesmaid's dress at *her* mother's wedding). She would be happy to wear jeans if she could have a new surname that didn't rhyme with cabbage. Even one that rhymed with another vegetable would do.

Brushed past, Belinda watched as her mother examined the inside of the door to the airing cupboard.

"Perhaps it's how they say Alison in Russia."

Timidly, she padded forwards. "Mummy?"

"Yes."

"What are you going to do with that screwdriver?"

"I'm going to get rid of this stupid lock."

"But -"

"One of these days, you'll get stuck inside the cupboard and I'll have to call the fire brigade to get you out. Arghhh!"

Seeing her mother's face crimson, Belinda held her breath waiting to see what would follow.

"Someone's only gone and painted the screw in place. There are layers and layers of the stuff!"

'Lick of paint'll fix that,' was their landlord's favourite saying. Biting her lip in an attempt to hide her delight, it seemed that Belinda's smile was intent on escaping the grip of her teeth.

"What are you still doing here? I thought I asked you to put your jim-jams on!"

Belinda could be as brave as a barrel full of bears now she

knew her hiding space was safe, at least until she outgrew it.
"Yes, Mummy."

"And don't forget to brush your teeth!"

CHAPTER TWO

When she woke, it was to darkness (or Worlds End's version of what passed for darkness). The curtains were fringed with orange streetlight. Female voices - her mother's and another's - vibrated up through her bedroom floor. Their spiralling rise and fall lured Belinda out onto the small and usually musty-smelling landing - something Mr Oo's sweet and sour pork and her mother's experimentation with sprays and candles had failed to get rid of. Now a smoky smell that flavoured the inside of her mouth was masking it nicely. Fire! Her heart began to race. The man on the radio said that more people died of house fires than any other cause. Why hadn't the smoke alarm gone off? Belinda was always reminding her mother to check the batteries, but now she couldn't remember when they'd last tested them. She needed to warn her! Navigating the geography of the woodchip wallpaper, Belinda padded down the steep stairs, counting as she went.

"What about beards?" Mummy was asking, her voice unusually lazy, like a smouldering summer's day.

There was one of those uncontrolled pig-like snorts that some ladies make instead of laughing.

"The only man a beard suits," the unfamiliar voice said, "is George Clooney."

"The others end up looking like Jesus," Mummy continued in her new joined-up voice (except that when she said it, it sounded like Cheesus).

"Or the *Joy of Sex* man!"

Breath caught in Belinda's throat: an Adult Word, one you could only get away with if you were Justin Timberlake. All thoughts of the flat burning down with everything they owned inside it forgotten, she didn't mean to eavesdrop, she really didn't. But was it her fault if they were talking loudly enough for her to hear?

"It's probably before your time."

"*Everybody's* heard of him."

"In that case... stop me if I've told you before..."

"What?"

"My one claim to fame. I modelled for him, you know."

"For the *Joy of Sex* Man?"

"For his book."

On the staircase, Belinda shivered in her thin cotton jim-jams, the legs of which hovered two inches above the sticky-out bones of her ankles. What strange conversations grown-ups had.

"That's not supposed to be *you* in the pictures, is it?"

"No! I was sacked, would you believe?"

"Sacked?"

"There were a few of us models, all from Soho and around. I told him - Charles, his name was - I'll want danger money for some of those positions."

"And?"

"He said, On yer bike. Or words to that effect. The pictures he used in the end? They're of him and his wife."

"If you want a job done properly..."

"Matter of opinion."

More laughter. Strange, too, the things grown-ups thought were funny. They didn't tell jokes, not proper ones like Belinda would. *Doctor, doctor, I swallowed a bone. Are you choking? No, really...*

"The closest I've come to doing anything like that is auditioning for the opening credits of a Bond film."

"Now, *that* sounds glamorous."

"Trained dancers, they advertised for. Then they had us all strip and bounce up and down on trampolines."

"You were a *dancer?*"

"Huh! For all the good it did me!"

There was a pause.

"But, to think: you were almost a Bond girl."

"No. I was only ever almost a silhouette."

Laughter rose briefly to a strange hysteria.

"There's no regular money in dancing, not unless you're the best. That was my last audition."

Mummy sounded sad. Belinda's teacher was always saying you couldn't expect to be the best at everything. Most people only got to be the best at one thing, and that was if they were lucky. Her teacher also said that there was no such thing as 'genius', only the Ten Thousand Hour Rule. Apparently, you could master anything you practised for ten thousand hours. The Librarian disagreed. She said there were Child Prodigies.

"Might they still do ten thousand hours?" Belinda had asked, and so they had done the maths: *416 days (14 months approx) = no sleep. 3 years and 6 months = full-time (with sleep).*

Together, they had read how Mozart (a musician from back in the olden days) had started playing the piano at the age of four and was already making up his own tunes by the age of five. But he was a Once in Every One Hundred Years Talent. "The exception that proves the rule," as her teacher said, giving her a look that said, *No one likes a know-it-all* when she reported their findings back.

For most people, ten thousand hours would take fourteen

years of practice, based on two hours a day. Belinda had found it hard to imagine that length of time, even after a page of complicated diagrams and the almost impossible discovery that she would be nearly twenty-one! "That's a *lot* of practice."

"It certainly is," the Librarian agreed.

"I'd better start right now!" Belinda said in panic, but as yet she hadn't managed to think of anything she might be good at, at least not anything that no one else would have thought of. If she was going to invest fourteen years of her life, she wanted to stand a good chance of being the best.

"I'm out of wine. Shall I get us a refill?" Her mother's slurring was slightly louder. Belinda stumbled forwards as the door opened inwards. Caught red-handed, she looked up, wide-eyed. Transformed by nicotine smog, the room oozed strange perfumes. Both stood staring at the other in a kind of shocked stand-off. Mummy was the first to recover her speech. "Belle, what are you doing out of bed?"

"I - I was -" Belinda managed to stop herself blurting out a lie. For all her mother knew, she might have just arrived at the bottom of the stairs. And she had a strong sense that her mother was equally appalled to be discovered with a wine glass in each hand.

"You were what?"

"I smelt burning, so I came to see if there was a fire." She pinched her nose and held her hand over her mouth for effect.

"Hello." A face appeared around the side of the door with so much smoke surrounding it that its hair might actually have *been* on fire.

Her mother gave a flustered look, her eyes unusually bloodshot. "It's just a cigarette or two."

What could have come over Mummy, allowing a visitor to smoke indoors? Worlds End rules were strict, and there were lots of them, because there was only one of Mummy and she didn't have eyes in the back of her head. A reasonable challenge of, "But everyone else is allowed to," usually led to the response, "Well, you're not everyone else!"

"But the smoke alarm -?"

"I took the batteries out."

Belinda felt as if her breath was being ripped out of her. She couldn't remember when she'd been more astonished.

"I didn't want it to go off and wake you up." Again, that insistence that everything had been changed on her account.

"But I *am* awake." Belinda could actually feel the smoke invading the fabric of her pyjamas, sticking to her hair.

"I can see that now."

On closer examination, from the way its eye make-up had slipped, the face peering round the door looked as if it had been crying. It was clearly putting on a brave performance. An old face, Belinda decided ('old' having been reassessed as above the age of thirty).

"Who do we have here?"

"This is Belle." Her mother brushed past, hands occupied by wine glasses, resorting to her *If you must* voice. Something in the child responded to the woman's delicious aura of danger. "Go and say a quick hello to Aunty Catherine while I get your drink of water."

The woman called Catherine used her teeth to strip the cellophane from a cigarette packet and then bent her head to light another, giving it her undivided attention. Minus the panda eyes, you could imagine her as a screen siren from one of the black and white films Mummy sometimes liked to watch. One who doesn't say much, but everything she *does* say sounds terribly important. *'Oh Larry! How could you?'* Looking closer, Belinda decided the woman might be a witch. Someone who, 200 years ago, would have been dunked in a river.

Seeing she was being watched, the woman beckoned. Small lines pointing towards her mouth and running all the way through her lips, gave her an expression that said it would be rude to refuse. Two steps into the warm October fog of the living room, Belinda offered herself for inspection. Her chest tight, she was forced to fill her lungs with foul-tasting air. Meanwhile, ignoring an even greater number of Worlds End rules, the woman had repositioned herself with *both* feet up to one side on the sofa.

"Between the two of us, I can do without the 'Aunty'. Call me Cat." She spoke with a husky voice, which, together with the narrow eyes of a practised smoker, deepened her allure. "So, you're Belle."

"Belinda," she dared correct her.

"And, you're what? Five?"

Insulted, Belinda made herself taller. "I'm six and three quarters," she said, which was very nearly true.

"Almost a grown-up," the woman said, although Belinda could tell she was being made fun of. Cat's tights were the type called fishnets. One of her big toes looked as if it had been captured while trying to escape. Her toenails were painted a purple so dark it was almost black.

The girl's throat burning, something more seemed to be required. "I can stand on my head," she volunteered impulsively.

"Really?" Taking a long draw on her cigarette, the woman raised her eyebrows, clearly reappraising her initial judgement that she was dealing with a baby.

Credentials established, Belinda nodded.

"That's something I haven't done for a looong time." Wasting no time in depositing her cigarette in the lip of an ashtray (something which had previously been for decoration only), Cat hopped down to floor level and knelt. She planted both hands on the floor, fingers splayed - "Remind me. Is this how you do it?"

Overcoming her disappointment at not being asked to

demonstrate, Belinda, whose expertise was rarely required, tried to be satisfied with being consulted. "Your head makes the top of the triangle."

"Like this?" The woman upended her head, coming up flushed and tousled a few seconds later.

"You might just need a cushion." Belinda selected one, plumping it helpfully. Not her mother's favourite, but one suitable for a visitor. (She had remembered about being nice.)

Returning with full glasses clinking, Mummy addressed Cat's bottom. "What *are* you doing?"

Embarrassed that something perfectly straightforward needed to be explained, Belinda said, "A headstand," as Cat kicked her fishnet-clad heels into the air.

"I can see that." Her mother scanned the room, completing an inventory of potential breakables.

Legs bent and the soles of her feet facing upwards, Cat stayed in position while the wobbling of her head reduced, getting used to the feeling of being upside down. "So far, so good," she said, although her face was turning worryingly red. Every sinew seemed to shake as Cat straightened her legs, pointing her toes in an impressive straight line. Her skirt wavered for a short while, then avalanched. The lacy black shorts Cat was wearing didn't impress Belinda particularly. (She had seen her mother's best underwear drying over the bath.) Neither did the sizeable purple bruise on one of Cat's thighs. (Belinda had had larger ones after she fell from the climbing frame in the school playground.) It was the moment Cat opened and closed her legs, north and south, east and west, as if she was doing the splits, that made Belinda's jaw drop.

"Now you!" Cat declared triumphantly, dropping down and sitting back on her heels.

"I can't do all that yet." The girl scissored her fingers.

"Never mind. Show me what you *can* do!"

Belinda glanced at her mother, whose tight-lipped expression made it very clear that the best way to prevent another gold star being removed from her good behaviour chart would be to say that it was time she was back in bed. If only the opportunity to show off wasn't so hard to resist.

"It's just the first bit really." Hands and head in place, she kicked up her heels. Her legs were suspended for a couple of seconds before they crash-landed. Little more than a bunny hop, she tried again with slightly more enthusiasm.

"Bravo!" Cat wolf-whistled and applauded.

Frustrated that she hadn't been seen at her best, Belinda said, "I'm better with a wall behind me."

"You can work on that. You're most of the way there."

"Alright, time for bed." Her mother held out the beaker of water. "Say goodnight to your Aunty Catherine."

From a kneeling position, Cat held her arms open to receive Belinda. "Come on." The further narrowing of her eyes said, *Never mind*, and, *I promise there'll be another time*.

"Goodnight, Aunty Catherine."

Cat didn't try to kiss her. The words, "Call me that in public and I'll kill you," warmed her ear. Although said in a jokey voice, Belinda thought there was every chance Cat might be serious.

"You'll do," said her mother, smiling and ruffling her hair. "I'll be up to check on you in half an hour."

Hair still settling, Belinda was halfway upstairs when the voice she now knew was Cat's said, "You didn't tell me you had a daughter. She's a sweetie!"

The girl paused to listen, expecting her mother to say, 'Yes, she is, isn't she?' but there was no reply. At least not one she could hear.

"Well, if you ever need a babysitter."

Belinda cheered up at the prospect of evenings with Cat, practising headstands and comparing bruises.

"What? You don't trust me?"

"Thanks, but I try not to go out in the evenings if I can help it."

"How does that work?" There was another elongated pause. "No! Don't tell me you have clients come *here*? But it's not safe!" Disapproval shaded the mature voice, and Belinda agreed. Shouldn't her mother have mentioned she was involved in dangerous work? Perhaps scratchy Uncle Sergei with the Russian-speaking dog had been sent to spy.

"Only a couple of my regulars. Don't look at me like that!"

"To let them know where you live... you have a child to think about!" There was something more than disapproval in Cat's voice. Something that was bound to make her mother cross.

"I think about Belinda! I wouldn't be doing this in the first place if it wasn't for her."

Belinda winced at the sound of her mother raising her voice while using her full name.

The woman called Cat spoke softly. "Oh, now. You don't mean that."

"Knowing there's a child here makes them better behaved. I've never had any problems."

"Take my word for it. Swim with the sharks and you're going to get bitten. And what if Social Services find out?"

"They won't."

"Why do you think you're the exception? It's only a matter of *time.*"

Now it was her mother's turn to pause. "Belinda's normally in bed. Fast asleep."

"Normally?"

"You know how it is. I have to fit around clients' free time."

"And where *is* Belinda when she's not asleep in bed?"

Crouching on the staircase, Belinda held her breath, afraid

that any minute her mother might come to check where she was.

"She's too young to understand what's going on."

"She's seems pretty smart to me. And she's just told me that she's six and three quarters -"

"She's barely six and a half! Listen, I know it's not ideal - but nothing about this is."

"What about your neighbours? They could report you and then what? You'd be out on your ear."

Glass eyes; spies; ears: there was much Belinda didn't understand, but that was all she could cope with for one night. She tiptoed upwards, careful not to make the stairs creak.

The next morning, after her *Rice Krispies* had popped their last, she asked when Aunty Catherine would be coming to help her with her headstands. Her mother set down her black coffee. "Oh, I don't think we'll be seeing Aunty Catherine again," she said cheerfully.

Just like that.

Belinda was stricken. People came and went at Worlds End. She was expected to be polite and entertain them, but just when she thought she might actually like someone, she was robbed of them.

"Because it isn't safe here?" she asked sulkily.

"Shall I tell you what's unsafe?" Her mother pretended to steal her nose. "Doing headstands in the living room, that's what!"

CHAPTER THREE

Belinda's best friend Emily was always saying, "You're so lucky to have a mummy who gets here on time to pick you up from school." Not today, she thought, as she watched her mother shift her weight from one foot to the other and give her the folded-arms treatment. On days like this she would be only too happy to be met by one of a string of childminders, even if they ignored you while they chatted on their mobile phones about absolutely nothing at all. She stuck her thumbs into the straps of her Hello Kitty backpack, took a deep breath and approached.

"I had a very interesting chat with your teacher earlier."

Straight to the point. Not even a 'How was your day?' Incapable of being embarrassed, Mummy didn't seem to be aware that she was blocking the gate. Belinda was going to be told off, right where all her class - and anybody else for that matter - could hear. There were smirks in the voices of girls who pointedly said, *"Bye, B'linda,"* before squeezing past.

She twisted her head, pretending everything was perfectly normal, replying, "Oh, bye, Shelley," and to her mother, "When?"

"She phoned me earlier, but I expect we should both go and see her -"

"See you tomorrow, Belinda."

Even when they didn't jostle her or say anything, she could *feel* them leering.

Not so easily distracted, her mother didn't waver. "Do you know why that was, Belinda?"

Hoping possibilities might be narrowed down, the girl suggested, "She was being friendly?" but her mother was already storming ahead.

"It would be easier if you stuck to the truth. I mean, *hiccups!* Who do you know who's actually had to go to hospital with hiccups?"

"It was in a book I read," she insisted. People hospitalised with hiccups was the sort of fact she and the Librarian collected, but it didn't interest her mother.

"Belinda, this is me you're talking to."

"It was, I swear!" But swearing was banned and her mother didn't look as if she was in the mood to hear about the American man who won a place in *The Guinness Book of Records* by having hiccups for sixty-eight years, which is longer than quite a lot of people live for.

Behind her, girls whose mothers and childminders were late played hopscotch and traded gossip under the watchful eye of teachers.

"And who *is* this Aunty Celia you've invented?"

"*Great* Aunty Celia is the rich one. She hides all her money under the mattress."

"Hah! I don't suppose she'll remember us in her will. Oh, and I forgot to say thank you. A chocolate taster is so much nicer than the last job you gave me. There's only one snag."

Uh-oh.

"Your teacher asked if I might be able to provide a contribution for the tombola."

Belinda winced.

"When she heard that there *is* no Great Aunt Celia and there *is* no dream chocolate-tasting job, she agreed with me that you, young lady, have a very vivid imagination."

Belinda didn't want to sound critical, but couldn't her mother understand that she left her with no choice but to make things up? Having experienced the full range of Mummy's pained expressions, she tried not to plague her with questions. Only that didn't stop everybody expecting *her* to come up with answers.

"Well? I'm waiting..."

Concentrating on the toes of her shoes, she squirmed inwardly. "Every Monday, we have to write about what we did at the weekend." It didn't appear that her mother understood the agony of this weekly torture, so Belinda added, "And then we have to read it out. In front of the whole class," for emphasis.

There was an impatient sigh, the sort that suggested Belinda should accept responsibility for the fact that what she was being taught was a load of rubbish. "And what do the other children write?"

Only last week, Amelia Nicholson had been to a roller disco for her sister's ninth birthday, a wondrous-sounding thing that Belinda hadn't even known existed. (It was a disco, but on roller skates.) Emily's exotic older sister actually now had a *boy*friend of her own (a word that made Belinda's insides turn to worms), although Emily couldn't write what *they'd* been up to, because it was top secret. Several children were racing furiously through a list called *Fifty Things To Do before You Are Eleven and Three Quarters*. But her mother didn't need to hear about hunting for insects and making mud pies. Not when she didn't like getting dirt under her fingernails. "I can't remember exactly."

"Just try to think of one thing. You usually have an excellent memory."

She shrugged and offered a snippet. "Andrew Welsh wrote about what he saw at the zoo."

Her left hand was snatched up and her mother uttered a none too reassuring, "Come on!"

Belinda was a girl who liked warnings. Several if possible. And reminders of what was going to happen when. Nothing spur-of-the-moment was ever a success where the two of them were concerned. "Where are we going?"

"It's a surprise. You like surprises, don't you?"

Belinda strongly suspected that she didn't.

They stood at the top of an escalator. *Be brave*, Belinda reminded herself. But the sight of a never-ending supply of ridged metal steps spewing out gripped Belinda with a variety of panic she'd never had to fret about before. Separating, the steps fell away so steeply she couldn't even see where they ended. Her eyes fixed on other people's feet; feet that simply stepped from the solid floor; trainers and lace-ups and the ones with the pointy heels. *The tiny animals surge forwards, their frenzy takes them plummeting down the terraced cliffs, creating avalanches of soil and rocks, the seemingly indestructible lemmings.*

"After three," her mother was saying.

They reach the final precipice, the last chance to turn back...

"One, two -"

Buffeted by a terrifying blast of cold air, Belinda stepped backwards. Taller people held onto a rubbery black hand-rest. "I can't," she insisted, chin low, hands high in her armpits.

"There's nothing to be worried about. Just hold on to my hand and we'll both step forward at the same time."

Why couldn't Mummy understand she was asking the impossible? A queue was forming behind them. People were side-stepping around them, overtaking on the left. Her mother crouched and said, "There's nothing to be afraid of. It's just a big conveyor belt."

But what if the conveyor belt speeded up? What if the

steps suddenly flattened out and sent you tumbling? What then? Belinda conquered the urge to lie down and kick her heels (she might be trampled) but a howl was building up, one she wasn't sure she could hold inside. Repeatedly accused of 'turning on the taps', she was never given credit for all the times she swallowed them down.

"Just take my h-" As Mummy was interrupted by a loud shriek, Belinda felt her scalp go very hot. A fresh wave of panic washed through her. Something had gone wrong, just as she'd known it would. Two teenage girls started to clamber back up the escalator, exaggerated movements of knees and elbows. It was clear they had been forced to go down. One made it almost the whole way to the top but she was carried away, looking vacant-eyed at Belinda.

Eyes prickling hotly, she might have asked, 'See?' but what Belinda said was, "What if we *don't* step at the same time?"

The way Mummy tucked her hair behind her ear suggested she'd got it into her head that Belinda was playing up, when she was genuinely, properly afraid. "I'll say 'one, two, three' and then we'll both -"

"What if my feet don't move? I might -"

Suddenly, Belinda found she was head-height with small rectangular advertisements: vitamin pills; clinics; theatres; a woman's eye blanked out with chewing gum. The black coat beneath her wasn't her mother's. She pummelled with her fists, shrieking as loudly as she could, heels kicking. Glad her training on what to do when kidnapped came rushing back to her, she was surprised that all her shrieks attracted was passing glares.

"Whoa, there!" her kidnapper said. "London Underground at your service. Your mother's right behind us. Look!" He spun around and there she was, laughing and waving. Belinda fumed. People didn't have a right to go round picking other people up just because they were little.

"Don't drop me!" But she was not, she realised, going to fall. She was riding high.

They waited for the green man at the side of a great wide road with flag poles and evenly spaced lamp posts. Looking at an enormous house at one end of the road, she asked her mother, "Who lives there?"

"The Queen. That's Buckingham Palace."

("Buckingham Palace has seven hundred and seventy-five rooms," the Librarian would tell her later and Belinda, who could only count five rooms in her own flat - excluding halls and landings - would ask, "What for?")

"Will the men in fancy dress be there today?"

"What men in fancy dress?"

"The ones in the metal hats with the feathers in."

"I think you mean *uniform.*"

But Belinda knew exactly what she meant. She had seen them on *Blue Peter*.

The grip on her hand loosened, she was set free inside the gates of a park where she came to an immediate halt, all thought of metal hats extinguished. "What is *that?*" Belinda was face to face with a comical-looking thing: a great white bird with a too-large head. At least as tall as she was, he reminded her of a dodo, something that should be extinct.

"That's what I wanted you to see."

She was in rapture. "What *is* it?"

"It's a pelican.

Belinda liked the feel of words that slipped neatly into place, like pieces of a jigsaw. Trying out the name inside her head - *pelican* - Belinda was dubious. Just as the duck-billed platypus did, it looked as if someone had made the bird from leftovers. The *pelican* was the Mr Potato Head of the bird world. A few too many feathers? Pass the glue. We'll just stick them here on the back of his head.

"That bit under its beak?" she laughed. "It's like the wobbly bits under a fat lady's arms."

"Ssshhh!" her mother said sharply. (It was an unfortunate coincidence that a very fat lady happened to be passing.) "That's his fishing net."

"What is he doing in the park?"

"There are several of them. They were a gift from the Russian Ambassador."

"Uncle Sergei?"

"No, not Uncle Sergei. Where do you get these funny ideas from?"

Having found Belinda lacking in interest, the bird waddled off along the path. "What's he doing now?"

"He's going for a walk, just like everyone else."

The pelican seemed at ease among the tourists. Americans weighed down by carrier bags from Harrods and Hamleys. Japanese teenagers in tartan kilts and cartoon t-shirts, with their cameras and machine-gun voices. Setting off in pursuit, Belinda fell into the pelican's way of walking, side-to-side and straight from the hip. When anyone paid him attention, the pelican's clapper-board bill snatched imaginary treats out of thin air. He crossed a bridge and turned right where another pelican - there were actually *two* of them! - sat on a bench. The second one was smaller. A lady pelican, Belinda presumed. Her webbed feet stuck out over the last wooden slat, expression quite offish, but every so often she risked glancing at the newspaper the old man sitting beside her was reading. The old man seemed to be minding his own business, as if he hadn't noticed that his wife was a pelican. Responding to an inner urge, Belinda moved closer.

"Uh-uh-uh! Don't touch!" came her mother's warning before she even realised she had reached out an arm.

Behind the rustle of his newspaper and under his hat, the man remained faceless.

Knowing that if she protested her mother would say, 'You were going to,' Belinda settled for a question: "What stops them flying away?"

"A supply of food - although someone told me that one of them flies over to London Zoo every day to steal the fish that is meant for the penguins' dinner."

"Yuk." Belinda pulled a face. The only time they had been to a restaurant, she had been served a fish with its head on, bulging eyes blind but staring. And there had been bones like sewing needles that had pricked the inside of her throat. From then on, if someone mentioned 'fish' she made sure they meant fish fingers, otherwise it was definitely a 'No, thank *you!*' "Look! There's another one. Over on the grass." Belinda pointed, her expression a question mark.

"Alright, go on. But don't run off where I can't see you."

She glanced back over her shoulder, without really looking. "I'm only going to -"

"Wait for me by the railings!" And, as an afterthought, "Remember: no touching!"

Belinda came to a halt beside a man in a peaked cap who was throwing chunks of bread directly into the pelican's bill, hardly a challenge for either of them. He delved into his Kingsmill bag and offered Belinda a crust. The smell of stale rose off it. "Want to try?"

No way, José. Mummy would be watching, plus, after her earlier experience in the Underground station, Belinda was done with strange men. Besides, she had already seen a sign saying *Do not feed the Pelicans,* which she assumed applied to her. (Mr Kingsmill might be there in an official capacity. Grown-ups often were.) She shook her head, clamping her mouth shut.

"Go on! Hey, I bet you haven't heard this one. *A marvellous bird is the pelican. His beak can hold more than his belly can.*"

Unable to stop it, a delighted giggle escaped from Belinda's throat.

"He can store in his beak enough food for a week -"

Having extended his arm, the man was holding the bread bag in front of her while looking the other way. She dipped her hand, took a slice, tore off a corner. Belinda misjudged her first throw (it turned out to be more difficult than it looked).

"And I don't know how the hell 'e can."

The pelican's clapperboard bill swung in her direction like the boom of a sailing ship. Instinctively, she pulled her hand back sharply and gasped.

"Alright, youngster?"

Laughing in the reckless way that is only possible when danger has been avoided, she asked, "Will you say it again?"

"You're pushing your luck!" the man retorted, but Belinda could tell he was only pretending.

"I'll remember it properly this time."

"Once more, then. *A marvellous bird is the -*"

"Pelly-can," she populated the gap he left for her.

Looking bored - no doubt he'd heard the limerick many times before - the bird waddled off and snatched greedily at the grass. What followed happened so quickly that the grey-spangled pigeon didn't see it coming - or perhaps he saw it but never imagined he was the pelican's target. Having been hoisted to shoulder-height by a man from London Underground, Belinda could appreciate how the smaller bird must have felt, caught up in the fishing net. A wheezing sound like a bicycle pump attracted more witnesses.

"Gee, will you take a look at that?" A female voice expressed the combination of fascination and horror Belinda knew she should be feeling. On any other day, the woman who had spoken would have held her undivided attention. Almost as wide as she was tall, she was wearing a wrinkled pac-a-mac and an *I love London* t-shirt over bosoms so large they were terrifying. "Jeez! I've gotta get this on film."

"What did I tell you? *His beak can store more than his belly can.*" Mr Kingsmill sighed with the regret of a prophet.

The woman rummaged deep in her rucksack - "Come on, come on!" - her eyes dipping impatiently as if they were a camera taking shots. At the same moment, appreciating the need for panic, the pigeon began to flap. Unable to tear her eyes away from the spectacle, the American operated by Braille. Eventually, she had the cap off the lens of the video camera and dangling on its elastic.

Feeling something press against the middle of her back, Belinda grabbed the arcs of the low railings for balance. She looked round to see if Mummy had come to find her, but saw that several rows of people had arrived, all of them keen for a closer look.

"Careful, careful!" The man with the bread stepped behind her, holding back the growing crush. Wedged between Mr Kingsmill and the amply-proportioned film-maker, the girl was safe to spectate, but there was no question about it: she was going to be in *big* trouble. Mummy wouldn't be able to see her. Nothing she could do about it now, so she decided to concentrate on what was probably the most exciting moment of her life. At last, here was something true that she could write about on Monday!

Nobody seemed sure how they should react. The pelican had raised his bill and was making swallowing movements. Bursts of laughter, nervous and disbelieving, fizzled out. The grown-ups clutched at their necks, exclaiming, "Oh, my God." (Even the foreign one knew how to say that.) Belinda pretended to be watching a cartoon; that what was happening wasn't real. Extending its wingspan, the pelican ploughed straight over the back of an indignant goose, squashing it down. Freed, the goose was prepared to provide an interview to camera, complaining loudly of the humiliation it had suffered, but the woman's attention lay elsewhere. "Come back here, come back!" she was yelling, assuming that pelicans spoke American.

"Do you know any Russian?" Belinda asked helpfully, trying her best not to look at the enormous bosoms. (It might be impolite to look and then *not* make a comment about something so prominent.)

"Russian?" The woman looked bewildered. "Ah, shoot. Throw it some more bread!" she bossed Mr Kingsmill about.

"I think his bill's already full."

"Yuk!" Belinda imagined her mouth crammed full of feathers, the dry texture of them on her tongue. A giggle formed of nerves and revulsion wormed its way out of her throat.

Another pelican - now so familiar, they had lost their novelty factor - sat in the grass, its too-large bill resting on top of a plumped-out breast. *Nothing to see here*, it seemed to say. The Mandarin Ducks and Canada Geese too, even his pigeon friends who might have been expected to be loyal. It was as if they'd all been instructed to ignore whatever was going on.

Still captive in the loose underarm skin of the bill, the pigeon flapped desperately. White down escaped as the clapperboard opened to protest: *why make such a fuss about being eaten?* As a folded grey wing reappeared, Belinda was reminded of how she once extracted from her mouth what she thought was a lump in her hot chocolate, only to find something shiny squirming on its back.

"What is it?" Her hand had jolted and she dropped the thing. It made her feel quite sick, something so ugly, armour plating and pincers, and probably covered in germs.

"It's an earwig."

"I almost *ate* it!"

"Stop scraping your tongue and put it away. The earwig's far more scared of you than you are of it."

But when she'd asked the Librarian to look up how earwigs got their name, the answer was that back in the olden days it was believed they climbed inside people's ears and burrowed into their brains at night (when most bad things seemed to happen). So, really, she'd been right to worry.

"*Belinda!*" Three syllables forced their way through the crush. "*Belinda!*"

Not now, she thought: not when something worth writing about is actually happening!

"*Belinda! Has anyone seen a little girl?*"

Discovery unavoidable, she shouted, "I'm here!" unenthusiastically, hoping the words would drift downwind.

"*Where?*"

"Hey, lady, we were here first!"

Bill facing down and neck taut, the pelican waggled its elastic skin from side to side. The pigeon - still very much alive - made a bid for freedom, forcing the pelican to clamp down and raise his head with several gulping movements.

"*Excuse me but I've lost my little girl.*"

"Let her through, for God's sake!" the American yelled over her ample shoulder. "Before my soundtrack's ruined."

The pigeon appeared to be moving down inside the pelican's neck. "It's jammed," the woman offered unhelpfully. Its grey bulge under the white feathers reminded Belinda of a Christmas stocking.

Her mother arrived out of breath, saying, "There you are! Thank goodness! I thought I told you not to run off." Belinda thought it was probably better not to point out that she had been told to wait by the railings, which was exactly where she was. That was called 'answering back'. Her mother turned and pulled on the jammed straps of her handbag.

Removing the lens of the video camera from her eye just long enough to look Mummy up and down, the squat American said, "I wondered who she belonged to. Asked me if I spoke *Russian*, if you can believe that."

The hand she had left lingering at her neck snatched away, Belinda looked up in time to see her mother's jaw drop. "My God, what *is* that you're watching!" she said, as if she would have liked to point the remote control and change the channel.

"He's eating his dinner." Belinda offered a distraction, knowing her mother wouldn't like to be spoken to in that tone. "But it isn't fish. Guess what it is."

The woman with the video camera carried straight on with her commentary. "See that? It's trying to get out!"

After experimenting with a range of expressions, her mother settled on disgust, which she directed with full force at the American woman. "You're *videoing* this?"

"Who's going to believe me back home otherwise?"

Belinda squeezed her mother's palm. "He swallowed a whole pigeon, Mummy."

"I can see that!"

Belinda thought that perhaps her mother wouldn't have been able to tell. She decided against saying any more. As the smaller bird fought back, she was struck by a thought: perhaps it was the pigeon who was waggling the pelican's neck, not the other way around.

"How long has this been going on for?" her mother asked, concerned, as always, with timing. *We're leaving in five minutes. Half an hour of television. Ten minutes until bedtime,* and so on.

Consulting her camera, the woman confirmed in a bored tone, "Eight minutes forty-two."

Her mother glanced over her shoulder, but there was no way out through the crush unless she was prepared to create a scene. Belinda watched her hand travel slowly down her mouth towards her chin, pawing and pulling at flesh where it hadn't appeared there was any spare.

Turning back to the main event, it was tricky for Belinda

to work out who to feel sorry for. She liked the pelican far more than she liked pigeons (although running at a cluster to make them scatter could be fun). The pelican, on the other hand, was just as big a bully as George Anderson, who acted like he owned the school climbing frame just because his dad was on the PTA. But would the pigeon - who was still alive, by the way - peck away the pelican's insides trying to find his way out? Would he flap about and give *him* tummy ache? That could be good, because then the pelican might spit him out, like the whale spat Jonah out when he couldn't stand any more of his singing.

The pelican shortened his neck and sat. People without the advantage of a front row view, forced to stand on tiptoes or angle their heads to look between gaps, were losing interest. Peeling away from the back, they remembered uneaten picnics, errands as yet un-run and whistle-stop tours that hadn't factored in time for a wildlife diversion.

"That's all, folks." The woman with the video camera sighed.

Belinda caught sight of a crooked sign in the grass that said *Don't Feed the Pigeons*. "Mummy, they should change that to Don't *Eat* the Pigeons." She laughed in encouragement. "Get it?" She had been about to say thank you for bringing her to see such an exciting thing.

Her reward was a brisk, "I don't want you to write about this at school."

"But -" Her mother was gripping her hand and pulling her along. Belinda had to skip to keep up. Surely they were here so that she wouldn't have to make things up!

"People will think you've invented it. You can write about your adventure on the escalator instead."

CHAPTER FOUR

Belinda felt a pinch of fear as she woke to strange screech-like sounds, similar to ones she had heard several nights before.

"It's only foxes," her mother had insisted. "Horrid things, poking around the bin sheds."

'Only' foxes wasn't much of a comfort. It was 'only' foxes who had broken into London Zoo and killed the penguins, even though they'd been doing nothing wrong. (Now, of course, she couldn't help thinking of a penguin stuck in the throat of a fox, and of the American woman with the enormous bosoms filming the whole thing.) And, of course, Mummy didn't realise she had fixed the cat flap so that Ink could come indoors if it was raining. A smallish fox could easily creep inside and come upstairs.

But, despite the threat of germs and the thought of being eaten, the girl wasn't convinced it was foxes. There were the familiar outdoor noises that she felt safe from in her bunk bed with its built-in wardrobe underneath (the only way to fit a bed and a wardrobe into what used to be called the 'cot-room'). She decided to investigate. The lights from the windows of the flats opposite were like hundreds of sparkling stars, spilling in through the parting her mother had left in the curtains. Kneeling up in front of the window, poking her head through the parting, the girl gasped at a ghostly outline. When she realised it was only her mirror image, she said, "You silly-billy!" Her nose went cold as she flattened it against the glass. To someone high up in the tower blocks, Belinda reflected, the light from their living-room window might look like a fallen star. Here at Worlds End, the rest of the world was suspended at arm's length. (It was embarrassing to remember how she used to believe the world stopped turning while she slept.) Raindrops pattered against the glass. Traffic churned steadily two storeys below, punctuated by the occasional blast of a horn. Shouts from older boys on their way home from the pub. She could hear Mr Oo as he gave chase with a raised fist - *"You boys no manners! No manners!"* A snatch of a football chant - *It's all gone quiet over there!*

There were familiar indoor noises, too. The constant murmur from the television set. The flush of the toilet. Footsteps on the staircase. Her bedroom door being nudged open, light spilling in from the landing. The silent pause while her mother waited to see if she was sleeping. Mostly, provided she was nice and cosy, she pretended she was fast asleep so she could enjoy the feeling of having Mummy watch over her. Her duvet would be fluffed or straightened or smoothed around her. Sometimes it was her hair or her forehead that received perfumed attention. She could hear breathing in the dark and it was nice to know that she wasn't alone. Sometimes Belinda forgot she was pretending and said, "I love you, Mummy," after Mummy whispered, "I love you, Belle."

This noise definitely sounded like an inside noise. Muffled, like the sound of her mother talking on the telephone, but, in the middle of the night, it was far more likely to be a monster or a ghost. Although she didn't really believe in them any more - at least not when it was light.

Back under the covers, she chanted, "You don't exist, you don't exist," but the noise ignored her.

"Mummy?" she called out uncertainly, voice trembling.

The noise paused.

"Mummy?"

"Go back to sleep, Belle. It's the middle of the night."

The sound of her mother's voice reassured her. "But I can hear the foxes again."

There was a pause. *"I can't hear anything."*

"Can you come and give me a cuddle?"

"You remember what to do if you're scared, don't you?"

As Belinda tented the duvet around her, the mattress bounced.

"Can you hear me, Belle?"

"Magic duvet."

"That's right. Nothing can get you while you're under there. And if that doesn't work?"

"Zap the shadows."

"That's right. And if that doesn't work, then I'll come in for a cuddle."

The noise started up again.

She clamped her hands over her teddy bear's ears. "Don't worry," she told him, her breathing loud in the confined cave. Six and a half was too old for this sort of thing really, but she needed to practise being brave. "This duvet is magic. We're invisible underneath here."

The noise got louder.

"Are you afraid of the dark? Because, if you are, I can always get Pig."

Allowing her hand to blindly tour her secret hiding place between the mattress and the wooden framework, it located something solid. Ouch! That was her Princess Aurora tiara. She walked her fingers around the crimped edges of the sharp plastic sleeve of her library book until they came across the torch in the shape of a pig; the one that didn't need batteries. "Oink, oink," she greeted it, and, "See, Teddy? I just do it like this." She pumped it in her hand, demonstrating in a worldly manner. "I thought it was broken to begin with, but it's easy to work when you know how."

The beam was cold and blue, and, with all the appropriate sound effects, she zapped the corners of the room and the space underneath her bunk-bed so that anything bad like foxes and ghosts and monsters would turn good. She began to feel a little better.

"Look! I can do one really bright small circle by pointing it downwards, or a bigger woolly shape by shining it from higher up." She found she could even create circles within circles. The beam highlighted ridges and creases in the sheet. "Did you know those mountains were there? I didn't either." It made the hand holding Pig seem too large for her wrist.

The noise still wouldn't go away. If anything, it was getting louder.

"What's that, Teddy? You want a story? Alright then. But only a short one, because I've got school in the morning."

If Belinda was completely honest, the book she was reading at the moment was a bit too difficult, although she had managed to fool the teaching assistant by skipping the long words and describing what she saw in the pictures.

"Once upon a time." But, even pointing to individual words with a finger, it was too hard to concentrate. Instead, cocooned under the duvet she began imitating the noise.

"It's like earwiggles," she told her teddy (this was the name she had invented to make them sound friendlier). "It's probably more scared of us than we are of it."

But then she had to stick her fingers in her ears, to be on the safe side. You never knew what might happen in the middle of the night.

CHAPTER FIVE

"Half an hour of television," her mother said, pointing the remote control at the set and switching over to BBC1. She scowled at *The Tweenies* (boring!) for a couple of minutes and then said, "Can I trust you to sit nicely while I make your dinner?"

"Yes," Belinda replied, confident that sitting wasn't something she could get wrong. She sat very straight on the sofa as if to prove it to herself, socked feet overhanging, heels not even close to touching the cushions. Two minutes later, the kitchen radio was playing something dancey. Knowing for a fact that her mother wouldn't be able to hear her, she turned over to BBC2. There was a typical lion - a larger version of Ink but with short sandy hair - who appeared to be having his dinner. A huge slippery tongue smacked and slathered at his lips. Just as the American with the video camera had provided a commentary in Pelican Park, as the lion picked up the whatever-it-was and shook it from side to side, a deep-voiced man announced, *"The gazelle isn't prepared to give up the fight."* And as soon as he spoke, it was obvious that those long dangly things hanging from the lion's jaws were spindly legs. Released, the poor dazed thing strained to raise its head on its fragile neck, only to be stilled by one of the lion's giant paws. The fact that animals were always eating each other wasn't shocking. When Custard the Dragon ate the dastardly pirate, it served him right for trying to shoot Custard - although a red trouser leg with a buckled shoe on the end sticking out of the dragon's jaws wasn't exactly something you'd want to watch immediately before macaroni cheese with hidden peas. What worried Belinda was how long being eaten actually took. She'd assumed that after one blood-curdling scream it would all be over. Questions about dying weren't the sort Mummy encouraged. She saved them up for Saturday mornings when they went to the library. The Librarian wasn't remotely squeamish, and never fretted about not knowing the answer. Mummy was always saying, "You aren't bothering this nice lady, are you?" But the Librarian didn't mind being bothered. She always said, "There are two kinds of knowledge. Knowing the answer, and knowing where to look it up."

The man on the television was now suggesting five minutes' pressure on the windpipe was needed to finish the poor gazelle off. Belinda experimented pressing her nails into the palm of one hand - something she knew could hurt quite a lot - to see how long she could stand it. She got to forty-three elephants and, still, the gazelle was insisting on hanging on. *Why don't you just give up?* Eventually it got boring, waiting for the thing to die, and she started channel-hopping.

ITV: some sort of old-fashioned film, Belinda guessed. A grown-up woman dressed to look like a cartoon character, hair tied in big bunches with white bows, a yellow watch (which the girl quite wanted for herself) and a yellow bikini. The woman moved her arms in and out as if it took a huge amount of effort. Questioning this, Belinda copied the movement - elbows out to the side, fingertips together, hands out in arcs, while a scrawny-looking man instructed, "And fling and in, and fling and in." The woman only managed two flings before her bikini top pinged off and hit him right in the face.

"Should you be watching this?" Belinda asked herself

when she had finished laughing. Sliding down from the sofa, she snatched the *TV Times* up from the coffee table to see if it had any good pictures. Underneath was a photo album, like any ordinary photo album, except that it was enticingly slim and black.

It wasn't hers. It was not for touching.

She eyed the living-room door for several moments. It didn't budge.

She looked at the album again. She would just pick it up and feel the weight of it in her hands. Just have a sneaky look to see what was on the first page.

Protected from sticky fingers in a plastic folder, a ballerina lady leapt out at her. As a dark thrill washed through her, Belinda could barely breathe. The lady's face was lifted to the light so she couldn't be sure. At least, not one hundred per cent. A chiffon scarf, held high above her head in both hands, streamed out behind her.

With a strong sense of things that were not supposed to be spoken of, the girl crossed her feet at the ankles and sank to the rug. Balancing the album on her knees, she was almost frightened to turn the page - and not just because she might get caught doing something she ought not to be doing. She didn't need to remind herself to hold the protective plastic sleeve by its crimped edges.

The woman was on tiptoes, her head and shoulders back, her arms like wings, a silk kimono slipping from her shoulders (Belinda knew those shoulders and she stared at the photo with awe); a black man was resting his cheek against her pale chest - where the girl's own head often lay - his eyes closed as if he might be sleeping. Breathing heavily now, the girl didn't know if what she felt was jealousy, anger or something new and disturbing.

The woman faced away from the camera, her profile in shadow, one hand on her neck. There had obviously been an accident because coloured paint was spilt all the way down her back. Yellow and red and green splashes on the floor where she knelt sideways on, naked. (Obviously, she'd been saving her clothes for best.) Belinda imagined her mother in the shower afterwards, the colours mixing together in the water that pooled around her feet.

Next, a picture of a man and a woman; the man, dressed in tight trousers, reclining on his back, his head raised; the woman sitting astride him, dressed in a satin nightie. One of her arms was lifted behind her at an unnatural angle. They were facing each other, eye to eye. It looked very uncomfortable. Her mother's face was angry-scared and, even though Belinda knew it was only pretending, there was something horrible about the way the man was staring back at Mummy. As if he thought she belonged to him.

Next, Mummy was dragging the man - the same one - backwards across the floor. She was so slight, but she looked just like a Superhero, something that made Belinda cheer inside.

This time the nightie was red satin and his trousers were black. The man was not helping. Perhaps he was supposed to be dead (probably killed by a lion). Shoulders back, feet planted far apart, her mother stared directly at the camera and, with an expression Belinda recognised, her eyes said she was not at all happy.

Here was something Belinda could do. She had been learning the crab position in Gym. Some of the older girls could bend over backwards just by putting their hands up by their shoulders and leaning. Afraid of falling, the little girl lay on the floor, flexed her wrists, bent her knees and pushed up through her feet until her tummy was higher than the rest of her. Just as Belinda was expecting praise, Miss Skelton had appeared upside-down, frowned at her, and declared it 'a work in progress'. In this photograph, Belinda could count

Mummy's ribs where her skin was stretched. She was even thinner at the waist than she was at the tops of her legs.

Now dressed in animal furs, her mother crawled over a mirrored surface, her head low, one leg bent at the knee, the other out to the side, very straight; her hands were spiders. Turn the page and Mummy was sitting astride a kitchen chair, dressed in a bowler hat and a low-cut top, which looked like a waistcoat. Her eyelashes were long and spiky. Her hands were on the rim of the hat as if she might twist -

Belinda saw the sheen of her mother's dark hair as her hand was pulled away from her mouth. Without realising it, she had been pressing her tongue into the dent between two fingers.

"What are you doing with my portfolio?" The voice was astonished.

Blood pounding wildly in her ears, Belinda could barely speak: "I -"

She pulled her knees in and cowered as the album was snatched away and snapped shut. Then the shouting began. "This is private, do you understand? Private." One of Mummy's hands was raised to her forehead. Her face was frightening, very different from any of the expressions Belinda had just been looking at. "You're not a little girl any more! I shouldn't have to keep telling you that not everything you find is for you to play with."

Belinda allowed her face to crumple but tears wouldn't come. The shouting had frozen her. "Are all -?"

A finger was jabbed and, even though it went nowhere near her, she flinched.

"Don't. Just don't. This isn't a discussion."

She had been about to ask what she already knew was true: "Are all of these of you?" And then, once her mother had sighed and said, "Before you arrived on the scene, yes," she was going to say, "You must have been very good at dancing." That's all. And she had been especially careful not to make fingerprints. But the *portfolio* was marched upstairs, her mother's footsteps so heavy you'd have been forgiven for thinking it had been carved from stone. *Thou Shalt Not Touch What Does Not Belong To You.* That was one rule God had missed off his list.

Left alone, cross-legged on the floor, Belinda felt very shaky and sick. She sat stock still, because Mummy hadn't told her she was allowed to move. Too old for the naughty step, sometimes she would be sent to her room until she was ready to say sorry, but this was not one of those times. The shock of being caught and the intensity of her mother's shouting faded, replaced by a silence that, in its own way, was equally disturbing. Miserably, Belinda pulled a strand of hair up under her nose, scrunched up her top lip to hold it in place, and tried to think, both knowing and not knowing what she had done to raise Mummy's temper to such a terrifying degree.

Still, her mother didn't come. A burnt toast smell oozed from the kitchen. Eventually she stood, pointed one foot and placed it behind the other, toes on the floor. It felt unnatural, as if she might topple over. She waited until her legs stopped wobbling, then she reached one hand up above her head in a curve, bent to the side. She didn't hear her mother come back downstairs, soft-footed without what she had called her *portfolio*. Belinda almost tripped over her own feet as she heard the joyless words: "I was a ballerina. A dancer. Ballet, tap, jazz, modern." Her mother's voice was impatient as she spat out facts - marvellous, wonderful facts - which seemed to cause her even more pain than talking about her family.

"But you stopped -"

"Yes, I stopped." The full stop made it all too clear that there would be no more answers. Not today; possibly not ever. Another unmentionable thing to add to the list.

Left to join the dots (or as the Librarian put it, 'read

between the lines'), Belle suspected this latest thing was at the bottom of why Mummy sometimes got tired and cross, and it had nothing to do with her growing or things costing so much money.

Mummy's voice wasn't angry any more, but it was still tense. "I started when I was about your age, and I took lessons for over ten years. It was how I earned my living before you arrived."

If her mother had started dancing at the age of six and finished at the age of twenty-one that was... Belinda counted backwards, something she had only learned recently. Using her fingers to help, she arrived at fourteen. *Fourteen years!* There was no need to ask, "Were you the best at it?" Expensive costumes aren't wasted. And even in the still, captured moments, the evidence had been there. This had been her mother's ten thousand hours!

"If you want, you can have lessons. You'll have to pick one type of dancing, of course."

Belinda was so amazed that she couldn't speak. She could barely return her mother's fidgety look. All she had wanted was to look at the beautiful pictures.

"Your dinner's getting cold. Quickly. Run upstairs and wash your hands."

Not needing to be told twice, Belinda fled, shutting herself in the bathroom, where there was no trace of anger hanging in the air. The girl knew that the portfolio was hidden. Somewhere she would never find it. She got the impression that her mother would rather rip the photographs into tiny pieces than allow her to look at them. It was *so* unfair. She had seen so few photographs of her mother before she was born, and none of her as a child.

"Where are they all?" the girl had once asked.

The unhelpful reply came: "In my parents' loft, I'd imagine."

There had been no choice but to take Mummy's word for

it when she said that she had looked nothing like her as baby, but almost exactly the same at the age of five.

Belinda ran the hot and cold taps, but she didn't wash the hands that had held the crimped edges of those plastic folders in case that might erase the memory. *Portfolio:* there was something delicious about the way it sounded. Like *amphibian* or *binoculars*. The thought of eating macaroni with burnt cheese topping made her feel sick.

CHAPTER SIX

"Do you pay for your prescriptions?" the white-coated girl with the chipped nail varnish asked.

"Yes, but not my daughter's penicillin."

"Or your birth control," the girl added absent-mindedly, scanning the white and green slip.

"No." Alison put her basket on the chemist's counter. On any other day she would have taken note of the way the girl rang the multipacks of Durex through the till and then left them lying on the counter, as though she preferred to have as little to do with them as possible.

"Is there anything else?"

"Canestan, please. Combi if you have it." Judging by the girl's reluctance to make eye contact, conclusions were being leapt at. Alison rolled the cuff of her white cotton blouse down as if trying to cover up an identification tattoo.

"Regular or double strength?"

A man was now standing close behind her, hands thrust deep in his trouser pockets. Alison stepped forwards, put her shoulder bag on the counter and lowered her voice. "Double, please. And a plastic bag."

In a manner that managed to be both disapproving and efficient, the girl pulled a flimsy transparent plastic bag from a roll and left Alison to pack. She knotted the handles of the bag together and buried the cargo deep in her shoulder bag.

Distracted, Alison was unable to say why it troubled her so much that Belle had accidentally stumbled across her past. One moment's carelessness and something else that had been private was no longer her own.

Her line of work didn't lend itself to friendships. It was hard to find someone to talk to; harder still to find someone she could trust with anything resembling the truth. Her beautician was the closest thing she had to a friend. Someone she no longer had to explain her likes and dislikes to. Who gave the impression of having seen it all before, even more so than the nurses at her clinic. Come to think of it, what Alison liked most about the beautician was her lack of curiosity. As a ballerina, Alison had always had to keep herself cleanly waxed, so when she described herself as a dancer, there was an element of truth to it, even though the chronology was adrift. It also explained why her thighs might be bruised sometimes, and why those bruises might resemble fingermarks.

It was better that she kept herself to herself. Alison had shown Cat the door after she had voiced her disapproval at the way she was organising her work. Cat, who had come to her for help, who worked the streets - something Alison could never consider. But she'd been right, of course! There was one hell of a difference between a five-year-old and a six-year-old. It was impossible to carry on as she was. Something had to change. But how?

Alison hadn't been able to see the future for some time now, but Belle was quickly becoming more aware. She was old enough to dream up increasingly awkward questions. Old enough to feel entitled to answers - and old enough to answer the telephone when it rang. For Alison's part, there were days when twenty-seven felt ridiculously old. If it weren't for Belle's persistent knocking on her bedroom door, she wasn't sure she would find the will to drag her bones out of bed each morning. She was so very, very tired.

With her shoulder bag bulkier than before she entered the chemist's, Alison made her way through a sterile housing development, too new for its trees to have outgrown their plastic tubes, let alone for any sense of community to have emerged. Where the forecourt of a petrol station had once been, she felt inclined to turn back. Only the thought of the time-wasters she had to endure - the last-minute cancellations after she had spent the best part of two hours plucking and preening - prevented her.

"Come in, come in!" The woman who bustled to open the sliding porch door of the modern bungalow was comfortingly elderly, with support stockings housing her thick ankles, and misshapen quilted slippers on her swollen feet. "You must be Edwin's eleven thirty."

"I'm a little early," Alison said, attempting to smile. The sole concession to what she had imagined on her two-bus journey here was a bamboo wind-chime, the uneven sound it produced like a child's attempt at playing the xylophone.

"Punctual!" the woman reassured, ushering her into a disappointingly ordinary hall and pausing beside a side table. She added a tick to an appointments' book of sorts, though it contained no names. Part of what had attracted Alison here was the anonymity.

"You don't mind if we get the formalities over with?" The woman, leaning on the table top for support, breathed noisily, like someone who used to smoke heavily.

"Oh, of course not!" Feeling foolish not to have volunteered what now seemed so obvious, Alison delved into her shoulder bag, careful not to reveal its contents.

"What a useful-sized bag!"

"It needs to be." She handed over a fold of ten pound notes that she had already counted out. Money taken from the tin in what she called the First Aid cupboard. One of the few

Belle couldn't reach by standing on a chair. There appeared to be an unspoken trust that made checking the amount unnecessary. Alison swallowed as she watched the money being locked away in a blue metal cash box, its tiny key attached by a narrow ribbon. She compared the sum - as she always did - to something tangible: her weekly supermarket shop. Their existence always felt hand-to-mouth. There was no monthly pay slip; no guarantee that she would earn enough money after paying the rent and the bills to put food on the table. If she or Belle were ill, or if a regular client was on holiday... besides, Alison refused to give up her mental arithmetic, because it might mean she accepted that this was who - and what - she now was.

"I could do with one of those myself!" The elderly lady turned to her. "Now we can both relax. Grab a seat in the living room and I'll make you a drink."

Although the place was spotless, it had a clinical smell. The room confronting her contained an ugly brown three-piece suite and a coffee table, but little else. No ornaments on the mantelpiece above the gas fire. No magazines on the table. Alison turned to ask for black coffee before she understood that there was no choice. A faint murmuring, like the chanting of prayers, permeated the thin walls. Otherwise, there were only the sounds of the house: a tinnitus-like hum that might have been a fridge; the steady pattern of a ticking clock, reminding Alison that time was money. She felt out of place. Sitting gingerly, she began to push back the cuticles of her fingernails.

The woman brought hot water with a slice of lemon, then rocked herself backwards into the armchair opposite, smiling expectantly. She had made nothing for herself. Sipping from the cup, Alison tasted sweetness, unfamiliar but not unpleasant. A spoonful of honey. And something else too. Something warming. Ginger, perhaps. The kind of comforting drink you might welcome when laid up with the flu. They sat without speaking, the woman breathing chestily. Although not accustomed to silence, it felt companionable. Aside from her passive role in this process, what felt peculiar was the lack of activity. At home there was always something that needed doing. A washing machine to empty. A stack of ironing. Activity and noise: those were the things that made it possible for Alison to shut off her feelings. Here, she was aware of every breath she took, the smallest movement of her body. Even as she raised the mug to her lips, she was conscious of a slight tremor in her neck.

A small click and the murmuring grew louder, punctuated by a higher voice. The odd word made itself known.

"Aha!" The elderly woman slapped her knees, levered herself to standing and shuffled out into the hall. Alison's gaze followed. Trying not to give the outward appearance of curiosity, she wondered if she would catch her first glimpse of Edwin. Instead, she saw a young woman, pretty, legs to die for, a slightly awkward way of carrying herself. She could work on that if she had a mind to. Rather than glance into the room, the young woman appeared newly focused. Seeing something she wanted in that expression, Alison felt reassured: this was a good choice. But still her stomach felt jittery with pre-audition excitement.

A moment later the elderly woman was back in the doorway. "So, now it's your turn."

She picked up her bag. Putting on a performance was what Alison was accustomed to, whether for a crowded theatre or an audience of one. Being on the receiving end: that was another thing entirely. Ushered down the hall to a room at the back of the house, she had the feeling of rescinding control, as you must in the dentist's chair.

"And remember: don't tell him your name."

The door was closed behind her, that same soft click. The

man sitting behind the desk was not what she had expected. Firstly he was young - possibly even younger than her. His head was shaven, but he had a neat ginger beard. He was wearing a velvet purple waistcoat. It was the Celtic cross hanging low against his chest that Alison least expected; something she associated with Christianity. *I am the Lord of the dance, said he.* That had been her favourite hymn at primary school. Her next thought was that her mother wouldn't approve of her being here, spending her rainy-day fund on something that might, after all, be a load of old rubbish. And, probably, she would be right.

Acutely aware of the value of her own time, the fact that Edwin kept his eyes closed made her prickle with irritation. It was all very well saying, "Don't tell him your name." Should she announce herself? Alison was used to commanding attention - being looked at - whether she wanted it or not. There was a seat on her side of the desk, but no invitation to sit.

After several more moments, she began to wonder if the silence, the lack of looking, had a purpose. The longer she observed him, the greater her impression that he was deep in concentration.

Nervousness turning to impatience, she glanced about for clues. Edwin's service was advertised as a 'reading', and yet she saw no tarot cards, no crystal ball. There must be something. Large picture windows overlooked the garden, which was small and mainly laid to paving. Its small square of grass needed mowing, a ten-minute job at the most. It was laziness not to bother. She turned her attention to an eye-catching object hanging in the window: one large hoop with four smaller hoops attached, each containing what looked like a cross between a spider's web and one of the lace doilies her grandmother used to have under her fruit bowl. There were feathers too, and plastic beads.

"It's a dream catcher."

Edwin's voice startled her. Looking at him, Alison found that he still had his eyes shut but was smiling serenely. She felt both defensive and curious. Had he read her last thought? And if he had, what else had he read and not responded to? Her natural inclination was to shut herself off - and yet she had come seeking help. Alison, who was all about masks and costumes, would have to allow herself to become vulnerable.

"A what?" The first thing she had said since entering the room sounded strange to her own ears.

"It's a protective charm. The Native Americans believe the webbing filters out bad dreams, so only the good ones can get through."

What a sensible, simple idea. She almost asked where she could buy one for Belle, whose current obsession was being eaten alive, but decided against giving away personal details. She would use this as a test. If he knew she had a daughter, she would trust him. As Edwin's eyes opened, Alison recoiled. They were clouded to opaque; not white, but the palest blue. Cataracts. She felt deeply ashamed. That explained why the decor was so bland. The house had been designed for a blind person, its contents chosen for ease of navigation; comfort rather than aesthetics.

"My mother caught rubella during her first trimester," he said.

How many times a day did he feel obliged to explain? Looking towards the door, she wondered if the elderly woman...

"I don't usually mention it, unless anyone asks."

The fine hairs on the back of Alison's neck stood on end. For a moment she sensed that Edwin could not only interpret her thoughts but could channel deep into her soul. He already knew every one of her hopes and fears. "B-but they can treat that," she stammered.

He smiled. "Ordinarily. In my case, the advice was not to."

His simple acceptance confounded her: surely treatments had improved over the past twenty-five years?

"Being able to focus my attention elsewhere has its advantages. Why don't you grab a seat?"

Alison realised why there was no crystal ball. His eyes did that job. She sat, meekly. Here was a man who couldn't gawp or leer. Who seemed, if anything, to gaze past her. His look was of such deep intensity that she found the need to glance over her shoulder. (Just an empty waste-paper basket.)

"Can you see anything at all?" she asked, feeling foolish, wondering if he would think she was intruding.

"Light and shade. That's all I need."

A rush of memory came, no less powerful than her first sight of footage of Nureyev hurtling onto the stage. She was Belle's age, sent into a darkened room, one cautious step after another, to be presented to a very old lady, who her mother had told her was completely blind. It wasn't even considered worth turning the light on - never mind that Alison made no secret of the fact that she was afraid of the dark. Of being instructed to step closer, closer. Of cold sandpapery hands coming at her out of nowhere. Fingers like bones searching out and then cupping the contours of her face, while she stood, barely daring to breathe. The things she imagined in those moments. That the fingers might press into her eyes. That the hands might close around her throat. But she did not turn and bolt. She didn't dare move.

"And *who* are you?" a bewildered voice had asked at last, not remotely witch-like. It was as if a cruel trick had been played on them both.

"Alison." Her voice, there in the dark, was tiny.

"Speak up. I can't hear you."

"Alison," she echoed stupidly.

"But I don't *know* any Alisons." And the jerking of the old lady's fingers on her skin was frightening, until it came to Alison that the woman had started to cry, tears the girl felt entitled to. She reached for those bony fingers, found the sandpapery hands they were attached to, pressed them together so that each might have a familiar friend, and returned them to the place where she estimated the old woman's lap was. Pushing her small soft hand firmly on top of them, she wanted to make sure that was where they would stay.

Her six-year-old fear turned to anger that rules about manners didn't allow her to vent. Although she didn't turn back, she paused in the doorway to switch on the light, and swore she would devise a way to punish her mother. This brief glimpse of herself at Belle's age threw Alison. She felt the residue of terror and anger, feelings she thought soap had long since washed off.

"Ready?" Edwin asked.

"Ready," she repeated, an automatic response, as she shuffled in her seat. It seemed impossible to say 'No', although if this unprompted taste of her past was representative of what was to come, how could she possibly be prepared?

"If you have a mobile phone, you might want to record our session. It's possible that not everything I see will make sense immediately."

His hypnotic narrative continued: he would describe things in the order they came to him, with no idea if what he saw was from her past, present, or future.

Alison said that she understood, but it wasn't true. She understood his words, not their context. It struck her then how much store she had placed in today. An urgency had been brewing, building up to this moment, and yet there was the very real possibility that the man sitting opposite her was nothing but a charlatan. The moment the thought entered her mind, she tried to squeeze it out: he might see it and take against her.

"Do I take it that I'm not exactly what you expected?" His accompanying smile dissipated the tension in the room.

Perhaps Edwin was simply someone like her, someone struggling to earn a living using the only means at his disposal. "I had no idea what to expect," she faltered. "To be honest, I've never done anything like this before."

"You're at a crossroads," he said. Such certainty! And Alison realised she didn't fear bad news. What she feared the most was that her life would remain the same. She had told herself that her circumstances were temporary, but that had begun to feel like a lie. Alison now feared they would carry on indefinitely; that their situation wouldn't worsen, but, at the same time, wouldn't improve.

In his soft, low voice, Edwin began to describe a person, someone Alison felt she knew, or had once known. It took a few moments to realise that the person he spoke of was her - the her who had existed what seemed like a lifetime ago. She hadn't expected this. Without asking a single question, he was delving into her past. Here was his assessment of her character, his summary of her earthly deeds.

The final epoch of the world's existence. Worlds End. A deliberate choice to laugh at herself and the unpredictability of the 'unchoreographed world', as Margot had called it. (In the arrogance of adolescence, the ballet students at the White Lodge had all referred to Dame Margot Fonteyn by her first name.) Alison had stopped laughing. Was it deliverance or reassurance she now wanted? Someone to listen and to say, *you're doing alright.* That thing she did for her clients. There was nobody to do it for her. Nobody. And it would be another lie. She wasn't doing 'alright'.

A vivid memory forced itself into her flow of thoughts: her first taste of ballet. *The Red Shoes,* based on a fairy tale. The shoes that never tire, forcing the person who wears them to dance beyond the point of exhaustion. It had been Christmas

Day and, much to her father's disgust, Alison had sided with her mother, who had vowed that she would not sit through *Jason and the Argonauts* one more time.

All through the opening credits, he had rubbished the film, saying it was 'all frills and froth'. Her mother had retaliated, recommending he go and peel the spuds rather than spoil it for them.

Alison had felt a tug of disloyalty when he shocked them both by announcing he would *prefer* to peel the potatoes. (In fact, he also peeled the parsnips, diced the carrot and turnip and stripped the sprouts of their muddy outer layers.) But Daddy was forgotten as she sat entranced, smitten from the moment the conductor silenced the rowdy ballet-goers by tapping his baton. It had turned out to be a surprisingly grown-up film - horrified expressions exaggerated by ugly stage make-up, kissing, dramatic talk of love and sacrifice. But, even on a small screen, the energy of the dancing had been nothing short of exhilarating. And she had practised being the flamed-haired, porcelain-skinned Vicky Page, diligently leaping around the living room, waving her arms this way and that, so that her mother would understand this was not a fad that would be cast aside to make way for the next. While her friends were singing into hairbrushes pretending to be Madonna, Alison's mind was firmly set on *Swan Lake*. It was something she wouldn't admit to later: how she had fallen in love with Moira Shearer - viewed as something of a traitor in the serious world of ballet for having succumbed to the lure of film. But the lessons of sacrifice learned from that film would haunt her.

Edwin was frowning. "There's something about the number five..."

Her first ballet lesson, dressed for the part - how she loved tying the satin ribbons of her new shoes! (Not red, but dusky pink.) Prepared to show off, she arrived early at the cold church hall with its breezeblock walls and out-of-tune upright, chords played heavy-handedly. She was greedy for more of the easy approval she had grown accustomed to, but no: it was all about discipline. The five positions.

First: heels touching, feet turned out, knees absolutely straight, arms curved in front. *"A straight line!"*

Second: step apart by the length of a foot, arms out.

Third: with the feet still turned out, the right foot was drawn in with the heel touching the middle of the left foot, the left arm curved in front.

Fourth: the right foot stepped forwards in the same position, the left arm raised in a curve above the head.

Fifth: the right foot was brought back in, heel to toe, toe to heel; then the right arm was raised above the head, meeting the left hand.

Repeat, repeat, *repeat!*

Alison recognised that, although her daily practice sessions had ceased, her dreams remained filled with these drills. That this had gone unacknowledged until now troubled her: surely she should have been aware that she had been replicating each painful hour spent at the practice barre? Stretching and manipulation. Those cruel contortions. *"Posture, posture, posture!"* Perhaps adding the crack of a whip for dramatic effect.

Her first teacher was by no means Alison's strictest. She only seemed that way because the young girl had never encountered anyone like her. Dyed red hair, crumbling cheeks, stick-thin, but at the same time shabbily elegant. So upright, she looked as though she had swallowed a broom. Years later, correcting her own position as she practised at the barre, Alison would imagine Miss Swale watching; her teacher's piercingly haughty words always present in her mind. *"Purity of line! Purity!"*

Only after she had mastered the basics was she permitted

to dance set pieces. But it was no longer about showing off. It was about perfection. That sought-after illusion of simplicity. Standing on stage to receive her first enthusiastic clatter of applause, armed with the knowledge of what it had cost her, she found herself unexpectedly humbled.

Alison asked herself, *Is this why I'm so strict with Belle?* She had told herself it was because she had to be both mother and father. Setting clear boundaries; making sure she didn't cave in. She had no one to back her up with a sharp *Do as your mother tells you.* Discipline - deferred gratification - was something that had been instilled in Alison, etched into muscle and memory. She was at her most impatient with Belle's apparent lack of discipline. But why expect it to come naturally to a child? That was hardly fair!

Tears prickled as Alison recalled how she believed she had failed her audition for the Royal School of Ballet. It had been such a slim hope. Eyes clenched, she had wished over her birthday candles more fervently than she'd ever wished for anything in her life. Even before she had caught sight of the older students practising their jumps, spied a feathery pile of discarded tutus flattened out like lily pads, she had so wanted it. But that meant being within the top two per cent and she had only thirty seconds to prove herself worthy. In her nervousness, Alison had made a technical error and had sworn in the most unladylike manner her mother was capable of imagining for a ten-year-old. But they called her back, saying they admired her passion and wished to see her dance again! Given a second chance, Alison leapt as if her life depended on it, holding her final position and containing the heaving of her chest until a stern voice said dismissively, "Thank you, that will be all." And even then, with no indication of whether she had scraped through, Alison walked tall, knowing that her exit was part of the performance: toes pointed, arms raised, every muscle taut.

For five years of her life, from the age of eleven, she submitted to a tortuous regime. "You are the clay," she was told. Entering the dance studio each day, she was moulded. Leaving her child's body behind, her upper back achieved an ironed-out flatness; her legs were twisted outwards from the hips; her feet, arched.

A conveyor belt of exams and rehearsals. There was nothing else. No room for weakness, for failure, for sleepovers or boyfriends. But it wasn't a sacrifice. By then, discipline was self-imposed. Every identically-proportioned, long-necked girl in her class represented competition. Although Alison moved as one with them, they couldn't all win a prized place at the Upper School. But even before graduating, there was the threat of humiliation - the shame of being 'assessed out'. Not even success would eradicate that persistent grain of self-doubt. Some found the constants of half-concealed anxiety and homesickness too much of a strain. The sacrifices Alison's parents made for her also weighed heavily. A grant had funded the boarding school fees, but it didn't cover her expenses, and there were thinly-veiled hints that they were 'going without'.

"You've always been your own harshest critic," Edwin was saying.

Perhaps. Alison got into the habit of doing more than was necessary. Perfecting every movement in front of the mirror. Dissecting each performance the moment it was over. *"You do not perform an arabesque: you are the arabesque!"* Hunger kept her alert. She took laxatives to keep her weight down, counterbalanced by glucosamine and calcium for energy and strength.

Allowing herself few friends, she preferred to spend what free time she had wandering through Richmond Park: sun glinting through foliage at the mysterious hours of dusk and dawn; the stark silhouettes of lightning-splintered trees; the gentle unfurling of prehistoric ferns.

On one occasion she had encountered a stag, misty-breathed as it crossed the path directly in front of her, turning its noble head, looking her boldly in the eye. And she met his challenge fearlessly, standing her ground on the muddy tract that cut through the russet ferns, then edging slowly towards him. Every muscle alert, he feigned disinterest. By now Alison had learned how to move while giving the appearance of stillness. In another life she might have been a skilled stalker. At any moment he could have charged towards her or bolted, but they contemplated each other - she and the stag - and to Alison it was as if she were looking in a mirror. His head held high, showing his pride. Something of her own humanity reflected back at her from a face that was clearly animal. She had a sense that they shared some ancient understanding. Even at that moment, Alison had known it would prove impossible to explain her learned wisdom, and so she kept it to herself. Used it, as she used everything, to add another dimension to her dance.

Edwin was blinking, as though he found it equally difficult to describe the things he saw. "I can see you standing in a room with a group of other people, but you're at a distance from them. I'm tempted to say that you're *keeping* your distance. Does that make sense?"

Alison's response - "Yes" - lodged in her throat. It was true. She had been accused of being remote. Other pupils found intimacy but, coming from a home where emotions were not expressed, the huggy-kissy atmosphere was foreign to Alison. There must have been something more. She had read, of course. If it is true that more than half of a ballerina's life is spent inside her imagination, then, between the covers of novels, that percentage increased for Alison. Yes, she realised. An only child, removed from her family home at an early age. In many ways, before Belle's arrival, she had always been alone.

Having already mentioned humility, self-control, resourcefulness, Edwin said it: "You harboured a ruthless ambition."

This brought Alison sharply back to the moment: the surprise that someone meeting her for the first time could recognise that she had once been ambitious. But ruthless? Had she ever been so hard? Naturally, she'd wanted to dance. It had sounded so simple at first. After turning professional, her understanding of what this involved grew, as did her desire. Desire became need, pure and simple - as essential as oxygen.

The stage, it was always the stage. The knowledge of the hushed audience, waiting, hungry for the sight of you; music filling your senses; strong hands spanning your waist: a potent and heady mix. A place where life was lived more intensely, where she was queen. Vicky Page had danced off the stage and onto the streets in her red shoes; she had danced with the late-night people and through empty streets long after the sailors and the prostitutes had retired; she had danced with only a wind-blown newspaper to partner her. It was impossible to do what Alison did for as long as she did it and be content. There was a martyrdom about it. Ignoring doctors' orders - doctors whose recommendation when consulted was to give up dancing - *give up!* Which dancer could perform with the most painful injury, whose toes bled the most. Her colleagues quoted statistics at each other: a ballerina's injury rate was eighty per cent, but a ballerina's pain threshold was one-third higher than average. Expected to be artists, at the same time they were required to be machines.

"You understood your own self-worth," Edwin said.

"Did I?" she scoffed self-deprecatingly, her mood darkening. Then she realised that he may not have been thinking in monetary terms, the way she was reduced to thinking about everything.

"Only a fool would put themselves forward for something

they didn't believe themselves to be capable of. The means by which you arrived there is immaterial."

The means.

Accustomed to the feel of her body being manipulated, Alison knew when hands lingered longer than they needed to; closer to her lowest vertebrae than they needed to be. She had embarked on her first affair with the ballet's artistic director tactically, discreetly. The real star, his dancers studied his notations with awe. This was one choice that had been a choice, a decision that had been a decision, a gamble she thought had paid off. She had watched *The Red Shoes* many times over the years. The last time she had been struck by the ballet director's close-up to camera, his cold, "You cannot have it both ways." Nothing to do with love; little to do with desire; her decision was about ambition. Her prize: a single piece, choreographed with only her in mind. Elegant, expressive. There was praise from the London critics, then a tour of the Far East. Talk had turned to the possibility of *conquering* America, as if they were about to mount a grand-scale invasion.

Edwin was frowning, shaking his head. "I'm seeing an interruption. A knee injury..?"

Un mal au genou: a sore knee - the explanation traditionally used by ballerinas to excuse their absences. Belle.

Others, accustomed to seeing her body displayed in Lycra, seemed to have known before she did - she who had always been so self-aware!

"Darling, I don't like to mention it but you're not your normal svelte sylph-like self."

"It's the change of diet. I'm bloated."

"I hate to break it to you, but that's not the rice."

But positive pregnancy tests don't lie.

"You work in a profession for the young, one that will come to an end very quickly," she was told as her cheeks burned. "You're good, but if you don't do it now - and I *do* mean now - it will be too late."

In ballet, rewards were unpredictable at best. It wasn't like footballers' pay, which compensated for the fact that careers would be short-lived. Other dancers planned for their retirements, just as other ballerinas planned their pregnancies - or brought them to an abrupt halt. Had Alison not fallen pregnant when she did - had she continued - the chances were that, at the age of twenty-seven, she would have only a few more years. Injury or age, two of the three ways to end a ballerina's career. The third... well, that was supposed to be marriage.

"Take a few days off. Go home. Discuss it."

Her parents fought her on this. They had not supported her all this time so that she could "throw it back in our faces." (Her mother's spiteful words.) Just when she was getting established was no time to take a career break. To them, the question of *who* Belle's father was seemed irrelevant once she'd made it clear that there would be no wedding bells. A mistake had been made. It needed to be put right.

And where was he? The man who was responsible?

His native Australia. Installed in a new directorship. Oblivious.

The sting of her father's slap left her cheek a vivid red. "I always went too easy on you," he said. "Your mother was right."

Looking up in shock, Alison found no softening in her mother's expression; no sympathy there.

It was only later, through the busy networks of gossip, that Alison had discovered there had been other girls. Of course there would have been! In ballet, girls outnumber boys and, of those available boys, a lower percentage prefer girls than in the unchoreographed world. But apparently none of those other girls had been so foolish as to neglect that one vital detail: the fact she would run out of birth control pills while on tour. How laughable it seemed now, thinking back to this morning's visit to the chemist's. The 'nice-girl' image she had of herself meant that, despite their ready availability, she had been too embarrassed to buy condoms.

"You won't be pushed into anything you don't want to do," Edwin was saying.

"I'm stubborn," she replied.

"No. You've always known your own mind."

Adoption wasn't the solution her parents had proposed. She had no strong feelings about abortion, never having had any reason to give it much thought. Perhaps it had been the sense of appearing to others as the fool she knew herself to be. Perhaps it had been because she railed against her parents' blackmail. Fought the fact that they thought they could decide this - the first adult decision she needed to make - for her.

"You don't own me!"

"Perhaps we don't owe *you either."*

It had stunned her, the depth and breadth of their vicarious ambition. Particularly the attitude of her mother, who had never before struck Alison as a Ballet-Mother-from-Hell. All she appeared to be able to think of was Alison as a tragic Odette. The feathered headdress. A perfect white tutu. Consolation for everything she'd been through, as if hers had been the greater sacrifice.

"You want to stand on your own two feet? Fine! But don't think you can come running back to us. You're on your own."

It was unsafe to dance after the first trimester. Besides, no one wanted to be responsible for partnering her, or risk injury. Alison felt her body, usually a finely-tuned instrument, change. She underwent a reckoning with her physical being, amazed at how it adapted, but aware of her new limitations.

Back in rehearsals only seven weeks after Belle's birth,

Alison confronted her reality. Thinner and frailer than she'd been before, she learned her body anew, feeling the essential changes to her musculature and skeleton. During her absence, others had risen through the ranks. And, of course, with the departure of the artistic director, she had lost her greatest ally. These things were to be expected. But resuming the position she had held had proved impossible. A single mother with a child who recognised no schedules. For someone who'd been so protected - although she hadn't known it - the outside world was bewildering. She had always assumed she had chosen a tough life, iron discipline, hardships. *"Lights go out and I die."* As true for any dancer as it was for Nureyev. Alison thought that ballet was all she was - it had been her whole life. And if she couldn't dance, then...

"You're asking yourself, *Who am I?*" Edwin's opaque eyes seemed to be boring into hers.

Who was she? Yes, that was exactly how it had felt.

Other possibilities opened up to her, at least at first. She tried not to view Modern and Jazz as lesser options. To own the stage again was the important thing, the only place where she was transformed. Auditions were humiliating affairs. What could she offer that others couldn't? She remembered reacting with shock and repulsion. Strange now, considering.

Later, misreading a situation: offering herself to someone who made it clear he had no interest in women.

But then Belle had entered a sickly stage - colicky and whiny - and Alison had been forced to let people down. Understudies had proved themselves technically competent. And considerably more reliable.

The way that Edwin was looking straight at her and yet looking straight through her was deeply unsettling. "Tenacity," he said. "Of all your gifts, it is the one that's helped you the most."

It wasn't how she remembered it. She had asked an agent

in one of her lowest moments, "Haven't you got anything else for me?"

"That depends."

"Try me." Not to dance at all was inconceivable.

Lap-dancing was the answer. Requiring her to perform in a club - a public place. Though ballerinas were no longer seen as pioneers and fashion icons, Alison had occasionally been papped walking down the street. Somehow, the rarity of the situation made it all the more difficult to handle. For someone to recognise her, wiped free of make-up, wearing dark glasses, they had to be either an arts journalist or a super-fan. Aware that some of the journalists who covered the ballet scene also hung out in lap-dancing clubs, she imagined their faces: the discovery that a perfectly-trained prima ballerina had been reduced to earning her living as a lap-dancer... Then she imagined her parents recoiling from salacious headlines.

"Thank you," she had said, preparing to head for the door.

He had shrugged in a 'suit yourself' kind of way. A confident shrug. One that said, *You'll be back.*

Alison's GP diagnosed her lack of interest in the world as post-natal depression, but couldn't understand that there was no *loss* of interest: she had *never* been interested in the outside world. She explained to several different people several times over that she had no intention of harming herself or her baby. Sometimes all you wanted to do was curl up on the sofa-bed - a single mother lying under a single duvet - watching your daughter sleep with abandon in her cot and listen to Damien Rice's breathy voice, his raw guitar-playing answered by a lonely violin. The depth of Alison's maternal feelings had come as a shock, but being unable to dance - to perform - was like a bereavement. Feeling as if she was an outcast, in her head she remained a dancer. And it was her dancer's stubborn martyrdom that told her, *Ignore the symptoms: 'K.B.O.'* as her father had always said.

"But what does it mean?" She'd pulled at his jacket sleeves, and at last he had dispensed with his stock answer, "None of your business," to say, "It means that, when things are difficult, you must just keep going."

"Then why don't you say 'J.K.G.'?"

"This is a motto and it's traditional for mottos to be in Latin."

Tenacity!

Alison had been brought up expecting life to be hard. She had also been brought up with a strong work ethic. Alison tried cleaning jobs, opting for those that allowed her to take Belle with her, even if night shifts were required or the pay was less. Existing in a state of constant exhaustion, trying not to think, she doggedly worked enough minimum-wage hours to meet the rent on her London bedsit where even *having* a child was frowned on, let alone one with such a highly-developed set of lungs. She hated the lingering smell of bleach and the rubber from the gloves. Retched at the stench of the men's toilets. There was no day on which she packed her ballet shoes and thought, *Goodbye old friends*. So when does a verb become a noun? At what point does the answer to the question, 'What do you do for a living?' change from, 'I clean,' to 'I'm a cleaner'? Is it subtle, or, if you catch the moment, can you rail against it?

And then a man, who couldn't possibly have imagined how unusual it was to find Alison perched on a stool at the copper-topped bar at one of her places of work - sipping a cocktail of all things - approached her and offered her fifteen hundred pounds to go to bed with him.

It had to be a joke. Someone must have put him up to it. Someone from Alison's old life. She glanced around the room nervously, but saw no one she knew.

No, he insisted. He'd been watching her.

Taken aback, she managed to be firm. "Look, I'm having

a quiet drink with my friend," but as she turned to present him with proof, Alison was dismayed to find that Karen, her co-worker, had tactfully absented herself. She was flustered, but he hadn't hesitated in apologising and skulking back to his stool at the far end of the bar.

It was only after the man had left her alone that irritation flared - irritation that she had attracted unwanted attention, dressed in her oldest clothes, the taint of bleach still on her skin. She leapt down Karen's throat when she returned. "Where the fuck did you disappear to?"

Karen shrugged. "I was trying to cadge a lift home. Why? What's up?"

"You're not going to believe what just happened."

"Don't tell me." Karen said, an amused expression on her face. "You've just been offered money for sex,"

Alison's lips peeled apart. Then she added, "Looking like *this!*" as if her appearance was the only issue.

"So? How much?" Karen asked smugly, sucking on her straw, the pair to Alison's cocktail, ordered by a customer moments before his taxi had arrived. ("Not so fast!" Karen had told the barman, who had been about to pour them down the sink. "I think you'll find those babies belong to us!")

"Karen!" Alison couldn't believe how completely unfazed she was.

"Oh, get over yourself. You're cleaning toilets for six pounds an hour."

"Not just toilets." *I may be taking antidepressants but at least I still have my sense of humour.* "Sometimes we get to scrape grease off the kitchen hob."

"So how *much?*"

Alison tried to appear casual as she glanced at the man, newly curious. Middle-aged, dressed in a well-cut suit, nursing a whisky, slightly awkward in his stance. "More than a month's wages," she said. He was not scanning the bar for potentially available women. He wasn't even doing what many male customers did - looking at their reflections in the mirrors that backed the shelves behind the bar.

"Imagine how much you could get if you showered."

It wasn't a Lottery win, but it was a very real sum of money. "What about Belle?"

"I'll watch her for you. If he's good for the full amount, you can give me fifty quid."

"I can't believe I'm even considering this." She removed the straw, threw back her head and drained her glass.

"Good girl!"

"Just this once. And if you say *anything.*"

Just this once became just this week.

Just this week became just to pay the gas bill.

It was not always a month's wages, but it was usually more than two days' worth. Enough to move to a one-bedroom flat within six months; enough to move to a small two-bedroom flat by the time Belle outgrew her cot. It was in a squat redbrick building above a Chinese takeaway, but their view was of Georgian splendour. You had to feel sorry for the barristers and the architects living opposite, whose outlook was the concrete 'square' used as a skateboard park, backed by ugly tower blocks whose angles and lack of symmetry distracted the eye. And all the time that their situation was improving, it was possible for Alison to justify why she did it. Sitting opposite Edwin, it struck her that she had no idea what had happened to Karen. Gutsy Karen, whose jokes were blue, and whose stories about her sex life were bluer. Who never seemed to feel defined by whatever she needed to do to pay the rent.

Here, in a blind clairvoyant's room, Alison came to understand how hard-won discipline had helped her to endure. It was just another performance. Others coped by using. Alcohol, drugs: things that would ruin you. Some enjoyed it, pay being a bonus. For someone with few other ways of meeting people - no friends to speak of, no family support - the companionship of her regulars was something Alison had grown to appreciate. And, of course, like the cleaning jobs, this was only ever going to be temporary. Just until she found her feet.

Her feet.

She had allowed the verb to become the noun! She had let it happen!

She blinked with realisation. Edwin appeared to be looking directly at her, his mouth a bemused smile. How *dare* you pity me! How *dare* you judge!

"A large white bird," he was saying. "The height of a small child."

Her spark of anger receded. She was back in her recent past, disappointed by the sense that he appeared to be winding down. "Was that important?" she pressed, wondering if she had missed an opportunity.

"I have no way of telling. Does it feel as if it might have been?"

It stung her like a slap: it was entirely possible that Edwin was the real deal, but that *nothing* he saw was significant. He was simply tapping into the minutiae of her life. Something inside her sank. "No. Just an outing with my daughter."

"All I can say is that things that don't seem relevant at the time sometimes turn out to be pivotal in the longer term. There's one last thing I have for you: rows and rows of bookshelves."

She remembered her father, holding a book open for her, paraphrasing Churchill (in his opinion, the greatest man to ever live): *"Look at it, Alison. It lies open like an angel's wings."* Alison had once loved the escapism of reading, but it involved both sitting still and quiet reflection - neither of which would result in any good, as today's futile experiment seemed determined to demonstrate. "Bookshelves?" she repeated.

"Does that mean anything to you?"

"The bookshop?" Alison offered, thinking of Worlds End Bookshop, whose second-hand paperbacks spilled out onto the pavement in orange crates and cardboard boxes, just on the curve of what Belle called 'the snake in the road'.

"No, this seems to be a house."

Nothing sprang to mind. And this felt like another failure to add to a string of failures.

"Do you have anything you'd like to ask me?"

A question so wide, so immense, that it wasn't even possible to begin. Alison had so wanted to see a clear path forwards, but her own version of Dorothy's yellow brick road had led back to the past, a place she'd been exiled from.

"No," she said, her throat tight as she fought back tears.

CHAPTER SEVEN

Once outside, Alison replaced her sunglasses and scolded herself: "Stupid, stupid, stupid!" Like Scrooge's ghosts, even if Edwin didn't have answers, he might have offered valuable insights. How many times did clients come to her thinking they wanted one thing only to find they wanted another? Comfort. Escapism. Reassurance. What right did she have to label what he had offered her 'humbug'? Alison took a deep breath, sucking air into her lungs.

It was a shock to realise the pang she was feeling was for her mother - of all people! Who even now, when she was obviously distraught, wouldn't be able to resist telling Alison how disappointed in her she was; what a God-awful mess she was making of her life. That had always been her mother's way, stating the painfully obvious. Dragging the 'I told you so' moment out to full dramatic effect, without a hint of whether help or forgiveness would follow. But Alison hadn't heard from her mother for a long time and doubted that she would.

When the midwife, seeing her circumstances, had asked Alison what support she had, she'd replied, "Very little."

"How little?"

"None, actually." She'd refused to cry. (Even in her darkest moods, tears rarely came, but *now* she found herself crying.)

"Not even your mother?"

And when Alison had shaken her head, and said, "She thinks I've let her down," the kind woman had replied, "She'll come round. They all do, you know."

Alison had written to let her parents know about Belle's arrival. A simple announcement. A single photograph, one of the few Alison possessed. After two weeks of waiting for the postman, she wondered if the card had got lost in the post, so she wrote again. Nothing. Alison had no choice but to accept that neither would show any interest in their granddaughter. It was as if, by ignoring her letters, they thought they could will Belle into not existing. Each time she'd moved, Alison had sent her change of address. There had been no communication in seven years; not a single birthday card. Prepared to be punished, Alison hadn't expected their bloody-minded self-righteousness to extend this far. It was brutal, this punishment of Belle for her own failings.

She stopped to blow her nose. (A mother, she never went anywhere without tissues.) What do you tell a child who comes home from school and asks, "Do I have any grandparents?" And later, when Belle understood about death and realised she might expect to have four of them: "Are *all* of my grandparents dead?" It was impossible to tell her the truth. "No, darling, they just don't want to see you." Easier to change the subject. But to make no attempt to provide a child with a *father*? Not even a hint of who he was?

Alison had always promised herself that she would tell Belle about her father when she was old enough. She had compiled a scrapbook of newspaper clippings so that she could point to a photograph and say, "Here. This is your daddy. Isn't he handsome?" (As if that were the only quality that mattered!) But she couldn't tell Belle without first telling *him* that he had a daughter. And if Alison hadn't found a way to announce she was pregnant - not even when he was leaving the country - if she hadn't been able to tell him about Belle's arrival...

She now accepted that she *had* been suffering from depression - not the post-natal depression that her doctor had suggested, but an all-encompassing grief that had made her question her worth. At what point *was* it appropriate to write? If she had worried that telling him all those years ago would have seemed like blackmail - an attempt to stop him returning to Sydney to take over the directorship of the Australian ballet - how would it have appeared when, less than a year later, she read about his engagement to a successful swimwear model? Or after his wedding photographs had appeared in *Hello!* magazine? (Congratulations - and by the way...) Perhaps on the birth of his first son? (I thought I should just correct the statement that this is your first child.) His second?

In his native country, where he was something of a celebrity (one article had called him a national treasure), the revelation that he had fathered a so-called love-child with a prima ballerina - an ex-prima ballerina, Alison reminded herself - would make the gossip columns. Even here, 10,571 miles away (she had checked - before reading about his engagement), it might be newsworthy if the papers were having a slow week. And she and Belle didn't need that sort of attention. Alison had been able to keep up to date with his progress through glossy celebrity magazines. Sometimes, sitting damp-tressed at the hairdresser's, towels piled around her shoulders, she came face to face with him. He was either captured deep in thought or smiling, shot against a backdrop of blue sky and Opera House, a tight-fitting t-shirt showing off his physique. He had aged, but his grey-haired and slightly craggy appearance suited him. She had run the tip of a finger around his outline, imagining flesh, and turned the page guiltily whenever anyone came close, as if she'd been caught reading a raunchy article. It seemed ridiculous now to pretend that a sky so blue could have been hers. But when no one was looking, she would discreetly tear those pages from the magazines and slip them inside her handbag.

"We girls have got to stick together," she'd told Belle when her daughter had asked about her daddy, hearing her own voice emerge, curt and bitter. She tried to remain upbeat when, sometimes, it was difficult not to weep. All she wanted to do was protect Belle against further disappointment.

Two out of four grandparents was all she had ever hoped to offer. But now Alison had reached the stage where she wasn't sure how she would react if her parents extended an olive branch. "You know what you can do if you think you can turn up and play happy families!" would seem appropriate, but that satisfaction couldn't be hers. Aside from the fact that she'd stall before the words were out, Alison didn't have the right to make that decision on Belle's behalf. Poor Belle, who had so little family that she took to inventing one for herself!

Pelicans, bloody, bloody pelicans! "Ha!" Alison laughed out loud, self-mocking, a single bitter syllable that attracted a startled glance from a passing jogger who clearly believed she had encountered a Care in the Community case. As she tried to still her wobbling lip, it struck Alison: *You're an idiot. Inventing conversations that will never actually take place.* She was a fool to be so miserable on such a beautiful day, when she had three hours to spare before she needed to collect Belle. Time: something rare and precious. She set off, newly determined, swinging her arms. She would go to St James's Park, a place she had loved as a girl. She would buy an ice cream, walk barefoot through the grass, sit cross-legged and make a daisy chain, her back against the gnarled trunk of a one-hundred-year-old tree. Try and put herself in Belle's shoes. Belle, who was not such a disobedient child. Who looked up at her, eyes pooled with all of her expectations and anxieties.

Alison harboured her own secret hope that today might still turn out to be the day Edwin had spoken of but, standing on the Blue Bridge with her elbows resting on the brass railing, she saw that the pelicans had retreated to the rocky outcrop. Squabbling and preening in relative privacy, only the zoom lenses of those standing on the terrace of the Swiss Cottage could reach them. Out of reach, they became less tame. Less like the misshapen people her daughter imagined them to be. No, today was what it was. Insignificant. A little money wasted. Money she could afford, she reminded herself. There was no need for the panic she had felt.

But some time between joining the queue at the kiosk and being served, Alison lost the appetite for ice cream. She asked for bottled water, balking at the price. Unwilling to abandon her original plan altogether, she chose a bench in full sun; tucked in her elbow to guard her shoulder bag, its bulk supported by the seat. All about her, groups of teenagers sprawled on the downy-feathered grass: skinny boys stripped to the waist; girls in strappy tops - apparently with no schools to go to. A middle-aged couple were feeding each other strawberries, taking it in turn to lean forwards and bite into the fruits' flesh. Hardly Troy and Bathsheba. The sight of juice trickling down their chins made Alison uncomfortable. It struck her, on this day of regurgitating the past, that she had never met a man in what you might call the 'normal' way. Introduced by a friend at a dinner party; locking eyes across a crowded bar, or whatever it was that was supposed to happen. Having spent so much time in close proximity to incredible physiques, it was unlikely that other men would ever measure up. But, except for that one notable exception, Alison had rarely *acted* on attraction. That iron discipline of hers usually prevailed. Her affair, now tainted with the knowledge that she had made a complete idiot of herself, had started with the calculated seduction of an older man.

It was she who had thrown herself at him and, under those circumstances, did she have any right - even with the benefit of acquired hindsight - to expect him to have insisted she stopped? To tell her there were others? And what if he *had* said, "Hey, slow down."? Would she really have stopped pressing herself against him, pushing him against the wall? Even now she could feel the breathlessness, her breasts flattening against his chest as they would under the bodice of a tutu. His mouth opening - had he perhaps intended to speak before she had made sure speech was impossible? His body reacting in the way she commanded, Alison had opened her eyes to capture the moment in the practice mirror, intending to make future use of the intoxicating sight of herself overpowering someone she had believed to be so controlled. Not for blackmail purposes, but in her dance.

She found she was blinking rapidly. Passing feet appeared to move in stop-start animation. It was impossible to answer those questions after almost seven years had elapsed and motherhood and disappointment had made her a different person. But Edwin had seen something of how ambition had caused her to become reckless. She had thought that she was wielding the power, when all she'd been was another fuck at the end of a long day spent observing slender young women in too-little Lycra.

Of course, the shame - that deep-seated humiliation that still distressed Alison if she allowed herself to dwell - was that it had been completely unnecessary. The other girls didn't have roles created for them. They weren't shown any favouritism. How could she feel pride in the fact that it was her artistry that had captured his attention? It was simply a punch in the guts. *Had* she known her worth, things might have been different. But what would she change if she could? Wishing for an alternative ending meant wishing there was no Belle. And that was unthinkable.

Looking for distraction, Alison deliberately turned her attention to a pair who appeared as shadows through their green and white striped deckchairs. She saw them through Belle's childish eyes: "Look, Mummy, look! Shadows with real feet." And, despite her mood, she managed to smile at the excitable expression she conjured up for her daughter. To Alison's embarrassment, Belle hadn't quite overcome the habit of describing everyone and everything she saw, pointing and occasionally jumping up and down. Alison had once met the steely glare of an extremely fat bald man Belle had described accurately. She had held her breath until his scowl softened and he said, "Well, she's not wrong, is she?"

Are you going to continually beat yourself up? she demanded of herself. *Do you imagine all of these people - these seemingly relaxed, surrendering-to-the-moment individuals - don't have their own secrets?* She could and would make herself relax. Belle was everything that was good about Alison's life. Belle *was* her life. She had answered the question of what she wouldn't do for her time and time again. There was nothing left to prove.

Slipping off her shoes, Alison rested her feet on top of them (the feet of an eighty-year-old, as they'd been described to her by a podiatrist). She raised her face, eyes closed. The insides of her eyelids glowed burnt orange. Yes. This was how you did it. Sitting still with the sun warming her skin gave Alison a feeling of well-being. Was the route to happiness really so simple?

She came to with the knowledge that the plastic water bottle had escaped her grip. Leaning forwards, she saw its precious liquid spilling onto the path, angry at herself for her momentary loss of control. After righting the almost-empty bottle, Alison's eyes followed the stream of water. Instinctively, she grabbed something from its path. Something with a tactile quality. A fat wallet, probably stolen then abandoned.

The thief was a fool: the supple leather was clearly expensive.

Opening it, she found a photograph of a couple of young boys gurning for the camera, the kind of forced smiles Belle gave whenever she heard the command, 'Say cheese!' *A family man*, she thought, scanning the grassed area behind her for the photofit face that was taking form in her mind: mid-thirties, intelligent-looking. Glasses perhaps, and a little stubble. Not one person fitted the bill.

The wallet hadn't been emptied, as she'd presumed. It was thick with bank notes and credit cards. Untamed possibilities vied for attention. *Recoup this morning's wasted money,* they urged. *Take the cash then put the wallet back where you found it: someone will retrace their steps to look for it.*

No: she couldn't leave the credit cards. Someone else would find the wallet and misuse them. *OK, take the whole wallet and cut the cards up when you get home.*

By now Alison had located a blood donor card - *A F Simons*. She felt ashamed that her first thought had been for herself. Why not do a good deed? Perhaps the park had a lost property office? But she suspected that whoever she handed the wallet to would pocket the cash, making her own self-control futile. And so she continued her detective-work, fleshing out her photofit.

Business cards. She shuffled them, looking for a match with the name on the bank cards. When she found it, she felt deflated. *Wealth Management*. She had imagined A F Simons in a creative profession. Architecture. Possibly an antiques dealer - the area was saturated with them. Not something so mundane. She could almost hear her father saying, "In finance, everything that is agreeable is unsound and everything that is sound is disagreeable." Without Churchill to quote, he would have been lost for words.

Alison knew the address, a five-minute walk away: "*She shall have all that's fine and fair, And ride in a coach to take the air, And have a house in St James's Square."* She was surprised that the nursery rhyme came back to her so neatly. In the eighteenth century, St James's had been the hub of London's thriving sex industry. Now its elegant Georgian stone terraces were home to the East India Club and the London Library, as well as businesses operating behind discreet front doors, where men presented themselves dressed in Savile Row suits, doused in cologne from the barber's in nearby Jermyn Street. She imagined a mock-Georgian streetlamp, a brass doorbell, a porch with black and white tiles, a bicycle chained to the iron railings - despite the so-called 'polite notice' asking cyclists to please refrain. Four storeys. Five, if you included the basement. Balconies at the first and second floor windows. Perhaps a Union flag. They tended to go in for that sort of patriotic display.

Perhaps the owner of the wallet had chosen to lunch in the park rather than a nearby restaurant. She decided to like him for making that choice, in spite of his dreary profession.

The eyes of the woman who opened the door slipped disapprovingly down Alison's body when she saw her standing on the steps, dressed in the anonymous daywear she so often chose. It was the outfit Alison felt was least likely to draw attention: large sunglasses; slim-fitting jeans - her good pair, she might have pointed out - and a crisp white blouse; hair secured neatly with a tortoise-shell clasp at the nape of her long neck. A neat figure, only slightly fuller than in the days when she rehearsed eight hours a day.

"Yes?" The woman seemed to want to keep her distance.

There couldn't have been a clearer message that this was yet another place where Alison didn't belong. So this was how it was to be. No pretence at pleasantries. Remembering her encounter with the stag, Alison removed her sunglasses and looked the woman directly in the eye. There was no sense that she was looking in a mirror now. "Is Mr Simons in?" she asked, chin up and smiling.

"Do you have an appointment?" The woman spoke as though she was operating a switchboard.

Unwilling to be put off, Alison reminded herself that Edwin had been able to detect that she knew her own self-worth. "I have something of his I'd like to return."

This only seemed to increase the woman's suspicion. She angled her head unnaturally, and her voice emerged a tone higher. "You can leave it with me. I'll make sure he gets it."

Making an appraisal of her own, as women do when being scrutinised, Alison decided: a snob, one whose skirt was too tight. To make herself feel better, she added unflattering knickers and an ill-fitting bra. "Actually, I'd prefer to hand it over to him *personally*." She couldn't resist making the word sound salacious. "I'll come back another time." Then, drawing on lessons learned bartering in the markets of the Far East, Alison deliberately made as if to leave (her exit always part of her performance), moving from porch to pavement. The black statue of William III on his high-stepping horse stood proudly against the blue of the sky, its stone plinth concealed by the neat hedge of the square.

"Wait!" the woman called out. Alison enjoyed the voice's urgency, suggesting fear she'd made an error of judgement. "Let me just see if he's available."

She turned, dismissing the offer as unnecessary. "Oh, I wouldn't want to put you out."

Too late for a welcoming smile, the woman did her best to appear civil, if not hospitable. "I won't keep you a moment."

Ushered in, Alison stood on the black and terracotta tile of the hall. Her nostrils prickled, assaulted by overbearing scent from an arrangement of Stargazer lilies. The original rooms of the house had been allowed to remain intact, which should have provided an informal setting for business. Instead, it added to the sense that visitors were intruding.

Her eyes beginning to smart, Alison noticed that the door of what appeared to be a waiting room had been left ajar. The herringbone design of the parquet flooring drew her eyes. She felt a shiver as she stepped over the threshold to take a closer look. Her eyes trailed upwards. *Rows and rows of bookshelves* - just as Edwin had said. A study! But there was no desk, just a couple of leather armchairs, a side table and an old-fashioned globe. A private library, perhaps. *Punch: 1880 - 1895, Picturesque England: Its Landmarks and Historic Haunts, The Passing of the Great Fleet.* She breathed in the familiar mustiness, hints of tobacco and coffee. Nothing could touch her here. There was no roar of traffic, no vibration of road works, no beeping to signal that a lorry was reversing. She couldn't even hear the slamming of a car door. What a waste it was, keeping a room in which time appeared to slow simply as a showpiece. And yet the books seemed to possess lives of their own, guarding secrets behind well-thumbed pages. Gilded titles read across rather than down the length of the spines: *A Bellringer's Guide to the Churches of Great Britain.* Alison could almost feel the weight of the books, the thickness of the yellowing pages. It was a room that should be loved. Look over here: *Margery Merton's Girlhood.* The collection painted a landscape of an England Alison no longer recognised: church and countryside and childhood. But it was the one she wanted to believe in, for Belle's sake. And yet, drawn as she was to the books, Alison couldn't remember the last time she had read a novel, let alone recall its title. She was reminded of her father quoting - or more likely *mis*-quoting - Churchill: *'If you cannot read all your books... let them be your friends; let them, at any rate, be your acquaintances.'*

Alison's hand was idly spinning the globe on its axis when her reverie was interrupted by the hard clip of metal-tipped soles on tiles. An impatient voice demanded, "Well? Where is she?"

"I -"

Someone else might have been intimidated, but Alison was used to dealing with the great, the good and the downright threatening. She announced herself - "I'm in here" - now understanding the frostiness of her original reception. With a pre-prepared smile, Alison turned to see a man she presumed to be Mr Simons sporting an expensive-looking tan and wearing a pastel tie. (She didn't like yellow on men.) He was neither attractive nor unattractive, but his impatience fuelled Alison's impression that he fell into the latter camp - that and the fact that he couldn't have been more different from the bespectacled brown-haired man of her imagination, to whose conjured credentials she had added someone who might pick up and read *The Poetical Works of Henry Kirke White of Nottingham* when taking a break from his ledgers. Not that people had ledgers these days.

"My secretary tells me you have something of mine," he snapped, not remotely embarrassed at having been caught out. He clearly wished it to be known that, in the world of Wealth Management, time was money, and his time came at a premium.

Well, her time had a value too and a not insignificant amount. "That depends," Alison said. In his mid-forties, if she had to guess. A well-cut suit. In both of these aspects, he fitted the profile of her typical client. Had he been a client, she might have employed a teasing tone, but he was not.

"I'm sorry," he said, sounding anything but. "Look, I haven't got time for games."

"Neither have I," she countered, approaching him briskly. "I have something belonging to a Mr A Simons and, before handing it over, I'd like to see some proof of ID."

The man performed an exasperated double-take, then tried the inside pocket of his jacket. His expression collapsed. Alison couldn't help rejoicing in his growing concern as he tried another jacket pocket, then patted the seat of his trousers. As far as she was concerned, this was proof enough, but he didn't wait to hear what she had to say before striding off down the hall and taking a door to the right of the staircase.

Several minutes passed before Mr Simons reappeared looking sheepish. "I don't suppose…"

What's the magic word? she might have said to Belle. Instead, she blinked, waiting.

Biting the inside of his cheek, he was working very hard to control a rising panic that it appeared might consume him. "I seem to have lost my wallet, and if you have it, you have almost every form of identity I own."

Detecting a tremor in his voice, Alison couldn't resist prolonging the torture. "Then, just so I can be sure I'm handing it over to the right person, would you mind describing a couple of things you have in there?" She met his anxious expression with absolute calm.

"Oh, yes, of course. Cash. Cards. Credit cards."

"Something personal, perhaps?"

He breathed out heavily through his nose, cupped his chin; then his expression softened: "Photos. My kids. Two boys. Goofing about for the camera."

Relieved he had redeemed himself in some small way, she reached into her shoulder bag, thankful she would be rid of the wallet and its temptations.

When Mr Simons opened it, it was the photos he turned to immediately and Alison found herself touched by his expression. He held the fold open for her to admire. "That's them: Will and Jim."

"How appropriate." She was slow to reverse her initial impression.

His eyebrows pulled together.

"Given where we are?" she prompted. "William and James?"

"Do you know, I've never made the connection. I didn't work here when the boys were born. Looking at this photograph," he studied it carefully, "I can't believe how fast they're changing. This was only taken a couple of years ago, but..." He shook his head.

Through fresh eyes, Alison saw the family man she had hoped to find. Someone who shared the same concerns as her.

Now, looking up from the wallet, he had the decency to appear flustered. "You must think I'm a complete idiot. I hadn't even realised my wallet was missing."

"You were lucky. I found it lying under a bench."

"Where?"

"In the park. Everything seems to be there - at least, the credit card slots are still full."

"And the notes!" He looked at her in disbelief.

Translating this as: *I can hardly believe you didn't help yourself,* she said, "You were lucky."

"I'd just been to the bank to stock up on petty cash!"

So, it wasn't even his own money. Had Alison taken it - or a portion of it - he could have written it off as a business loss.

Shaking his head, he started to extract some notes. "Please. Let me give you something for your trouble."

Tempting as it would have been to accept, the situation felt uncomfortably familiar. She recoiled. "No, you really don't need to -"

He held a fold of money at arm's length, nodding towards his hand. "I insist." It seemed the transaction he was proposing was equally distasteful to him.

This riled Alison in a way that would have been difficult to explain, so she ensured her voice was light: "You're in no position to. I won't allow you to ruin my good deed for the day." Especially since her first thought had been to pocket the money.

"Then at least let me call you a cab."

"Again, thanks, but no." She was almost at the front door when she began to sneeze. Whether their encounter was preordained or not, the quicker she escaped the suffocating scent of the lilies the better. "I already have a travel card. Besides, it's a beautiful day. I'll walk."

Alison had paused on the pavement outside the office to look at the statue of William III, when she heard the door behind her.

"My card." Mr Simons was breathless, leaning out from the shade of the porch into the sunlight. "Should you ever need me to return the favour…"

She was unable to resist pretending to read it for the first time, knowing full well what it said. "*Wealth Management.* How thoughtful." An unscheduled memory visited: her father accompanying her to the bank to cash in all of the half-pence pieces from her piggy bank (together with those they had dug out from down the back of the sofa) before they were taken out of circulation. Copper for silver had seemed a good exchange. She had come home and announced, "I'm rich, Mummy!"

"It's just as well one of us is," her mother had said ruefully.

"I'm doing my best," her father replied.

Alison had offered the small plastic bag containing her haul of silver, but her dad had said, "Don't be so daft."

It seemed that the morning's session with Edwin had awakened snapshots from her former life that she hadn't realised she'd stored away.

Mr Simons shrugged: "Just in case?"

Opting for what seemed like the easiest way to extract herself from what had become an awkward situation, Alison took the card between her index and middle fingers.

He added, almost as an afterthought. "You didn't have to do this."

"I'd like to think that someone would have done the same for me."

Walking away, Alison wondered if it was too late to turn back and say, 'On second thoughts, I will have that money.' She could have used it to treat Belle. But she was proud, and that had always been her downfall.

Rounding the next corner, she stopped and closed her eyes briefly, emitting a small sound of exasperation. Opening them again, Alison noticed a red telephone box. Well placed for her purpose: a discreet street corner; a good area.

Pretending to be about to cross the road, she checked that no one was looking. She then retraced her steps and removed some of the more extreme of the eighty or so vice cards on display. Alison started to replace the cards with the thirty she distributed daily. The source of a reasonable percentage of the so-called 'means' that Edwin had spoken of. Relatively low numbers compared with some of her colleagues (if that was an appropriate way to refer to people she'd never even met). Thankfully she also had her regulars who welcomed a discreet call to see how they were. No call with Alison ended without an appointment being arranged.

CHAPTER EIGHT

Alison's stomach jolted at the sound of knuckles rapping on a rectangle of glass. *Stay calm*, she cautioned herself on catching sight of a uniformed sleeve. It was hard even to draw breath.

"You startled me!" One hand was high on her chest, fingers splayed. If her gesture was designed to distract, the sentiment at least was genuine. "I was just removing some of these awful cards -" Speaking with an authority she didn't feel, Alison tried to channel calm. Without knowing what the police officer had seen, her legs wanting to buckle, she stepped outside and handed the cards over. Included among them - unavoidably - was one of her own.

"So I see." There was a moment when Alison thought the policeman would accept her explanation of what she had been doing. He shuffled through the cards then looked up at her pointedly. "Who are you working for?"

"Look, I'm sorry -" It wasn't too much of a challenge to sound indignant. As a mother, she was horrified at the thought that Belle - or any other child for that matter - should be exposed to the explicit adverts for BDSM, fetish and oral. A group of five-year-olds at Belle's school had, to the PTA's horror, invented their own version of Pokémon, swapping glossy prostitute cards they had managed to collect among themselves. "Where did you find them?" they'd been quizzed. The children, although knowing they had done something slightly mischievous, couldn't comprehend the furore their little game had created. "They're all over the place," they'd shrugged. An estimated thirteen million cards are tacked to the surfaces of central London's phone boxes. Within reach of sticky fingers, apparently, given a leg up. So commonplace, adults have become blind to them.

"Who employs you?" the policeman demanded, any pretence at pleasantness having evaporated.

Of all the stupid -! Alison swallowed. The last thing she wanted was to be associated with people-trafficking. There was no time to weigh pros and cons. "No one," she said, with resignation. "I work alone." The words were out before it struck her: the policeman might just have been fishing.

"And you're..."

"The ballerina." She pointed to a discreet card, embarrassed by her self-deprecating pseudonym. The thought that the details of her life were about to be examined under a microscope made Alison feel sick to her stomach. All of those things she had managed to keep hidden.

His eyebrows twitched upwards ever so slightly, as he opened his mouth. Stars clustered behind Alison's eyes. After six years of getting away with it - so much so that her constant fear of discovery had eased - she was about to be arrested for the one illegal, but also the least dangerous activity, that her job entailed.

"I'm arresting you for displaying vice cards."

"But I provide an escort service!" she protested.

"You do not have to say anything -"

Alison gasped, not because of the slap of humiliation, but because of the realisation that there were only forty minutes until she needed to collect Belle from school. She had never once been late, let alone failed to show up. All of the names on her emergency contact list invented, the threat of Social Services loomed large. And - her mind racing - for the life of her, she couldn't think of one person - not one! - of whom she could ask a favour. Fond of Belle, Mrs Oo might do it at a pinch, but it would be hypocritical to ask. Alison had never been a friend to the Oos. Besides, she saw how her neighbours pitied Belle; how they attempted to compensate for what they obviously saw as her inadequacies in the parenting department. And for how they imagined Belle would react when she eventually realised how Alison managed to pay the rent. Because the Oos must have a pretty good idea. How could they not? Men arriving in expensive cars, traipsing past their kitchen door and up the back steps at all hours. They had never once complained. They were far too polite.

"- but it may harm your defence -"

How long do these things take? she wondered. Would she be kept overnight? In which case...

"- if you do not mention when questioned something which you later rely on -"

"In case you ever need me to return the favour." She felt inside the back pocket of her jeans for Mr Simons's business card. Thick. Embossed. Except... no. She didn't know him. But she'd seen the way he looked at his sons' photographs. He was clearly a man who loved his family. And she knew where he worked.

"Anything you do say may -"

Mr Simons had *made* the offer. Pressed his card on her. And what choice did she have? It was this, Social Services, or begging her mother. And she couldn't face that particular conversation, not under these circumstances. There was no time to think. "Can I make a call?"

The police officer glared at her, apparently put out to have been interrupted mid-flow. She sympathised, having fumed whenever audience members used to throw her concentration with a ring-tone or a camera flash.

"May be used in evidence," she completed the sentence for him. "I need to arrange for someone to pick my daughter up from school."

His mouth curled into a sneer.

"Please. She's six years old! I'm entitled to one call, and we're here, in a phone box."

"You don't have a mobile?"

"I left it on the table by the front door." She stopped herself. This compulsion to protect herself by telling the first lie that came to mind had to end. The policeman didn't know that she had neither a table in the hall, nor a front door, but he could easily find out for himself, and what would that say about her character? "I won't be a minute." Alison turned and picked up the receiver, sensing that her best approach was to assume the only reasonable answer was *yes*. As for Mr A F Simons, she wasn't so confident what his would be.

Away from the police officer's gaze, Alison closed her eyes momentarily, a sigh surging from her lungs. *Wealth Management*. She tried to centre herself, but her hands were shaking as she punched the direct dial number printed on the business card into the phone. *Pick up, pick up, pick up!*

"Mr Simons?" Alison asked before he had the opportunity to speak, her heart pounding violently. "I'm the person who returned your wallet. You said I was to call if I needed anything."

Half expecting him to hang up, instead she heard him laugh; not nastily, but as if he was taken aback. "That was all of five minutes ago!"

"Did you mean it?" Alison pressed. Shaking his head, the policeman released his hold on the door and it swung shut.

"Of course, but…"

She placed the business card on top of the phone and reached into her bag for her mobile. Slim, black and silver, she hoped it would be possible to leave it behind unnoticed. There was an unwritten code that she would never reveal the names of her regulars. The mobile vibrated under her moist palm, as if determined to draw attention to itself.

"I wouldn't ask anything for myself, but it's my daughter. I've been called away on an emergency and I may be gone overnight." The growing lump in Alison's throat made speech increasingly difficult. "I can't get hold of anyone else…" Aware how lame it sounded, she couldn't think how better to dress it up. When Mr Simons didn't reply immediately, she added, "I need someone to pick her up from school and take her home with them."

"You'd trust your daughter with someone you don't know?" The horror in his voice was palpable. Surely he'd understand that only someone desperate would dream of asking?

Must I beg? She closed her eyes, as if that might make it easier. "You're obviously a family man and, frankly, I'm out of options. Can you do it or not?"

"I can't -"

The only way to counter tears was with anger, aimed at herself and her whole sorry predicament rather than at A F Simons. "Shit -!"

"Hang on! I was about to say that *I* can't, but my wife might be able to. Give me a few minutes."

"I don't have a few minutes. I only have this -" Trying to get a hold of her breathing, Alison could no longer ignore the policeman who was pointing to his watch, adopting similar sign language to the gestures she used at Belle's bedtime. "- This one call."

"You've been arrested." Mr Simons's voice flat, it wasn't a question. Alison swallowed but made no denial. "Well, it's obviously not for dishonesty!"

"No. It's nothing like that. Look, I'm sorry to press you but I need a straight yes or no."

"Yes."

"Yes?" She laughed with relief, wiping a tear from the corner of her eye.

"Don't make me change my mind. I'd better jot down the details. Give me the name and address of the school."

Being as succinct as possible, Alison listed the name of Belle's class, her teacher, the headmistress and a few of her daughter's likes and dislikes. (Under no circumstances would she eat olives). He reciprocated with his home address - something she, in panic and gratitude, had forgotten to ask - adding, "As far as my wife is concerned, we'd better say you're a colleague. Agreed?"

"Agreed." But her mind was racing: "But Belle's school? What shall I tell them?"

"About my wife? You don't need to say anything other than that she's a friend. Her name's Collette."

"Collette," she repeated. "Will you make sure she has some ID on her? You know what schools are like."

"To be honest, I'm glad they're so strict. I'm sure she'll think of it herself, but, yes, I'll remind her."

Alison breathed shakily, trying to reassure herself that this wasn't the most irresponsible thing she'd ever done.

"But what about you? Do you have a solicitor?"

"I'm hoping it will all be relatively straightforward."

"Insist on legal advice. Once you've done that, you can't be questioned until you've got it."

"But Belle -"

"Don't worry about Belle. My wife will feed her and we have a spare room if needs be. OK?"

"OK." Alison repeated, sighing heavily. What a strange question. None of this was 'OK'. This was what she'd always dreaded. And that it should happen today of all days, when she'd decided to take stock of her life! Remembering her manners, she said, "I don't know how to thank you."

"I counted the money. It was all there, every note." There, in his voice, was the gratitude Alison had wanted to hear earlier, when she'd imagined she was entitled to take the moral high ground.

"I'd better go. But I may see you later."

The policeman was facing the square. His arms were folded. She could see his hands tucked around his sides. Thumbing through the contacts in her mobile, she found and then dialled the number for Belinda's school. "I'm afraid I'm having a bit of a nightmare," she told the secretary, cutting through her sympathetic preamble. "My mother's been rushed into hospital, and - would you believe it? - not *one* of the other people on my emergency contact list is available. I've just managed to get hold of a friend. The only thing is, I'm a little worried that Belinda won't recognise her. We haven't seen her for the last couple of years. I wondered if her teacher... Oh, thank you. Thank you."

Noticing that the policeman was opening the door of the box, she put her hand over the receiver and turned her head.

"Time's up," he said.

She raised her hand, indicating *one minute*. To Alison's relief, exhaling in exasperation, he let go of the door.

"I'm really sorry," she told the secretary. "The doctor's just said that he needs to speak to me urgently. My friend's name is Collette. Collette Simons. Would you mind taking care of everything for me?"

Having been assured that things like this happened occasionally, but agreeing to update her emergency contact list as soon as she could, she hung up. Her mobile phone was now in full view, if the policeman cared to look.

Stepping outside, Alison performed a double bluff. She twisted her neck, looking reluctant to leave.

"OK, enough stalling." The policeman took her firmly by the elbow. "If you can't find anyone, we'll put in a call to Social Services."

"No, no, everything's fine, but I really would like to call my mother..."

"You're chancing your luck. Come on!" He steered her away.

The sanctuary of the phone box left behind, it was still a beautiful day as they headed towards Savile Row. Alison had done all that she could. Belle would be taken care of and she could be reasonably confident that her clients' identities were safe. The likelihood of an honest soul handing her mobile in at a police station was remote.

CHAPTER NINE

Alison experienced the sensation that she was sleepwalking through familiar and yet unfamiliar processes. It wasn't that they didn't register: they were simply things that happened, over which she had no control. Just as she'd done in order to dance on a fractured toe for a whole season, Alison cut herself off. Straddled between two spheres, she signed for her personal belongings. The knotted plastic bag from the chemist's was held up, suspended and spun around like a fairground carousel.

"Sarge." The man on the desk whistled to summon the policeman. "You might want to take a look."

She made no comment. Admittedly, her latest purchases would make denying her occupation difficult. Few mothers of six-year-olds enjoyed sex lives that demanded supplies in these quantities. Her leather bag was turned inside out, the seams of the lining checked for holes, eyebrow tweezers extracted (she'd wondered where they had disappeared to) and everything was locked away.

Through the photographs - asked to hold a card with a number written on it, to turn to the left and to the right - she imagined Maria Callas singing from Bellini's *La Sonnambula*. The sleepwalker.

Through the fingerprinting - while her right hand was

manhandled; her thumb held and rolled across the black ink pad - in her mind she was Allesandra Ferri, hair flowing, holding a candle out in front of her, the sleeves of her luminous nightdress billowing, incandescent, unearthly.

"Your left hand, please."

Placing it on the card, it appeared alien to her. Her knuckles looked particularly pronounced under the harsh lights. She flexed her fingers momentarily; turned the hand over and made a fist.

"Flat on the table, if you don't mind."

No one treated her badly. No one attempted to make the experience any more degrading than it already was. Her responses were automatic. As each finger in turn made its black contoured mark inside a white box, in Alison's mind she was moving on pointe, performing that extraordinary *pas de deux* duet, while the audience believed absolutely that she was fast asleep.

Through the hour during which she sat alone in a cell, her body restless, she focused on a performance from another production of the same ballet: How watching Nikolaj Hübbe's absolute control had taught her that standing still - especially when everyone else is shifting in semicircles and diagonals - can hold an audience rapt and breathless. And with what he described as 'a little experience under his belt', Hübbe understood how to display his physique. Plain white tights; a white sash tied diagonally over his tanned torso: that is how an uninvited guest makes a stir on arriving at a ball. Underdress, and everyone else's finery looks ridiculous. In command of the whole act, he owned everything on stage.

A rap at the door: "The duty solicitor's here to see you."

Throughout the consultation Alison tried to appear patient, nodding and frowning while things she already knew were confirmed. That, argue all she liked, no one was going to believe she only provided companionship; that it was an offence to allow a child or young person between the ages of four and fifteen to reside in a brothel, but that, since she worked alone, her home wouldn't be classified as one.

"What can I expect?" she asked.

"For a first-time carding offence? You'll get a penalty notice."

She found herself nodding: a penalty notice didn't sound so bad.

"But you might find you receive a home visit from Social Services."

The thought was sobering. This was exactly what Alison was trying to avoid.

Then the questioning began: she was asked if she had a problem with drugs. (The police were entitled, the solicitor had told her, to test for heroin and crack cocaine.)

"Are you taking laxatives?" they had asked routinely at the Royal School of Ballet. And, *"You're not purging, are you?"*

"No," she said, knowing that she didn't look like someone who had a drugs problem. There were no telltale bags under her eyes, their whites were clear and she imagined her pupils would appear normal; her complexion was good, her teeth white.

Who else lived off her earnings?

"Remember the sacrifices that have been made so that you can be here."

"My daughter. Belle." At this point she concealed a wave of nausea. Had her instinct to trust Mr Simons been right? Perhaps his wife had been busy...

"Age?"

"She's six." Her mouth was dry.

It was only when they asked how Alison thought her six-year-old daughter would feel about her mother being a prostitute that her nostrils prickled and flared. "I'm an escort," she repeated. It didn't matter to her that they refused to see the distinction; that it wasn't *helpful* if she continued to insist on it. Holly Golightly settled on the term *American Geisha*. How would it sound if she used the English equivalent? Would that be *helpful*? she wondered. The thought made her smile wryly before she checked herself. The biggest problem Holly faced was that she might fall for a guy with no money. Alison had Belle to think about.

Asked if she lived in a flat or a house, the rebellious part of her nature wanted to say, "A luxury penthouse."

Who else lived in the building?

"There's a Chinese takeaway on the ground floor. A Mr Oo and his wife live above it. We have the second and third floors."

"We?"

"My daughter and I."

"And there are no other sex workers?"

Alison flinched from the term, lifting her chin: "I work alone. I've already told you."

They didn't like that, she saw. If she wouldn't accept their help, there would be no option but to charge her and require her to attend meetings with a supervisor in order to address the causes of the conduct which constitute the offence.

On hearing *the causes of the conduct*, her father's face elbowed its way to the front of Alison's mind. *"This is what we're going to do. I'm going to shout at you for a while and you're going to cry."* She pushed him away.

Encouraged to access support services, Alison was asked if she would like help to find a way out of prostitution. What other skills did she have?

"I can dance the role of Giselle to perfection."

"Giselle?"

They obviously hadn't made the connection with her business card. And why would they? "Never mind," she said.

"We'd like to think you're taking this seriously, Miss

Brabbage. Do you realise we could inform your landlord?"

Eventually, just as they appeared to be losing patience, it was confirmed that she would receive a conditional caution.

Alison jerked back to life. It was the time of day some might still call late afternoon. She suspected a more serious crime was demanding their attention. In the twenty-fifth biggest city in the world, a whore operating independently was small fry.

She hurried to Victoria station, dismissing the thought of returning to the phone box for her mobile phone. Her contacts' names would mean very little to someone with an unenquiring mind.

It was already too dark for Alison to see the green rise of Brockwell Park from the train. She stood as they approached Herne Hill station, impatience building. She was the first to disembark, the first up the stairs. It was only as Alison passed a florist's stall in the station forecourt that she broke her stride. Flowers! That's what an ordinary woman would buy when her boss's wife picked her daughter up from school. She checked the contents of her purse, reminded of food shopping not yet done. After a few moments' indecision she settled on sunflowers, their heads large enough that a few stems would make an impact. Disorientated by unfamiliar surroundings, Alison studied a map of the local area before deciding which direction to take, passing a deli and a café. She had the sense that she'd arrived in a neighbourhood she might have enjoyed coming home to, had her circumstances been different. The sunflowers proved awkward to carry, making her feel ham-fisted as she presented herself outside 25 Melberry Gardens and rang the bell. Nerves had accumulated in her empty stomach, not assisted by the realisation that she had no idea what Mr Simons's first name was. *What employee wouldn't know the name of her boss?*

Through the door's frosted glass insets, she saw the approach of a hazy outline. Unhurried. Pausing to turn and yell, "It must be your mummy!"

Hearing those reassuring words, Alison suddenly felt exhausted. But she couldn't relax yet: she had a part to play.

Never entirely comfortable in the company of women, Alison fully understood that there was something unsisterly in what she did for a living. The majority of her clients were married. Happily so, more often than not. But the woman who opened the door was someone Alison found herself wanting to impress. Like those girls at the Upper School - the ones with the razor-sharp cheekbones - who wore ever-so-slightly amused expressions, as if they were in on the latest joke and had the power to decide whether or not you were to be left in the dark. Who wore the clothes you wanted, be it the coveted *Swan Lake* tutu (no matter that it stunk of stale sweat) or the latest slouch-wear. Alison found herself admiring expensive versions of the well-fitting jeans, pumps and masculine white shirt she also favoured. "Collette?" Alison enquired, angling her face around the sunflower heads.

"Come in, come in!" The woman stood back, holding the door open. The hall, Alison noticed, was wide and, apart from a pair of stray trainers, uncluttered. Coat pegs were hung with hats of various shapes and sizes (flea-market finds, she assumed, clearly never worn by their present owners). "You must be Alison."

"These are for you." She was glad to be rid of the burdensome flowers.

"Oh, you shouldn't have!" Collette looked genuinely touched. "You found us alright?"

"Mummy, Mummy!" Belle's excitable voice reached them and Alison had to resist the urge to run to her daughter and hug her.

Instead, she called out, "I won't be a moment, sweetheart." Then she said, "It was fine. This really is so kind of you. I just hope Belle hasn't been too much trouble."

"To be honest, I've been enjoying myself." Collette lowered her voice discreetly. "I have more spare time now my two have reached that age when they prefer to make their own way home. They're always at one after-school club or another. I think it was chess and football today, but I find it impossible to keep up." She proceeded at normal volume. "And how's your mother?"

Not quite sure what Mr Simons would have told his wife, but seeing Collette's eyes full of concern, Alison opted for, "She's in the best place she can be."

"So the hospital's keeping her in?"

"For a couple of days, yes."

"Mummy! Mummy! I've got baked beans *and* peas *and* sweetcorn with my fish fingers."

"Lucky you!"

"I'm afraid we're running very late. The kids are only just finishing their dinners." Collette explained, leading the way past framed portraits. A picture of the family lying in bed, a baby the focus. Parents, back to back, each holding one child. A picnic. Alison felt a pang: Belle would never be at the centre of a family group. At least, not one that included both parents. As she passed the cupboards under the stairs, Collette closed a door that was slightly ajar, restoring the clean line.

"There you are!" Alison exclaimed at the sight of Belle squirming. Her heart gave a lurch. Her daughter looked particularly small, sitting at a large table set in the middle of a vast glossy white kitchen - the type Alison might pore over in a magazine while waiting her turn at the hairdresser's, doubting the owner's claim that it was easy to keep clean. Chewing conscientiously in that way of hers that brought her whole head and torso into play, Belle was expending far more energy than she stood to gain from a mouthful of peas. An orange square, already pronged on her upright fork, was being waved about. She swallowed, an action which involved the whole of her neck, and declared, "Yum!"

"It's nice to see someone enjoying their food," Collette said.

"Can we get down from the table?" asked an older version of one of the boys who had appeared in the photograph from the wallet. Just as Mr Simons had implied, goofiness had been replaced by emerging pre-teen cool, including - apparently - a lack of tolerance for small children and adults.

"After you've said hello."

"Hello," they said in unison, enthusiasm notably lacking.

"Hi." Alison mirrored their economy, and then added something particularly parenty, by her standards. "I expect you've got loads of homework that needs doing."

"Go, go, go!" Collette clapped her hands. Not waiting to be told twice, they skulked past, heads down, although Alison noted how one of them - either Will or Jim - raised his eyes to the level of her breasts. "Come and tell me when you've finished," their mother called after them, and then turned back, shaking her head as if indulging some slight misdemeanour.

Alison glanced about for evidence of havoc her daughter might have wreaked. There were signs of cutting-out: round-ended plastic scissors and pages from a glossy magazine with jagged shapes missing. One of those red retro kitchen mixers Alison craved was upended, its triangular blades doughy. Not that she ever baked, but she might feel more inclined with a kitchen as spacious as this, and an oven that wasn't caked in grease from previous tenants' culinary disasters. It would be possible to be a different person if you lived here, in the light, with decking beyond the full-length windows running the width of the house, and fresh herbs overflowing from terracotta pots.

This was the home Belle deserved. One Alison would never be able to give her.

Feeling suddenly tearful, she walked around behind her daughter and kissed the top of Belle's head, then rested her chin there for a moment to breathe in the spring scent of her hair and scalp. Her hands were shaking as she ran them through Belle's unravelling plait. Removing the elastic band, Alison pulled the three sections apart. And as she smoothed out the kinks, she had a sense that the hands she could see were her mother's hands, and somehow it was she and not Belle who was saying, "Ow, Mummy, you're pulling!"

"Have you been good?" Her own voice was gravelly as she scooped up a neat ponytail.

"Yes," Belle replied in a new bored-sounding tone, reaching for a beaker of milk.

Collette laughed. "Why don't you show Mummy the Get Well Soon card you made? Grab a seat, Alison. I expect you could murder a cup of tea."

"Why would anyone murder a cup of tea?" Belle asked, pushing an already dog-eared folded sheet in front of her. (Her daughter, she saw, was sitting on a cushion, also white.) "What's it ever done to you?" She had drawn a painfully-pink sexless character, suggesting that a limited number of felt-tips had been available. The character was wearing a green triangle on its head, an eye patch too far down its face and had red circles for cheeks. Like most of Belle's people, this one had arms that stuck out at right angles from its body.

"Uh, uh, uh, don't be so cheeky. It's just a saying." Alison found herself speaking as if she were reciting lines from a script. She must guard against the possibility of saying 'we must skedaddle' or 'okey-cokey'. "Who's this you've drawn?"

"She's a queen pirate. That's her wooden leg and that's her eye patch because her glass eye would fall out if she didn't wear it, and that's her parrot and that's all the treasure. See?"

For once Alison was grateful for the kaleidoscope quality of Belle's imagination. There was always an order and a logic that needed to be grasped, based on Belle's slightly skewed understanding of how the world worked. The treasure had its own rays, like the rays of the sun. "A pirate with very shiny gold." The paper shook as Alison opened the card to read what was written in her daughter's downward-sloping scrawl. She still found it odd that schools taught children joined-up writing before they insisted on correct spelling. Applying a little guesswork, she deciphered: *To Grammy. I hope your leg gets better soon.* A lady pirate with a wooden leg for a supposed grandmother with a bad leg: it had a certain gallows humour. She hoped to God that Belle hadn't told Collette that her mother actually *had* a wooden leg. She imagined Collette suggesting that it was made of plastic or carbon fibre and Belle refusing to tolerate a substitute. Poor Belle! It was hardly her fault that she had found herself in a stranger's house having to make it up as she went along. "Love and kisses, Belinda," Alison read out loud. "Granny's going to be very pleased with this."

Belle beamed. "We made chocolate chip biscuits too."

"Did you, now? I wondered what that lovely smell was." Noticing her daughter's cheek was daubed with tomato ketchup, with the strange sensation that she was looking at her own mirror image, Alison found herself licking the side of her own mouth, surprised when the taste she expected didn't arrive.

"You'll have to take some home with you." Collette deposited a white mug on the table. "Unless you'd like one to go with your tea?"

What Alison really would have liked was fish fingers and baked beans, but she took a biscuit from the Tupperware box, bit into its sweet and still slightly warm shortbready texture, and, cupping a hand to catch falling crumbs, made an approving *mmmm*.

"Aunty Collette taught me a pirate song! *Fifteen men on a dead man's chest. Yo ho and a bottle of rum,*" Virtually tone-deaf, Belle began, rhythmically but tunelessly.

"Not while you're eating, sweetheart." Alison barely noticed that she was employing the nagging phrase her mother had chipped away with, making mealtimes a misery. Tone-deaf she might be, but Belle never had any problem memorising words. Her head was moving in a way that suggested she had a whole choir singing inside it, and she made a pantomime of swallowing the mouthful of fish finger before asking Collette, "What comes after *Done with the Rest?*"

"If in doubt, try *Yo ho ho* again."

It bothered Alison that she couldn't remember teaching songs to her daughter. Belle picked them up at school, of course - a curious mix of hymns, folk songs and chart music, accompanied by action routines that incorporated sign language. But Alison had grown up in a house with a piano, inherited from her mother's mother. Never at home long enough to justify lessons (thankfully), it had been her job during the school holidays to polish the keys, first the yellowed ivories and then the blacks. She had lingered over the task, experimenting with her arabesque (*adagio*), slowly extending one leg behind her as she drew the damp cloth towards her. ("Never side to side, because moisture will seep between the keys.") The lid would be lifted to reveal the keys she had shined so beautifully and visitors would be coerced into joining in with something from one of the few sheets of music they owned: *When I'm Sixty-Four* or *She's Always a Woman to Me.*

She observed Collette watching her daughter, absorbed by Belle's lively chatter, amusement transforming her face. Alison marvelled at how quickly her daughter befriended someone new; how quickly she trusted.

Their voices became muffled. All Alison could hear was

the causes of the conduct which constitute the offence. The words were chilling. More real than Collette's beautiful jawline, her wide green eyes. Her ready laughter and serious nodding: exaggerated expressions designed for young children still learning to recognise emotions. This instinct for what children needed seemed to come effortlessly to Collette. Although the threat of Social Services hadn't reared its troll-like head, Alison felt like the outsider, cast aside in favour of an attentive newcomer. Belle was no longer that clingy little girl. She was growing up too fast.

Alison came to, as if jerked out of a deep sleep.

"Mummy!" Her daughter had lolled heavily against her.

"Yes, Belle," she replied automatically. Her solidity and warmth were so sweetly familiar.

"Mummy, I'm *tired*," she announced, in a way that suggested the onset of exhaustion so complete it couldn't be fended off. She became a slightly younger version of herself, the one who had said 'par-cark' and 'telebision.' Who had to balance the edge of her plastic beaker on the table as she angled it towards her mouth and released a loud 'Ah!' every time she took a sip.

"I'm not surprised," Collette said, glancing at her watch as if she, too, had suddenly remembered herself. "Andrew will be home soon." And again she transferred her green gaze to Alison. "I hope he doesn't keep you at the office too late."

"It's difficult for me to manage overtime, I'm afraid." *Andrew: so that was his name. Not Adam, as she'd imagined.* "Come on, Belle. Two more pieces of fish finger and then we must think about getting you home to bed."

"Aw!"

Alison foresaw a tantrum and wasn't sure she had the energy to deal with it. "I could have sworn you said you were tired!" she countered.

"But I was going to sleep in the lilac room." Belle's

shoulders folded inwards, suggesting that a promise made was being retracted.

"It's my fault." Collette admitted, slightly guiltily. She was a woman whose hair fell back perfectly into shape after it had been ruffled. "I showed Belinda where she could sleep if she needed to stay the night. You took rather a fancy to it, didn't you?"

Even though Belle was a little too heavy for it, Alison heaved her into her lap - "Come on, poppet" - and tucked a stray hair aside. She nuzzled her daughter's cheek and spoke directly into her ear: "You can sleep in your own room, with all of your things." A jealous part of her was afraid that her daughter seemed to prefer what a new friend had to offer.

"Oh, that will be much better, won't it?" Collette coaxed.

Into these negotiations walked Andrew, angling his neck as he loosened his lemon-coloured tie.

"You *wore* that?" Collette asked, apparently horrified.

"Of course I wore it!" he declared defiantly, wasting no time in removing it, rolling it round an index finger, and pushing it into a gap between the espresso machine and the wall. "Our son bought it for my birthday."

"I hate to say it of a child who's inherited my genes, but Jim has very questionable taste." Collette turned back to them and dramatically clasped the arm that was tucked around Belle's middle. "Everything he wears has to either be black or have skulls in it, preferably both. Even his jim-jams. On the other hand, he seems to think that middle-aged men should all wear yellow." She said it in such a way that suggested yellow was far worse than skulls, and quite possibly worse than earwigs, Belle's current least favourite thing. Alison contemplated the sunflowers resting in water in the stainless steel half-sink, blinking. Out of place among the cool white gloss and hot red accessories.

Squirming in her lap, Belle was giggling and quite clearly

pulling faces, enchanted by all the attention she was receiving. "Is today your birthday, Mr Simons?"

"Oh, it's not -" Alison said, grasping what her daughter had said, embarrassed that this might have been an even larger favour than she had envisaged. Again, as soon as the words were out, she was aware that this was the sort of thing an employee would be expected to know, especially given that Andrew's company was so small.

"No, no. It was yesterday."

She would have bought her boss a card at the very least; she might have even pushed the boat out and made him a cake. "You kept that very quiet!"

"At my age, you don't advertise that sort of thing."

"Too late. I've make a note for next year."

"Quite right. Embarrass him," Collette said, apparently convinced.

Andrew undid the top button of his shirt and exhaled as if it was for the first time that day. "Thank you, darling." After bending down to kiss his wife's forehead, he addressed Alison, "I hope you didn't have any difficulty finding us. How was...?"

"My mother. As well as could be expected." Short and to the point, as might be appropriate when you wished to assure your boss that your personal life wouldn't intrude during working hours.

"Good. Good." Just the right amount of sympathy/relief. *How had he become such a practiced liar?* she wondered. For Alison, lies were the glue that bonded the threads of her everyday existence together. And yet, even surrounded by evidence that everybody did it, Alison managed to retain the idea that she was the only one desperate to make a good first impression, measuring how much was too much to give away. And for someone whose job entailed constantly giving away little pieces of herself, she cherished the fact that she alone had the power to decide. If the answer was, 'Nothing', then her power increased.

"And unless I'm mistaken, *this* beautiful young lady," Andrew was saying, switching seamlessly, "must be Belinda."

At the sound of her name - possibly at its unusual association with the words 'beautiful' and 'young lady' - a sticky popping sound suggested Belle had just extracted her thumb from her mouth. Alison captured her daughter's fragile wrist inside a circle of thumb and index finger and saw the glistening nail and skin. She pretended she was about to take a bite when Andrew continued, "And tell me, Belinda, do you live in a little white house?"

Alison was surprised by the speed with which a question tumbled out of her daughter, fully formed: "Do *you* know what the pirate had in his flagon?"

It was so unlike those occasions when she would repeat, "Mummy, Mummy, Mummy," and Alison, occupied by other things, said, "Just a minute, Belle." Yet when she eventually gave Belle her full attention, her daughter either had nothing she wanted to ask at all, or it was obviously made up on the spur of the moment, suggesting she had simply wanted reassurance. Alison never ceased to feel guilty, even though she believed children should be taught to wait.

"So you like a bit of skullduggery?" Andrew asked, to which Belle responded with enthusiastic nodding.

"Pirates, pirates... You see, you're pushing on ahead. I'll have to start from the beginning." And with a very solemn expression that seemed to impress Belle even further, Andrew frowned and sighed, apparently working his way through the verses.

When Belle opened her mouth to speak, Andrew made one hand into a *stop* sign and turned for the hall, as if he might find fewer distractions out there.

Collette loud-hailered her hands and shouted, "Cheat!" at

her husband's retreating back.

His head reappeared briefly - only his head - stern, shaking and tut-tutting.

"He's gone to look it up," Collette whispered loudly and very slowly.

"In a *book?*" Belle whispered back, agog. Alison saw how amazed her daughter was that there might be a book in which her poem was *written down*.

"Don't tell him I told you so." Collette beckoned and Belle leaned forwards. "He pretends he remembers it, but I expect he really only knows the first few lines."

"It's best to look things up when you don't know them." Belle confided with a knowledgeable hiss. "That's what I always do."

"Very sensible," Collette said.

"The Librarian helps me and then I write them down so I remember for next time."

Minutes later, the whole of Andrew returned, declaring like a magician about to unveil something extraordinary, "I have the answer!"

Belle bounced in Alison's lap, colliding with her chin. "Ow!"

"What is it? What is it?"

"Grog."

There was a pause while Belle seemed to be considering whether or not this was the right answer, before she asked, "What's grog?"

"Rhymes with dog."

"Yes, but what does it *mean?*"

"*Everybody* knows what grog means."

The women exchanged glances. "I'm not sure I do," Collette goaded. (Even her smirk was the sort of expression Alison wished she could mimic.)

"It's what all pirates keep in their pocket flagons."

"Which is?" his wife prompted.

"Rum, of course!"

"Yo ho ho and a bottle of rum?" asked Belle in her best pirate's voice.

"Precisely!"

The kitchen filled with laughter, with Belle exactly where she liked to be, but rarely was: the centre of attention.

But the atmosphere deflated just as swiftly with a subject-change.

"So, do you think you might make it in to work tomorrow?" Andrew asked. "I mean, if you can't, don't worry. I'm sure we can manage without you for a day or two."

"I'll try my best," Alison said, her initial impression of him completely reversed now that she had seen him in his own home, with his wife, who wasn't remotely scary. (Much the reverse, in fact.) She noticed that Belle's thumb had crept back into her mouth as soon as she thought people weren't looking. It was late, and she needed her sleep.

"You'll call to let me know?" He said this looking into her eyes, as if to drive home a point. Confused, Alison was uncertain exactly what it was he was asking. The idea that they might wipe clean the memory of their disastrous first encounter wasn't entirely disagreeable. Feeling dishonest that negotiations of any sort should start in front of a woman - possibly the first Alison had taken a liking to in some time - she found it difficult even to agree.

"Of course she'll call," Collette interjected, with mock exasperation. "Unless she can't, in which case you'll know she's had to go to the hospital."

Alison was grateful to her hostess. The intensity of Andrew's gaze had unsettled her. It was time to leave, and she gathered up her daughter's strewn-about possessions, while Collette made a few additions to Belle's backpack: biscuits, the lovingly drawn Get Well Soon card for the grandmother who didn't even want to meet her - and a green felt-tip pen she had particularly liked, as she asked, "Where do you have to get back to?"

"Just off the King's Road, near Parsons Green."

"We have a clock that goes backwards," Belle contributed.

They recited their litany of goodbyes and thank yous, to all intents and purposes respectable visitors. Her daughter played her part to perfection, even down to dragging her heels as they walked up the path to show just how hard done by she was, not having been allowed to sleep in the lilac bedroom.

Belle settled on the train, her head on the plastic armrest that separated their seats.

"You don't look very comfortable," Alison said.

"Well, I am."

And when Alison thought her daughter might already be asleep, she said, "I'm really sorry I wasn't there to pick you up from school today, sweetheart."

Belle opened one unfocused eye. "That's alright, Mummy. I had fun."

"You did really well this evening. You know," she ventured uncertainly, "I don't really work for Mr Simons."

"I know that. We were all just pretending."

Choked by the fact that her daughter could harbour so little self-pity and ask so few questions caused Alison to turn her smarting eyes to the window. The train's brakes made a grinding noise. She pretended to be looking out into the deepening gloom to see where they were. "You liked Mrs Simons, didn't you? She wasn't pretending."

They were nowhere she recognised. She watched a spattering of raindrops leave tails on the window as they raced horizontally, like notes on sheet music. *When I'm Sixty-Four.* Belle *should* have people like Collette in her life. Her daughter had no grandparents to speak of; no godmother. Alison needed to make more of an effort to foster friendships and, if not friends, then a support network. Names to fill her emergency contact list.

"Not all of the time, she wasn't." Cat-like, Belle yawned. "But when Mrs Simons said I was welcome any time I liked. Then she was pretending."

Alison wondered if it was possible to feel more of a failure as a mother. Her mouth was behaving strangely, as if her face were trying to crumple in on itself. There was a whole host of things Alison needed to do better. She would buy Belle a poetry book. Make peace with the Oos. Use hotels more often. Or, if her clients frowned at the expense, keep her appointments to the daytime. Facing the window of the speeding train, afraid that her daughter might see her cry, she experienced the sensation that, despite its slight rocking, the carriage was standing still while the world raced by.

CHAPTER TEN

"You could be a model if you wanted to."

"Thank you," Alison replied, kneeling on the hotel bed, slowly buttoning her sheer blouse.

He was watching her intently, lying back on the pillow with one hand behind his head. "Have you ever thought of doing anything like that?"

She'd had an inkling the moment he walked into the lobby that he was going to be the type who wanted to save her. Once - what felt like a long time ago now, but perhaps only two years had passed - there'd been a regular. One who'd suggested she give this life up and let him take care of her. Any other single mother would have leapt at the offer. And she'd liked the man. More importantly, as far as Alison was concerned, she'd felt that he respected her. But crossing the line was dangerous. However overdramatic it sounded for a twenty-seven-year-old, Alison doubted she would ever have an ordinary relationship. One that didn't involve keeping time by a clock. Where you woke in the morning, turned over and found another person's head on the pillow beside yours. But if that elusive thing was to be hers, she didn't want it to start with his agreement of her rates, checking her availability. And, from what the man knew of her - the little she'd given away - his expectations would have been distorted. She would never have been able to be herself, never relax. Imagine his horror, arriving home to find that his bath hadn't been run, his whisky wasn't poured, and with her, standing there, grease underneath her fingernails, having spent the afternoon trying to scour the oven, saying, "You know what? I'm a bit tired." Besides, you can't rely on a promise; you can only really ever rely on yourself. So that had been the end of that. Alison had lost both a good client and the closest thing to a friend that she'd had. On the whole, the idea of friendship appealed more than a deeper, complicated relationship. Collette, she knew, would be a better bet than Andrew. But why would a woman like Collette want to be friends with her?

"Sorry." She tried to disguise a sigh, realising that the man lying on the bed, putting off his return to reality, was waiting for her to reply. "I'm too short to be a model." (But an ideal dancer's height, she'd been told.) "Come on, you!" She whipped the duvet off him playfully.

"Do I have to?"

"You asked me to remind you about your meeting at three."

"I did, didn't I?" He threw his legs over the side of the bed. "You could be one of those body doubles. You know, when the actress doesn't want to strip off."

Turning off the trouser press (when paying for a hotel, they all liked to get their money's worth), Alison immediately thought of *Pretty Woman*. Having worn thigh-length boots to play the part of a prostitute, Julia Roberts objected to posing in them for the movie posters. Since the cinema-going public had thought the PVC-covered legs in the poster were hers, and her reputation hadn't been damaged, you had to wonder what the fuss was about. Still, Alison suspected that being a body double wasn't as glamorous as her client imagined. Exposing yourself to one person at a time was one thing, but, as her brief trial as a Bond girl had taught her, exposing yourself to an entire film crew was another.

"Michelle Pfeiffer's used one."

She laughed in disbelief, asking, "For what?" as she handed him his pressed trousers. "I can't imagine why *she* thinks she needs one." Alison had seen footage of Fonteyn, an experienced forty-six-year-old, playing teenage Juliet, intricately entwining her forearm with Nureyev's as Romeo, and there wasn't a single audience member who didn't believe she was fourteen years old.

"For the hot-tub scene in *Tequila Sunrise*," her client explained. It wasn't a film Alison had seen, but she could imagine. Given what they had been doing ten minutes earlier, Alison was bemused - almost touched - by her client's obvious embarrassment. He turned from her, stepping ungracefully into his trousers. "I read about it in one of my wife's magazines."

Alison had honed her own theory about why happily married men sought her out. They were all trying to recreate their first sexual experiences. Stolen moments; something (or someone) forbidden, clandestine. The back of the bike sheds. A distant cousin's hand on their thigh under the dining-room table. The hour when mothers nipped down to the shops saying, "Be good." The two of them suddenly alone in the house, unable to wait for the click of the front gate before launching themselves at each other, peeling off jumpers and t-shirts that caught on ears and earrings; falling as one to the carpet.

At first, the thought of sex in a double bed bought from Ikea, in a bedroom they had decorated (her, wearing dungarees and reminding him of Jennifer Aniston in her *Friends* days), in a property they'd taken out an eye-watering mortgage on, may have seemed liberating. No more sneaking around, they told each other. No need to keep the noise down. No wondering who was going to burst through the bedroom door. But, unless they could recreate the frisson after the kids arrived, it was the complicated arrangements they missed, the urgent and heady collisions, and, halfway through, the "What was that?" "I thought I heard something." "Shit! Where's my underwear?"

Understanding what she was made Alison good at her job. Big on pretending, she could be the person that was demanded but, at the same time, she could also be Ondine, Giselle or Marguerite. She could personify the dying swan; harness that same sense she once enjoyed: the ballerina as a sacred being. She could be her opposite.

A quick glance at the hands on the hotel alarm clock: five minutes, and she would need to leave to collect Belle. Time to hurry things along.

"What else did you read in your wife's magazine?" She retrieved his silk tie from the floor, threw it over his shoulder, brought him his shirt and stood him in front of the full-length mirror.

"Joanne Whalley used one too. In *Scandal*." He slipped his arms into the shirt sleeves.

"I don't think I know that one."

"It was based on a true story. She played the part of the girl who had an affair with that politician."

"And what did she use a body double for?"

"Her behind."

"What? She accepted a part in a film about an affair. Didn't she think there would be sex in it?" He allowed her to move his hands aside; she lifted his collar. Then, with the tie hanging loosely around his neck, she began to button his shirt.

"I wonder if she got to choose her own bottom double. Imagine being a fly on the wall in those interviews."

Alison arched her eyebrows. He had no trouble, it seemed.

"It's not just women. I had a mate who was in *Braveheart*. You remember the scene where they turn round and lift up their kilts?"

"Yes?" She concentrated on the task. The thing was to make it appear that whatever she was doing was the most important thing in the world. Working from the bottom upwards, her body no more than a couple of inches from his, she reversed the process of undressing him. Collar downwards might have felt as if she were his mother getting him ready for school.

"Third from the left."

"Really?" Alison collected anecdotes: the ordinary and extraordinary things people chose to share. They came in handy when she needed to break an embarrassing silence, except that Alison would refer to a friend of a friend, as if she was positioned in the centre of a vast social network.

"They waxed him, mind."

Enduring her own battle against hair growth, Alison grinned devilishly. "I feel his pain."

"Seriously, though," he said, and she knew that he was watching her reflection in the mirror. "If acting bothers you, even models use body doubles."

"Surely they just airbrush the photographs?"

He lifted his chin as she folded down his collar. "Not if they're being filmed for an advert."

"What's the point of a fashion model who needs a body double?"

He shrugged. "I'm just saying."

She enjoyed this exchange, as an office worker might enjoy a business lunch, but there was a loneliness in knowing none of it was real. Her client would go to his meeting, then home to his wife, and she - she was a social castaway. Belle was Alison's only reality; her anchor.

Alison adjusted the knot of his tie until it was just so. "There we are. One hundred per cent respectable." She stepped aside so that he could see his reflection. Standing behind him, looking over his shoulder, she watched as he went to touch the knot, his hands stopping short of making contact.

Instead, he stroked his chin and turned his head pretending to examine his afternoon stubble critically in the mirror - although she knew he was watching her reflection as she pulled her slim black trousers over her hips. "Sometimes you're not even looking at the person you think you are," he mused. "It might only be their face. Or maybe it's them, but with someone else's feet."

"Not mine!" Alison said, wriggling the toes of her slightly turned-out ballerina's feet; feet that still caused her pain, even though it was six years since her entire body weight had rested on her toes. "Maybe *I* should find a body model." She certainly needed to do something.

Mummy was standing just inside the school gates, under the trailing fronds of a willow tree, Belinda's scooter leaning against her leg. As always, she was alone. A short distance from the other mums, it appeared that she hadn't been invited to join in.

"Why are they all so mean to you?" Belinda had asked. Mummy had explained it was the other way around. She preferred standing alone than spending ten minutes discussing nappy rash, before realising she'd been volunteered to run the cake stall at the summer fair. And her own mother - gammy-legged Grammy - had always insisted on talking to the mothers of children Alison couldn't stand.

"One day, I found her talking to the mummy of a girl who bullied me and we had to stand there until they'd finished, pretending we were friends."

Over time, Belinda had seen that it was true. Mummy would always nod and say hello, even when an arriving mother looked her up and down to inspect what she was wearing (usually a variation on her film-star sunglasses, denim-and-cotton theme), but she never tried to make friends. Today, Belinda was relieved to see her mother's expression brighten the moment she saw her.

Clinging to her upper arm, dragging the soles of her shoes across the faded painted lines on the tarmac, Emily was moaning, "Ohhh!"

If she carried on much longer and Mummy heard, she would announce, "And the Oscar for best actress goes to…" But Belinda didn't want Emily to have the pleasure of hearing her own name so she asked, "What?"

"You're *so* lucky."

"I don't see -"

Newly impish, Emily gave Belinda a small sideways shove. "Your mummy's got her hands behind her back, stupid."

"Hello, Emily!" One of her mother's hands emerged and, when she waved, Emily giggled, because Belinda knew her best friend had what teachers called 'a crush' on Mummy. She had confided that she liked how she was… different.

Belinda sincerely hoped that the whatever it was that set her mother apart wouldn't reflect badly on her. And so, Belinda had begun to study Mummy more closely, finding it hard to find names for what she discovered. Occasionally, when the Librarian used a phrase she thought might do the job, she would stop her mid-flow and ask her to write down what she had just said.

"If this is for a story you're writing," the Librarian would say, "these words are quite grown-up. You might want to keep it simple." But she would write them down, adding a helpful definition, because all knowledge was good. Belinda's notebook resembled a sparsely populated dictionary. She had collected 'self-contained' and 'guarded', knowing deep down they weren't the whole story.

Today, her usually controlled mother looked fit to burst. "Which hand, Belle?"

"Go on!" urged Emily and skipped off.

Was it a trick? Mummy wasn't normally playful in public.

Reaching out and tapping the left one, Belinda was rewarded - for what, she wasn't sure - with a tube of Fruit Pastilles. "Wow!" Her eyes boggled, then she leaned in confidentially. "You know you could have swapped hands behind your back, Mummy."

"I was too excited. Anyway, don't you mean 'Thank you'?"

"Thank you, Mummy! Can I go and give Emily one?"

"If you're quick. I want to leave in two minutes!"

Not waiting to be told twice, already several paces away, Belinda span on the spot when she heard: "Remember to ask her mummy if it's OK first!"

The outer circle of mums were gossiping over the heads of largely-neglected children. At the very centre was a pushchair so overladen with baby paraphernalia it resembled the donkey in Buckaroo. Belinda was amazed there was still room for a grizzling infant underneath.

"What did you get?" Emily asked straight out.

"Wait. I have to ask." Belinda stood, looking up at Emily's mummy, waiting for a gap in the conversation. *Sometimes I think the builders will never finish. Does anyone know how to get rid of grass stains?* Thirty seconds of fidgeting later, understanding that they would never stop (not even to breathe), she raised her voice: "IS IT ALRIGHT IF I GIVE EMILY A SWEET, MRS AMBROSE?"

Emily's mother gave one of those downward 'Who's making that noise?' glances, and carried on yapping: *White vinegar; ammonia. Ooh! Have you tried toothpaste?*

"That counts," said Emily. "She didn't say 'No.'"

Very formally, Belinda peeled back the foil.

"Blackcurrant!" Emily clapped her hands, but then did that big doe-eyed thing, as if to ask, *Are you sure?*

Regretting her generosity, Belinda reminded herself it wasn't always possible to have what you wanted exactly when you wanted it. "That's OK. There's always more than one."

The tube refused to co-operate. Emily had to wait while Belinda tore at the green wrapper to reveal the next sweet, which was an orange (both a colour and a flavour). "First one to chew loses!"

Familiar with the rules, they simultaneously stuck out their tongues, placed the sweets in position and watched the other's face for signs of movement. The sugar felt gritty against the roof of Belinda's mouth. She began the ritual of moving her tongue against the pastille's underside until the granules dissolved.

"Don't I get one?" Mrs Ambrose asked, having realised there was reason to pay attention.

Alarmed by the potential for her treat to be further reduced, Belinda looked despondently at the tube. Luckily, the next sweet was her least favourite: green.

"Belle!" Rescue came in the form of her mother whose index finger was jabbing at her wristwatch.

She rolled the sweet to the side of her mouth, like a hamster would, said, "Gock to go!" and scarpered before anyone else could muscle in.

Her mother declined - "No thank you, sweetheart. They're your treat," - just as she'd known she would. "We need to pop to the supermarket."

It remained a point of honour not to chew, even without Emily as witness. Tomorrow, they would discuss how it had gone and Emily would find some way of claiming she had won. That was how their friendship worked. "OK," she replied. Perhaps her mother's buoyant mood could be taken advantage of. "Can I have a dog?" Belinda got off her scooter and wheeled it into the Co-op, even though some ignorant parents allowed children to scoot inside shops.

"We live in a flat." Her mother stooped to pick up a basket.

"Please, please, *please*. Just one small enough to put in your handbag?"

"There's not enough room in my handbag as it is. And imagine if it wee'd."

"Then can I have a rabbit?"

"No!"

Inside, the air was instantly cooler. One difference between the people in the adverts and real people in supermarkets was that, in the adverts, they were always smiling. Another was that the staff in the adverts never just stood round chatting about their boyfriends. Real staff wouldn't pay you a blind bit of notice until you picked up a magazine and started to read it, or stroked a peach to test if it really did feel like the skin of a mouse, and then they demanded stroppily, "Are you going to *buy* that?"

Mother and daughter bypassed a crate of strawberries, shiny, plump, green-capped and releasing the most delicious saliva-producing scent. Belinda was about to offer to put a punnet on her scooter, but her mother was striding ahead through Fruit and Veg and the girl had to run to keep up. It was always her fault if she got left behind, never mind that her legs were shorter and that the scooter was a handicap when you had to trundle it.

"There you are," Mummy said as they passed the deli counter, where most of the interesting-looking things were, but they refused to buy anything that wasn't packaged because, once, they had seen a fly with its feet splayed on a slice of honey roast ham. Only they're not really feet, just suction pads. The Librarian had told Belinda that flies actually taste through tiny hairs on their legs, which means they try a bit of everything they land on. The next bit was *really* disgusting. Because flies don't have teeth, they vomit saliva which breaks food down into liquid so they can suck it up. *If this sounds unhygienic, that's because it is,* they had read together. Also, Belinda was averse to anything that had been too near an olive.

There were runner beans and broccoli in the basket. Belinda hadn't seen that happen. "Can I have a guinea pig?" she asked.

"No." They had stopped in front of the tins of spaghetti. "Worms or hoops." (This was what her mother always called them, although the labels quite clearly said 'spaghetti' and 'rings'.)

"Alphabet," Belinda answered without hesitation.

"That wasn't one of the choices I gave you."

"Aw, that's not fair!" Even saying the words made Belinda's forehead wrinkle and her bottom lip push outwards.

Her mother's mouth fell open and Belinda felt an Oscar coming on. She was blinked at, as if she was kicking up the most awful stink because *it was all supposed to taste the same.* (If Mummy actually ever ate tinned spaghetti, she would know it didn't.)

"Quickly, Belle. Make up your mind."

She stood on her scooter, in case being taller might help, but if she couldn't have the one she wanted, when it was right in front of her *on the shelf*, how was that a choice?

With a sigh, her mother picked up the two cans and held them uncomfortably close to Belinda's face - *Hoops, worms, hoops, worms, hoops, worms* - but she couldn't just *make* herself want something she didn't to suit somebody else. She stepped back down.

"Shall I choose for you?"

"Hoops," the girl blurted quickly, shifting the now-smooth orange pastille, surprised to find that, rather than anticipating that she would want to say *No, wait!* once the so-called worms had been put on the shelf, all she felt was relief.

"That wasn't so difficult, was it?"

They were on the move again. Pasta. Rice. World Foods. "Can I have a chipmunk?"

"For tea?"

"For a pet!" Her scooter's wheels picked out the dents between every floor tile.

"Do we have to start that again? I thought we might talk about something else."

"What about a chinchilla?"

"What *about* a chinchilla?"

It was infuriating how quickly her mother lost track of conversations. Perhaps she had ADD, like Russell, a boy in her class. Her teacher was always saying things like, *If we could just have one moment of your attention, Russell* and, *If you could just wait your turn, Russell.* "Can I have one for a pet?"

A food label was scowled at and rejected. "I'm not even sure I know what a chinchilla is."

Sometimes it was difficult to believe her mother actually went to the library once a week. "It's like a big fat mouse with huge ears and a bushy tail."

Mummy did that thing where she was pretending to think about it. "No."

"Can I have a hamster, then? It won't take up much room."

"Hamsters smell." A loaf of wholemeal bread, a jar of crunchy peanut butter.

"Can I have a budgie?"

"No. I don't like the thought of keeping animals in cages."

Two pints of milk later (blue top for her, red top for Mummy), they were on their way to the tills.

"It's a bird."

"I don't like the thought of keeping birds in cages."

"Alicia?" A very old man (and, by that, Belinda now meant someone over the age of fifty), a basket suspended from the crook of one arm, reached out and touched her mother's shoulder. His eyes were bright. "I thought it was you!"

It might have been that they were passing the frozen food, but Belinda felt her mother tense. "I'm sorry." She stared at the man's hand as if she was talking to it and, at the same time, pulled Belle to her hip, which left the scooter sticking out at an angle. The girl wasn't entirely sure if this was an unscheduled hug or if she was supposed to be shielding Mummy, but the scooter was definitely a trip hazard.

"I'm sorry, do I know you?" Mummy asked in her put-out voice.

The man looked down at Belinda, as if she might somehow rescue him, but she was distracted by the thought that she might get the blame if someone tripped. People were always suing when they had accidents that weren't their fault. All you had to do was pick up the phone to one of those solicitors who looked like the women on the make-up counters in Peter Jones, then walk with a limp for a week or two. Also, Belinda was keen for the man to get a move on so that she could ask her next question before she forgot it.

"I thought I did, but..." The skin of the man's throat reddened. "Not only do I not recognise the faces of old friends, but now it seems I'm starting to think I know people I've never met! Sorry to have bothered you both." The man squeezed her mother's shoulder slightly before removing his hand.

"Mummy!" Belinda tugged her mother's sleeve.

"Just a minute, Belle." Mummy smiled a tight smile and did something strange: she took off her sunglasses and looked the man directly in the eye. "That's OK. I find myself doing the same thing."

"So it's not my age, then?"

"I think it comes from living in a big city." Her mother's voice was gentle, considering that he was a stranger, which meant that he mightn't be safe to talk to. "You've probably seen me shopping here before."

"That must be it!"

After the man had disappeared up the frozen goods aisle, Belinda forgot his face so quickly, she doubted she would even recognise him if he came and stood behind them at the till.

"So." Mummy's heels clipped. "What was so urgent?"

"We're not supposed to talk to strangers."

"He was just a lonely old man, Belle. We might be the only people he speaks to all day."

"So, we can talk to *old* strangers?"

"If you're in a safe place like a supermarket and someone says 'Hello', there's no harm in being polite. OK?"

"OK." Belle shrugged, unconvinced but with urgent matters to get back to. "Can I have some roller skates?"

"Yes, you can."

In her shock, Belinda swallowed the half-dissolved pastille. "I can?"

"If you still want them in two weeks' time, you can have them for your birthday."

Stunned, the girl thought about what had just happened. She had named everything she knew her mother would most definitely say no to, and then thrown in one completely different thing - the thing she really wanted - right at the end! Had she uncovered the secret of how to get her own way?

As usual, her mother paid the gum-chewing check-out lady in cash.

To be honest, body-part modelling wasn't the worst idea Alison had ever heard. The fact was, she couldn't afford to dismiss anything before she'd looked into it. With Belle installed in front of CBeebies with a glass of milk and a peanut butter sandwich, she spent the best part of half an hour Googling the subject. A foot model boasting earnings of one thousand pounds a day and working up to sixteen days - emphasis on the 'up to' - a month blogged, *'Fortunately for me, most catwalk models have ugly feet from years of squeezing into ill-fitting shoes.'*

"Try pointes!" Alison mourned her crippled toes. Some

women spent hours removing layers of dead skin from their feet, but Alison had kept hers, the only thing between her and blisters.

'*I massage Vaseline into my feet before putting cotton socks on at bedtime and have hot wax pedicures three times a week.*'

"I bet you do!" Sipping from a mug of black coffee, Alison discovered a model whose hands had appeared in adverts for a well-known brand of washing-up liquid, earning her three thousand pounds a day. '*Few people go to the lengths I do to keep their fingers looking tip-top. I never do any gardening or housework.*'

"That sounds like the one for me," she told the screen.

Her new mobile rang: the regular she had bumped into in the supermarket. She switched roles seamlessly. "No, Eddie, of course I'm not upset with you. No damage done. I prefer not to be approached when I'm out with my daughter, that's all. It's far better if you use this number. So, would you like to get together? I'm available tonight. No, wait, tomorrow afternoon would be better... Wonderful. I look forward to it."

The advice she located on an agency website was considerably more honest and, Alison suspected, a few steps closer to the truth: '*Although some body models are in demand, this is only part-time work. Get yourself another income.*'

CHAPTER ELEVEN

Alison stared long and hard at the telephone handset nestling in its plastic cradle. Two days had passed and she owed Andrew Simons that telephone call, yet here she was, nervous that she might feel compelled to tell a man she barely knew secrets she normally guarded. Listening to the burr of the dial tone, she punched the number embossed on the business card. Closed her eyes. Breathed out through her mouth.

"Simons," a confident voice replied.

She held her breath so she might not be heard. Perhaps it wasn't too late to hang up.

"Hello?"

"Hi, it's Alison," she blurted.

"Alison! Hi. Hi. How's your mother? Jenny, can you give me a minute here?" There was muffled pause when she imagined Andrew putting his hand over the receiver. "Where were we?"

"You were enquiring after my fictional mother."

"I was. And how is she?"

"Still sufficiently poorly to keep me from my fictional job." Although she was its instigator, Alison disliked the flippant turn the conversation had taken. She had hoped for something real. "Listen. I just wanted to say thank you. I feel I owe you an explanation." Slow down, she told herself, aware that her gushing sentences weren't fully formed.

"You owe me nothing. But I *am* glad you've called. Collette's been asking after you. I feel bad lying to her. Now, at least I can say we've spoken. She liked you."

Alison found that she was smiling. "You say that as if it were strange."

"Let's just say she wouldn't keep it secret if she didn't take to someone. I've gone up in my wife's estimation. Apparently, I'm becoming a far better judge of character."

"Well, I liked her too. As did Belle, whose judgement has always been excellent."

"Yes." He left it at that, leaving Alison to conclude that Jenny had decided his minute was up.

She felt bolder now that mention of Collette had lent legitimacy to the conversation. "How about lunch?"

"Let me check my diary."

"Today?"

"Yes, one o'clock would be fine."

"Your bench, Pelican Park? That's probably St James's Park to you."

"I look forward to it."

Alison arrived with time to kill. She wanted to make sure that today was a pivotal day; a day worthy of one of Edwin's premonitions. Leaning on the railings of the Blue Bridge, looking towards the arc of the London Eye, she saw three birds bobbing together in the lake. Young, by the look of them. The middle one was beating its wings on the water's surface, its feathers still an adolescent brownish hue. She clasped her hands together. A paper bag hung from one of Alison's wrists, inside it, three rounds of sandwiches, a flapjack and a chocolate brownie, a smoothie and an orange juice. The results of her bet-hedging exercise. She reflected that her feelings towards the pelicans had changed since the pigeon-eating incident. They no longer made her want to smile. There had been a cruelty about it. Something she hadn't intended to expose Belle to. And as for the fat American with the video camera!

Instead she focused on what Belle had insisted was called a 'zebra goose' on account of its black-and-white-ness, even after she'd shown her daughter the sign which clearly showed it was a Bar-headed Goose.

"A scoop." A voice close by made Alison's stomach lurch. She turned to see Andrew nodding downwards, having apparently materialised at her elbow.

"You crept up on me!" His brow had a hot weather sheen to it and he had abandoned his suit jacket in the office. "Is this going to be like the 'grog' conversation?" she asked.

"It's the collective term for pelicans. I thought you might be able to impress Belinda. A caravan of camels. A murder of crows. Kids like that sort of thing."

"I'll only be able to impress her if I can tell her *why* 'scoop' is the collective term for pelicans."

"Oh." He rolled his eyes. "She's reached *that* age."

"She was *born* that age." Alison laughed, straightening up. "And she's very big on facts."

The bridge teemed with the usual mix of tourists (some of whom were - inexplicably - photographing a cluster of pigeons), day-trippers, office workers, students, lovers and - even at midday in the middle of a heatwave - joggers.

"Hello, by the way."

"Hello."

She held up the brown bag. "I've brought a picnic. Are you hungry?"

"Always."

"Shall we?"

They walked pathwards, the fig trees and shrubbery that fringed the lake to their left. She was pleased to see that

'Andrew's' bench was vacant. Alison didn't want to find herself sitting on the grass, not knowing where to look. Already, she could see a young woman whose dark hair was piled in a top-knot, lying on her front, clearly topless, the waistband of her running shorts rolled down to reveal the upwards curve of her buttocks.

"Tell Belinda that pelicans bark. Like a dog. Jim pointed that out to me."

"And you didn't ask him why?" A moorhen, perfectly safe, made a kamikaze dash across Alison's path.

"I missed that opportunity. Damn!"

As they closed the gap between themselves and the bench, an elderly couple who looked in greater need took up residency.

"Look at that!" Alison stopped in her tracks to demand, "Did they ask for your permission?"

"Don't tell me: you forgot to make a reservation," he countered. "Let's push the boat out and hire deckchairs. My contribution. Over by the bandstand."

The deckchair is a great leveller. It's difficult to be formal when sitting so close to the ground. Even though they adjusted their chairs into more upright positions, there was already less of a lunch-with-your-fake-boss and more of a picnic feel, Alison reflected, as she peered into the brown paper bag.

"I didn't know what you'd like, so there's chicken and avocado, poached salmon and watercress and BLT."

"I can't make that kind of decision!" Andrew insisted, one hand on top of his head. "Not in my lunch break."

"How about we share?" She placed one of the recycled paper napkins on the knee closest to her and began to tear at the recycled packaging.

"So," Andrew said pointedly after anchoring the fluttering napkin with a hand.

"So," she replied, almost breezily, offering him the open

triangular carton. "It looks as if I need to think about making some serious lifestyle changes. Mainly on the job front. I certainly can't carry on as I am." It was so infrequently that Alison opened up to another person that she hadn't thought about the process of saying the words out loud. How they might sound to her own ears, let alone another's. *Shit*, she thought, nostrils prickling. *I'm going to cry.*

Andrew sat forwards, elbows on his knees. "I repeat. You don't owe me an explanation."

One corner of Alison's mouth twitched and she nodded: *I know*. When she spoke, her voice emerged clipped and tight. "I was caught leaving my cards in the phone box in the square."

"Cards?" As Andrew interpreted her meaning, she saw his face crimson and he thumped his hollow-sounding chest. Bending down, she retrieved the bottle of juice from its upright position by her feet, twisted the lid off and handed it to him. "Here. You'd better drink this." She heard him swallow painfully and gasp.

His colour returning to normal, Andrew said, "Jenny - my PA, that is - thought you must be a girlfriend. That's why she was so severe with you. Not that I have a history of girlfriends, I hasten to add." He bent his head forwards and ran one hand upwards over the shorn hair at the nape of his neck. "God, listen to me rambling on like an imbecile!"

Feeling immensely grateful that he'd turned the tables on himself, Alison offered, "The cards: they're quite tame. I'm an escort."

There was a girl seated in a deckchair close by. Her eyes were shaded by dark glasses and she was reading, her legs crossed. The rise and fall of her chest under her spaghetti-strapped sundress was visible, suggesting that her novel was racy. But at the mention of *an escort*, the heel of her suspended foot dropped cleanly out of its flat red pump, leaving the shoe dangling.

"Independent," Alison added, remembering that she had seen *Independent Financial Advisor* on Andrew's business card.

The word seemed to prompt a reaction from him. "And that pays, does it?"

So, they were to discuss practicalities. Why not? "Not so much that I'm in any danger of needing your services. But enough to make it difficult to imagine how I might earn the same amount elsewhere."

"An intelligent woman like you?" He spoke with a self-deprecating tone, the message that he knew he was a bit of an idiot.

"An ex-ballerina with little experience of anything else and a six-year gap on her CV. And don't forget I'm a single mother, so I'd need flexible hours. Would *you* take me on as your secretary when you could have your pick of the latest graduates?"

His answer was to bite one corner off the half-round of BLT.

Shooing a pigeon away that had ventured too close to her ankles, Alison noticed daisies in the grass by her feet. "Don't worry. It was a rhetorical question."

"It's not that. It's the financial services regulator. I wouldn't be allowed to."

It's not you, it's the regulator was one put-down Alison hadn't seen coming.

"Other industries might also be closed to you, I'm afraid... if you have a criminal record."

"Then it's just as well I don't."

"They're not going to prosecute? Well, that's fantastic. I'd presumed..."

Although she didn't see much cause to celebrate, Alison leant over and touched her smoothie bottle to his juice bottle. "First offence."

Andrew winced and then lowered his voice. "A caution will still show up on a CRB check. If you've signed one..."

Even fake smiles fade. Alison had been so relieved at the prospect of being released that she hadn't thought the implications through. She had admitted her guilt. "So no working with children or in healthcare," Alison stated what Andrew seemed nervous to voice. "But seriously, assuming I *can* get an office job, how much do you think I could expect to earn?"

"Starting from scratch? Oh, I don't know, twenty, twenty-five..."

She winced. It was hopeless.

"That might even be a little on the high side, I'm afraid. Ours isn't really a typical firm. How much do you think you'd need?"

So this was her reality. The figures simply wouldn't add up. "My single biggest expense is rent. It's ridiculous, how much my landlord charges. And getting a mortgage has never been an option."

"So?"

"They say your rent should be one-third of your take-home, don't they?"

"Not in London, I'm afraid. Let's say we work on half."

"Then I'd need three thousand five hundred a month. After tax."

Andrew switched his phone to the calculator function, using his thumbs as he spoke. "Times twelve equals..." His pause said it all.

"You may as well tell me the damage. Go on."

"Fifty-eight thousand pounds."

"In other words, *three times* the salary I could ask for. *If* I could get a job."

"Perhaps we should work on rent being two-thirds of your take-home." He started thumbing more numbers.

"Stop right there. Even if the figure comes down to forty

thousand, it would still be out of reach." *So much for 'the causes of the conduct'! How about 'the cost of being a single mother'?*

Andrew closed his eyes as if in pain and exhaled loudly.

She responded by placing a chicken and avocado sandwich on top of the napkin on his knee. "I'd probably go stir-crazy behind a desk anyway."

"The stupid thing is that there's a flat going spare above my office. It's a good size too - although it wouldn't be big enough for a family of four." He peeled back the top slice of bread, looked inside, and patted it back into place. "I stay overnight every now and then, but most of the time it just sits empty."

Alison was incredulous. "You don't rent it out?"

He shrugged, a wan smile on his face. "If I'm being honest, I can't stomach the idea of strangers traipsing in and out. Even talking about it makes me uncomfortable. And before you ask, yes, I've thought about putting in a separate entrance. But what I loved about the place the moment I walked in was the hall."

"Hmmm," she agreed, remembering its generous proportions. "And the library."

"I have the solution to your dilemma," he said thoughtfully. But Alison wasn't so naïve that she could ignore the slow grinding of cogs. *There's no such thing as a free lunch,* she reflected as she contemplated the triangle of poached salmon and watercress sandwich she had lost interest in. "I didn't invite you here to bribe you with sandwiches and demand even more favours. That was strictly a one-off."

So why are you here? she asked herself the next logical question. *To admit you misjudged him?*

A football that had lost its momentum drifted over. As Andrew hauled himself up from his deckchair to kick it back, a picture came to mind. When Andrew sat back down with a groan, Alison said, "There's a square near where we live. One with a private garden. You wouldn't think a small rectangle of grass could be so attractive until you surround it with iron railings and put a lock on the gate. Poor Belle stands there clinging to the bars. There's a sign which says, *No Destructive Ball Games*. Of course, she wants to know what a *destructive ball* is. It actually stopped her sleeping, she was so worried about it."

Rather than laugh as she'd intended, Andrew said ruefully, "I'm really not as nice a person as you think I am."

She felt a pang of empathy. "You're a businessman. If you have something valuable, you're hardly going to give it away." Inhaling air tainted with cigarette smoke, she turned to see a topless teenage boy who seemed keen to draw attention to himself, flexing his muscular arms. "Let's not go back to that subject. How about dessert? I can offer you a chocolate brownie or a cherry almond flapjack."

"I'm supposed to be on a diet!" But he needed no further encouragement. "Halves?"

"I thought you might say that."

"You mentioned that you were a ballerina?"

"Yes." While tearing the packaging from the cakes, Alison could tell that Andrew was studying her with a level of concentration it was only possible to respond to with flippancy. She broke the end of the brownie off for herself and offered him the rest. "Trained by the Royal Ballet, no less." She anticipated his next question, the one that usually followed if ever she shared this detail about her life. "Go on. I can tell you're dying to ask."

"What?" He spoke with his mouth full.

"Was I any good?"

"And were you?" He caught a falling crumb.

"I trained for five years."

"Almost as long as a doctor!"

Having heard the comparison before, Alison knew it wasn't strictly true. Still. "I was flawless. Exquisite, in fact."

The sky above them was almost impossibly perfect, as if they were on a film set, or outside the Sydney Opera House. "But Belle arrived, and it became completely unworkable." For the second time in the space of quarter of an hour, Alison thought that she might cry.

"And you tried -?"

Irritation prickled enough for her to fight back. "Everything. I tried everything." She remembered the depression, the despondency, and the feelings were raw and immeasurable once again.

"Of course you did."

Closing her eyes, she tried to let go. *He has no idea*, she reminded herself, taking a moment to breathe. He couldn't possibly know that a choice is not always a choice. Choice can only happen when preferences aren't outweighed by need. Would he understand her better, perhaps, if she referred to *uneven playing fields?*

Driven by a peculiar compulsion to have Andrew know something real about her life - aside from the cost of her rent - she contemplated out loud: "I don't expect you to understand this, but anything other than ballet could only ever be a means to an end for me. I was put here to dance and now that I can't... any other job would be a compromise." Her words sounded overdramatic. Alison compressed her lips while she composed herself. "It was only ever supposed to be temporary. I set myself an ultimatum, which passed a long, long time ago, and I still haven't come up with a better plan." And now, it seemed, her options had diminished.

Andrew was leaning towards her attentively. Listening without interrupting.

"They used to lecture us on the fact that ballet is a young person's profession. There *is* no going back. And the combination of the fact that I'm not getting any younger and Belle being that bit older... I don't want her to know. Not just *how*

I earn a living. I don't want to burden her with the knowledge of *what* I gave up. It was bad enough that my mother blamed me for the loss of her figure! At least this way I'm my own boss. I'm not absent, like so many of the other working single parents at Belle's school are. I get to prioritise being a mum."

"So, well-paid, part-time work, flexible hours and a little more respectability."

Said light-heartedly, it confirmed that this was an impossible dream. "And security," she added for good measure. "Don't forget the security."

A drumming sound started up nearby, drawing Alison's attention. A group of nodding teens sitting on the short grass flanked a cross-legged boy with a set of bongos wedged between his knees. She could just about see his hands - elegant hands - hitting the centre of the skins alternately with his fingertips and then the heel of one hand; hitting the rim and producing a higher pitch with the sides of his fingers. The drummer then added another movement, twisting his hand to produce a different sound with his thumb. Every so often, he introduced a new element to the hypnotic pattern, without altering the rhythm.

"I am not," Andrew began and, snapped out of her trance, she turned her head towards him at the moment he paused and winced, "unfamiliar with your phone box."

It was Alison's turn to raise her eyebrows. It seemed such a strange - possibly even an inappropriate - direction for the conversation to take. She hoped Andrew wasn't going to make a confession.

"Not for myself," he added hastily. "There is an expectation that I will..." He shifted in his seat, his discomfort palpable. "Entertain clients. They tend to be alone in London on business. Collette was never keen before the boys arrived. Now she refuses point blank. And however good Jenny may be at her job, she is not -"

Wanting to save him further embarrassment, Alison said what seemed obvious. "No." The drumming continued, but now it was a background noise.

"And when I am not actively entertaining, I might be asked to arrange for... company."

Chin held high, Alison felt every part of the mechanism of swallowing. "Let me get this straight. Are you suggesting that you act as my *pimp?*" Her throat seemed to fight the word, as though it was repugnant to her.

"No!" Looking appalled, Andrew lowered his voice. "I didn't know that an escort would use a pimp. I provide my clients with a business card, no more."

"From the phone box."

"It seemed the obvious place to look. But, if you were to make yourself available, I'd be happy to pass your cards on instead."

She could see that Andrew's awkwardness was not because he was judging her. He seemed intent on focusing on what was going on around them. The drummer. The reading girl. Anything rather than look at her. It struck Alison that he was worried *she* would be judging *him*.

Relenting, she said dismissively, "It sounds like evening work. That wouldn't work out."

"But if you weren't paying rent, you'd be able to afford childcare. And my clients aren't exactly short of cash. If the money was better, you might not have to work so often."

So this was to be *in return for use of the flat?* Astonished, she remembered her first client. A month's wages. The shock that anyone could value an hour of her time so highly. "And my regular clients?"

Protective of them, in all but one case, 'like' was the wrong word to describe how Alison felt about them. But it would be equally wrong not to acknowledge that attachments existed. Pillow talk when there is no need to seduce or impress is very different from the pillow talk that takes place between married couples or lovers. Alison knew the small details of her regulars' lives. Things that had caused them pain. Partners who, previously passionate, now flinched at their touch. The humiliation of indifference. She had been entrusted with memories of intimate moments. *"She had such a beautiful little body before the cancer. Beautiful."* Tender words that made her wonder if their partners knew this was how they felt, that this - and not necessarily the sex - was what was missed. Alison couldn't just say, "I can't see you anymore."

"If you needed to keep your other clients on, provided they're presentable... You look shocked."

"I am!" she acknowledged with a disbelieving laugh. "This is turning into an extremely weird day."

"If it's any consolation, it's taken me by surprise as much as it has you. You know," - he leaned his head close to hers and she wondered what else he was going to reveal - "I was expecting you to tell me that you'd been arrested because you were a political activist. Greenpeace or something!"

Pleasantly surprised, Alison laughed. "Is that how you saw me?"

"You seemed to have a certain - how shall I put it? A rebellious streak. I could see you fighting the system."

She raised her eyebrows. "Chaining myself to railings?"

"Let's both think about how this might work. But in the meantime, Collette has asked me to invite you to lunch on Saturday."

Alison blinked. It had been forever since someone had invited her into their home, let alone for something as civilised as a meal. She tried to place herself in the cool white oasis of calm that was Collette's kitchen.

"Both you and Belle, that is. I told you she liked you."

"That's sweet of her. You'll have to think up an excuse. Blame it on my mother."

"No one says no to my wife and lives to tell the tale. If I say you can't make this Saturday, you'll be invited next week, and the next."

"You actually want me to *accept?*"

"Don't panic. There are no strings. Lunch is just lunch. Of course, if it's awkward…"

"No. Not *awkward*, exactly. But…" Alison barely knew what her next question should be, let alone how to phrase it. *Why* would he want her to say yes? "What will you tell her?"

"Nothing. Yet. As I say, we need to think about how we could make the arrangement work. For both of us."

CHAPTER TWELVE

There was to be a new outfit. A dress, if Belinda liked. Something suitable for a lunch, but also for birthday parties. It was difficult to imagine being more excited. Belinda sat on the back step a full quarter of an hour before they were due to leave, notebook stowed in backpack, waiting for her mother. She spoke to Ink from a distance, not wanting to risk him brushing up against her and depositing hairs, or anything else that might spoil the day for that matter.

"We're going to walk down the King's Road, but if we get as far as Peter Jones we might catch the number 22 home again."

Mr Oo backed out of his kitchen door carrying a stack of cardboard packaging for recycling. Batter mixture. Hot and spicy noodles. Something called *Hung Fook Tong*. "Wha' sa' you say?"

"I was just telling Ink that we're going shopping for a new dress."

"For the ca'?" He lifted a pizza box off the green wheelie bin, opened the lid, pressed down on its jack-in-a-box contents, dumped his cardboard inside, pressing down on it too.

"No!"

"For Mrs Brabbage?"

"For me!"

Empty-handed once more, he applied his fists to his waist.

"Is your birthday? Happy birthday!"

"No!"

"Is special day?"

"No."

"I think mus' be special day. Only one way to tell."

"What's that?"

He disappeared inside the kitchen and was gone a couple of minutes.

"How should I know?" Belinda shrugged at the cat.

"Here." Mr Oo was holding something out to her. "I give you fortune cookie. Only for very special customers."

"Really?"

"Our secret." He glanced towards their front-door-that-was-really-a-back-door with a hint of nervousness. It was ajar but remained still. His voice was urgent. "You read message inside and tell no one. Understand? No one."

Meaning her mother. A fortune cookie was food but, strictly speaking, neither of them was breaking the rule unless Belinda ate it.

"You can read, can't you?"

"Of course I can!"

"That's good. If someone else read it for you, it won't come true. Okey-dokey?"

"Okey-dokey."

Inside the wrapper, the cookie was shaped a little like a croissant, egg-shell hard and egg-yolk shiny. Belinda lifted it to her nose and sniffed it. Nothing. She licked it. Not unpleasant. Definitely sweet. She nibbled one end carefully (it could hardly be called 'eating'), avoiding her wobbly tooth. There was little more to detect. Just the flavour of lightly-sweetened cardboard. And so she snapped the cookie in two and pulled at the edge of a small piece of paper, the size of a joke from a Christmas cracker. It read, *Not all closed eye is sleeping, or open eye is seeing.*

"You keep that very secret, OK?" Mr Oo said, his hand lingering on the doorframe.

"OK," said Belinda, trying hard to look grateful.

"Fol' it up and put it in back pocket."

There was frantic shouting from the kitchen, unintelligible to most ears but, as with whatever the cat said, she got the general message.

"You should probably go and see what Mrs Oo wants."

"Ah! Very wise!" Mr Oo launched into his own tirade, as if stepping over the threshold had caused his transformation. Chinese was an angry language.

Belinda sat staring at the words printed on the small white strip of paper, willing them to take on different shapes. Shapes that meant something she could understand. Learning to read had been like this. A combination of guesswork and latching onto the slow-motion sounds the Librarian made, trying to drag them out, moulding them.

"Is that a word?" she would ask about the resulting syllables.

"It's not the one we were looking for, but I don't know that it's *not* a word. Shall we look it up in the dictionary?"

"It's not a word, is it?" Belinda would ask when the Librarian had run her index finger all the way down the page without stopping.

"If enough people start using it, it might find its way into the dictionary."

"You mean I can invent new words?" The thought was mind-expanding.

"Well, *somebody* invented all of these." The dictionary was snapped shut so that she could see the width of it.

"Not the same person?"

"Lots of different people. Do you want to see where your word would go?"

Gradually Belinda would string words into sentences. Into impossible-to-argue-with facts and stories with her own illustrations.

"Oh dear," said Mr Oo, startling her. His hand was held out towards her. "I jus' realise. I give you wrong cookie. You muss give that one back."

"But you said -"

"My mistake. My wife tell me you are dragon."

"I am?" Belinda's eyes opened. She was paying attention now.

"Born year of dragon."

"I was born on the first day of the new century," she said importantly, standing up.

"Yes. Year of Metal Dragon. I give you one for sheep. That's no good. Give me back." When she didn't cooperate immediately, he closed his hand and opened it again. Mr Oo's face was sterner and more impatient than she had ever seen it.

"Now you have this." He handed her a piece of paper folded very small. No cookie. "Same rule. Wait until I go before you read it and tell no one. Not even no-good ca'. OK?"

"OK."

Belle looked over her shoulder and watched until she was sure he had disappeared inside. Then she unfolded the piece of paper. *New clothes brings great joy and change to your life.*

There is little, save a second-hand book shop, to hint at paisley-print bohemia. Little to suggest that, in the Sixties and Seventies, the King's Road was where it had all happened: 'Youthquake'; The Saturday Parade; the swinging velvet patchwork city. Jean Harlow has long since been whitewashed. Changing-room curtains of glass beads have been replaced with practical linen. There is no special permit or bribe that would allow you to keep a lion cub in a furniture shop specialising in reconditioned pine. Rhinestone and appliquéd velvet suits hang mothballed in the backs of wardrobes. You won't see a man in a bowler hat twist his head to frown at androgynous sex appeal of the kind not seen since the Twenties: a spectacle of boyish hair combined with three layers of false lashes. Look about at your fellow shoppers: not a felt hat, a feather boa or a dead animal in sight! Drape jackets, brothel creepers, shiny satin shirts: nothing. You might find a lace doily under a cut-glass fruit bowl on your granny's sideboard, but you'd be shocked to learn this was a remnant of the microdress she got married in at the registrar's office you're walking past. "Don't tell me," she'll scoff as your jaw drops. "I suppose you think Kylie invented hot pants!" And she'll tut, enjoying herself immensely, liberated by the memory of the glory her varicose-veined legs once were in their Mary Quant tights. Naturally, she'll do all this without losing the right to criticise what you're wearing, because she has lived - yes *lived!* - and you with your gadgets and your *X Factor* have not (and, if the pitying look she throws you is anything to go by, probably never will).

For 'Apple', think computers. Ask any teenager about *Too Fast To Live Too Young To Die* (if you can distract them from their electronic devices) and they might confuse it with a sequel to *The Fast and the Furious*.

Safety pins might be used to attach price tags to clothes in expensive boutiques, but won't be found combined with tartan, a lavatory chain and a studded dog collar. You cannot identify your enemy by his slicked-back hair and sideburns while your own is dyed green and spiked with clear gel glue. Vivienne Westwood, who once put spokes in the system, has taken up gardening. Malcolm McLaren? Wasn't he something to do with motor racing? SEX is no longer capitalised.

No one is worthy of staring at. Certainly not a mother and daughter, holding hands as they traipse down the double-yellow-lined, low-emission road, stopping off to view marvellous familiar sights.

Having reached the stage where she must read everything, Belle was enjoying the feel of words as she rolled them around her mouth: Paddy Power Bookmaker, The Worlds End Distillery and, opposite, Bespoke Italian Chandeliers ("What's that, Mummy?") and Artistic Features. She questioned everything. Why were the trees planted in sand when they were squillions of miles from the seaside? Why was that telephone box not standing up straight? And struggling to come up with sensible answers, Alison lightly slapped Belle's hand away from the cracked bark of a tree she'd begun to pick at.

They paused to measure the progress of the grapes at the Worlds End Nurseries, peering through the overflowing ivy and wrought-iron railings at the magical oasis beyond. Chinese dragons, Buddhas and Victorian urchins sat among Box shrubs clipped into neat rounds and towering spirals. Then they crossed over to visit the clock that goes backwards, its hands spinning, until Belle announced that she was feeling dizzy, and could they please go and visit the blue plaques? There were several Alison might have chosen, but Carlyle Square was home to two of Belle's favourites, Sir Osbert Sitwell and Dame Sybil Thorndyke, both of whom had featured extensively in the bedtime stories Alison made up for her daughter: Sir Osbert Sitwell who sat upon his sit-upon and Dame Sybil Thorndyke who, in her own mind, was a RuPaul and Paul O'Grady hybrid. Belle pulled out her notebook to sketch the top of Osbert's iron railings and asked, "What would you call that shape, Mummy?" and Alison replied, "A Zulu spear." She tried to correct Belle's spelling when she wrote 'Zooloo', but her daughter scowled, clearly finding the look of it very satisfactory as it was.

They detoured down Burnsall and Godfrey Streets to

see what they referred to as 'the beach houses', a better description wanting for the colourful terrace, where you could choose between living in the bright blue house or one of its lemon-yellow or pink neighbours. And then, as they usually did, they paused outside an estate agent's window to pick their next home. Should they plump for a three-bedded penthouse in Cadogan Square at three thousand five hundred pounds a week or stretch themselves and buy one outright for six million pounds? "Monopoly money," Alison called it, laughing.

A waiter wearing a black apron and using his silver tray as a gong tried to tempt them inside a café, insisting a second breakfast was a necessity for two people going shopping, but Belle was far more interested in investigating why some nearby scaffolding had been wrapped in what appeared to be material used for lagging boilers. One of the Polish builders let her try his hard hat on, but she was happy to give it back, because as well as being too big for her, it was actually very dirty. Then they began in earnest their search for something suitable, something that said, 'Of course we are fully equipped for Saturday lunches. We do this all of the time.' A disguise of sorts.

Watching her daughter parade in front of the mirror in one of the dresses she had picked out, her mouth set in the shape of a smile, Alison was agonising over whether she'd been right to accept Collette's invitation. *What am I doing?* she asked herself. She had offered Belle the invitation as proof that Mrs Simons liked her. She wanted her daughter to know that it was *her* invitation, because Belle had behaved so nicely. Before this moment, Alison hadn't admitted how lonely she was. She had been telling herself that she needed a support network for Belle. Some genuine names to add to the emergency contact list. She had ignored the fact that *she* was in need of a friend.

"Will there be anything I like?" Belle had asked as they sat at their own kitchen table, marked with felt-tip pen from when colouring-in had proved more of a challenge, and where Belle had her own 'special' cushion so that she was at the right height.

"To eat?"

"It won't all be *olives*, will it?" Belle sometimes liked cornflakes for lunch, and it was difficult to say that she shouldn't, because Alison often ate breakfast cereal at odd hours.

"You had fish fingers last time. You enjoyed that, didn't you?"

"Do you think *those boys* will be there?"

"If by *'those boys'* you mean Will and Jim, seeing as they live there, I suppose they might. Don't you like boys?"

"No."

Belle was so sure in her response that Alison felt brave enough to tempt fate. "Then you don't think you'd like to have any brothers?"

"No!"

Her spirit lifting, the movie-perfect sky didn't feel so threatening. "What about a little sister? Would you like that?"

"Why do we have to have anyone else?" Belinda scowled. "I like things the way they are."

Alison's ribcage expanded. "I do, too. I just thought I'd check."

"Hmn. Mummy, will we all have to sit round a big table?"

"Probably."

"For hours?"

It hadn't occurred to Alison that lunch wouldn't interest Belle. So she had dangled a carrot of the most enticing kind - a new dress - and it was decided.

Then Belle had asked one further heart-rending question that brought Alison crashing down to earth: "Will we have to pretend?"

A question Alison had attempted to block out, busily applying suntan lotion to Belle's face, neck and arms, instructing her that she should pack her bag and be ready to leave in half an hour. Mummy was just going to take a quick shower.

Belle was now strutting the length of the changing room, one hand at her waist, looking back over her shoulder and pouting.

"Darling, you don't have to walk up and down. You can just look at yourself in the mirror."

"I'm modelling the dress. This is what you're *supposed* to do."

It was disturbing, the way her daughter put her hands behind her head, jutted out a hip. Poses that would have been provocative had they not been clumsy. Where had Belle learned this behaviour? Was it something she'd watched on television? Some dance routine she and Emily had rehearsed in the school playground?

Alison stopped herself as if she had been slapped: a memory of her mother snatching a hairbrush out of her hand. Pretending to sing, she had been dancing along to a music video showing on MTV. A song called *Tease Me*. Copying the woman in the tight black trousers with the oscillating hips, she had thought the way she was sticking her bum out was funny. There were no angry words, just the shock of the television being switched off and her mother storming out, being left alone to reflect: *What just happened?*

Alison didn't allow her daughter to watch music videos. Was it possible that Belle was copying something she'd seen *her* do? Her daughter was going through a phase of finding excuses to delay going to bed and then getting up during the night. She'd had another of her impossible-to-describe nightmares. No longer populated by giant killer jellyfish who lived off the coast of Australia, there was nothing so specific that Alison could have her daughter draw a picture of and rip it into pieces. Something far more sinister for its vagueness was out to kill them in their sleep. (Belle had a thing about people going to bed and not waking up again.) It was too hot. She was thirsty. She had growing pains. And when all other excuses failed and the luminous hands of Alison's alarm clock confirmed it was 3:00am, she had appeared in the doorway, complaining of being bored.

Alison returned her focus to her daughter, who was asking, "Do you like this one, Mummy?"

It was a pink princess dress. "Yes," she lied, deciding not to impose her own taste on Belle on this one occasion. "The real question is, do you?"

I have accepted an invitation to a woman's house knowing that I'm going to have to lie to her. And to ask Belle to go along with it. Alison could use Belle's word and call it 'pretending', but Belle wasn't known for her subtlety. The thought of what she might come out with… And if Alison told her daughter it was OK to pretend in front of the Simons, how could she then insist that telling the truth was important?

Belle frowned at her reflection and blinked. "I don't know."

What kind of mixed message would she be sending out? "Then why don't you try the purple dress with the butterflies? That's very pretty."

"I like pink." Belle hugged the dress possessively.

"All your friends wear pink. Wouldn't it be nice to look different?"

"I suppose," Belle replied, her anxious-sounding tone creeping back in.

Alison was tempted to say, *We don't have to go. Not if you don't want to.*

Holding hands between shops, their palms grew slippery in the heat. Alison's shoes were pinching her feet and, feeling her scalp burning, she fretted that Belle had come out without a hat. Belle seemed determined to try on every dress in every shop, and Alison became convinced that this was only a display to show willing. Several hours from now they would be back in the first shop with the pink princess dress. She wished she'd sounded more encouraging. A familiar coffee shop sign appeared like an oasis.

"I don't know about you, but I could do with a little sit down and a drink."

"Can I have hot chocolate?"

"Don't you want something cold? What about lemonade?"

"Hot chocolate."

Alison sighed. Foot-sore and flushed, she conceded: "I suppose you'll want marshmallows."

A sharp tug on her arm, Belle had stopped walking. "There!" she said with unreserved enthusiasm, eyes gleaming.

"Where?" Alison turned and looked in the window they had just passed. It was not pink, did not have tiny shoulder straps, a tutu for a skirt, sequins or glitter. Neither did it shout Saturday lunch date, but Belle was looking at the miniature Chinese-style dress - white with a green dragon design - as if it was the most beautiful thing she had ever seen and, frankly, Alison was more than happy to bring their overheated expedition to an end.

There was something celebratory about the fruit frappés they were persuaded to sample. Belle insisted on sitting on a high stool at the 'wavy' bar and they perched, watching the pedestrians and slow crawl of buses, straws in their mouths, making a game of catching each other out by grabbing at arms with ice-cold fingertips.

"Come in, come in!" Collette said, opening the door inwards. "And look at you! You win the award for the best-dressed visitor."

"Is there a prize?" Belinda asked, taken aback: no one had thought to tell her the rules.

"It's just a figure of speech," said her mother, stroking her hair, which was plaited so tightly it was more than likely that she would get a headache. "We have Chinese neighbours," she added, as if Belinda's outfit needed to be explained.

"Well, there's cake. And that's as good as a prize. *Andrew! Our visitors have arrived.*"

Belinda presented Collette with the flowers (red, to go with the kitchen mixer) and noticed how she put one hand flat above her bosoms and then bit her lip. She must have really liked them. The girl could see into the front room where the boy with the skull t-shirt was sitting in front of a giant television and playing some kind of computer game with shooting and explosions. She ventured a timid "Hello" from the doorway, glad when it seemed he hadn't heard her.

"*There* you are!" Collette's husband said, appearing from another door off the hall. It hurt Belinda's neck to look up at someone so toweringly tall. "Ah! I see you're wearing your Custard dress."

Mummy and Collette stared at him as if he had said the most ridiculous thing. In fact he was the only one to have noticed. "Yes!" she agreed and confided, "My neighbour says dragons are for luck."

"And prosperity," he added.

"Pros…" she faltered.

"Perity."

"Will you write that down for me? The whole thing, please. I have my notebook." She unhooked her backpack and fished about inside.

"*Don't forget,*" Mr Simons read out loud. Crouching down, he took her pink biro and, resting the book on one knee, started a new page. Belinda could see all the way up one of the legs of his shorts. His legs were really hairy. "Prosperity means 'good fortune'. I'll write that as well, shall I?"

"Your speciality," Collette commented as she passed on

her way down the hall with Mummy following, dressed in her maxi-dress and flat gold pumps. "I thought we'd eat outside."

"Like a picnic?" Belinda was pleased with how everything seemed to be fitting neatly together.

"That's right. It'll be more relaxed."

"There we are." Mr Simons closed the notepad and handed it back to her, revealing even more of his hairy legs. "You look very pretty. I, on the other hand, am just trying to keep cool in this terrible heat."

The girl remembered about being polite. "Is it working?"

"Not very well, no."

"I'm sorry about that." Realising that she had received no instructions on how to address him, Belinda asked, "Should I call you Uncle?"

For a moment it seemed that there was something wrong with Mr Simons's eyes. "Andrew will be fine, if that's OK with you. I get called Andy a lot but, to be honest, I don't really like the short version."

"Mummy calls me Belle but I prefer Belinda."

"Then Belinda it is. For some reason," he looked at the oak floorboards very intently and then cleared his throat, "my wife has got it into her head that your mummy works with me, and I think she might feel a bit silly if we tell her that she's... misunderstood."

"That's OK," said Belle, lowering her voice to match his. "I know all about pretending. If anyone mentions it, you could just say something like, 'I don't think we should talk about work.'"

He nodded, giving it some serious contemplation. "I don't think we should talk about work?"

"And then you could maybe say, 'While the sun is shining.' And if you wanted to be *really* sure you could say, 'I forbid it!' But make it sound so serious that everyone knows it's really a joke, otherwise they might be scared. Do you want to have a practice?"

He stood, raised a stiff arm, (it was alarming, how tall he was) and said it loud like a really bad actor, "I forbid it!"

"Like that! Yes!"

"Keep it down, you two!" came a voice from the front room.

"Ten minutes more, Jim, then I'd like you to come outside and join us."

"Fifteen!"

"Where's your brother?"

"Not back yet." Jim spoke without turning round, so Belinda didn't have to attempt to say hello again.

"You can have until he gets back, but then I want to see you both outside. OK?"

"Kay." He said it like it was the last thing on earth he intended to do.

Andrew shut the door to the front room and shook his head, and Belinda wondered if even he thought he'd given in too easily. "What do you think we could talk about instead?"

"You could ask me about school, or even how Grammy is if you get really stuck. I've worked out what's wrong with her."

"Oh?"

"It's called Deep Vein something. The Librarian told me about it. You get it from flying or sitting around and doing nothing. Old people do a lot of that."

"Deep Vein Thrombosis," Andrew contributed.

"Maybe. I've written it down, but I don't worry too much because no one expects me to remember long words. It's the one where a blood clot from your leg gets into your chest if you're not careful."

"Is that what happened to your granny?"

"No. They caught it in time. She's back at home now, taking things slowly."

"So it's good news."

Belinda shrugged. "I couldn't pretend a funeral. Not when I've never actually been to one."

"Best to keep things simple, otherwise you might get mixed up with your real granny. Assuming you have a real granny." He appeared to be struggling to keep up. "Do you? Have a real granny, I mean?"

"Maybe. I'm not really sure."

"Oh?"

"It isn't something we talk about." Since making the discovery that this was the best way to stop questions coming, Belinda wasn't scared to own up to this. "Do *you* have a real granny?"

"No! I'm terribly old."

"How old?"

"Forty-four."

It was only polite to look properly impressed. "Wow!" she said, because you only said *OMG* to friends.

"But I do have a real mummy who is the boys' grandmother. And a mother-in-law, who is the boys' other grandmother. If I forget her I'll be in big trouble. Would you like to hang your bag up?"

"No, thank you. I'll probably need something from it. I have a wobbly tooth and if it falls out I'll need to put it in my jam jar."

"Show me?"

It was a strange request but, being a visitor, she obliged, opening the mouth of her backpack and peering inside. It was a miniature jam jar, the type they give you when you stay in hotels. It had once had a label with a picture of blackcurrants (or was it blackberries?) but that had come off in the sink. Perfect for stray teeth but otherwise quite unremarkable.

"Not the jam jar. Your wobbly tooth!"

Belinda laughed. "I thought you meant..." She pulled a serious face, stood soldier-straight, and did the *Ahhh!* thing you did for the dentist, then pointed to the bottom row and demonstrated how far the tooth was moving. (The truth was, it was really hard to leave it alone.) "Most likely, it'll come out when I'm eating lunch."

"It's possible," was Andrew's assessment, which was a very satisfactory answer as far as Belinda was concerned. "You'll have to be careful not to swallow it."

"Otherwise I won't get any money from the Tooth Fairy." She was hoping for a shiny pound coin for her Peppa piggy bank.

The white of the kitchen felt very bright against Belinda's eyes. Laid out on the table, at a height she could just about peer into were various salad bowls and plates of quiches, chicken pieces, some kind of green dip. She approved of the cling film: no danger of household flies - although what would happen when the food was taken outdoors, where there was the added possibility of wasps, she didn't know. Inevitably there were olives, but they were quite separate. (Even the green ones and the black ones were in different bowls.) Belinda counted three things she liked and two more that she was prepared to try if her mother insisted.

"Andrew?"

"Yes?"

"Do you go in planes very often?"

"When we go on holiday or if I have to go on a business trip, yes."

"I take the bus. Mostly. What's that orange stuff?" It looked all rubbery.

"That's smoked salmon. Have you ever tried any?"

"No. We're a no-smoking family."

"We are too, but we make an exception for salmon. How about a drink?"

"Yes, please. What are you having?"

"I think I'll have a beer."

"Oh." Disappointed, Belinda stood on tiptoes to look out into the garden where Mummy and Collette were sitting under a parasol with tall glasses in their hands. "What's Mummy having?"

"That looks like Pimms to me."

"I'll have one of those, please."

On hearing the commotion of a rock-fall and surprised laughter, Alison turned to see Andrew demonstrating the ice-maker on the wardrobe-sized fridge. Belle was being allowed to press the button, her backpack still on. She pointed her index finger slowly then jumped backwards.

"More!"

"Carefully!" Alison called out.

Biting her bottom lip, Belle began to walk in pigeon-steps, gripping a clinking glass containing something orange and fizzy, with a curly plastic drinking straw and a paper cocktail umbrella sticking out at angles. She paused at the threshold between kitchen and decking, and inched one foot tentatively over the sill.

"What have you got there?"

"Pimms!" Belle announced proudly. Behind her, Andrew shook his head and mouthed, "Tizer".

"Lucky you," she said, trying not to sound disapproving. (Alison wasn't keen on her daughter having sugary drinks.) "Do you want to put it down on the table so that you don't spill it down your new dress?"

As soon as the glass was safe, Belle bent her head, sucked greedily at the straw and gave a satisfied *Ah!*

"You really need a strawberry in that," said Collette, doing the honours, then looking at Alison in alarm. "Oh."

"What?"

She winced. "I think that strawberry may be highly alcoholic."

"The strawberry's just for decoration, Belle. You don't eat it."

"We have plenty of other strawberries that *are* for eating,"

Collette explained by way of compensation.

The curly straw proved problematic. Belle couldn't see the liquid loop-the-loop while she was doing the drinking. It was a miracle the glass wasn't upended when she attempted to angle the straw upwards. Alison leant over to right the glass then beckoned her daughter over and lowered her voice: "If you don't keep the straw in the glass, I shall have to take it away."

Belle scowled and moved beyond arm's reach, clutching her straw protectively. It took her less than a minute to make a discovery.

"Look, Mummy! If I put my tongue over the end the Pimms doesn't fall out."

Andrew came to the rescue. "Do you want to sit down to drink your drink, or would you prefer to explore?"

She jumped up. "Explore!"

"How about I show you the boys' tree house?"

"Keep to the shade," Collette instructed. "Mad dogs and Englishmen and all that."

Belle's eyes widened in alarm. The prospect of rabid canines made her glance behind her.

"Don't worry, sweetheart. It's just the title of a silly song. There aren't any dogs in the garden"

"Just one very old tortoise," Collette confirmed. "Although we do call him Rover." She turned to Alison. "If you're looking for a low-maintenance pet, a tortoise is what I recommend."

Both women sat basking as Andrew escorted Belle to the end of the garden.

"Rover?" Alison found herself repeating.

"The Wild Rover, to give him his full title. He makes the occasional bid for freedom. We've had to paint our address on his shell."

"Belle's after a chinchilla."

"Sounds messy to me."

Alison sipped her drink. "She settled for roller skates."

Deep in conversation, Belle was clearly trying to contain her excitement as she and Andrew crossed the expanse of parched yellowed grass, keeping to the shade. Everything else was so neatly kept that the decision not to water must have been deliberate. Alison could hear her daughter explaining that she was very good with ladders because, in actual fact, she had to climb up one to get into bed every night. "It's like a bunk bed, only I have my wardrobe and my desk underneath, for when I get homework."

"Did he build it himself?" Alison asked, as Andrew showed Belle - still refusing to part with her backpack - how high the ladder to the tree house was.

"He built the original. I'd have warned Belinda off that. Guaranteed splinters. No, this is the bigger, better model."

Bigger, better was said with a certain wistfulness. Alison waited, exercising that skill she was told she was so good at: listening.

"At one point, there was talk of solar panels." Collette sighed. "It's only in the last few years that Andrew's business has taken off. Things were really tight when the boys were younger, but we used to spend time doing things together. Decorating. Putting up crooked shelves. Now, if anything needs doing it's, 'You organise it, I'll write the cheque.' Not everything is better when you have money."

Alison was amazed at how quickly this virtual stranger appeared to have decided she was someone to confide in. And how powerful her desire to be taken into Collette's confidence was. It struck her that she would have to make a choice: explore Andrew's offer about the flat or have a new friend. Accommodating both would be impossible.

"You've not had your lucky break yet, but, from what Andrew tells me, it won't be long."

"Oh, I don't know about that..." Alison looked away.

Feeling her sun-warmed shoulders relax, she sensed something she hadn't felt for some time. Was she on the cusp of becoming a someone again?

"You're too modest! I'm not saying that I have *any* understanding of what it is you mathematical wizards do. Compound interest rates mean nothing to me. All I can say is that he's never talked about Jenny the way that he does about you."

Alison found herself blushing before she reminded herself. The someone Collette was casting compliments at wasn't real.

"But I'm warning you: treasure the here and now, because no matter how much you think you want to be a city big-shot, there will come a day when you have the money but no time to spend it." Blinking rapidly, Collette paused and took a drink, and her elongated neck, with its thin silver chain, was very elegant. "Don't think I'm complaining. It's just the way it is."

If it were a choice, straight down the middle - the flat or Collette's friendship - which would Alison opt for?

"Anyway." Her sigh signalled a subject change. "It's good to see Andrew relax. We don't see this side of him often enough these days." Collette's nails were French polished; the stone on her platinum engagement ring a large shining oval. "I know your work is stressful. I don't imagine he tells me the half of it. Even when he doesn't work late, he finds it hard to switch off."

Alison shifted her focus, aware she'd been caught staring at the diamond. Afraid that the straps of Belle's backpack might have caught on something, she was relieved to see Andrew now wearing it. Still holding his beer bottle, he steadied the ladder as Belle climbed under his patient direction; counting out loud as she brought one foot up to meet the other.

"Give yourself a break," Collette coaxed, breaking with her wistful expression. "He's quite trustworthy."

Alison heard her own sharp intake of breath as her daughter's foot slipped from one of the ladder's rungs. It was neatly caught and guided back.

"As I said. *Quite* trustworthy."

"Sorry." She smiled. "I never feel that I can take my eyes off Belle."

"You're used to being in control." Collette frowned briefly in a way that suggested she wasn't entirely convinced about her husband's choice of shorts. "Come autumn, I should start thinking about finding a job myself," she said, sounding newly distant.

"Why autumn?" Alison experienced the feeling that she was playing at being a grown-up: sitting outside on the decking, sipping Pimms, listening to Andrew and Belle singing *King of the Castle* in the near distance, on tempo but out of tune. But countering that pleasantly guilty feeling was a possibility. *This is the person you're supposed to be.* The mother who holds down a serious-sounding well-paid job, who is appreciated by her boss, and who gets to let her hair down at the weekend.

"Jim - our youngest - turns twelve in October." Collette leaned across the table to top up Alison's glass.

"Woah!" Alison said instinctively as the liquid gushed past the ice Collette held back with a spoon.

"Oh, you'll be alright. This is weak by Andrew's standards. I stopped him from adding brandy."

Glowing from the inside out, Alison knew this not to be true, but it was a lie she wanted to believe. She couldn't remember if she'd ever drunk in front of Belle before, and wasn't sure she should.

"No, the boys don't need me here when they get home from school any more. But, if I'm completely honest, I'm putting the whole thing off."

Alison raised her eyebrows.

"It's hard to argue that we need the money. God knows, plenty of youngsters could do with a job more than I can. And there's worse unemployment to come, if what Andrew says is true. So there's that side of it."

Although Collette raised her glass to her lips, Alison could tell there was more to the pause than satisfying her thirst. "But…" she prompted.

As she twisted round conspiratorially, the cotton of Collette's dress fell open, exposing another inch of golden skin. "I've had this mad idea."

Standing on the wooden platform, Belle was showing Andrew her discoveries; forgotten things that the boys must have discarded. Toy cars. Soldiers. An enamel mug. And he was expressing equal measures of surprise and delight. *"What do you think this is?"* A screwdriver that Alison was pleased to see him confiscate and stow safely in a back pocket. "How mad?" she asked.

"I think I want to try for another baby. A girl."

Taken aback, Alison swallowed.

"I'm still the right side of forty." Collette was quick to confirm. "Just."

The tree house was far enough away and Andrew and Belle were creating enough of a racket that it wasn't necessary to lower their voices. "What does Andrew say?"

Collette smiled secretively. "I didn't know myself," she said. "Not until the night your mother fell ill."

For a moment, Alison had forgotten the lie, but she recovered herself. "You haven't discussed it with him." There was no question mark.

In the instant Collette turned her gaze to her husband, Alison grasped why she and Belle had been invited to lunch. *Collette wasn't in the market for a new friend. She was trying Andrew out with Belle.*

"It's too new an idea to say out loud. Your daughter's quite something. I'm not usually a fan of other people's children. Even my own two have turned into monsters. Speaking of which, they're being suspiciously quiet."

Alison felt unexpected pride welling in her chest. Clearly, Collette had selected Belle as a favourable example of a little girl.

"When Belinda was tired and she launched herself against you - I wanted that." One of Collette's hands was a fist. "I *want* that."

Alison reflected on the woman's intensity. When Collette wanted something, she seemed to want it violently. Alison suspected there was no talking her into delays or compromises. "You'd go through all that under-fives' stuff again?" Alison still found it overwhelming, her daughter's need to be near her and watch over her while she did the most mundane things. "Being followed into the loo?"

"Even that! I wanted to be sure I wasn't just feeling hormonal - worrying that this might be my last chance." Deliberately overdramatic, Collette either shared or had adopted the same self-deprecating mannerisms as her husband. "I don't think it does any good in a marriage, appearing to be changeable. I prefer to be one hundred per cent sure before I speak up."

She was quite unapologetic about her tactics, something Alison couldn't help but admire. "And how sure do you feel?"

"With a drink inside me, the sun shining, and neither of the boys making outrageous demands? Oh, I'd say, ninety-nine point nine per cent. Sober, the sun still shining and no outrageous demands, I'd say eighty." She shrugged her bronzed shoulders. "Or thereabouts."

Alison resisted the urge to cry out as, from the corner of her eye, she caught the moment when Belle leaped off the wooden platform, launching herself into Andrew's arms. There was no disaster, no tears, and once grounded, Belle immediately scampered back up the ladder again, shouting, *"Again!"* Jumping off ladders would become her new craze, and Alison wasn't sure she wanted it to be encouraged. "Perhaps I should rescue Andrew."

As she went to get up, Collette put one hand on her wrist. "He's fine." The gesture was gentle but, at the same time, restraining. It said, *I need you.* Alison knew she wouldn't argue. She pulled her focus back, deciding she had no choice but to trust that Belle wouldn't prove too much of a challenge. She was almost disappointed when Collette removed her hand to bat an inquisitive wasp away from the Pimms jug. "No, if I'm going to push for this - no pun intended - I want it to be for the right reasons. Not just because I'm trying to fill a void. And I'm old enough and ugly enough not to think that my husband would spend more time at home just because there's a new baby." Collette was sitting back, observing her shrewdly. "What would you do?" she asked.

Put on the spot, Alison felt drained of much of her newfound confidence. "Oh, mine are *very* different circumstances," she faltered.

"*If* you were me."

Alison glanced back at the kitchen extension, as if it might provide an answer. The boys were contemplating the contents of the fridge, squabbling over the last of the cola.

"Four bedrooms," Collette said without hesitation, clearly having gone through the process of eliminating any space-related objections. One elbow on the back of her chair, she twisted round. *"Boys! If we're out of Coke, there's some ginger beer in the cupboard.* Sorry. You were saying."

Amazed that someone who barely knew her cared about her opinion, particularly on something so important, Alison was ambushed by a memory of the instant she realised that her pregnancy was not 'unwanted'. After getting over her disbelief - all of the *I'm not ready for this* - seeing Belle's heartbeat on the screen for the first time, the reverse became true. The realisation: *this is actually happening - right now.* And, with her eyes trained on the monitor, even while she was terrified, a part of her couldn't help but think, *And it's amazing.* Alison had many regrets, but Belle had never been one of them. "I think I would, yes," she said.

"You would?" Collette looked pleased.

"It's possible to talk yourself out of anything."

"So I should go with my gut?"

"Your gut, your hormones, whichever part of you is trying to tell you something."

"Is that what you did?"

Conversation with another woman a fairly unusual event, for Alison, the question felt deeply personal. She looked critically at her fingernails. "Not getting pregnant in the first place, no. That was an accident." What *was* it about these people that demanded her honesty? Making a small noise in her throat, Collette gave her a look that said, *I wondered...* "But afterwards..." The scariest thing that had ever happened to her was also the only thing - besides being on stage - to make her feel completely alive.

"So you and Belle's father aren't together any more?"

"Oh, we were never together." It was sometimes a conversation killer, but that was fine. Far cleaner to have any misunderstandings out of the way.

"It was a one-night stand?"

"No. Not exactly." She managed a wry smile. "I think that when you have no intention of giving the other person a choice in the matter, it's not fair to burden them."

There was a pause while Collette contemplated this, neither agreeing nor disagreeing. "Andrew says that you were a ballerina. Before."

"Yes," Alison said, wondering how Collette was tapping into her thoughts. What other confidences had Andrew shared?

"Once he'd told me, it seemed so obvious."

"In what way?"

"The way you hold yourself. It was either that or you'd

been sent to a finishing school where they taught you to walk while balancing a book on your head - although I'm not sure they do that any more."

Feeling under scrutiny, pretending that the sun was in her eyes, Alison averted her gaze.

"I'd be more than happy if you wanted to add my name to your emergency contact list for Belinda's school." When Alison looked at her, Collette blurted, "Just to be on the safe side. And while we're talking shop, why don't you take the flat in St James's Square?"

Alison felt her hands being grabbed in a way so unfamiliar that her instinct was to recoil. "I -" Astonished, she made a false start.

"Move Belle to a local school, lose the commute."

"But it was only mentioned as a possibility..."

"What's there to think about? You'd have two hours of your life back every day."

Feeling as if she'd passed some kind of test, it dawned on Alison that it might be possible to have both a friend *and* explore what sounded like a profitable arrangement. But still she hesitated.

CHAPTER THIRTEEN

It was a bad session. The worst she could remember.

Alison felt very different on the inside to how she looked on the outside. Her strength came from within. Of all her regulars, she had always felt that Jay was the one who had something bubbling under, that thing she didn't like to dwell on - a propensity for cruelty. As Cat had once lectured her, *If you swim with sharks, you have to be prepared to run into a Great White.*

Jay used an escort - or so he told her - because he had a taste for things his wife preferred not to do. This didn't mark him out as unusual. His justification for infidelity was that he never did the things he did with his wife with another woman. No kissing had been his first rule. But this boundary as he saw it - this distinction - together with the question of payment, reinforced his belief that he was entitled to behave in a certain way. Wariness had led Alison to set ground rules of her own. Although she'd told Jay they were routine, it wasn't something she'd ever found necessary with other clients. Her first rule was respect.

"Hey, not so rough."

Having given him the first warning, now he was calling her 'bitch'. It was the tone he used as much as the word. A tough-guy voice. "Do you like that, bitch?" he repeated.

Was he trying to provoke a reaction or was it possible he had mistaken her rapid heartbeat for excitement? She had two choices: ask him to stop or let him finish as quickly as possible. She chose the latter.

Focus on the money.

Jay weighed twice as much as Alison did. She had been taught to endure pain, the body's way of telling you it's under attack, but this was invasive. Pinned down, she drew on an inner source of anger and drove it deeper still: *How can you expect respect when you don't respect yourself?* Rather than risk confrontation - or the possibility that a 'No' might have excited him further - she was hurt in a way that would prevent her from working for the next couple of weeks. *Do you think you're the exception?* Cat had demanded. The truth was, Alison had thought she was in control. Prior to this moment, she'd always believed herself well-equipped to deal with sharks.

If she couldn't mentally cordon off the pain, the best that she could do - and it wasn't much, Alison knew that - was to turn to what she knew best. Think: *The Invitation*. She must become the young girl - a part danced by Lynn Seymour - who, on misinterpreting an older man's attention, had responded playfully. There was violence in the moment she realised that he didn't only want to dance with her. The musical accompaniment was jagged and strange. You'd be forgiven for thinking it improvised, almost *un*musical. There was a struggle. A series of lifts with his hand thrust between her legs, and, even then, she wasn't sure what it was he wanted. Then, as he threw her about, spread-eagled, hooped her around his body, it became brutally clear. Clenching her jaw, Alison hated Cat for being right. Horrific to watch, those who didn't turn away from the stage felt as if they had borne witness. Finally, when it was over, she slid down his body to the floor.

Critics had praised MacMillan for refraining from

'toppling art into sensationalism'. But this wasn't the stage: it was Alison's home - supposedly her sanctuary.

She abandoned the bed the minute it was over, but not before she saw the bloodstain on the sheet. No one would believe she was a victim. Real victims make it clear that they want no sexual contact with their attackers. They don't just say, "No". They yell for help, struggle to escape, fight back, leaving the attacker with vivid scratch marks. Though visibly distraught, the victim won't be prevented from reporting the attack straight away. It's only in the aftermath - the following days and weeks - that she'll be too traumatised to function. The further a rape departs from this formula, the less likely the victim is to be pitied. An escort, paid for her services in advance with a recent police caution for carding...

"Hey! Our time's not up yet."

Slipping into her robe, loose hair falling into her eyeline, Alison wrapped the cool silk about her, making no attempt to disguise how she felt. "You crossed the line." Her legs felt weak. A chill had started in her chest and was moving outwards. She could feel her body struggling to rearrange itself from the inside out. "I'd like you to leave now, if you don't mind."

"What if I *do* mind?"

Even if he'd reacted with kindness, Jay couldn't be anything other than repellent to her now. Nodding towards the sheet, the place where she'd lain, she said, "You hurt me. I'm bleeding." It was almost as if she could track the altered flow of blood through her veins.

"Perhaps you've just got your period."

She heard breath leave her mouth. "Don't you think I can tell the difference?"

Jay threw his legs over the side of the bed and sat up, hunch-shouldered, an oversized sulking schoolboy. He showed no signs of leaving. "If you don't say, how am I supposed to know?"

Standing there in disbelief, Alison felt that she shouldn't have to answer that question. She could still feel her scalp where he had grabbed a fistful of hair; still feel his grip on her shoulder. "Get dressed," she said, her breath very high in her chest.

He stood and hissed at her. "You don't get to say when this is over. *I* get to say when this is over." Unresolved as the situation was, there seemed to be potential for it to accelerate into violence, but as his eyes dropped from her face to a spot of blood on the carpet, Alison saw doubt.

Though the voice that said, "Go home to your wife," was strangled, she hoped that using that word - and all of the authority it carried - would work.

Jay was dressing now. Although she pretended not to look, Alison saw the moment he slipped the used condom into his jacket pocket and checked the bed to see if there was anything else he should consider taking. She fought the urge to yell, *Have it all! Take everything!* But that would only aggravate things. Needing him gone, she was relieved to see him slink past.

"Remember." One of his hands lingered on the doorframe (Alison understood full well how holding a movement adds emphasis). "I know where you live. I even know where your little girl goes to school."

Enraged that Jay dared mention Belle, if only while lashing out, determined not to sound intimidated, Alison replied, "A stranger hanging around the school gates these days? They'd have you arrested." Rage and restraint: these two opposing forces in measure.

She listened to his footsteps on the staircase and, though her shoulders jumped, welcomed the slam of the front door. Moments later, Alison's mobile buzzed. A self-pitying text. She replied, her thumbs angry: *How dare you use my daughter to threaten me! Never call this number again.* She cast the phone down on the bed, distancing herself from it. Then, at the sound of a car engine starting, Alison made her way downstairs; a clawed hand gripping the rail, a crab-like walk, bringing one slow foot down to meet the other. She bolted the door, top and bottom. Needing to be absolutely sure, wincing, she knelt to lift the letter box and looked out. Jay's car was gone - *gone!* She let the letter box clatter, exhaling with relief as she sat back on her heels.

Minutes passed before Alison became conscious that she was kneeling on the rough jute mat in the tiny square between the foot of the stairs and her front door, staring at the scratched and yellowing plastic of the cat flap. Tears erupted suddenly, as if someone had grabbed her shoulders and was shaking her. Admitting how frightened she'd been, Alison repeated to herself, *He's gone* and *You're safe,* but safe wasn't the word she'd choose to describe how she was feeling.

Locating the top of the first step by touch, her flat palms found the rise. Then, hooking her thumbs onto the second step, she eased her left knee upwards, then her right. Weight on her hands, her feet walked backwards and she perched. Alison blinked, chasing various scenarios around her mind. Of how it might have been worse. A constant quick-fire, identified as Mrs Oo's chatter, should have been a comfort. But even knowing someone was at home next door, Alison felt utterly alone. There should have been someone - someone - she could pick up the phone to.

Cat would understand. If she could forgive how Alison had turned down her attempt at kindness. But Alison pushed everyone away. *"When things are tough, we just keep going."* And that meant being on your own.

"Enough," she announced, trying to launch herself upwards. Her joints locked, she threw a hand out to steady herself. Everything was going to take twice as long as usual. No matter. There was an hour and a half before Alison needed to pick Belle up from school. She ripped the satin sheet out from under the mattress, tore the covers from the pillows, and crammed it all into the washing machine. Crouching to program a hot wash, a drop of blood splashed between her feet, a deep red reminder on the kitchen floor. *What am I doing?* she thought. And she fetched a black refuse sack, opened the door of the washing machine, transferred the linens, knotted the sack and dropped the whole thing down the steep stairs. The carpet wouldn't be so easily dealt with. Taking a damp J-cloth and Trouble Shooter 1001 into the bedroom, she scoured cowlicks into pile until her knuckles were raw.

Back in the kitchen, her gaze landed on Belle's artwork that decorated the fridge, her latest a combination of painted pasta, cotton wool and glitter she had called 'Mummy'. Now that everything was defiled, Alison did what she would never normally do. She reached for what she called her medicine cabinet, locating a miniature bottle of whisky. *Bell's, Extra Special*, salvaged from a hotel. Cracking the seal with a twist, she put her lips around the bottleneck; hesitated momentarily to see if second thoughts would arrive, then threw back her head. Liquid hit the back of her throat with a shock that left her gasping. Heat and flavour travelled unexpectedly: back into her mouth, rolling around her tongue as well as downwards. Honey, peat and something sharp and biting. The second swig went down smoothly, following the volcanic trail from her throat to her stomach. She held the third mouthful over her bottom lip until it felt swollen and numb, while she told herself consoling things. *At least Belle wasn't here.*

Alison took the half-empty bottle into the bathroom and turned on the shower. A fourth swig while she waited for the flow to reach body temperature. The roof of her mouth ablaze, her teeth felt as if they were melting. She nudged the plastic bottle between Belle's Cheeky Cherry shampoo and her own Liquid Shine.

The water's cruel sting made her curse. Nothing but questions to be gained from a visit to A & E. Better off keeping next week's appointment at the clinic. Thirty-five minutes she spent under the shower, chin raised, eyes closed, avoiding every area that felt tender. The bathroom was awash with steam, mirrors fogged. When the ball of magma that had replaced her stomach burned less fiercely, she stoked it: sip five.

Perching on the cold edge of the bath, Alison studied herself carefully using a compact mirror that needed regular de-misting, but she didn't want to go into her bedroom. Not yet. Her face the last thing she dared look at, it seemed remarkable that she looked no different. *Belle need never know.*

The bedroom now unavoidable, she checked the dregs of the bottle. One swig's worth. Cheers. No honey, just the acrid burn. Empty, the small plastic bottle looked inconsequential. She dropped it into the bathroom bin and braved the upstairs landing. Her skin crawled. From the door, her stripped flesh-coloured mattress looked naked. Nothing to be done about it now.

Blood: she remembered the blood. A panty liner. A bra. No: no bra. Loose-fitting clothing. Her head throbbed. No time for make-up. Sunglasses, then.

At least Belle need never know.

The downstairs landing: her shoulder bag was too heavy so she decanted her Oyster card, loose change and keys into her pockets. She had no use for her mobile phone. She would change her number.

"OK," she said, facing the front door, the black refuse sack in her grip. And, because there wasn't a part of her that seemed inclined to cooperate, she said it again. The door she closed was not the door to a building she wanted to call home. The concrete apron in front of the garages was cracked and ugly; the wheelie bins were overflowing. She hid the black sack behind the bins.

I can't stay here. She contemplated the Simons's offer. No longer simply an option - a *possibility* - it was something that *had* to be done.

About to disrupt her daughter's life, she sped up. Pain was unavoidable. You had to prep Belle gradually, telling her things umpteen times before she understood. The girl liked to run through the worst case scenario of what might go wrong. She liked to have every 'But what if?' argument out of the way. All the facts had to be at her disposal, written in the notebook that went everywhere with her. And Alison, well Alison had to say things confidently, with authority and out loud before she acted on them. Collette was right. Appearing changeable did no good. Once something was out in the open, it couldn't be taken back.

CHAPTER FOURTEEN

Something inside Belinda deflated at the sight of her mother. Not her usual neat outline, but all baggy, like the clothes women wear when they're expecting babies. Not standing alone by the willow tree but tripping over her own feet in a hurry to get to her. Dropping down to one knee to hug her.

"What are you?" Mummy said, planting noisy kisses on different parts of her face, so that it was equally difficult to avoid them or to say, "I'm not perfect, but I'll do."

Muffled by cotton, Belinda writhed about in an effort to free herself. She was distracted by a joke she really didn't want to forget the punchline to, but seeing Mummy wince she frowned. "Why are you wearing your decorating clothes?" Belinda tried to reach for the arms of her mother's sunglasses so that she could look her in the eye, which was how you knew if someone was telling the truth. As Mummy ducked playfully out of the way - "Uh, uh, uh!" - Belinda sniffed. "You smell funny."

"That's not a very polite way of saying hello." The smell was stronger when her mother spoke in her overly cheerful voice. "I can only answer one question at a time. Which one's it going to be?"

"But you *do* smell funny. Like -" But there was nothing in

Belinda's experience that it was like. Only things that it was not like. Her mother's usual smells varied between coconut oil, baby lotion or her going-out perfume, but always something clean and fresh. "Not like you."

Mummy turned her head away. She pretended that she was very old and made a groaning noise as she stood up. "That's not a question. So now it's my turn. I have one for you."

"Ooh! Can I just do my joke first?"

"Seeing as you look like you're about to explode, I think you'd better."

They were walking towards the gate, but, unusually, Belinda didn't have to skip to keep up. "It's a really good one. You're going to like it. An elephant goes into, no, hang on. An elephant robs a bank and the policeman asks the manager, 'Would you recognise him again?' and the manager goes: 'No, he was wearing a *stocking over his head*.'" Hoping her laughter would be catching, she looked up. Her mother's mouth was turned up at the edges, but only just. "You'd still be able to tell it was an elephant," Belinda explained, wondering if she had remembered it right. "Even with the stocking."

"What if there was more than one elephant in town?"

"There wasn't," she sulked, disappointed that everything had to be reasoned out. Mummy had ruined the whole point of the joke.

They wove through a tight cluster of sporty-looking pushchairs and handbag-sized poodles. The gunshot slamming of heavy car doors faded and the foot traffic thinned. Having seemed so keen to get the joke out of the way, Mummy had fallen quiet. Belinda held her breath. The only sound was the click of her mother's boots on the pavement. The thing was to watch for clues, only it was hard to play detective when you didn't know what signs you were supposed to be looking out for.

"I'm sorry," Mummy said at last. "I didn't mean to spoil your elephant joke."

This apology was so remarkable, Belinda wasn't sure whether to say 'That's alright', or ignore it.

"I'm afraid I had something else on my mind. How would you feel about moving?"

"I *am* moving," she insisted, because she was keeping up very nicely.

"I meant moving house."

Belinda was stunned. "Why would we move house?" She had learned the numbers of stairs in the flat so that she could go down them in the dark in case of fire. Things like that take time.

"Don't you want to know where we'd be going?"

Belinda had asked 'why' because that was what she wanted to know but, now that the 'where' question had been planted, it seemed sensible. "The other side of the road?"

"Further away than that."

"Near Sir Osbert?"

"Further than that."

'Further than that' meant away from everything Belinda could remember. Mr and Mrs Oo. Ink. Bus numbers and timetables. The bakers that did the special bread she liked. The backwards clock that made her dizzy if she watched it too long. "But *I* thought you'd tried everywhere else," she protested. "That's why we ended up in Worlds End."

"Not this place."

Her mother wasn't just asking a question. There was a definite plan.

"Are we moving to Grandma's?" Belinda asked. Without waiting for an answer, questions began queuing up. Would Grandma's house have side streets where Mummy would smile at the traffic warden who stuck notices on the windscreens of large cars she called 'farm vehicles', or laugh when sports cars parked underneath trees became splattered, because she said they were things they never had to worry about? Would there be shops Mummy would comment on, saying that the tattier the shop front, the more likely its name would begin with Chelsea? *Chelsea Plumbing and Heating, Chelsea Bikes, Chelsea Food and Wines.*

Belinda's arm went limp as her hand was dropped. "What on earth gave you that idea?" Her mother had squared up.

"I - I don't know." The truth was, the child had thought that only something that huge might explain such a monstrous idea.

They took a few steps in silence (apart from the clicking of her mother's boots) before her hand was taken up again, because the rule was that you had to hold hands when you were walking. (It didn't apply if you were scootering because scootering needed both hands, but then you had to stop when you got to the road.)

"It's near Pelican Park," her mother said.

"Near the big road?"

"Close by. It's on a lovely square with a private garden in the middle. The flat belongs to Uncle Andrew and Aunty Collette."

Objections and impossibilities rose up. "That would be too far to get to school. I'd have to get a different bus." And too far from school meant too far from Emily's, and too far from Emily's meant -

"You have to change school when you're seven anyway. We had this conversation, remember?"

Belinda's primary school only went up to age seven and then you went to junior school, but some other primary schools went all the way up to age eleven. Belinda remembered that a form had been filled in on the computer. But when a six-week holiday seemed like forever, turning seven still felt a long way off. She definitely remembered that her mother had said there was no point worrying about it just yet. Belinda felt a tummy ache coming on. "When would it be?"

"Not until you've broken up for the summer holidays."

She tried not to panic, gathering up facts to drape around her like a magic duvet. "Near Pelican Park?"

"*If* the plan works out it will be less than five minutes' walk."

"Why *if*?"

"It might be somewhere else."

The move was happening. There was no stopping it. Once Mummy got something into her head, it always happened.

Her bedroom sprang to mind. She had been told that it and everything in it was hers. But what if it wasn't? What if everything belonged to someone else? What if she was left with nothing?

"Tell me what you're thinking," Mummy asked, a request that suggested it was only reasonable to think of one thing at a time, not that different thoughts might shove and push at each other without excusing themselves. No one understood that being inside her head was like being attacked from all angles. *Can I take my bed? Will there be foxes? What about the big road? How do you get across? And what about the Librarian? How could I have forgotten her? I should have thought of her first!*

"What about the library? We always go to the library on Saturday mornings."

"Now, that's something you're really going to like. There is a little library inside the building, and Andrew says you can use it if you're very careful. Some of the books are really old."

"Does it have its own librarian?"

"No, but I'm sure there's a public library close by. And Piccadilly has the biggest book shop in the world."

Mummy was completely missing the point. In a new place, it was going to be more important than ever to have someone who could answer questions. "But who helps you look things up?"

"They have assistants, Belle." A frustrated tone was creeping into Mummy's voice. "All you have to do is ask."

This definitely isn't going to work. I should run away. Can you live in a library?

Alison had managed to get some pasta inside her daughter but Belle was still mad at her - just as she would have been if the tables were turned. Still young enough to remember the impotence she had felt as a child, there had been no option but to trust that her parents would make the right decisions. But did she really have a clue what she was doing? *I'm running away.* Alison looked at herself warily in the bathroom mirror as she placed two pink Nurofen tablets on her tongue and washed them down with cold water scooped up in one hand. She leant against the side of the sink, contemplating the plughole. *I can't stay here. I can't.*

Even the thought of going back into her bedroom made Alison feel sick. She pottered about in the bathroom. The imprint of Jay's presence had left a ghost-like residue. What she hadn't acknowledged at the time, she knew she would feel if she had to lie in the same bed again. Alison shuddered, her body leaden.

How had Andrew said the arrangement would work? He hadn't, she realised, at least not in detail. It seemed he had done his thinking out loud with Collette, and since she'd been all for it, his reasoning must have made sense. But could Alison *really* play the part of Andrew's assistant well enough to convince his wife? *Why worry about Collette? Your main concern should be how this charade will impact on Belle.* Alison tried to recall when she'd first started challenging the things her parents told her. The Tooth Fairy! It seemed so harmless. But Alison's childhood had hardly been typical. Attending boarding school meant fewer conversations and more letters. An English teacher had been the first adult Alison decided was an idiot. The woman insisted it was possible to know what an author had been thinking at the time he wrote this or that. She would have been no more than nine. Was two more years to be her revised ultimatum for turning her life around? If only she could earn enough so that there was money left over to squirrel away.

Hesitating in the living room doorway, Alison observed her daughter. Could a little girl be persuaded that her mummy could earn a reasonable living by dressing up in nice clothes; accompanying men to restaurants and clubs? No. She had to make sure there was more to the job than that. Something to lend it a degree of respectability.

Belle was kneeling in front of the coffee table, humming seriously and tunelessly to herself as she coloured something in. Occasionally she paused and angled her head to admire her progress before carefully selecting another garish felt-tip. It was such a studious activity that Alison felt as if she were intruding.

I even know where your little girl goes to school. She shuddered. "Ten more minutes until bedtime, Belle."

"Almost finished!"

"Belle," Alison started. "Would you mind if you were upstairs on your own tonight?"

The pen in her daughter's hand froze and she looked up in horror. "You're not going out, are you?"

"No, sweetheart. I'd never go out and leave you on your own." She perched on the edge of the sofa and eased herself back gently, nervous of applying too much pressure or moving too quickly. "I just thought I might sleep down here on the sofa." She could sleep right now, sleep and never wake up. And yet she was afraid of closing her eyes. Afraid what her mind might show her when there were no distractions.

"Are you ill?" Belle twisted her head and scooted around on her hands and knees, as she sometimes did when she was being a dog chasing its tail. A dark green line ran scar-like across her cheek.

"No!" Alison protested. "No, it's just that I want to give my mattress a really good air. Could you run upstairs and fetch my pillows for me?"

"From *your* room?" Colouring-in abandoned, Belle was up on her feet. Alison removed a felt-tip pen from her daughter's waving hand and snapped the lid back on.

"Just the pillows. I'll use the spare duvet from the airing cupboard."

"But I'm not allowed in your room!"

She was right, of course, but what had happened was a rule-changer. "Not without asking, you're not. But I think I can trust you not to touch things that don't belong to you, don't you?"

Her daughter frowned momentarily, a sure sign that she was conducting a mental stocktake of all those things that might demand investigation given ten minutes of her time. Then the cloud lifted. "Ooh! Can I sleep on the small sofa? Then it could be like a sleepover party."

"That's a good idea. We'll both sleep down here."

"With our feet on the sofas?"

"We'll take our shoes off first, but, yes, we'll have to have our feet on the sofa."

"So is shoes off the new rule?"

Tonight, Alison knew, Belle would push as many boundaries as she could get away with. "Shoes off has always been the rule."

"I thought no feet was the rule."

"Shoes off and no jumping is the rule."

Belle looked doubtful, as if she was waiting for something more to be said. No doubt she was wondering what else she could squeeze out of the situation. "We could have snacks, Mummy!"

"How about popcorn, seeing as it's a special occasion?"

"What special occasion is it?"

"A girls' sleepover party."

"OK," she agreed eventually, securing the upper hand. "I'll go and get my pillows as well."

CHAPTER FIFTEEN

Alison woke with a dizziness she couldn't account for. It was as if she'd been pirouetting to an unending piece of music. Although she couldn't see her daughter's outline, she sensed that Belle was awake and close by.

"Belle, sweetheart?" she said, waiting for her eyes to adjust to the dark.

Her daughter was a standing shadow. She heard the sticky extraction of her thumb, then Belle grizzled, "I had a bad dream," in that half-asleep state of hers.

This was not Alison's bed. This was not her bedroom. She remembered: they were in the living room. Remembering why, she shuddered. "Do you want a cuddle?"

A grunt of agreement and a loud sniff. Assaulted by a cold waft of air, Alison scooted back against the back of the sofa to make room. She felt Belle's weight, inhaled her warm and familiar scent, felt the thrust of her daughter's head and arms. Worse than any pain her daughter could inflict, Alison imagined she could still feel Jay's touch on her skin. Untangling one arm, she stroked Belle's hair away from her brow. "What was your nasty dream about?"

"I was running away."

"You ran away? Where did you go?"

Her daughter's face was crumpled in the dim light. "I knew

I had to run away even though I didn't want to."

"Then why did you go?"

"I don't know. I suppose I just wanted to be found."

Belle shuffled about, trying to find the most comfortable position. Alison didn't complain. Such simple, childlike logic. She, too, was running away, and what for if not to be found?

"Well, I'm here now." Already making plans for their escape, she felt awful, knowing herself to be the cause of this bad dream. "I've found you. The only way you're running away is if I'm allowed to come with you. Is that a deal?"

"Deal."

Although Belle wouldn't remember their conversation in the morning, it didn't sound like much of a deal. Alison cocooned her daughter in her arms and nuzzled her. Children moved house all the time. And they got over it. Didn't they?

CHAPTER SIXTEEN

"Hello, you must be Jenny." Belinda was coming down the staircase, her sock-feet sinking into the pile of the plush carpet. "I'm Belinda."

Carrying a tray of sliding coffee cups and a plate of chocolate digestives, Jenny scowled. "I already know who you are."

"I live upstairs. Did you know that?"

"I'd heard a rumour that there was a little girl, but I thought it was a herd of elephants stomping about."

"I don't think so! I'm sure I would have noticed if there were elephants!" She laughed a little encouragement but Jenny was in the middle of a balancing act, turning her back to the office door and about to bump it open with her bum. She decided against telling Jenny her elephant joke.

"Wait! I can get that for you." Belinda rushed to grab the handle and was rewarded with a tight smile. "I'm allowed to use the library, so we'll probably be seeing a lot of each other."

"Are you on your way there now?"

Although Belinda missed the Librarian and often wondered what she was doing, it was cool to live in a house with its *own* library. You were allowed to touch provided you were careful, because some of the books were very old and valuable. Few had pictures, so Belinda mainly read the titles. Some titles were spelt wrong, like *A Helpe unto Devotion*. Some of them were funny and went on forever, like *A Journal of the Forces which sailed from the Downs, in April 1800 on a Secret Expedition under the Command of Lieut.-Gen. Pigot, 1802.* You needed a very deep breath for that one.

"I am," she said. "I'm learning a poem. But don't worry. You won't hear me. I can do it inside my head."

Five minutes later Jenny appeared with a glass of warm Ribena for her and only the slightest look of disapproval.

It had taken Belinda two weeks of trawling to stumble upon the copy of *An Oxford Treasury of Children's Poetry* that Uncle Andrew had hidden between the leather-bound volumes. He had left a note in it: 'For Belinda's eyes only, on long-term loan'. She hadn't even shown it to her mother. Even with its torn paper jacket, it was a beautiful thing. An illustration for each poem. Normally, the lives of books were mysterious. You didn't know whose hands they'd passed through. This book had been written in: *To Andrew, on the occasion of your fifth birthday*, the same Andrew who was the builder of tree houses and writer of secret notes. He had even promised to show her how to make invisible ink so they could write to each other without anyone else knowing, but she needed to get her own candle, a lemon and paints, because grown-ups didn't keep those sorts of things at work.

Now that there was space for shelves, Mummy had started to buy books. Carried home in plastic bags, they were put in alphabetical order, like the ones at the library, and their spines were tickled every week with a feather duster. Belinda didn't think the books were actually ever read. The library downstairs was different. The books in there weren't really supposed to be for reading.

What Belinda liked most about the apartment in St James's Square wasn't the size of her new bedroom, or its tantalising view into the private square, or even the fact that they had their very own key to the gated garden, or the Zooloo-spear railings glossed in black. It was that, once Uncle Andrew and the lady called Jenny left for the evening, Belinda was allowed to take off her shoes and slide up and down the slippery hall. She was amazed something so rebellious was actually allowed. That her mother didn't shout at her to stop before she broke something. Instead, "Are you going to polish the floor?" and "Can I go downstairs and polish the slippery floor with my socks?" were the new phrases they used. Belinda would pad down the big staircase, step down from thick velvety carpet to deliciously cold floor. You never actually knew where you were going to stop when you skidded. You just took a run-up, put your arms out, yelled *Geronimo!* and then measured how far you had gone on the squares of the tiles.

Mummy was happier in St James's Square. The oven was new, so she didn't have to be cross so often, and she had nicer dresses. She said that the flat, with its high ceilings and tall doorways, made her feel like Alice from *Alice's Adventures in Wonderland*, and when Belinda insisted that she didn't know of any Alice or any Wonderland, bedtime stories were reinstated. It was the downstairs hall, with its many doors, most of which were locked, which felt most like Wonderland.

Mummy's hair changed and when Belinda said that she liked it better, her mother asked her if she would like hers cut too. They went together the next time and, sitting in matching leather chairs, they both read magazines. There were still rules, of course, but there were also treats. They kind of balanced out, so it was fairer.

The only thing Belinda really didn't like about their new home was the new childminder called Kirsty. Now that she was seven, her mother sometimes worked in the evenings, and you weren't allowed to stay at home on your own until you were at least twelve. You couldn't even argue that you would be in bed asleep because it was the law, and if you broke the law you got sent to prison. Her mother had said that having Kirsty was 'an experiment', which meant that if she didn't work out, no one would be in trouble. They could take another look on Gumtree, or maybe even put a card in a shop window. There were always plenty of teenagers looking for work, although it had taken a while to do all the interviews and get references.

Kirsty had boobies and the indent of her belly button showed through her thin cotton t-shirt. Belinda couldn't help wondering at how her flesh bulged over the top of the waistband of her tight jeans. The teenager threw Belinda a mean glance, and she knew there was no way she would be able to make Kirsty like her, not even by being nice.

Even though Kirsty oozed best behaviour in front of Belinda's mother, it was obvious it was all pretend.

"That's a really amazing dress," the teenager gushed.

"Thank you," Mummy replied in her sing-song voice, sounding like she meant what she was saying, even though she didn't. But it was true: it was an amazing dress. To begin with, it looked as if you were covered from shoulders to ankles, but when you looked closer you could see that some of the original black material had been cut out and replaced with see-through material. Mummy, who was busy trying to decant the contents of her enormous shoulder bag into a tiny rectangular clutch bag, thought that being clever and kind was far more important than being pretty. She did a smile she didn't really mean. "I've written my number down in case you have any problems. Oh, and there are snacks in the fridge in case you get hungry. Belle has a plain biscuit and a small glass of warm milk just before she goes to bed. And no later than seven thirty. Don't let her play up."

Belinda could tell that most of what Mummy said was for her benefit.

"Don't worry: I won't." (That too.) Kirsty had taken her shoes off without being invited and was standing with one bare foot on top of the other.

Mummy looked as if she was in two minds. "She might want you to test her on her spelling. She has a test tomorrow she's a bit nervous about. Or she might just want to read. I'd prefer it if you didn't turn the television on until after she goes to bed."

"That's fine. I always help my sister get ready for her spelling tests. They have them almost every week."

"And how old is your sister?" The things that didn't fit were being posted back into the shoulder bag.

"Eight."

Belinda could tell her mother was struggling to think of something to say about eight-year-old girls. "You should go now, Mummy," she piped up. "You don't want to be late."

Her mother bent down and did a bear hug but no kisses because she had spent ages putting lipstick on. "You'll do," she said and, "Be good for Kirsty, won't you?"

Belinda was terribly grown-up, waving her mother off, even though it was odd having a stranger close the flat's front door and trap them both inside. Especially a stranger who could make her feelings plain without saying a single word. Kirsty hip-swayed up the hall. Ignoring Belinda completely, she put one foot up behind her as she sat on the sofa. When Kirsty leaned back, everything jiggled.

"You're supposed to test me on my spelling," Belinda reminded her, holding onto the belief that the childminder would carry out her mother's instructions before texting her boyfriend.

"Your mum said I *might* want to test you. The first thing you have to understand is that when I'm in charge, I'm the boss."

Belinda waited in the doorway, bewildered.

"Has nobody ever told you it's rude to stare?"

"I'm not staring."

"Yeah? You could have fooled me."

"I'm waiting to see if you might want to test me on my spelling."

"What do you think?" Kirsty slouched further down the sofa and held a cushion over her boobies, crushing it with folded arms. Her voice was mean.

"That's not very friendly," Belinda said. She had understood that the childminder was being paid to do a job.

"That's because we're not friends."

Mummy had been wrong. It wasn't just the height of ceilings and doorframes that could make you feel as if you'd drunk the potion that made you shrink. Kirsty was making Belinda feel shorter than she had ever remembered feeling.

She pointed the remote control and the black screen of the television sprang to life.

"But I'm not allowed to watch television before I go to bed."

"Suit yourself."

"I heard Mummy tell you." Something told Belinda she had further still to shrink.

"Again, you weren't listening properly. She said *I'd prefer it if you didn't*. She didn't say I couldn't. You've only got half an hour anyway."

It was hard to argue. Kirsty was using her mother's exact words, but she was twisting their meaning. Only the fact that Mummy had said that she was to be good *for Kirsty* stopped Belinda from answering back. "Then I should probably just have my milk."

"I'm not your slave. You know where the kitchen is."

Belinda stood there, wide-eyed.

"Fine!" Kirsty launched herself upwards and strode straight past. When she opened the fridge, everything inside the door rattled. Before Belinda could point to the green-lidded bottle, Kirsty had poured her mother's special skimmed milk into a grown-up glass. She took one look at Belinda's dismayed expression and said, "What now? It's a glass of milk, isn't it?"

Belinda felt her eyes fill. She couldn't see properly. She heard the fridge door slam and the bottles in the door settle, then an exasperated sigh.

"It's on the table if you want it. I'm missing my programme." There was a slapping and sliding of bare feet.

The sip of cold milk tasted wrong. Not gone-off, but different. Belinda brushed her teeth, up and down and side to side, had a wee and put herself to bed. There was no one to three-quarter close her door so that just enough light from the hall came in, and no emergency water on her bedside table.

Some time later, she heard sounds of movement in the lower floor of the flat. Belinda hoped Kirsty was looking for her and was panicking that she couldn't find her. There were lots of hiding places. One of the first things she'd done once they had moved in was to uncover them all in case anyone wanted to play hide-and-seek, or in case robbers came and wanted to hurt them. Perhaps Kirsty would have to use the emergency number and interrupt Mummy at work to explain that she'd lost her. Belinda held her breath, listening out for the phone, but there was only a creaking on the small staircase, then the sounds of cupboard doors being opened and closed, especially in the bathroom. Small though she was, Belinda wouldn't be able to fit in the bathroom cabinet, even if she took the twelve-pack of toilet rolls out.

After a while her bedroom door knocked against the side of her bedside table and the big light was switched on.

"You're in bed!" Kirsty said accusingly.

Guarding her eyes with both hands, Belinda squinted upwards. The teenager was looking around her room, scowling at all of her private things: her drawings, her sticker book and her bookends. Even the socks she had left lying on the floor.

"Did your mummy and daddy get divorced recently?"

"I don't have a daddy." Belinda was still up to her chin in duvet.

"Whatever. Your mother's boyfriend, then. They just split up, right?"

"Mummy doesn't have a boyfriend."

"Then where's the money coming from? This place must cost a fortune," Kirsty said.

"It belongs to Uncle Andrew." The girl was too nervous to yawn. "It's something to do with Mummy's job."

"What kind of job is that?"

Belinda didn't like being on the receiving end of so many questions. This was worse than school. "I'm tired and I have my spelling test tomorrow. Please can I go to sleep?"

"Hard luck. I'm the boss when your mum is out and I want to talk."

"Can you at least turn the big light off? It's hurting my eyes."

Kirsty didn't look particularly pleased but this was one compromise she seemed willing to make. "Better?" she asked, but she said it as if Belinda was a baby.

Hopes that the childminder would soon want to watch more television faded when Kirsty sat down on the bed. Belinda slid towards her as if she were falling into a rabbit hole.

"Tell me about this job your mum has."

Belinda scrambled backwards so that no parts of them were touching. There wasn't enough flat surface and she felt as if she might slip back. "It's secret." She wished she still had the bunk bed with the ladder, but that had stayed behind in Worlds End. Their old landlord had probably slapped another coat of paint on it by now. There was no longer any need for space-saving solutions.

"Secret? You mean like the Official Secrets Act secret?" the older girl demanded. "Spying or something?"

Belinda shrugged. She didn't want to say that Mummy's job was dangerous because things she said had a habit of coming true.

"Dressed like that! What, is she a Bond girl or something?"

That rang a bell. "What's a Bond girl?"

"What's a Bond girl!" Kirsty said as if she pitied Belinda for being so stupid. "The girls who go out with Double-Oh-Seven. Now, don't try telling me you don't know who he is."

Belinda lay very still. She imagined zapping Kirsty with her pig-torch and turning her into someone nice. Perhaps if she just pretended to be asleep.

"Daniel Craig? Never mind. Is this the book you're reading?" The teenager picked up her copy of *Matilda*, studied the cover, then flicked through the pages. A small rectangular shadow that must have been Belinda's bookmark fluttered to the floor.

"Remind me what Matilda's surname is."

It was too dark for reading and you could tell Kirsty wasn't really that interested. "Wormwood."

"And the headmistress?" The childminder was pressing the closed book between her hands.

"Miss Trunchbull." The way that she seemed to agree made Belinda wonder if she could read with her hands, like blind people did. Then, she shoved the book back on the edge of the bedside table, half-on, half-off and all crooked.

"What else can you tell me about this job?"

"Mummy has to learn different languages."

"Which ones?"

"All the foreign ones. And she reads the boring newspapers." Belinda risked edging one hand out from under the duvet and squaring the book up. She wasn't brave enough to go rummaging for her lost bookmark, even though things that ended up on the carpet had a habit of disappearing during the night.

"Before I come back next time you need to find out more."

Belinda was supremely confident that Kirsty wouldn't be coming back. When her mother heard how she had ignored all of the rules, that would be the end of the experiment. Perhaps Mummy wouldn't go out at night anymore and that would be even better. "What else do you want to know?" she asked.

"This is for your benefit! You only have one parent, she's in a dangerous job and you haven't even asked what it is. That's negligence."

"What does negligence mean?" Belinda asked, realising that Kirsty had come up with 'dangerous' without any encouragement. She crossed her fingers for protection.

"It's worse than stupid. Get yourself a dictionary."

When Kirsty still showed no signs that she had remembered there were snacks waiting in the fridge, Belinda - who thought she'd been studying her mother for ages - said, "Mummy doesn't like it if I ask questions."

"None of them do. You have to trick them into giving things away."

And Belinda thought about all those times she had found it difficult to name the small things she learned about her mother. The phrases the Librarian had used: 'Self-contained' and 'guarded'. And the nagging doubt that, even though she knew about Mummy's ten thousand hours, it wasn't the whole story. Belinda was fairly certain she would never see Kirsty again, but some of what this teenager said made sense. "How?" she asked.

"You say things like, 'Where are you going wearing that beautiful dress?'"

"No."

Kirsty frowned down at her. "What do you mean, *no?*"

"She doesn't like people saying things about how she looks."

Kirsty whistled. "Most attractive women *expect* to be told how beautiful they are."

"Not Mummy. She always says that being clever and kind is more important than being pretty. Do another question."

"OK. You ask, 'Why do you always have to work at night?'"

"But she doesn't. She only works *some* nights."

"Duh! Look, Little Miss Know-It-All, you're reading *Matilda*. So you know you've got to look out for yourself. I can't think of everything for you."

With everything jiggling, Kirsty hauled herself up and walked straight out of the door. But now Belinda was up on her elbows. She wanted her back.

CHAPTER SEVENTEEN

Alison leant on the polished scroll of the banister as she shouted up the wide staircase: "Come on, Belle, you'll be late for school!" Then she winced apologetically as Andrew appeared at his office door. She hadn't thought him particularly tall when she first saw him standing in the hall. The doors in the St James's Square building were giant eight footers. But Alison no longer felt intimidated by the granite and the marble, the ceiling height and the ornate coving, and, once her suspicion of Andrew's motives had diminished, the desire to gush with gratitude every time she bumped into him was also fading. It was now the collision of family home and place of work that was hard to reconcile.

"Oops," she said, anticipating a mild ticking off. Perhaps a note of sarcasm.

"Good morning," he replied cheerfully, handing her what looked like a letter. "I thought I heard you."

It was too thin to be a card. "Is this my eviction notice?" she joked, looking between his expectant face and the envelope as she ripped it open. Her mouth fell open as she saw the figure written on the cheque. "What's this?" She looked at Andrew, startled.

"Call it a bonus." He appeared to be pleased with himself.

"A bonus?" The name of the account on the cheque wasn't

one she recognised. She blinked, trying to take it in. Foreign clients were known for being particularly generous with tips, but she would be wary about accepting this amount of money.

"It's proportionate, I assure you."

Proportionate? To *what*? "I - I don't understand."

"It's quite simple. After meeting with me several times, Mr Khalil had settled on investing one figure. After one evening with you…"

Alison snatched her arm away. "So this is from *you*." She was stunned. Surely her rent-free arrangement with Andrew covered situations like that? How much *had* Mr Khalil invested? She remembered nothing that singled their appointment out as extraordinary. If anything, it had been tame. Dinner at the Oxo Tower (he kept referring to the river as 'her' Thames, which she'd found endearing) followed by *The Merry Wives of Windsor* at the Globe Theatre - all of Shakespeare's usual twists and turns. To be honest, Alison found the sixteenth-century English so difficult to follow that she had struggled to come up with something suitable when Mr Khalil required a translation. "This is what you like to watch?" he had asked, bemused by the whole affair; everything from the crush of students standing in front of the stage, down to the chill of finding himself outdoors (she hadn't accounted for being exposed to the sky when deciding what to wear) and having to pay extra for cushions for the hard wooden benches. Alison had laughed and admitted, "No, it's not really my thing at all." She picked her way gingerly over the Bankside cobbles in her heels, clutching a cashmere pashmina around her shoulders. The lights of the buildings of Upper Thames Street threw long reflections into the river, and beyond was the dome of St Paul's.

"And what is 'your thing', if you don't mind my asking?"

What a question! Ask her ten years ago and she wouldn't have struggled to answer. Had he *seen* her ten years ago, asking wouldn't have been necessary. And Alison never spoke to clients about Belle. Not any more. "Oh." Trying to search for something impersonal, instead, she found herself under a blanket on the sofa with her mother. A temperature had kept her home from primary school. Her pre-dancing days. They had watched *Harvey* and *All About Eve* back to back. "Films," she said. "Black and white ones."

"Ealing comedies." He had nodded, as if he understood her.

"I prefer American films, actually."

"Then you mean movies!" he corrected her.

"Yes. I suppose I do."

They had been polite. Careful with each other. How she imagined a first date would be.

"The bonus is from the company." Andrew stood, one elbow resting on the banister, one size twelve shoe on the bottom step. "Hopefully it will compensate you for the fact that you've let go of some of *your* clients to make room for mine."

"But the name -?"

"Our trading name. Old family names stand for discretion, but they don't crop up very often on Google's search results. Don't look so horrified. I've also done very nicely - or should I say that Collette has." Andrew snatched at the envelope playfully. "Of course, if you don't want it, I'm sure she'd love to spend it."

"I want it." Alison gently tugged it away from his grip; nudged the cheque back inside.

"Are you sure?"

"I'm sure." She whisked the envelope behind her back.

"Hopefully, this will be the first of many. And good morning to you, Belinda."

Giddy with possibilities, Alison smuggled the envelope into her shoulder bag, but she needn't have worried about prying eyes. All her daughter's attention seemed to be taken up by the painfully slow business of coming downstairs.

Andrew was asking her, "What is it today?"

"Can't you tell?" Alison observed as Belle continued her walk downwards, without taking her hand from the polished banister. "It's a spelling test." The dark bags under her daughter's eyes weren't shadows cast by the brim of her straw boater. Alison had tried to correct Belle's misunderstanding that the change in schools was to blame for the increased number of tests. But there were so many, it was difficult for an anxious child.

Andrew pulled a face. "Rather you than me."

"A few nerves are good," Alison assured Belle as she joined them, standing a couple of steps from the bottom, their heads almost level. "You'll be fine. Kirsty said you were nearly perfect." This second-hand praise was greeted by a *hmpf*. "She *also* said how nicely you read for her."

"So the new babysitter's working out?" Andrew asked.

Alison flared her eyes at him. "The *childminder* is working out, yes. She had nothing but good to say about Belle." Her daughter's eyes shot up to meet hers, as if Belle had been expecting a telling off. Well, so what if there had been a minor mishap or two? The fact that Kirsty wanted to cover for her suggested the two had bonded. "You can relax, Belle. She said you were no trouble at all. We both liked her, didn't we?" Alison ran her daughter's plaited hair through her hands, but Belle simply scowled.

Enthusiasm was not cool at her daughter's new school. Alison couldn't ignore the changes in Belle. Exposed to children as old as eleven, Belle was displaying nerve-inducing hints of pre-teen behaviour. She remembered those girls at the White Lodge with their knowing glances. Mostly she remembered wanting to be just like them, and being like them had meant acting like them. ('Acting up,' her mother would have called it, but she hadn't been on the receiving end.) Becoming one of the inner circle was a process of osmosis. You proved yourself worthy. Ironically, it was Alison's loner status that had eventually singled her out as being cool.

"Hello, Jenny! How are you?" Belle piped up with a contrasting burst of energy and manners, grabbing the balustrades with both hands and peering through them.

"I'm fine, Belinda, thank you for asking. And you?"

Twisting her head, Alison saw that Jenny was walking up the hall carrying coffee mugs, grimacing in lieu of a smile. She wondered if Jenny had also done 'very nicely' out of Mr Khalil's investment. What explanation had Andrew given for the fact that it was she and not Jenny who was asked to take clients out for cocktails or to dinner? Andrew insisted there was no jealousy. Though his knowledge about his assistant's personal circumstances was vague, the one thing he *did* know was that, come five thirty, she always rushed home to feed her cats. They were like her children, he joked.

"Shall I do the door?" Belinda asked, trotting down the last few stairs and navigating the transition from plush red carpet to tiled floor.

"If you wouldn't mind."

Oblivious to any tension between the adults, Belinda was the recipient of one of Jenny's face-transforming smiles. It was just as it had been with the Oos. The wary looks they cast Alison and the glowing expressions they reserved for her daughter.

"And what's on your agenda?" Andrew asked.

"Me?" Alison turned her attention to him. "Oh, the financial papers, the gym and then Mandarin lessons." She reacted quickly to his raised eyebrows. "It's no big deal. Just a beginners' conversation class."

It was Andrew's turn to blink, and he also shook his head, as if he'd had his suspicions. "Both here and at home, I am surrounded by brilliant women."

"How is Collette? I've been meaning to call her."

He removed his elbow from the end of the banister and tapped its wooden scroll. "Over the worst of the morning sickness, I'm glad to say. She says it must be a girl. I certainly can't remember her suffering this way with either of the boys."

Having arrived back at elbow height, Belle asked, "Aunty Collette isn't ill, is she?" with a good deal of concern.

Andrew circled her shoulders with one arm. "Not ill, no. She's expecting a baby. Or *we're* expecting a baby, as everyone reminds me I should say these days."

"Gosh, a *baby!*"

"Yes, a *baby.*" He gave Belle's shoulders a squeeze. "I can hardly believe it myself."

"Send her our love, won't you?" Alison said, trying to move the conversation towards the front door. "And now we really need to get our skates on."

Andrew walked with them. "Just one other thing. I thought we might have lunch. Tomorrow - if you're not doing anything, that is?"

"No."

"Good. There are a few things I'd like to discuss with you. Work bits and pieces. Nothing major."

Alison herded Belle through the door as he held it open. "One o'clock-ish?"

"You know where to find me."

"Behind his big desk!" Belle added helpfully, the lift in her voice suggesting she thought playing with computers was a strange occupation for a grown man. But once the front door was closed, she demanded, "Do you and Uncle Andrew often go out to lunch?"

Alison didn't know why, but she felt defensive. "You heard what Uncle Andrew said. It's not for fun. It's about work. Like a meeting."

Beau Brummell's statue stood at the entrance to the Piccadilly Arcade, inscribed with the words, *To be truly elegant one should not be noticed*, an echo of Alison's sentiments and state of mind. Now, as in Brummell's day, Jermyn Street was a place where you could be assured of discretion. The reason Alison gave Belle for spending so much time in Waterstones was that, statistically speaking, nicer people went to bookstores than almost any other type of shop. The real reason was that Alison thought it unlikely she would be recognised by her clients (or, more importantly, her *former* clients) there. Its back door on Jermyn Street, the enormous steel-framed building was wedged between traditional gentlemen's clothing stores dealing in everyday essentials, such as monogrammed slippers and silk smoking-jackets.

The bookshop offered six seductive storeys of secluded corners in which Alison could lose herself, but firstly she liked to devour the papers in the calm of the basement café. Feeling the need to be informed - and not just about the business world - she lapped up details of things that visitors for whom money was no object might want to sample while in the capital. Restaurants (judging by the number of awards he was winning, Gordon Ramsay's was still the place to be), clubs, casinos, plays, galleries, exhibitions, films: she had opinions to offer on all of them, albeit that they weren't her own. It wasn't necessary to read *The Kite Runner* to be able to discuss it, although Alison was careful *who* she discussed it with, her understanding of exactly where her clients came from woolly at best. The one thing she might have had a strong opinion of her own on - ballet - Alison preferred to avoid. It was too much to sit in the audience, knowing... Alison was not a 'has been', not really. In her mind, she was still a 'might have been', which, in many ways, was worse.

And yet she had found herself at the front of the stalls,

witness to Darcey Bussell's final performance, with every hair on the back of her neck on end at the audience's rapt silence. Returning her companion's sideways smile, her chest expanded in ragged stages as the string section softly began.

Much was made of Bussell's being 'only' thirty-eight. As any ballerina knows, thirty-eight is a good age for a dancer. "My plan was to go out feeling good," Bussell told reporters at the end of the evening. Alison couldn't help but wonder from the set of her mouth if she'd been plagued by second thoughts. It wasn't until the age of forty-two that Margot Fonteyn had first partnered Rudolph Nureyev, and their curtain calls had been frenzied. Bussell might have had two more years in her, maybe four. But Fonteyn was childless; Bussell had two children to consider. She had gradually been cutting back.

Her curiosity fuelled, a few days later Alison had watched BBC footage of Bussell revisiting the White Lodge. (She had graduated to Sadler's Wells shortly before Alison joined.) There it was, just as Alison remembered: the columned architecture; the grassy avenue cut cleanly through the trees, drawing the eye into Richmond Park. The interviewer asked Bussell, "Are you nervous?" as they were getting out of the black cab. It had seemed a strange question; strange to imagine that someone who had reached the top of her profession, so obviously at home on the stage, might be. But instead of denial, Bussell hesitated, the camera zooming in on her neck as she swallowed. The residue of those same nerves Alison had felt walking through those double doors for the first time. The senior girls in their red tracksuits, feigning disinterest. The boys in their blue twisting their necks, smiling knowingly. The brass statue of 'Margot', fingertips shiny where they'd been touched by generations of smaller hands. "For luck," they'd said, hoping something of her essence would rub off on them. Bussell recounted how a teacher had told her, "If you're going to cry in every class, this isn't for you."

And so it was that Alison found herself daydreaming while waiting her turn at the coffee counter, a thick wad of newspapers tucked under one elbow, as Alessandro asked, "And how are you today?" and would she like her usual brought over? (The fact that she had 'a usual' lent her a sense of belonging she had rarely felt anywhere else.)

Installed at her corner table, she spread the broadsheet in front of her. *A Theory of Prostitution.* According to the article, it followed that prostitution *needs to be well-paid because the prostitute must give up the financial advantage of marriage.* Alison silently protested. She knew several escorts who were either married or in long-term relationships - although not all of their partners knew how they earned their livings. Other sources, she read, claimed that as many as fifty per cent of university students were sex workers, with that percentage likely to accelerate in line with planned increases in fees. These students didn't intend to trade lifestyle for marriage. No doubt, they would manage to have it all.

The olive-skinned barista approached, singing *Umbrella-ella-ella* to announce his arrival. With no fear he would associate its content with her, Alison didn't hurry to cover the article as she might once have done.

Sliding her Americano onto the paper-covered table, he read over her shoulder and a gave a slow whistle: "Five thousand pounds a night!"

"Apparently, that's not unusual." The figure was inflated as far as Alison was concerned, but by a smaller margin than it used to be. She wondered, not for the first time, how the barista made ends meet.

"I may have to reconsider my chosen calling." Alessandro caught her eye, arched a single brow and said, "I have blueberry muffins. I don't suppose I can tempt you…?"

"Not today, thank you." Alison wished she was more practised at harmless flirting, by which she meant the unchoreographed type.

"When do you ever try my muffins?" he exclaimed in that wonderfully passionate way Italians have, licence to be perhaps a little rude because there is an understanding that nothing is to be taken seriously, except the coffee. In many ways, he would have made a wonderful ballet dancer. He certainly had the temperament for it.

Refusing to rise to his bait, Alison sipped. "This Americano is wonderful."

"Pah!" He threw up his hands as he skulked away, clearly delighted but unable to drop the pretence.

For the first time in Alison's life, financial independence seemed like a possibility. Saving half of what she earned, she estimated that two years from now she would have a tidy nest-egg - especially if the cheque tucked inside her purse was to be the first of many. Her revised ultimatum (two years, definitely no more) no longer sounded unreasonable. They wouldn't be able to afford to live in London, that went without saying, but a modest home... When Belle was nine, she would be thirty. Too late to resume a dancing career, but she'd already come a long way from the young woman who, in desperation, had turned to a medium. Was this lightness of feeling optimism?

And then, bringing her crashing down to earth, on the very next page, the other end of the scale: an update on the Ipswich Serial Murders. Reading the name of the man who was to stand trial, Alison's blood froze. She stared at its letters: Steven Gerald James Wright. What her father would have called a solid name. One a boy could grow into. Trembling with hatred, she turned the page, wondering that she was capable of smoothing the paper on the table, knowing *that* name was still there, on the underside. It shouldn't be possible. Not when people she knew from what she thought of as her former life - Cat among them - enjoyed none of her newfound security.

She had friends now. Andrew and Collette wanted her to succeed almost as much as she did. Andrew did 'very nicely' out of her little contribution, and Collette - well, she assumed Collette was in the dark as to exactly what Alison contributed. But Collette frequently expressed gratitude that she had received a last-minute call asking her to pick a little girl up from school. She had realised what was apparently missing from her life before it was too late to do anything about it - this 'last-chance' baby of theirs. Looking at the family portraits in the Simons's hall, Alison hadn't noticed that anything was missing. She had only seen what was lacking from her own life. Security. Companionship. Someone to share the responsibility with. And what she had been unable to provide for Belle: a father.

But Collette's friendship was more than enough to be getting on with. Ignoring the white lies she told out of necessity (repeated so many times Alison almost believed them herself), it was one of the few things in her life she felt good about. Having been introduced into Collette's circle, Alison hadn't been made to feel small or intimidated. She had never found the need to roll down the cuffs of her blouse to cover an imaginary identity tattoo. These days she found herself bounding out of bed, scooping her daughter up and running with Belle giggling in her arms to deposit her in the bathroom.

In return, because he had demanded nothing, Alison kept herself informed about the issues that concerned Andrew and this horrible *regulator* of his. Since the start of the recession, everybody had heard of the FSA. Studying the financial papers: more on the Bank of England's bailout of Northern Rock. She wondered if the Treasury Select Committee's chairman, John

McFall, regretted the words he used in an attempt to calm the bank's panic-stricken customers, who had queued round the clock to withdraw a combined one billion pounds; scenes lifted straight from *It's a Wonderful Life*. "We've had sixty quarters of continued growth, the world economy has grown for the past five years. So it's against a strong background. Don't let's predicate everything of doom and gloom..." But doom and gloom seemed to be exactly where the country was heading.

Opposite, an article about soon-to-be introduced money laundering regulations. The history held greater interest for Alison than the crime itself. She read how the law had been tightened after a chink in the Court's statutory armour forced them to release £750,000 of funds confiscated during a 1970's drug-trafficking case. Alison tensed. Bringing up a child in Central London, exposure to drugs featured high on her list of parental fears, a list that also included child abduction, the early sexualisation of children and a possible repeat of the terrifying 2005 London terrorist attack.

The Courts were permitted to confiscate items used while *carrying out* the offence, but not to 'strip drug-traffickers of the total profits of their unlawful enterprises'. Little wonder the drugs culture had risen to its current level! Was she to understand that, beforehand, they'd simply *got away with it?* No doubt, the poor sod who pulled the short straw served time while the others huddled in a seedy back room counting piles of so-called 'dirty' money, which was fed back into the banking system. (This, she'd grasped, was the 'laundering' part.)

With the loophole closed, the confiscation regime empowered Courts to freeze assets at the beginning of criminal investigations. Alison found nothing to object to in the logic behind the assumption that they - together with income earned during the six years prior - were also the proceeds of crime. At the same time, Alison made a mental note: she must sort out her bank accounts - especially if bonuses were to be regular occurrences. In fact, she would make a point of opening a new savings account right now, before she went to her Mandarin class. Andrew's company cheque would be her first deposit.

CHAPTER EIGHTEEN

The waiter whisked away the silver domes that covered the bone china plates he brought to their table, all very over-the-top for a special order of Eggs Florentine. Andrew waited until Alison had pierced one of her poached eggs, spilling the gold of the yolk onto the rich green of the wilted spinach, then she watched with detached amusement as he disassembled his architectural Chicken and Bacon Stack on Toasted Rye and, setting the iceberg lettuce aside, constructed something as close to a common or garden sandwich as he could manage. She could almost hear Collette tutting, "Why didn't you order something you actually wanted to eat?" But she had no intention of becoming a stand-in for Collette.

Andrew caught her smiling and raised his eyebrows. "You won't tell on me, will you?" The ice in the wine bucket rattled, rearranging itself as he removed the bottle to top his glass up. "Are you sure I can't tempt you?" The neck of the bottle was wrapped in white linen.

"Not at lunchtime." She sat the tea strainer on her teacup and poured the Earl Grey from its silver pot, then added a dash of milk from a tiny china jug.

"Philistine!"

"If you say so," she luxuriated. "I just like it the way I like it."

"I know that! It's straight from *When Harry Met Sally*," he enthused, as if taking part in a pub quiz. "Something to do with apple pie."

"I've never seen it."

He pretended to be horrified. "Never seen it?"

"I've heard of it, obviously, but I was too young to see it at the cinema."

"Ouch! I forget you're not the same age as us. I'll lend you the DVD. You, with all of your special requests, are more like Sally than anyone I've ever met."

It was Alison's turn to raise her eyebrows. "But it's OK to order something you don't really want and then muck about with it?"

"I'm British. It's expected of me."

Smiling, Alison contemplated the décor. It wasn't clear who its wavy lines had been designed to appeal to. *Not unlike a stage set*, she mused. "So," she fed him a prompt. "We're here because…"

"Mmm!" Acting as if she'd just reminded him there was a purpose to their lunch, Andrew chewed thoughtfully and swallowed. "I have a couple of requests, favours, whatever you want to call them."

She had no fear that diners within earshot would think they were anything other than colleagues discussing an ordinary business transaction over a bite to eat. The egg was just how Alison liked it, the hollandaise sauce sufficiently lemony, the muffin crisp on the outside, soft and doughy on the inside.

"The first is a straight yes or no."

"No," Alison quipped, pretending to be wary (although a reservation lurked at the back of her mind that the bonus placed her under a new obligation).

"It would be well worth your while money-wise. I have a client who'd like to book you for a whole weekend. Three days if you count the Friday night."

As Alison did the maths, she felt her mouth fall open. "I'm not sure about leaving Belle with the new babysitter for an entire weekend."

"You insisted I call her a childminder!" Andrew teased, taking a sip of Sancerre.

"She's just a sixth-former after a little extra pocket money. She can cope with putting a seven-year-old to bed, but she's hardly a pro. And, besides, it wouldn't be fair on Belle."

Andrew waved aside her objections with his fork. "We'll have Belinda."

Enormous ice cream sundaes with names sounding like cocktails were being delivered to the table next to theirs. Arming themselves with long-handled spoons, its four female occupants nibbled the corners off fan-shaped wafers while planning how to mount their assaults. Alison wrote a mental Post-It note: she would bring Belle here for a birthday treat. The Parlour wasn't as stuffy as some of the store's other restaurants. They would sit on a high stool at the bar and share a banana split.

"You will?"

"Of course!" Andrew said.

"Wouldn't it be too much for Collette?"

"She'll be in her element, dressing up, cutting out, shopping. All good practice. You never know, she might not even notice if I escape for a game of golf."

Alison considered this while the waiter topped up Andrew's wine glass. Bottle still in hand, he turned to give her a stiff nod of enquiry. "No, thank you." She covered the rim of her empty wine glass. "Belle won't need convincing. She's been dying to stay in your lilac room."

"I thought you'd painted her bedroom lilac."

"So did I, but apparently it's the wrong shade."

He winced in empathy. "Girls!"

"What excuse will you give Collette? There are only so

many times my poor old mother can end up in hospital."

"I thought I might tell her you'd offered to take my place on a business trip. She's always saying I should push you forward a bit more."

Alison nodded. "You'll make it sound as if it was *her* idea."

"I generally find that's best." He pressed a linen napkin to his mouth. "So, it's not out of the question?"

"Advance warning would be nice, but no. Not if Collette's happy to help out."

Andrew smirked, looking guilty.

"It's this coming weekend isn't it?" Breath caught in Alison's throat, then she nodded with realisation. "And you've already said yes." This was the first time she felt as if assumptions had been made.

"Is it do-able?" He redeemed himself by leaning towards her over the debris on the table and looking concerned. "I'd take Belinda home with me on Friday after work."

"Two days to organise myself and plan an entire weekend?" She crossed her knife and fork on her yolk-smeared plate and a waiter appeared at her elbow to clear.

"Two and a half. Go on. You have more friends in high places than anyone I know."

"The way you describe me, you'd think I'd be in demand as a city hot-shot's PA!"

"If only I could afford you."

She saw Andrew's neck colour and relented a little. *Think of the money.* "I suppose the man on the half-price ticket booth in Leicester Square might be able to pull a few strings."

Andrew cast her one of his pleading *Oh, come on* looks.

"Is there anything I should know about this client of yours?" Alison moved her cup and saucer to a more central position.

"He's very professional. Middle Eastern, I believe."

"Can you narrow it down?"

"Not really. They're all the same, aren't they?"

Tempted to protest, Alison acknowledged that, even if she had the information, she might not understand the implications. She sipped her tea. "Does he speak English?"

"Enough for telephone negotiations. He's very to the point."

"Blunt, in other words!" She wondered what would happen if they didn't get on. Fifty hours was a long time to spend with a stranger. But it was also an awful lot of money to turn down. "I suppose you'd better give me his details."

Andrew leaned towards her conspiratorially. "He does like opera, I'm afraid. I know you're not a fan." When he leaned back, there was a piece of paper on the table with the name Tanvir Hussein underlined, his arrival details and a five-digit number scrawled underneath.

"What's this?" she asked.

"His budget for the weekend."

Alison reflected that she was not quite so shocked as she would have once been. "Dollars?"

"Good old-fashioned sterling."

She tried not to blink. Far better to give the impression that Andrew was putting her out. "Does that include my time?"

"No."

"And you'll let me have a float for deposits?"

"I will."

Alison sighed. "Opera it is, then." She watched Andrew's shoulders relax, the way he dipped his head in victory while his mouth stretched into a smile. Would he feel let down, she wondered, if she didn't manage to squeeze a little more out of Mr Hussein? "What was the other favour you wanted to ask me?"

"Oh, that!" He shook his head dismissively, as if Alison could discount it. Something so trivial it was hardly worth mentioning. "It's just that the big boss is coming down to

London in a couple of weeks' time. An audit of some kind."

"I thought *you* were the big boss."

"It's like a franchise, really. I'm my own boss. I employ Jenny. This is more of a regulatory arrangement."

"Ah, the *regulator!*" She referred to the body as if it were an eccentric uncle whose presence was tolerated at family gatherings.

"The thing is... I was wondering if you and Belinda wouldn't mind making yourselves scarce."

Smiling indulgently, Alison acknowledged, "She can be a bit noisy. I recently had to ban her from singing *Supercalifragilisticexpialidocious* after a bath-time performance nearly drove me to insanity." Even now, just thinking about it, the cartoon band of pearly kings and queens was invading her head again.

Andrew winced. "He's rather used to having the flat at his disposal when he's in town."

It was like her father's slap. Stinging. She waited a moment to see if anything else would be said. The lunch-time clatter continued around them. When Andrew didn't meet her enquiring gaze, Alison moved her napkin from her lap to the table. "Have I got this right? Do you want it to look as if no one lives there?"

"As if I stay occasionally, perhaps. A few things in the kitchen cupboards won't hurt." Andrew's relief at how quickly she had grasped the situation was apparent. Her cooperation appeared to have been taken for granted: a reminder of how few rights she had. "He won't go into Belinda's room. If you hide everything in there, we can lock it."

With a chill spreading from her core, Alison lowered her voice and hissed, "Is the flat actually in your name?" At the sound of a champagne cork popping, there was a small cheer from the far side of the restaurant. Watching how Andrew bit his lips, top and bottom, and then pursed them, Alison realised she had hit the nail squarely on the head. "Is *that* how you can afford not to charge me rent?"

"The lease for the building's in my name, but I re-charge the cost to the company."

"Shit!" she heard herself exclaim, rather too loudly for Fortnum & Mason but caring little when the white-haired lady seated to her left turned to glare. Every muscle in her body tensed. *Free accommodation! Was it possible that Collette knew?* Not wanting to dilute the heady feeling of having been welcomed into her home as a guest, Alison had glossed over why Collette had been so keen for her to take Andrew up on his offer. The flat could have been let to a Japanese bank, boosting the family coffers. Now it was clear: it hadn't been the declaration of friendship she'd been so willing to believe in. It was simply that, with someone else already footing the bill, there would be no shortfall in the family's income. Because although Collette denied that money was important to her - that family was all that mattered - Alison had witnessed the reckless way she thrust her credit cards at shop assistants. It was as if she felt entitled to compensation for being denied a husband twelve hours of the day. Alison watched the numbers clock up and thought, *comfortably off.* In her parents' house, that had meant being able to afford an occasional ice cream when you went to the park.

"There's nothing for you to worry about." Andrew's patronising tone grated.

Throwing him a look, Alison saw everything that she had first found unattractive. The slight double chin. The contrast between his ruddy colouring and straw-coloured hair. Anger flared. "That's easy for you to say! I moved Belle away from everything she knew - I made her change schools - because I thought it was a home, not just somewhere temporary -"

"Calm down." She flinched when he placed one hand on her arm and saw that the hand at the end of her own arm was clenched, her knuckles white, the outward expression of inner seething. It came from a deep place and she was breathing hard. His touch was uninvited. Andrew had cut her short but, even as she was speaking, Alison had known that wasn't the whole truth. She had accepted his offer only when staying at Worlds End was no longer an option.

I even know where your little girl goes to school.

"I've got your back, remember. It's the pair of you I'm thinking about." Andrew's head was low and his voice soft, as if he were placating a child. "I don't want you coming under scrutiny."

Although her blood was still boiling, Alison forced herself to relax. She had done many things, but she had never before felt herself capable of violence. When she flexed her fingers, Andrew released his grip. Seeing the sense in what he said, she wondered if this brief surge of insanity wasn't perhaps because her thoughts had returned to Jay's threat. But she couldn't help questioning Andrew's motives. Was his real concern that he might be found guilty by association? *I'm really not as nice a person as you seem to think I am,* he had told her. Slowly, silently, she counted to ten. "I wish you'd told me, that's all." Her voice would have sounded pleasant to anyone within earshot. To Alison's ears, it sounded forced.

"What was there to tell? Look at how far you've come. This has been a great move for Belinda. She's thriving - as are you. There's no need to overreact. It's one or two nights a year, that's all. And, again, you'd be more than welcome to stay with us."

"No, it's fine." Alison felt foolish on so many levels.

"Look. I'll plan it better in future. You tell me when you're going on holiday and we'll try to work around that."

Feeling herself trembling, Alison craved fresh air. She no longer wanted to be in a public place with this man.

"Friends?"

Forcing a smile, she contemplated that the possibility seemed far less certain.

"And you're still alright for the weekend?"

Andrew was obviously concerned he had caused offence - perhaps even permanent damage. *This situation might be more short-term than you envisaged*, she told herself. *Make the most of it.* She would buy the best opera tickets her contacts could source; earn herself a fat tip. "We're fine, boss." Alison pushed back her chair without bothering to go through the pantomime of offering to pay her share. "Actually, I should probably start on the planning, if you don't mind." As she stood, her reflection appeared unexpectedly in an angled mirror. Her body double. A person she no longer wanted to be.

"Of course," he replied, reaching inside his jacket pocket for his soft, fat wallet. There was no contradiction. "You go ahead."

CHAPTER NINETEEN

Mummy stopped applying mascara, squatted down next to Belinda, put one hand on her back and the other on her chest and asked, "Do you need to go to the toilet?"

"No."

"Well, can you please stop jigging up and down? You're distracting me."

She stopped jigging and instead swung on the bathroom doorframe.

Her mother froze, the mascara wand almost in position again. "Is there something you want?"

The truth was that Belinda was bursting to tell Kirsty everything she had discovered. Each time it appeared that her mother was ready to go, she noticed something that wasn't quite perfect. An eyebrow that required smoothing. Just a touch more lip-liner.

"Mummy?" Belinda began.

"Yes, darling?"

She stopped herself from saying that her mother didn't need to worry because she already looked very beautiful. "You don't want to be late for the taxi."

"Gosh, is that the time? You're right. I don't." Her mother turned and crouched down again.

"That's alright. I don't need a kiss."

"Ah, but I do," she said, pointing to her forehead. Her nails were very purple and matched her dress. They were called French nails and they had come out of a packet. It had been Belinda's job to pass them to her mother, one by one. "Just there."

She complied, a quick peck so as not to disturb the delicate layers of foundation and powder. Her mother's hair smelt fresh and clean, but it was stiff like candy floss.

"What are you?"

"I'm not perfect but I'll do. Mummy?"

"Ye-es."

"Hmm. Will you come and check on me when you get back?"

"Of course I will. I always do." They did rabbit noses at each other until Belinda was out because she was the first one to laugh. "You know," her mother slapped her thighs and then pushed herself upwards, pretending to creak like an old lady. "I'm not even going to bother telling you to be good, because I already know you will be."

Belinda beamed, all the time thinking, *the taxi.*

"OK." Mummy was businesslike, all signs of nerves vanished. They walked down the small stairs side by side, her mother lifting the hem of her dress clear of her heels. "I'm off, Kirsty," she announced from the hall. Kirsty looked up from where she was sitting on the sofa, reading a magazine and pretended to pay attention. "You know the drill. I'll text you when I'm on my way home."

"Have a nice time."

Belinda kept watch until her mother had closed the front door behind her and then ran into the living room, skidding just slightly in her socks.

"So?" Kirsty asked. She already had both feet on the coffee table.

"She's a tour guide."

Kirsty was straight-faced. "Uh-uh," she said. "No way is your mum a tour guide.

"She *is*," Belinda insisted, cross that everything she said was rubbished so readily.

The teenager sighed as if she was saying *Do I really have to explain everything?* "Listen to me. Tour guides wear blazers. They have blue badges."

"Mummy shows rich businessmen around London. That's what tour guides do."

Kirsty licked the end of one finger with its chipped pink nail varnish and scooped up a page of her magazine. Belinda thought of all the germs. "At night?"

"Not just at night! The other weekend I went to stay with Aunty Collette. I had the lilac room." She remembered the way that Aunty Collette had said that it was her room whenever she wanted it, until Uncle Andrew had reminded her about the small matter of the baby they were having, who might need use of the room, perhaps.

"Listen to me!" Aunty Collette had laughed at herself and rubbed circles on her tummy. "I almost forgot."

"That's OK," Belinda had offered. "I don't mind sharing. I don't mind babies." Although she'd never had the chance to test if that was true.

And Belinda had been allowed to put her ear to Aunty Collette's hard round tummy to listen, but she hadn't been able to hear anything that sounded like a baby growing.

Kirsty looked at her with a double chin. "You stayed for the whole weekend?"

"Yes! We made butterfly cakes and Aunty Collette took me to her grown-up yoga class and we did breathing through one nose and then the other -"

"Nostril."

"Excuse me?" Belinda asked, because she had been banned

from saying *what*? (even though she'd caught Mummy saying it quite a few times.)

"You only have one nose. The word is *nostril*."

"You block the holes, like this." Belinda demonstrated and it felt like a seesaw all over again.

"Forget yoga. Forget your weekend. Right now I'm only interested in where your mum was staying."

Belinda back-pedalled to what she'd been saying. "And, anyway, I was wrong. It wasn't a secret. I asked Mummy and she told me. She took the man all over London to see all the places he wanted to."

"What sort of places?"

"Restaurants and an exhibition and the theatre. He wanted to go to the opera and Mummy didn't like that very much. They sing high enough to break mirrors." Her mother had done a very funny impression, singing their shopping list as she wrote it out. *And then we will go to Tesco Metro on Piccadilly for iceberg lettuce, cucumber, new potatoes, wholemeal bread, sliced ham for your sandwiches and not to forget the toilet rolls!* "She said she could have done with ear-plugs." Belinda eagerly offered up all the proof she had collected, expecting at any moment to be congratulated. "Sometimes if they don't speak English, Mummy tells them what is being said. One time, she had to read a speech in front of one hundred and fifty people. She didn't like that because no one thought to tell her about it before so that she could have a practice."

"OK," Kirsty conceded. "*Some* of that may be true." Her hand reached down deep into the magazine rack that lived in the gap between the big sofa and the armchair and came out with half a dozen theatre programmes in it. She fanned them out on the coffee table and left them lying there, then walked over to the sideboard, pulled open a drawer, and took out an envelope.

Belinda was astonished. These were all private things that

were not for looking at, let alone touching.

The childminder waved some yellow theatre tickets she had extracted. They still had their stubs on. "What?" she asked. "Don't tell me you didn't look for clues?"

"I didn't need to. Mummy told me everything."

"Right. She told you *everything*."

Belinda couldn't understand why Kirsty kept on repeating things. It was almost as if she didn't believe her. Then she remembered another detail: "And I checked."

"How?" Kirsty demanded.

Keen to convince the teenager that she'd done a thorough job, she explained, "I told Aunty Collette what Mummy had said and she knew all about it. She told me lots of other things about the man."

"What sort of things?"

They hadn't been very interesting. "Just that he was Uncle Andrew's client and that if Mummy did a good job we would all do very nicely out of it."

"The same Uncle Andrew who owns this flat?"

"Yes. He works downstairs. He's the boss."

"I read a sign on the door as I came in. It's something to do with investments, isn't it?"

Belinda shrugged. These were very unnecessary details. "He has a big desk with two computers on it."

Kirsty moved her mouth to one side and it pulled her face out of shape. Then she brought it back. "It's always men your mum shows around London, is it?"

"I'm not sure."

"And she doesn't have a boyfriend?"

"No!" Belinda was immediately defensive and more than a little bit shocked. "Mummy's never had a boyfriend."

"Don't you think that's strange? Someone as stunning as your mother *never* having a boyfriend?"

Belinda didn't understand what boyfriends had to do with

her mother's job. Neither did she see why Mummy should be criticised for not having one. Girls looked after each other. Sometimes you needed a man to fix the leaking tap on the kitchen sink, but then you could look for one on the Internet. If there was more than one plumber who lived close by, you could choose them by how friendly they looked. (She had chosen the last one because he looked like a chipmunk.) She tried to sound worldly: "You don't have to have a boyfriend. It's not the law."

"No, it isn't." (Kirsty was having boyfriend trouble. Belinda had heard her arguing on the telephone.) The teenager marched past without saying a word, as if she owned the place.

"Where are you going?"

But the childminder didn't reply, so Belinda ran up the small staircase after her, amazed to find she was quite blatantly twisting the handle on her mother's bedroom door.

"Mummy won't like you going in there," she warned, although a thrill was rocketing through her chest.

"Damn!" Kirsty said, rattling it. "It's locked!"

"What were you going to do?" she asked, wide-eyed with awe but more than a little disappointed.

"Does your mum usually lock her door?"

"I don't know."

"How can you not know?"

"The door's always shut. I've never checked to see if it was locked before."

Kirsty looked exasperated. "Do you always do exactly what you're told?"

Judging by all of the times she was told off, it had never struck Belinda that, by some people's standards, she might be considered well-behaved.

"Check! Check every day until she forgets."

"What should I check for?"

"Clues, of course!"

"I don't need clues." Belinda trailed Kirsty to the top of the staircase.

"Yeah, you do," the sour-faced teenager insisted, one hand on the banister.

She spoke with such cold authority that all of Belinda's question marks gathered force and somehow made a decision for her. "Mummy's left her make-up bag in the bathroom. We could see what's in that." She felt surprisingly guilt-free. In fact, Belinda was very pleased when Kirsty froze.

"We could." Retracing her steps along the landing, the childminder managed to look shocked and impressed at the same time. Belinda felt as if she'd been awarded a shiny gold star. Nudging open the door, Kirsty pulled on the cord of the light. Her face lit up.

Petrified the older girl would just tip everything out of the bag and onto the bathroom floor, Belinda yelled, "No!"

The childminder used a nasty baby voice: "Have we changed our mind?"

Belinda felt giddy, like she had done after Mummy allowed her to taste some of her coffee. (It had been disgusting.) The first time she had ever broken her side of the girls-sticking-together rule, she had a strong inkling that, like everything else in life, even *breaking* rules had to be done properly. "We have to remember what's on top. Mummy will remember what she used last."

"Well, well, well," Kirsty said, snapping the eyebrow tweezers within close range of Belinda's nose, as if they were crocodile jaws. "I think we'll make an excellent little sneak of you."

CHAPTER TWENTY

Belinda arrived home from school, panicked to find that her bedroom had shrunk.

"Mummy!" she shouted.

"Just a minute!"

At a second glance she saw that a number of large cardboard boxes had been piled high against one of the walls in her bedroom. Those on the bottom layer had 'Alison' written on their sides in big letters; two of them were labelled 'living room', two 'books'. Even the kitchen had its own boxes. The ones on the top layer were too high for Belinda to look inside. A suitcase lay open on her bed, one side taken up with her mother's things, the other side with her own, all folded in neat squares.

She heard footsteps on the small staircase. "Almost there, Belle!" When Mummy arrived she was slightly out of breath, standing there with her skin glowing from so much rushing about, her long hair tied back from her face.

"Are we moving again?" Belinda asked with dismay. "I thought you liked it here."

"I do like it here." Her mother looked quietly pleased with herself as she sat down, making the suitcase bounce. "And no, sweetheart. Uncle Andrew needs his flat back for a few days, so we're putting everything in your room, then we're going to lock the door so that all our things are nice and safe."

"Is that why you lock your bedroom door?" The words flew out before Belinda had time to think what she was saying. Her face was almost at the same height as her mother's. Cold with terror, she held her breath.

"How do you know that, you little monkey?" The playful words were there but the jokey tone that should have gone with them was missing.

"There was this one time Kirsty got lost when she was new." Belinda faked a laugh in the hope of sounding convincing. "She thought it was my bedroom door and that I'd locked myself in, so she was rattling the door and I came up behind her and shouted 'Boo!'"

"Shhhh!" Her mother covered her ears. "Not so loud."

A crisis appeared to have been avoided. "Why can't everything go in your bedroom?"

"Because Uncle Andrew wants to use the grown-up room."

"Where are we going to sleep?"

"Actually, I thought we girls could have a few days away together."

"Like a holiday?" Belinda had never had a holiday, but every Monday she had been forced to listen all about them from other children.

"Not *like* a holiday. An actual holiday. A mini-break, anyway. You'll have to miss two days of school."

"Which days?"

It was as if her mother had guessed what she was thinking. "Not spelling test days, I'm afraid. Tomorrow and Friday."

That was terribly soon. "Where will we go?"

"I thought I'd show you some of the places I enjoyed going to when I was growing up. How do you like the sound of that?"

"Am I going to meet your mummy and daddy?"

There was a visible stiffening of her mother's back and

neck, and a silence crammed full of things that were never said. It struck Belinda that, within the space of two minutes, she had twice failed to stop and think before opening her mouth. Surer than sure, the promised holiday would be placed out of reach on a shelf, but the voice that followed was a tone higher than usual and very cheerful. "We're going to Richmond, where I went to school. We can visit the park and I thought you might like to have a ride on a pony, so I've booked that."

"A pony!" *She was not in trouble!*

"Does that sound like fun?"

She nodded, but felt her eyes go wide. "I might be a bit scared."

"Well, that's OK. The stables has gentle ponies especially for people who haven't been riding before. First of all, you try sitting on one and, if you decide you don't like it, you can just help feed and groom them, but if you *do* like it, you can go for a little ride."

"I think I probably will like it."

"I think you will, too."

Entering the park via Richmond Gate, Belinda seemed delighted by everything she saw. She read the notice out loud in that lilting, gulping way of hers: "Wild deer roam freely in this park. Please keep at least fifty metres away from the deer and be…"

"Alert." Alison prompted. "It means that you have to pay attention."

"Do not touch or feed the deer. Do not photograph the deer at close range. What's 'range', Mummy?"

"Close range means close up."

"So no touching."

"We won't be near enough to even think about touching!"

Transfixed by the sight of London, rising like a Utopian

mirage out of the tree tops, she demanded, "What's that?"

"That is the City of London."

"Where we live? Wow! I never knew it looked like that."

As the weather man had predicted, the low sun was unnaturally warm for October. Everything was light and shade. To Belle, silvered branches scattered about the scrub were the skeletal remains of some ancient beast. Her shadow seemed almost as substantial as her small person.

"Listen!" she demanded, crunching through acorns and twigs and dry leaves in her new spotty Wellington boots.

"Don't touch!" Alison warned, panic catching in her throat, as Belle crouched in front of a cluster of 'fairy' toadstools she had found nestling in a crook between the roots of a tree.

Once they started to trek up the Queen's Ride - not nearly as straight as it had been in Alison's memory - they were plummeted into shadow. The sky, shut out by the tall oaks, was oppressively narrow. There was a sense of walking up an aisle, of something formal and solemn, but Belle, with no preconceptions and concerned only with enjoying herself, clearly couldn't sense it.

"It looks like a very long way," she said complainingly, hanging onto the straps of her backpack as if they might provide support.

"It's not as far as it looks," Alison encouraged. She had set herself the challenge of standing in front of the gates of her old school, curious to know if she would experience the rush of nerves that Darcey Bussell had displayed. "The King cleared the trees over three hundred years ago to give his visitors the best view of Richmond Park."

"It had better go somewhere good," her daughter muttered, trudging forwards, dragging the soles of her Wellingtons through the sandy soil.

"This path leads to the White Lodge."

"What's the White Lodge?"

A simple question, deserving a simple answer, Alison stuck to the facts. "It's a very old house that used to be lived in by some of the Royal Family." Alison could feel her throat tightening. "But it's a ballet school now. I went there for five years. I lived there too. It's what you call a boarding school."

Belle came to a halt. "Didn't you live with your mummy?"

"I went home to see my parents during the holidays." Alison could almost see the cogs of Belle's mind whirring, arriving at unpalatable conclusions. "I wasn't sent away, darling. I chose to go." Quick to correct her, at the same time she realised how foreign this unlikely truth sounded. An illogical sense of panic gathered in her chest: How might she feel if Belle announced that she wanted to do something that would take her away from home?

"Because you didn't like your mummy and daddy?"

"No! It was because I wanted to be a ballerina and this was where the best teachers were." She didn't wonder how her mother had felt, if her sacrifice hadn't been purely financial. Perhaps she, too, had been in training: teaching herself how to give things up so that her final goodbye had appeared painless. To Alison, she herself had been the only one who gave things up.

"I don't think I'd like to live at school."

"It wasn't all that bad. Imagine having this as your back garden." Trying to lighten the mood, Alison threw out her arms and spun around, allowing the trees to blur, but her daughter still failed to look impressed. "Oh, Belle! Going away to boarding school isn't something you'll ever need to worry about."

"You won't send me there?"

"Never! I'm afraid I couldn't afford to, even if you really wanted to go." Alison dropped down to Belle's level again and saw the slight tremor in her daughter's lip. "Did you think that was why we had come? You thought I was trying to get rid of you?"

Belle shrugged dismissively.

"Don't be daft. We girls stick together. Always."

The tremor was becoming a wobble. "But *you* asked if I wanted dancing lessons."

"And if you do, there's a dance studio less than five minutes from home. Not everyone who has dance lessons wants to be a dancer. Hey, come here."

It had started then, just as Alison gathered her daughter up in an embrace, the ghostly baying. She felt a fresh creep of anxiety.

"What's that?" Belle froze, standing wide-eyed on the sandy tract, all thoughts of being sent away extinguished.

Alison's pilgrimage now seemed self-indulgent. Even without the noticeboards on display, having lived within the park's gates for so long, she should have remembered: early autumn was mating season. Although it was rare for stags to attack, every pupil had a horror story to tell about an exception they'd heard of (always a friend of a friend). Each severed and silvered branch looked as though it had the potential to be a set of antlers. There was no knowing which clump of russet ferns a stag might rise from. The bellowing continued, and this time it had acquired an eerie echo.

"It's deer," she replied, trying to sound confident. Following the sound as best she could, Alison saw him through the trees: a shape less distinct than Belinda's shadow had been. He wasn't fifty metres away, but he was at what she judged to be a safe distance. Relieved, she pulled Belle closer, pointed, and whispered: "There. Can you see?"

Standing in a place where light was in greater supply, he turned and they saw the branches of his antlers. He was an impressive specimen.

Belle gasped. "Is it a wild deer?"

"'Wild' only means that they're not kept in cages."

"Why's he making that noise? Is he hurt?" Belinda asked

as the stag threw back his head once more.

"No." And Alison shivered, because the sense that she was leading her daughter into a trap was rapidly gathering pace. "He's calling to his friends. There! Can you hear them answering?"

"Maybe he's lost."

"Maybe."

On edge, the fall of every dry leaf now had Alison glancing back over her shoulder. She was keen they moved away from this place. "How about a piggy back? Hop on."

Five minutes later, Belle had recovered sufficiently to be calling her 'horsey' and demanding she sped up.

"Almost there."

The central portion of the Lodge came into focus, a Georgian mansion with its external staircase branching off to the left and to the right, and its grand columned entrance. Alison swallowed, slowing instinctively just as they arrived at the edge of a clearing the size of a football pitch. It was backed by several steel-grey tower blocks. Glad to have her daughter where she could control her, glad to have something substantial to hold on to, Alison counted nine large deer. A lone stag stood proud, slightly distanced from the females he had claimed as his own. His warning call was the echo they had heard. With the stag aware of, but seemingly choosing to ignore them, Alison judged it safe to cross the open ground.

"Will I be able to see the bed you slept in?" her daughter asked.

They passed a dead tree trunk that resembled a totem pole; another with branches like witches' fingers.

"Oh, I don't think we'll actually go in."

The threat from the deer receding, it now seemed as if Alison had invented it to distract herself. Continuing in a straight line, her eyes trained on the house, she moved as if she were stalking something. The enthusiastic shouts of a sports lesson reached them, such an ordinary, everyday thing that her fear seemed displaced. Alison was slowing, slowing, crossing the road, her view of house and sky widening.

"Whoa!" Belle kicked her heels, and she crouched to allow her daughter to dismount, bringing herself up to her full height again slowly, smoothly. "Look! Zooloo spears, Mummy!"

Alison hadn't anticipated experiencing an absolute sense of not belonging. The wrought-iron gates topped by gold-painted Zulu-spear shapes, the gates she had unlatched on a daily basis, seemed impassable. Five long years, and yet there was nothing here that told the story of who she now was.

The crunch of gravel. "Alison?" Unmistakable French pronunciation. She twisted her head sharply, expecting to see a twenty-two-year-old.

"But of course it's you. I would recognise you anywhere!" The boy had been replaced by a thirty-year-old man. He was removing a cigarette that had been dangling from his lips. "You have come to visit us, *n'est ce pas?*"

Completely taken aback, Alison managed to say, "Jean-François!" Despite having never been lovers, both in rehearsal and on stage they'd been more familiar with each other's anatomies than newly-weds. She said the first safe thing that came to mind. "You still smoke, I see."

"Well, we don't all have your self-control. And I am French. It's almost obligatory." He waved the packet of Gauloises at her.

"You always give up quicker with a pack of ten," they said in unison, and Alison, who had never ceased to be shocked by the percentage of ballerinas who smoked, found herself laughing. "So. You're still here?"

"You make it sound as if I never left! You know, I have danced on the world's stages. But now that I've retired" - he gave a little indulgent shrug - "I teach a little. And what better place could there be?"

"You teach?" It struck Alison in the guts. *Cleaning toilets. The man at the bar. The humiliation of not knowing how to fill in tax returns. Having no one to ask.* Wanting to double over, she reached breathlessly for Belle's shoulder.

"You should not look surprised. I'll have you know, I am magnificent. My pupils adore me, *naturellement*. And those who should go on to do very well."

She raised her eyebrows and intoned slowly: "Those who should?"

"*Bof!* There is only so much you can teach. Nobody can help the others, you know that."

Alison recovered her humour sufficiently to quip, "I'm glad you haven't lost that legendary modesty we all found so endearing."

"How can you say that? I am the most retiring of God's creatures, *non?* But, you know, my pupils: they are just the same as we were. They still invent Russian-sounding names for themselves, most of which turn out to be desserts. I always thought that you would -" He looked from Alison to the Lodge and back again.

"Teach? No one suggested it to me." She managed to dismiss the idea, as if it was inconsequential.

"What?" He laughed. "Were you waiting for a personal invitation? I re-trained as a teacher! Three years, it took."

"Three years." The fact that it would have been impossible calmed her.

"Three looong years. In fact, I wish I had known what I know now when I was performing. Ah, but who is this *tres* chic young lady? Aren't you going to introduce me?"

Placing both hands on Belle's shoulders, Alison indulged a smile. "This is my daughter, Belinda."

"But, of course!" *Un mal au genou.* A sore knee. "I remember! And do you dance as beautifully as your mother? You know, she was... she was..." He pursed his lips and let the opening of one hand render his kiss airborne. "The most beautiful. Here." He beckoned. "I will let you into a little secret. I worshipped this woman."

While Belle giggled (she found foreign accents disproportionately amusing), Alison felt her chest expand in response to his flattery - although it differed substantially from her memory. There was no worship. Sparring partners, they had also challenged each other.

"I do gymnastics," Belle volunteered, and Alison felt a pang, hoping that her daughter wouldn't kneel down there and then to demonstrate her version of a headstand.

"And you, Alison. Please tell me you still find time in your life to dance."

"I chose to be a mother."

"*Mais, bien sur*. Of course you did." But his eyes said that he didn't believe that, for people like them, a settled life was possible. They said, *For you, I will pretend*. Then his hand was touching her elbow. "But you will come and meet my class? They will want to meet a real-life prima ballerina."

"Oh, I -" Alison looked down at her daughter.

"Can we, Mummy?" Belle was up on tiptoes, her eyes imploring. "I want to see."

"You will do this for me," Jean-François said, and it was not a question. The way he said it left no wiggle room.

"Well, I suppose -"

"There is no *suppose*." Ushered through the gates, walking with gravel underfoot, Alison drew on Jean-François's sense of belonging that, together with Belle's curiosity, was strong enough to carry all three through the grand entrance. Inside the foyer, his arm circled Alison's shoulder. "We will find some practice clothes for you, some shoes…"

"Oh, no." She shook her head.

There was Maurice Lambert's life-sized sculpture of Margot posing on pointe, the fingers of her brass hands shiny, legs rumoured to have been modelled for by Georgina Parkinson, eyelashes, strands of wire.

"Oh, yes! You will partner me." Walking backwards, he pulled her by both hands.

"But I haven't danced in years!" She was giddy with the thought of it. There were the tutus, stacked, just as they always had been, like giant lily pads.

"You may think you have forgotten up here." Still walking, Jean-François released one of her hands to tap the side of his head. "But the muscles of a ballerina don't forget the music. When I don't dance during the day, my dreams make me dance all night. Ah!" He threw back his head a little, and she remembered the beautiful line of his jaw. "I see you know how it is to wake feeling exhausted, every muscle aching!" He stopped, bent his knees slightly, blinkered her vision with his hands and looked very closely into her eyes. "I miss you," he said solemnly, and he seemed to want his expression to convey many things. He had not been a friend, they had crossed too many boundaries for that. But Alison remembered him as one of the best partners she had ever had. She re-lived his proximity; the smells of his breath on her face and his sweat; his touch, the grip of his hands around her waist, and it wasn't something she wanted to flinch away from. She remembered adrenalin-fuelled nights when they had gone straight from stage to nightclub, euphoric. Music throbbing, they found a podium, danced provocatively. It seemed that he remembered how to push all her buttons. Now he said with premeditated devilry, "You and I, we are not like other people. We are never truly alive unless we are on the stage!" Alison could feel her heart racing, the flutter of wings in her stomach. "We were born for the limelight. To us, applause, it is like oxygen. Without it, something inside us dies."

The sound of blood pulsing in Alison's ears might have been the onset of the audience's pandemonium after the heart-stopping silence of curtain-fall.

"OK," he said, and again it wasn't a question. His voice was calm, full of confidence that she couldn't refuse him. But Alison was alarmed by the feeling of something in herself awakening after a long winter's hibernation, frightened it would demand to be fed. Somehow, because Edwin, a clairvoyant she had only visited once, hadn't foreseen this - whatever it might be - Alison knew it shouldn't be happening. To Jean-François, it might have seemed he was asking something small. *Dance with me.* But she suspected not: she suspected it was a challenge.

Aware of her daughter close beside her, although she couldn't see them, she knew that Belle's eyes had wandered to the tutus and that she was already transfixed. The tutus, worn by generations of students, the stiff bodices absorbing sweat and ambition. Her own ambition, stacked in the corner of a corridor - where it belonged.

"No," she said, and it was if she was locking antlers with the stag who had crossed her path. Her refusal was absolute and unretractable. The reason she needed to flee was because she wanted so much to reclaim the person she'd once been. She was as certain as she had ever been about anything in her life. She shouldn't have come back here. If she could have physically pushed Jean-François away from her, she would have done. Stepping backwards, unsupported, Alison, who had always been so co-ordinated, struggled to regain her balance. "I can't."

Startled, Jean-François laughed, a single breathy "Ha!" Disbelief. *"No* isn't a word I've ever heard you use before."

"Oh, *I* have," said Belle from the sidelines. "She says it all the time."

The tension dissipated, Jean-François threw back his head, and his laugh acquired an echo. "You, my angel, are priceless!" He chucked a giggling Belle under the chin and turned to look Alison in the eye, a note of regret. "And you, my angel, were peerless."

"Actually," she cleared her throat, "we're just on our way to Belle's first horse-riding lesson."

"But, Mummy -"

Alison didn't want to give Belle the opportunity to sacrifice her lesson for the opportunity to see her dance. "Sorry, darling. Not today. We don't have time. In fact..." She took Belle's hand firmly in hers.

Jean-François looked at Alison sadly, but not with pity. "I will see you again?" he asked.

Alison felt the corners of her mouth twitch. "Perhaps."

CHAPTER TWENTY-ONE

Arriving home at Saturday teatime, bumping their wheeled suitcase up the front steps to the porch, Alison heard voices. Female voices.

She wiggled her key free from the lock in the front door - "Wait a minute, Belle" - grabbing at her daughter's backpack, the only part of her that was accessible.

"It's Jenny and Kirsty!"

While her daughter bounded into the hall pretending to be on horseback, and announcing loudly that she had ridden a pony, Alison found herself bristling at the unusual pairing of two familiar names. Why should they be coming downstairs from the flat?

"Hi," Alison said, as the small group congregated at the foot of the wide staircase. Her voice was curt. She parked the suitcase in front of her like a shield. "I didn't realise you knew each other."

"We don't," Kirsty cut in. "I've lost something and I thought I'd drop round and see if I left it here. Turns out I hadn't."

"I - I let her in," Jenny said, reddening. "I popped in to make sure the cleaners had done a half-decent job. Andrew's busy with his family, otherwise he'd be here himself."

Belle was prancing about on the plush red carpet of the lower steps, her feet marking out a pattern, bringing one foot up to meet the other and then stepping back down again. Her hands were lifted as if she were holding reins.

"I didn't realise you had a key to our flat."

Belle blew air through her mouth to make a snorting sound.

"Oh, *I* don't," Jenny said. "Andrew keeps the spare in the office safe."

Alison turned her attention to Kirsty. "What was it you lost? The flat was being used by someone else this weekend, so we had to box everything up and lock it in Belle's room."

The childminder glanced sideways at Jenny, who shook her head and said, "I tried to tell you."

"An exercise book. Notes for a school project. I usually type them up straight away, but not this time, worse luck."

Alison felt her mouth twitch. "I don't remember seeing it. Do you, Belle?"

Belle whinnied in response.

"What colour is it?"

"Stupid thing is," Kirsty said. "I can't even remember. I'll recognise it when I see it."

"Well, how big is it?"

"It's just a normal exercise book." Kirsty shrugged in such a *whatever* way that Alison wondered if she'd asked a stupid question. You had to feel sorry for the girl's mother.

"I'll keep an eye out for it while I'm unpacking. If I find anything, I'll give you a ring."

"I guess I should be off, then. See you around, Belinda. I said *see you around.*"

"I can't speak. I'm a horse."

"Well, see you around, *horse.*"

"And the audit?" Her mouth tight, Alison turned to Jenny, who was frowning after the teenager as she headed towards the front door. Alison glanced over her shoulder to see what she was missing, but the door was already closing. She couldn't put her finger on the reason her own brow furrowed as she returned her attention to Jenny. Probably the prospect of Belle starting to behave more like Kirsty. "Did it go well?"

"It's hard to say, really. He didn't give very much away," the woman said, with the nervous eyes of someone looking for an opportunity to bolt.

"No," said Alison, remembering her many examiners. "They never do."

"I should probably get home myself. Feed the cats," Jenny said, as she skirted round the suitcase.

Watching her move towards the front door, it struck Alison: "Aren't you going to put the spare key back in the safe?"

Jenny rolled her eyes as if chastising herself and tried the handle of the office door. It didn't give. "I must have locked it!" she said, shaking her head. "Andrew's so security-conscious, he makes me paranoid."

But Alison couldn't ignore the fact that the alarm was set, over-cautious by anyone's standards, particularly someone who had only nipped upstairs for a moment or two. She also noticed as she hauled the suitcase upstairs that Belle wasn't cantering about on the landing. Nor was she sitting cross-legged with her back to the door, waiting to be let inside.

"Belle?" she called.

The door was ajar. Pushed lightly, it swung away from Alison.

"Here, Mummy!"

So much for security! she boiled inwardly, depositing the suitcase in the hall, then striding back to the top of the flight of stairs, hands making fists. Waiting for Jenny to emerge from the office, Alison had more than enough time to count to ten. *It's not worth it*, she told herself, deciding against confrontation. *She'll only say that you disturbed her before she had the opportunity to lock up.* But going from room to room,

Alison experienced a sense that her personal space had been violated.

She carried out an inspection, looking for signs that things had been disturbed. But if anything was out of place - she straightened the frame of a mirror - how would she know who had moved it? The whole point had been that the big boss was to use the flat. Now she had learned that, in addition, the office cleaners (did they, too, have their own key?) and Jenny and Kirsty had been there - without anyone thinking it necessary to ask her permission. She had half a mind to ring Andrew and insist on some ground rules if this was going to happen again. But what would her complaint be? That he'd tried to make sure she came home to a clean flat? This only reinforced the feeling: the flat wasn't theirs to call home. The sense of living hand to mouth - the very thing Alison thought she'd left behind at Worlds End - was not as far away as it had seemed.

Unpacking the tower of cardboard boxes, returning each thing to its rightful place, Kirsty's lost exercise book slipped Alison's distracted mind.

CHAPTER TWENTY-TWO

The race towards the end of the year accelerated following Belle's October half-term holiday. Frustrations that, a month prior, had kept Alison staring at the ceiling at night seemed to diminish in the wake of small joys and successes. She graduated from the beginners to the intermediates class in Mandarin. Confident enough about her finances to consult an accountant, he was more than understanding about her situation and helped her to register as self-employed. Legitimacy felt good. Finally, she had a sense of control. Then Belle came home carrying a scroll she was reluctant to be parted from - a certificate for having come first in a spelling test. Alison had it framed, since, with a fitted kitchen, there was no scope to hang it on the fridge door - the place traditionally reserved for such things. Belle also had a small - but very important, she was keen to stress - part in her school Nativity play: the innkeeper's wife.

Throughout November, she practised her lines with everybody. Passing each other in the hall, Jenny and Andrew would give the child her cue during the hour or so towards the end of the working day when their lives collided.

"Not another traveller!" one or other of them would declare, taking the part of the innkeeper. "No, we have no spare rooms at the inn tonight."

"Take pity on them, husband, for you know not when you will be in need of a bed. And that good lady is near her time."

Andrew even took to addressing Belle as 'wife', causing confusion when Collette - who really *was* approaching her time - dropped in unexpectedly. She was on her way home from Christmas shopping, laden with bags which swamped the hall.

"How many relatives do we have?" Andrew asked after learning that there were still more to bring in from the taxi.

"Friends *and* relatives."

"Then by this time next year we must make an effort to lose a few of each."

"Don't be such a Grinch. I need everything organised before the beginning of December - while I can still fit through the front door, preferably!"

"Speaking of which, give me a hand with the door, will you, wife?"

Collette's jaw dropped in protest (she had only just squeezed into the leather armchair in the library) but Belle came sliding forwards, saying, "OK, husband!"

"Well, then," Collette said after the identity issue was ironed out. "I'd better play the part of Mary. I don't think I'd make a very convincing Joseph."

"Mummy can be Joseph!"

"Oh, can I?" Alison retorted ungraciously.

"It's only acting, Mummy," said Belle, handing her a checked tea towel. "Here. You need to put this on your head."

Alison saw little point in refusing.

"Not like that, like this!"

"It's only *acting*," repeated Collette, compressing her lips to stifle laughter.

Andrew cleared his throat. "But we only have the stable, wife."

Belle threw the giggling pair a look that said: *See! Uncle*

Andrew did as he was supposed to do, so why can't you behave yourselves? "Then offer them the stable, husband!" The centre of attention, in charge of casting, and as actor and director, Belle was in her element.

"Bravo!" Jenny applauded from the office doorway, and Belle turned, beamed and curtsied.

All of the adults professed to be bitterly disappointed when a missive was sent home from school saying that each child could only bring two guests, but Belle was very grown-up about it. She chose Jenny.

"Jenny?" Alison repeated, trying to hide her surprise. "Are you sure?"

Admittedly, it was Jenny who, on December 1st, had asked for Belle's help to decorate the Christmas tree in the library, and who had resisted the temptation to rearrange the baubles that Belle had hung from the low branches within her limited reach; Jenny who had sent Belle a postcard from a weekend trip to Margate to visit her sister.

"Uncle Andrew is always talking about the boys' school plays. Aunty Jenny doesn't have one to go to."

Alison couldn't ignore the fact that, in her daughter's eyes at least, Jenny had been promoted to 'family'. And it was a good answer, given in true Christmas spirit, with a child's absolute belief that no adult Christmas could possibly be complete without a Nativity play. As Belle solemnly illustrated Jenny's invitation with a galaxy of five-pointed stars, Alison hoped that her daughter wasn't building herself up for disappointment.

"It's during the working day, sweetheart. Jenny may not be able to get time off."

"That's OK." Belle shrugged, adding the brightest and pointiest star over the roof of the stable. "She'll still know I wanted her to be there."

But when they traipsed downstairs to the office - "Knock,

knock!" - to present the invitation, Jenny's face melted. At the sight of the handmade envelope, complete with its drawing of a stamp, unexpectedly, she gave an enthusiastic yes. Alison contemplated the prospect of sitting next to Andrew's secretary, and then made a conscious decision to compensate for her uncharitable thoughts.

"It would be lovely if you could come back afterwards for mulled wine and mince pies."

"To the flat?" For a moment this seemed to be an imposition too far on her time. But Belle was standing there practically bursting with anticipation and with such large and hopeful eyes that it must have been impossible to contemplate not saying, "Thank you, that would be lovely."

Alison met Jenny's upward gaze for a moment intending to say something that expressed the gratitude she felt. It wasn't important whether she was liked or not. That Jenny would do this personal kindness for Belle meant more than Alison could put into words. But she saw the mild panic in Jenny's eyes as Belle performed a victory star-jump.

"Come along, innkeeper's wife," Alison said, ruffling her daughter's hair. "We've caused enough disruption for one afternoon."

"Will we all go together?" Jenny piped up as they reached the office door. "Travel there, I mean."

"I'll already be at school but you and Mummy can go together!" Belle replied on Alison's behalf, as if nothing would make her happier. "And we'll be getting a taxi back because I'll be wearing my costume."

Alison winced: "It would mean leaving at about two thirty."

Andrew replied, a faceless voice, from behind his two computers: "Anyone would think it was Christmas!"

"Bah, humbug!" Alison replied without thinking, then wondered if she'd spoken out of turn.

"So, it's all settled!" Belle announced gleefully, clapping her arms to her sides.

"That's me told," muttered Andrew, frowning at the graphs on his duo of tinsel-framed screens.

The *Nutcracker*-themed Christmas decorations went up in the windows of Fortnum & Mason. Mesmerised, Belle stood in thrall as she watched the clockwork components move. A toy train circled the Christmas tree. The owl on top of the clock opened its eyes, its head rotating through 360 degrees. Lifelike dolls sprang to life. The Mouse King nodded sagely while the Sugar Plum Fairy pirouetted. And, of course, everywhere were baskets overflowing with tea from China and coffee from Arabia, candy canes and marzipan fruits. Somewhere between explaining how all the elements fitted together and trying to coax her daughter away, Alison found that Belle - who had never been to the cinema, let alone the theatre - had extracted a promise that she would take her to her first ballet. But, to Alison's surprise, unlike their disastrous visit to the White Lodge, the prospect wasn't daunting. Instead, it felt as if this was something she could share with her daughter. *See, this is what Mummy used to do.* And maybe it would pave the way for one of those serious conversations she continually scripted and rehearsed over and over inside her head.

In the event, it was Jenny who gasped at the innkeeper's wife's timid entrance on the small tiered stage (which looked makeshift to Alison's professional eye); whose hand seemed to rise of its own accord and ripple as Belle's darting eyes, anxious for reassurance, searched the pair of them out; who mouthed Belle's cues, nodded encouragement, and who shed a few tears when Belle's voice emerged, far smaller and more mechanical than it had done in the high-ceilinged hallway. Alison, much of whose life had been spent on a stage - a place where emotion had to be restrained - didn't question why she did none of these things. Instead, she wondered if she'd been right to allow the adults in Belle's life to buoy her up with confidence so that she was unprepared for the possibility that she might be overcome by shyness. But she understood why Jenny looked at her questioningly, as if to ask, *Aren't you proud of your daughter?*

It might have been different had it been Collette sitting beside her on the small and uncomfortable plastic chair. Collette would have gripped Alison by the arm, placing her other hand over the hard round mound of her stomach, given her a sideways smile that suggested her heart was bursting. And, rather than the clunkiness of the delivery and the piano that sounded as if it hadn't been tuned for years (or perhaps it was that the thirty-four voices singing *Little Donkey* were off-key) Alison would have focussed on the hope invested in this new life-to-be, how it was Belle who had brought them all together, and that thought would have made Alison proud beyond measure. In imagining this alternative scenario, she found herself reaching into her shoulder bag for a travel-pack of tissues, offering one to Jenny and using one herself.

"And which one was yours?" another bloodshot mother twisted round in her seat to ask Jenny. Jenny looked towards Alison, embarrassed to have been singled out, but Alison nodded her consent.

"Innkeeper's wife."

"Ahhh. She was precious."

"And yours?"

"Shepherd Number Two." And the mother mimicked the hammed look of surprise her son had adopted as Shepherd Number One had caused a collective holding of breath when he underestimated how heavily he was dropping to his knees. A painful thud, it had only been after an extended pause that he uttered that well-known biblical exclamation, "Wow!" and everybody (including the angel, who seemed to have forgotten his cue) was heard to exhale. And they had both laughed, shaking their heads in wonder at how it was possible to get quite so emotional over costumes hand-stitched late at night from old sheets, and half-forgotten lines; language borrowed from the King James Bible and clumsily blended with Estuary English.

The pre-Christmas trip to see *The Nutcracker* at the Royal Opera House was a triumph, the colour and grand sets and the costumes and the orchestra, but only once Belle had mastered her velvet tip-seat. She had approached it warily, pushing it down with her hand and then letting go.

"It's not going to bite."

"It might."

Rather than being overwhelmed by their opulent surroundings, voicing her newfound expertise, Belle declared that ballet was almost exactly like a play, but with dancing instead of words.

Belle chose a lull in the score to ask why the men had forgotten their trousers and the next logical question that followed: what did they have down the front of their tights?

"It's called a dance belt," Alison explained, which bought a few minutes' quiet, until Belle complained, "They're wearing them all wrong," and the woman to Alison's left hooted loudly, leaned in and asked, "No brothers?"

"Only child."

"Then it's time for that talk."

"I think it probably is," Alison agreed, her focus turning to that other talk she needed to have; the one that concerned what the word 'family' really meant. And maybe, maybe it would be alright. Though she pretended to watch the stage, the second and third acts were taken up with how the stage lights reflected on her daughter's rapt and enchanted face, which occasionally turned to her for reassurance: *Did you see what I just saw?* Alison, to whom the steps were so familiar, had no need to watch. She needed only to listen to the orchestra to experience muscle memory, her restless feet questioning why she wasn't on stage.

Maybe it wouldn't be as bad as she had imagined. Belle would look at the cuttings Alison had compiled of her dashing father and his new family set against the backdrop of the Sydney Opera House, and would see nothing of herself in his face or - in her half-brothers'. Selfish though it sounded to adult ears, maybe the phrase, "I wanted you all for myself," would wash. But first, before any conversations took place, Alison intended to make sure that her daughter had the best Christmas ever.

CHAPTER TWENTY-THREE

Mrs Brundle, Belinda's teacher, let it be known that the first day of the last week of the Christmas term wasn't a good evening for her mother to decide to be late to pick her up from school. Not only did she have an awful lot of shopping to carry, but, now that she had missed her train, it was more than likely that she would freeze to death waiting for the next one. Belinda, who had been anxious about this very prospect after she'd first heard it mentioned, had asked the Librarian: was it actually *possible* to freeze to death? The answer they found online wasn't all that comforting. A person would die long before their body actually froze. Rather than dying, it was far more likely that their fingers and toes would turn black with frostbite - and once they'd turned black, well, you might as well chop them off for all the good they would be. After that, Belinda's mother had never needed to remind her to wear mittens.

Belinda was far more anxious about her mother, who, she was absolutely sure, would never *decide* to be late to pick her up. It wasn't really evening yet, even though the sun had gone down. It had, however, been deemed too cold for standing outside, and the pair huddled inside the main entrance, peering out through the gaps in Year One's cut-out snowflakes into the four o'clock gloom. Every few moments Mrs

Brundle's feet shuffled and the carrier bags between her legs clinked, then she removed her hand from Belinda's shoulder to check her watch. You'd be forgiven for imagining a growing army of people wondering where she was. Inhaling noisily, as if what her watch told her was displeasing, she thumbed another furious number into her mobile phone.

Mrs Brundle made one thing crystal clear: she expected her pupils to take full responsibility for the behaviour of their parents (it was just as well Belinda only had one). Perhaps, for the first time, the seven-year-old felt the weight of this responsibility. She began to wish that someone - anyone - would turn up. No matter who it was, she would claim them for her own, and have done with all the tutting and sighing. And then Belinda wished that person would be the Librarian, realising with a pang that she'd been so busy, she hadn't given her much thought. Or perhaps Mr or Mrs Oo, who would more than likely have a better range of snacks. Or even Uncle Sergei with his Russian-speaking dog.

But it was Aunty Collette who was startled by the flood-lighting as it flashed into action.

"It's my Aunty!" Belinda announced, pushing on the door and producing only a slight jarring movement.

Captured in the act of wheeling the new buggy across the tarmac, Aunty Collette was wearing her pregnancy coat, because her tummy was still big - although now it was squashy like a deflating balloon. She'd said it wasn't like the last time, when she'd been back in her 501s within ten days.

"And Ben," Belinda sighed.

The baby had been a disappointment to them all. It was a boy, and so it had been impossible to call it Belinda. Her mother had asked her please not to make a fuss, because Aunty Collette had really wanted a little girl, so she had tried not to mind. In actual fact, Belinda had surprised herself by feeling nothing very much. With an enormous Christmas tree to welcome her in the Simons's hall, she felt rather like one of the wise men bearing gifts from afar.

"Come and meet Ben." Aunty Collette had invited, looking as if she was about to offer a consolation prize.

It was just a baby swaddled in a manger ("It's a Moses basket," her mother had said): bald and not very interesting, especially compared with all the pine cones and candles in the fireplace; the silver tinsel and the red and green baubles; the clove-studded oranges hanging from the mantelpiece by red ribbon. She'd tried to show willing by singing it *Silent Night* while Mummy and Aunty Collette sat together on the sofa whispering about grown-up women's things, and Uncle Andrew lolled in an armchair swilling red wine around a large glass as if he was daring it to spill.

At some point during their visit, Uncle Andrew had said, "Of course, it will have to go back," and there was an embarrassing moment when Belinda thought it was Ben he'd been talking about. Instead, it turned out that Aunty Collette had stocked up on an awful lot of pink. Apparently there was no right to return children. You had to accept what you got, like it or lump it.

No, the main reason that Belinda was disappointed was because when she'd agreed to share the lilac room, it was on the understanding that the baby would be a girl. Now there was even talk that the room was to be painted blue.

Mrs Brundle helped Belinda with the awkward bar on the door and they stepped outside to meet the inrushing air, blown straight from the Arctic.

"I'm *so* sorry I'm late!" Aunty Collette gushed from behind a woollen scarf that was looped round her neck so many times it must have been suffocating her. She stood in the porch, all damp-haired, puffy and breathless. The see-through cover of Ben's buggy was spotted with raindrops. Apparently, it was very unlikely that *he* would suffocate, because it wasn't made of normal plastic, like Mrs Brundle's clinking carrier bags. "I'm Belinda's Aunty Collette. I was at the doctor's with this little monster when I got Alison's call. And the traffic! It must be Christmas shoppers."

"Well, you're here now, that's the main thing," Mrs Brundle said, making a mental note of the time and checking the list that stopped her from handing you over to a stranger. "Collette...?"

"Collette Simons," Aunty Collette said, helpfully pointing to her name. "There I am."

Apparently satisfied, Mrs Brundle picked up her carrier bags, two in each hand, and adjusted the handles like you had to so that they didn't strangle your wrists. All hope of putting up her umbrella was abandoned and, somehow, Belinda imagined she would be blamed for the fact that her teacher was going to get wet.

"Where's Mummy?" asked Belinda, and when there was no answer she added, "Grammy's not ill again, is she?" because she had a strong sense that they were supposed to be pretending.

Aunty Collette squashed her lips together and sighed. "Yes, darling. Mummy's had to take her to the hospital."

"Will I be coming home with you tonight?"

"Hood up, poppet, it's miserable out there. Yes, I think that's best, don't you? We don't know how long Mummy's going to be." And Aunty Collette gave Mrs Brundle one of her *you know how it is* looks, which seemed to make even her teacher's expression defrost. "It might be me again tomorrow, I'm afraid. We'll have to see how it goes."

A bad leg wasn't going to convince anyone. Perhaps pneumonia was a good thing for an old person to catch at this time of year. There seemed to be a lot of it about.

They walked towards the gates, the wheels of the buggy whooshing. A certain awkwardness was caused by the adults' need to talk when they couldn't really think of anything to say. Mrs Brundle asked questions she wasn't interested in the answers to, like, "So, you're Mrs Brabbage's sister?" and "And how old is the little one?" and Aunty Collette reeled off replies ("A friend of the family, actually," and "Just over two weeks"). Belinda didn't join in. She needed all her concentration to look out for reflected light that showed where puddles were lurking, so that she could leap around them.

Aunty Collette had parked right on the yellow zigzags outside the school gates. Belinda had a pretty good idea why the boys didn't want her to pick them up anymore. Having a parent who parked irresponsibly could get you into all kinds of trouble. But, more concerned whether her carrier bags would hold under the strain, for once, Mrs Brundle made no comment.

"Jump in!"

"There's no child seat," Belinda said as Aunty Collette held the door open for her.

"You're a big girl now. You can use the seat-belt."

She gulped so loudly, Aunty Collette must have heard her.

"Come along, Belinda. Ben's getting cold."

Feeling the onset of panic, she faltered, "I'm not supposed to get in a car without a child seat."

She heard a sigh and was snapped at. "I'll tell you what. Just sit in the front while I sort the buggy out. I think the old booster seat might still be in the boot."

"But -"

"I said *sit inside!* We won't be going anywhere for a while yet."

Scrambling in silently and sitting up straight, Belinda wondered if she hadn't actually preferred staring out into the dark with Mrs Brundle. At the same time, she felt very bad to be putting Aunty Collette to so much trouble. Her lovely hair was plastered to her face. Although she didn't say anything, she was breathing hard and her red hands worked furiously, so you could tell she was very cross. Mummy wasn't mentioned at all and it was impossible to ask. Experimenting with everything that looked as if it might move, Aunty Collette converted Ben's buggy into a carrycot and strapped it into the back seat. Then she took the folded-up legs and wheels and started rummaging about in the boot. A shoulder-tensing slam later she was back, struggling with something much more bulky. Belinda made sure she sat very still. Only her eyes moved, alternately blinking at the blurred lights in the darkness and checking in the mirror. Her breath was raggedy in her chest. Aunty Collette was right: the cold was bitter, just like *In the Bleak Mid-winter*. Her fingers felt as if they might have turned black inside her mittens. The car rocked about as Aunty Collette checked that the child seat was secure. Seeming very unsure about the whole thing for a grown-up, she muttered an exasperated, "I don't know," several times. Then, with a, "That'll have to do. OK, Belinda, let's have you in the back! Quickly!"

Terrified, Belinda did as she was told, gripping the sides of the seat the whole way to Herne Hill.

"Haven't you got your keys?" Jim demanded, opening the front door inwards. As Belinda traipsed past, keeping her head down, he added, "What's *she* doing here?"

"Number one," Aunty Collette manoeuvred the buggy up the doorstep and over the threshold, "I have my hands rather full with your brother and number two," she unjammed a wheel with a carefully-aimed kick, "Belinda's staying the night, so could you *please* be a little more welcoming."

Belinda felt a short-lived triumph as the buggy was parked in the hall that no longer looked quite so spacious. Still, she kept her head down. The oak floor was littered with pine needles. (Aunty Collette said this was going to be the last year they bothered with a real tree.) Jim ignored her but the burning eyes on his black t-shirt made it seem as if he was staring right at her.

"What time's dinner?"

Ben was low-key grizzling, as if it was hardly worth the effort of trying to attract his big brother's attention.

"James!"

"What?"

"You really are the limit!" Aunty Collette freed herself from the confines of her scarf.

"It's a reasonable question." Jim crossed his arms. "Or aren't we allowed to ask questions anymore?"

Since their last visit, Christmas cards had been wedged in the frame of the mirror in the hall: gilded angels' wings and jolly cartoon reindeer.

"I haven't even got my coat off yet, and Ben needs changing. I don't suppose you thought to turn the oven on?"

The cue to take her own wet coat off, Belinda folded it neatly and hid it out of the way on the floor under the buggy. She also rescued her reading book so that she had a homeworky excuse in case she was asked if she wanted to help change the baby's nappy. She had made that mistake last time and it had been the most disgusting thing she had ever seen.

"How was I supposed to know what we're having?"

"You might try looking in the fridge for clues."

He shrugged as if this had nothing to do with him. "If we won't be eating until half-past six again, can I have some crisps? I'm starving."

"If you really can't wait, I'd prefer it if you had a piece of fruit." Her pregnancy coat shrugged off, Aunty Collette now had Ben slung over one shoulder, his legs frogged up, and was patting his back. He was wearing the blue and white-striped babygrow that Belinda had helped her mother choose in Baby Gap. The spaces for his feet hung empty. His face very red and out of shape, he was making white baby dribble on Aunty Collette's shoulder.

"There isn't any."

"I bought bananas and blueberries only yesterday!"

Jim shrugged. "Dad used them all to make a smoothie for his breakfast."

Of the things that hadn't gone quite to plan, this was the one that made Aunty Collette burst into tears. She marched upstairs with the baby and slammed a door. Having never seen a grown-up cry before, Belinda looked open-mouthed at Jim, hoping for a suggestion as to what they should do to cheer her up. He threw her a mean look and said, "What?" before trudging into the living room and slumping down in front of the television with his back to the door. Blinking fairy lights were reflected in the large screen and he began shooting zombies again.

No one had put the oven on.

Belinda took herself and her book into the calm white kitchen. Mistletoe had been hung in the doorway but, once inside, there were few signs of Christmas. Nothing to suggest that anyone might have been baking cookies.

She stood in front of the gleaming stainless steel dials with their numbers and complicated symbols, not sure of what to do, wanting to help. In her imaginary worst case scenario, she set the house on fire. Sometimes Mummy told her that the most useful thing she could do was to sit quietly and not get in the way. The fact that Belinda found herself alone suggested she had already succeeded in not getting in the way, so she took a seat at the table and opened her reading book, trying to make herself small and inconspicuous.

It was difficult to concentrate on *The Worst Witch* with so many thoughts jumbling up her mind. Something told her she was the cause of all this upset, but she didn't quite know what she'd done wrong. Belinda wondered if Aunty Collette had stopped crying and when she was going to remember she hadn't told her where Mummy really was. If a foreign businessman had needed an emergency tour of the South Bank, wouldn't she have just said so?

Aunty Collette at last appeared, lugging the baby's Moses basket. Looking wild and worn out, she wedged the basket on the kitchen counter between the empty fruit bowl and some sterilising equipment, then stood staring red-eyed at the stainless steel dials. Belinda could see she was biting her top lip. After slamming a cupboard door, she scooped the lasagne from its foil tray into something that would go in the microwave. An iceberg lettuce got the brunt of her anger. As she attacked it with a knife, Belinda was too afraid to ask about her mother. Aunty Collette might start crying again.

Jim's expression changed to disgust when he saw his new brother on the kitchen counter. Will trailed moodily behind. They scraped back chairs on the opposite side of the table and deliberately looked everywhere but at Belinda. Their main obsession was how unfair it was that they had to divide their two-person lasagne into three, even though Aunty Collette rescued the empty packaging from the recycling bin and shoved it right in front of their faces. "Look! It feeds two fully-grown adults."

Pretending she was invisible, Belinda found an interesting spot of crusted food on the shoulder-height table top to stare at. It was difficult to ask for a cushion while she was invisible.

"We're still growing." Will already had his knife and fork at the ready. (He was sulking, having made it clear that he thought he should be allowed to eat in his room because he had got to a crucial bit of his history essay.)

"Yeah," said Jim. "You're the one who's dieting."

"There's no need to keep on pointing it out!" Collette said tetchily.

Belinda broke cover to volunteer, "I'm not very hungry,"

which earned her a watery smile before she melted into the white background again.

While the boys shovelled food into their mouths, clashing metal with teeth, Belinda chased a bit of chopped lettuce in circles around her plate. She was aware that Aunty Collette's red-rimmed eyes kept straying towards the clock over the kitchen doorway (just the numbers and the hands, with no surround).

"Your father will be home any minute," she said occasionally, a statement which excluded Belinda (proving she was invisible) and failed to interest those it had anything to do with. This sentence gradually transformed itself into, "What's keeping your father?" but still Aunty Collette didn't hint at what was keeping Mummy. *Could the same thing be keeping them both?* Belinda fretted. The boys got down from the table and Aunty Collette barely noticed that they hadn't excused themselves. Both of her hands gripped her mug, as if they were glued there, but her tea went undrunk. Belinda pretended to read about Mildred's broomstick crashing while an idea formed of many jigsaw pieces slotted into place inside her head. She had suspected Uncle Sergei of being a spy all that time ago, but she hadn't realised until now that he must have been looking for dancers for the Russian Ballet. Her mother had said no because what she wanted was to be a mummy. They'd had to move from Worlds End so that he wouldn't be able to find her when he came looking again, but Mummy had made the mistake of going back to her old school, where she'd been recognised. And, having refused to dance with Jean-François - clearly foreign and quite possibly Russian - they had followed her home from *The Nutcracker*. No wonder her mother had been so cross when Belinda found her portfolio! It was the only proof that she'd ever been a ballerina. And now Mummy had been kidnapped by the Russian Ballet. Though the jigsaw still had one piece missing, the more the girl thought it through, the more she realised it was the only possible explanation.

Watched pots do boil eventually, and at the sound of a key in the front door, Aunty Collette shot up from her chair.

"I expect that will be Andrew."

Before Belinda could agree that she expected so (who else would have a key to the house?) Aunty Collette was off out under the mistletoe. Momentarily, hope rose in Belinda's throat. There was a slim chance that her theory was wrong and her mother would walk in out of the cold evening with Uncle Andrew. Holding the seat of her chair with both hands, she leaned to one side and angled her head - but no, he was alone, absent-mindedly kissing the top of Aunty Collette's head, ignoring the baby dribble. Knowing it would be 'negligent' (Kirsty's word) not to eavesdrop, Belinda slipped out of her seat and, bending backwards, carried her white plastic chair over to the worktop so that she could stand on it and look down into Ben's Moses basket. She would pretend to be babysitting; making sure he was still doing whatever it was babies were supposed to do.

The chair rocked slightly. "Oh!" she said, feeling silly to have been startled at finding herself face to face with a baby. What had she expected? Ben was slightly jaundiced, which gave him an oriental appearance, more like an Oo than one of the Simons's boys. His eyes were tightly shut but his lashes were an extraordinary length and they rippled like a fish's fin. Belinda barely dared breathe so that she could hear the adults' low murmuring. Something was said in a tired voice that sounded like, "They'll throw the book at her this time," and the only book that Belinda could think of was her mother's portfolio being snatched away from her.

Then the murmuring was muffled by Uncle Andrew's study door and Belinda was left actually keeping guard over the Moses basket (which she still maintained wasn't very different from a manger). Ben's hands stuck out from under the fleecy blanket, fingers like starfish. His ears were almost see-through.

"My mummy has been kidnapped by the Russian ballet," she whispered to him, filled with importance and dread. "I expect we'll be sharing the lilac room tonight."

They had both been forgotten.

CHAPTER TWENTY-FOUR

The walls were painted brickwork; slate-coloured up to waist height and whitewashed above. Alison paced the sparse interview room, covering the same few feet of lino again and again.

Seated at the table, the duty solicitor, a young woman, seemed determined that Alison should join her. "Are you sure you won't sit down?" she asked for the third time.

Holding one hand over her mouth, Alison shook her head in refusal. Blood pulsed violently in her ears. How could she? Her method of dealing with real-life drama was refusing to think about it. Not just to play the part, but to actually *become* someone else. This time she couldn't seek refuge. She needed to face reality. Both hers and Belle's.

They had come for her. She had buzzed them in through the entry system after one had announced that he had an appointment to see Andrew. It happened occasionally. Both Andrew and Jenny would be stuck on the phone and visitors would try Alison's doorbell. Meeting them in the hall, she showed them into the library. (Two of them, inexpensive suits.) "Take a seat," she'd said. "I'll let Mr Simons know you're here. I didn't catch your names..?" But one of them had closed the door. Hearing it click behind her, she had experienced a dredging feeling and she had known. All the time they spoke in soft tones, lowered voices, Alison had remembered how, the first time she had explored the library, she had thought that nothing could touch her there. No sirens, no sounds of roadworks; not even the slamming of a car door. She couldn't have been more wrong. But this time, she wasn't sure how it had happened. She still didn't understand. How had they found her?

"OK," the solicitor said. "It's likely that you'll face two charges. One for tax evasion and one - possibly more - for money laundering."

Alison stopped pacing. She was aghast. "Money laundering?"

"It's how the proceeds of crime make their way into the legitimate banking system."

"Yes, yes, I know what it is, but..." Not sure what the appropriate question to ask was, she settled for: "How?"

"It's alleged that you've been receiving substantial sums of money from parties that the police suspect have criminal - and quite possibly terrorist - connections."

Terrorist? Alison put one hand on the table to steady herself and sank into the chair. Certainties rapidly fracturing, it was as if she was watching the loop of low-quality CCTV footage from that horrific day in July 2005. Four bombers - ordinary-looking boys, not men in well-cut suits. A man arriving at Luton station carrying a rucksack. Wounded passengers staggering out of underground stations, blood mixed with dust. The number 30 bus, its roof ripped off, debris thrown into the air. Blind panic exacerbated by a communications meltdown. Those were her images of terrorism. Fifty-two dead; 700 injured. Alison's only role had been looking to see how close she'd been at the time of the carnage (Belle was already safely at school; she had been on her way home after dropping her off).

"You're shaking your head."

Unaware she'd been doing it until she stopped, Alison looked at the young woman sitting opposite her. Not unkind, but there to do a job and then to get on with her last-minute Christmas preparations. Two plastic cups of water had been placed on the table. Alison's shaking hand took the one that was still full, raised it to her mouth and she sipped. Enough to moisten her mouth, no more. She tried to construct a sentence from inadequate tools. "Impossible."

If only she had stayed in Worlds End. Stuck with her regular clients. If only she had never found that bloody wallet! Never set eyes on Andrew. Nureyev had been right. *"Everything betrays you sooner or later - only your work betrays you last."*

Things she had thought were hers were slipping away. Everything in Alison's life was interconnected: the place she called home; the people Belle had grown to trust - she supposed her daughter might even call the feeling 'love'. The entire support network Alison had constructed, so that there would be help if she ever found herself in a similar situation. It shouldn't all come crashing down at once, leaving her staring in anguish at a cloud of dust.

"I'm afraid not. They appear to have good reasons for their suspicions."

"Someone trying to launder money through a -" Alison heard the breath leave her mouth. She had almost used that derogatory word - a noun she never used - to describe herself.

The duty solicitor raised her eyebrows. "Not so unusual, I'm afraid."

"I thought the whole point was that money launderers used legitimate businesses." But Alison already knew from her accountant that if a prostitute's services are organised in such a way as *to constitute a business*, then it would be classed as legitimate - at least as far as the taxman was concerned. The duty solicitor's pitying smile wasn't reassuring.

"But I don't understand. *How* would I have committed a

money laundering offence?"

"Simply by receiving the proceeds of crime."

"Even if I didn't know?" Her heart was beating wildly.

"I'm afraid so."

"I've brought this on myself, haven't I? I've put myself on the radar." Fingernails dug into Alison's left palm; she tightened her fist further, her knuckles whitening. "They would have left me alone if I hadn't filled in that bloody self-assessment form!"

The woman left what felt like a deliberate pause, one that warned: *Be careful what you say.* "For what it's worth, I don't think H.M.R.C. are that efficient. Besides, the police tell me they received an anonymous tip-off."

Alison sprang up from the chair. So that was it! "Jenny!" The name was also out before she could stop it. Her hands were around her neck, fingertips meeting at its nape.

"Jenny?"

She remembered that evening not so long ago. Mulled wine and mince pies. Belle steering awkward conversation to common ground. A clumsy air-kiss goodbye. "My -" She had been about to say 'my boss's secretary', but in her world 'boss' was a term with serious connotations. "My landlord's secretary. His office is on the ground floor of my building." There was no doubt in Alison's mind that Jenny was her Judas.

"Is there any particular reason you think it would have been her?"

A clear image of Jenny and Kirsty coming down the stairs crowded to the front of her mind. Ignoring the teenage childminder and her blatant lie, Alison said, "She's never made a secret of the fact that she disapproves of me."

"You're saying she knows how you earn your living?"

Alison bent her knees and sat back down, compliant. "She suspects."

"Alison, I can't promise that you won't be charged - or that you won't hear from H.M.R.C. Both the crimes I've mentioned carry custodial sentences."

Something inside Alison splintered. She jerked her head away. She had heard what happened to children when single parents went to prison. She saw a social worker; Belle, carrying her possessions from carer to carer in carrier bags. This couldn't be her daughter's future. It couldn't! There was little to separate her from hysteria.

A moment later she felt the touch of the duty solicitor's hand on her forearm. The woman's voice was gentler now. "But you must know it's not you the police are after."

So now *she* was the means to someone else's end! "That's not much consolation when I'm going to lose my daughter!" Hour-long visits once a fortnight. Not allowed to hold hands, let alone kiss. Tortuous goodbyes. Better no visits than that.

"No, no it isn't." With pain in her eyes, the woman nodded acceptance. "But if you co-operate, it might not come to that. They'd be more inclined to go easy on you."

"Do you have any children?" Having practically accused the duty solicitor of being uncaring, Alison's fingers flickered as if they might grab at the words: too late.

"I don't, no." Sensibly, Alison reflected, she allowed a moment to pass before continuing. "The last time you found yourself here, you received a caution for carding. But your list of clients... they're hardly the sort of men who lurk in London telephone boxes."

Alison compressed her lips. In the past, she had chosen to be a loner. Now she had reached a place where no one could help her. "They're the sort of men who like to be ferried round in limos with blacked-out windows," she said bitterly, dark humour to match the darkness spreading from her core.

"It won't take the police very long to find this information out through other channels, so I think it best you tell me. How do your clients find you?"

Her mobile phone already confiscated, Alison supposed that men involved in terrorist activities would be the sort for whom phones were disposable. They would know better than to leave a trail. The names thumbed into her contacts wouldn't be real names. And her laptop - that would already be in the hands of the police. She had kept records as the accountant had suggested, meticulous records, because the logic of it pleased her. The same would apply to those.

And her purse! She knew full well that Andrew's business card was in one of the credit card slots. *A F Simons. Wealth Management.* She certainly didn't want to be mistaken for someone who needed his services. That would do her no favours.

"Andrew Simons," she said, and the admission brought a strange calm. "He runs the investment company downstairs. They're his clients."

Her mind turned briefly to Collette, the woman who had professed to be a friend. And although naivety had led Alison to this despair, part of her still wanted to cling to the belief that their friendship had been real. For Belle's sake, if not her own, she would like to offer the small comfort that Aunty Collette had not been pretending.

"So Mr Simons acts as your agent?"

Alison winced. There was a complication here. Two complications, if you included the flat. "If they ask where they might find an escort, he... points them in my direction. That's all."

"To the upstairs flat?"

"No. I never carry out business on the premises. Except for making appointments."

"And you make those directly. By phone?"

"Andrew usually arranges an introduction."

"Who pays you?"

"I'm paid by the men." But, of course, her accounting records would show receipts from Andrew's company. And although the name on the cheques differed, there would be a connection somewhere, even if the legitimate business was only a front. "Usually."

"Usually?"

"Sometimes Andrew gives me what he calls a bonus."

"Based on what?"

"The difference between how much his clients say they're planning to invest after his initial negotiations and how much they actually invest."

"After meeting you?"

Alison remained silent.

"Are you sure he wasn't buying your silence?"

"I had no idea, not until you told me... Do you think he thought I *knew*?" Each question gave birth to another. She could barely take it all in.

"How does he sell the service you provide?"

"He doesn't." Alison shook her head, certain of this one thing, at least.

"OK, let me phrase that another way. When one of his clients says that they'd like an escort, does he tell them that you're working for him?"

"I don't think so." It was mortifying to have to admit that she didn't know. She had only worried about balancing her books. "I think they just find that the whole experience of doing business with him is far more pleasant than they'd imagined." Indifferent to the woman's feelings towards her, Alison didn't bother to explain the extent of her services. What did it matter now that she could make herself understood in Mandarin? That she could understand enough of several European languages to act as a translator?

"Do you source clients from anywhere else?"

"I used to. Before I moved to the square. Since then there's been a steady stream." Alison's chest rose and fell. "And the fact that I have fewer overheads means I don't need to work so often. I get to spend more time with my daughter." It struck her that this present-tense description was no longer hers to lay claim to. The thought was chilling.

"Fewer overheads?" The duty solicitor raised her eyebrows. "What else do I need to know?"

"I have a rent-free arrangement with Andrew."

"Rent-free?" Clearly a slave to a London landlord, she blinked. "Based on what?"

"The fact that the flat was standing empty, and the understanding that I would make myself available." Said out loud, it struck Alison anew how terribly naïve she'd been not to have insisted that they went over the fine details of their arrangement. "My daughter..." she began, but it was all that she could do to find breath and grip the edge of the table.

"Belinda?" The solicitor coaxed, pushing the plastic cup towards Alison.

She shook her head, her chest tightening as a fresh wave of panic flooded through her. "She's... she's staying with the Simons... They know I've been arrested!"

"But not *why*."

"They're not idiots," Alison snapped. "They'll suspect."

"I really don't think you need to worry about your daughter's safety, but I'll arrange for a phone call. The police will be keen for you to put Mr Simons's mind at rest. They'll want to keep a close eye on him. And the contents of his bank accounts. See if his behaviour changes."

"And the contents of my bank accounts?"

"If the money laundering charge sticks, I'm afraid they'll be frozen."

"Even though I had no idea who the men were?"

"The law makes it the responsibility of anyone working in financial services to check. We have to assume that either Mr Simons didn't, or that he knew exactly who he was dealing with."

Alison closed her eyes, but her mind was racing. "If what you say is true, whatever I tell him, Andrew will have good reason to worry that any trail from me will lead straight to him."

"Then we'll work out a story to throw him off the scent."

"We'll have to leave the square. *Then* Andrew will know." But one look at the duty solicitor's face told Alison that she wouldn't be going anywhere, at least not immediately.

"Is it possible to make a defence based on lack of knowledge?"

The duty solicitor's expression suggested that she wanted to be cautious. "There is precedent - recent too. But the case was unusual. And it only relates to the tax evasion charge. The money laundering is another matter."

"Give me something, that's all I'm asking for." Alison would have grabbed at anything.

The woman took a deep breath. "A sex worker has just been cleared of tax evasion after claiming she hadn't realised it was payable on illegal earnings. But she was extremely lucky. There was no doubt that she was running a business, and the advice on the H.M.R.C. website is crystal clear."

Alison had been surprised to find prostitution listed as a trade. Thinking he was providing entertainment, her accountant had regaled her with stories of how Lindi St Clair had accused the Inland Revenue of living off immoral earnings when they asked her to pay over £100,000 in back income tax. *"The tax man is a pimp and the government is a pimp as well."* Her accountant had laughed, but he wasn't telling the story of his own life.

Her head pounded violently. "I need to make arrangements for my daughter."

"Does she have a father?"

Alison heard a sound catch in her throat.

"Grandparents, perhaps?" The poor woman thought she'd touched a different type of raw nerve.

"She has both -"

"Good."

"- but she's never met them."

"Do you keep in touch with them?"

"I don't, no." The corners of Alison's mouth twitched. "But I know how to contact them."

"Whatever you want -"

Whatever I want? Incredulous, she cut the duty solicitor off. "What I want more than anything is that Belle shouldn't have to get tangled up in this! Because of who I am - or rather who I *was* - I imagine my case will attract more publicity than this sort of thing normally would."

Glancing down at her neat notes, the young woman looked confused. "I was about to say 'whatever you want help with.' But who *were* you?"

Ashamed at her outburst, Alison closed her eyes. "It won't mean anything to you."

"Try me."

She opened them. "I was Alicia Serafina." It was painful, uttering that over-blown name in her present circumstances. It brought to mind her final performance - although she had never imagined at the time that it was to be her last. The curtain call. How arrogant she'd been, that young woman who'd shown so much promise!

The woman's brows knitted together, as if she were mining the depths of her memories. "Remind me."

"There's no reason you should have heard of me. I was -"

She looked at Alison afresh. "Not the ballerina!"

It was Alison's turn to be surprised, although it was difficult to feel flattered. "Yes."

"When I was a student, I once queued round the block for returns to see you! It was pouring with rain but there must have been hundreds of us, huddled under our umbrellas. The people at the front of the queue had camped overnight."

Alison tried to smile appreciatively, but failed. She noticed that the young solicitor was wearing a black sequinned cardigan over her tailored black dress. Dressed for a night out. A Christmas party.

"We waited outside the stage door. I saw you being set upon. You had to leave your jacket behind because someone wouldn't let go of it." The woman's eyes were gleaming.

Alison remembered the evening, or another almost like it. Finding herself at the centre of a scrum. Alternately claustrophobic and laughing as she was pawed and grabbed at. A short-lived madness. Strange that she'd forgotten slipping free from the jacket until now. She assumed she had lost it. Left it behind in a changing room. "I liked that jacket."

She paused, frowned. "You were billed as the next big thing, but then you just… disappeared. I always wondered what happened to you."

"My daughter happened to me. The rest, I brought on myself." It felt good to be honest.

The duty solicitor looked awkward. "I don't know what to say," she said.

Alison's mouth twitched. "If it's any help, I didn't expect to find myself here, either." Her second career choice had been another option with little security and a limited timespan. And it had led her to this moment.

"If you're resigned to making arrangements for your daughter -"

"If I don't, then Social Services will!"

"I put that badly. I'm sorry."

"No, I'm the one who should apologise. I didn't mean to

jump down your throat. In fact, I should be thanking you for staying so late on my account. You look as if you were on your way to a Christmas party before I ruined your plans."

The duty solicitor ran the edge of her cardigan through her fingers self-consciously. "Drinks at a barrister's chambers, actually. Just me and a bunch of old men! No, I was trying to suggest that you might want to consider a different approach. Beat the press at their own game."

Make the announcement *herself*? "Isn't that illegal?"

"It would be up to the defence to take issue. And if they did, well, then it would be a civil matter rather than a criminal one."

"How does that work?"

"The prosecution would have to raise an objection that their case had been prejudiced."

"You don't think I have a defence." It wasn't a question and her answer was another pause.

"If you tell your story in your own words, you might discover you have a great deal of public sympathy."

It was kindly meant. "By some people's standards, I've been living a life of luxury!"

"You're a working mother, trying to support her daughter. Women will identify with that. I have a friend who works in PR. If you like, I could let you have her contact details. Then you can decide."

It was another choice that didn't feel like a choice, and it wasn't only hers to make. The key thing was to make life liveable for her daughter. "I need to ask Belle's father. He has his own family now."

"Either way, he probably won't be able to avoid publicity."

Alison covered her eyes. "What a way to find out you have a seven-year-old daughter!"

"He doesn't know?"

Shaking her head, she no longer feared that he would think she was blackmailing him. With a growing acceptance of her own fate, it sounded foolish to say it. "There was never a good time to tell him."

CHAPTER TWENTY-FIVE

Early morning. Frosted dew was clinging to the grass in St James's Square and Alison stood looking warily at the glossed front door. This was the building she had called home. Instead of putting faith in herself, she had sunk so low that she had allowed herself to be swayed by the visions of a blind man, without knowing whether what he saw was good or bad; without knowing whether, when *she* encountered the very things he described, she should have allowed herself to be drawn towards them or run as fast as possible in the opposite direction. *Those* were the questions she should have posed when Edwin gave her the opportunity. *Those pivotal events you mentioned? Will things get better for us?* At the time, Alison acknowledged, she would have blocked her ears if he'd hinted that worse was to come - that she might actually stand to *lose* her daughter. But the prospect of a flat overlooking St James's Square had had such a 'drink me' quality about it that she hadn't stopped to think.

"*You'd have two hours of your life back every day. What's there to think about?*"

That was unfair: she had stopped to ponder the possibility that the bottle might be marked 'poison', but not nearly long enough to think of the other dangers Alice had been alert to: getting burnt by a red-hot poker or eaten by wild animals (things that would almost certainly have crossed Belle's mind).

Warmth a distant memory, that heady summer's day assumed a dreamlike quality. A glass of Pimms, sun lightly toasting her skin, Alison had been ready to be persuaded by someone whose lifestyle she thought she had wanted. Collette's deep-rooted dissatisfaction had gone undetected. The something that made her believe that if she had one more thing - a Kenwood mixer, a new pair of knee-high boots, an adorable baby girl - she'd finally be content. Had Collette become a problem that Andrew needed to throw more and more money at? Money he didn't have?

But Alison was in no mood for forgiveness. In all likelihood, if Andrew suspected anything at all - and how could he not? - her work would dry up. And if work dried up, why would he let her stay in the flat?

Why, for that matter, would she want to stay?

Cheeks taut with cold, she let herself into the building. Wiggling her key free from the brass fitting, the scent of citrus invaded her nostrils. She noticed that an expensive wreath had been hung on the front door: pine, dried oranges and tartan ribbons. Jenny was there in the hallway, a cup in one hand. She murmured a cursory, "Hello."

"How could you?" Alison demanded, finding that, exhausted as she was - thinking she'd wanted nothing more than a hot shower and a change of clothes - she had energy left for a fight.

"How could I *what?*" Open-mouthed, Jenny was a rabbit in the headlights.

"Don't play innocent with me! Well, you've got your way now. I just hope you can live with your conscience."

She barged past and already had one foot on the bottom stair when Jenny called warily: "Honestly, Alison. I have no idea what you're talking about."

Turning, she spat out angry words: "So, you didn't tip the police off?"

"The police -?"

"You've never thought I was a fit mother!"

Jenny squared up to her, indignant. "Actually, you couldn't be more wrong. In my experience, children never turn out the way they do by accident. I'm not terribly fond of children, but even I know it's the parents who are usually to blame. You, on the other hand - all the evidence suggests you're an excellent mother." She smoothed her skirt, as if she'd finished having her say.

Memory beckoned: the last act of *Swan Lake*. Dancing as part of the corps, one poor swan couldn't keep pace with the chaotic patterns of the final act. Twenty-three swans went in one direction; she, alone, went in another. Now Alison was that confused swan, blindly trying to find her way. Belle's runaway, praying she would be found.

The combative glint had disappeared from Jenny's eyes and she was all concern. "What's happened? Please tell me that Belinda's OK."

One hand covering her mouth Alison found she was gazing down at the tiled floor - the floor Belle so loved to slide up and down. If it hadn't been Jenny, then *who?* Her shoulders caving inwards, she gave way to the tears she'd been too shocked to shed at the police station. Jenny's voice came as if from a distance - "Come and sit down." Though the hand on her shoulder was real, the words, "Come on," were distorted and fuzzy.

She allowed herself to be led into the pine-scented library and seated in the leather armchair. *Row upon row of books.*

"I'll get you a coffee. I've just made a pot. Black?"

"No sugar," Alison responded, finding herself staring at the concentration of baubles towards the lower branches of the Christmas tree: Belle's uncorrected handiwork. The fairy lights blinked. Unable to settle, she stood, walked towards them but got only halfway. The antique globe stopped her. Spinning it on its axis, her gloved hand journeyed from the United Kingdom - such a small, strangely-shaped island - ignoring the vast continents that she had toured, through a distance of 10,571 miles. Australia, as Belle had pointed out, looked a bit like the head of 'one of those dogs'. Her father would want to take her there. In his position, God knows, she would. *My Bonnie lies over the ocean.* She spun the globe again, reflecting on the terrible distance. *My Bonnie lies over the sea.*

"Drink this," Jenny was saying, holding out a cup to her.

Alison's hands wrapped around its warmth and she sat. *My Bonnie lies over the ocean.* The coffee was good and strong. Its aroma combined with the comforting leather of the battered armchair and the tobacco from the old book-bindings, the beeswax polish and the pine needles. These things brought her back, grounded her, but her surroundings no longer felt safe.

"I was arrested," she admitted weakly.

If Jenny's astonishment, expressed as a single syllable of laughter, wasn't genuine, she was a very good actress. "Arrested? For *what*?"

"Tax evasion and money laundering."

Jenny took a step back and sank into the only other chair in the room. "It's serious, then?"

"My solicitor thinks the charges will stick." Removed from the interview room, repeated out loud, it seemed almost impossible.

"You know," the woman began tentatively, "I've never really understood what it is you do, or what your relationship with Andrew is."

"Apparently, I didn't either."

"So, it *is* connected with the business?" Jenny sighed and

nodded, as if with realisation.

There was little point in holding back. "I provide escort services for your clients. Not all of whom are what they seem, apparently."

Breath rushed from Jenny. She fingered a small gold cross hung from a delicate necklace at her throat. Something Alison hadn't noticed before.

"I'm sorry," she began, concerned. "I've shocked you."

"No, no. Well, yes, actually."

"I always thought you suspected."

"Give me a minute. Hot flush, I'm afraid." Jenny fanned herself with a pale green pamphlet that was possibly an antique. "I had no idea. And now I'm rather afraid this *may* have had something to do with me - but that was never my intention, believe me."

Alison sat forwards.

"The recent audit... it uncovered some irregularities. I answered the questions that were put to me, no more."

"What questions?"

"I thought it was fraud they were suggesting. Given that an employer doesn't normally steal from his own business, I imagined *I* was under suspicion. I told the auditor that I had no knowledge of the accounting entries, of course, but I didn't think he believed me."

This, at least, made sense. "Would he have gone to the police?"

"He'd have been under a legal obligation. There's a formal reporting procedure." Having acclimatised herself to the news, Jenny chewed her lower lip thoughtfully.

"Then I've just put you in a very difficult position." Alison also realised she had given away the very information she'd agreed to keep close to her chest.

"No, no. Actually, you've set my mind at rest. They don't appear to be looking in my direction for answers any more.

And I've been doing a little digging of my own. That's why you've seen me here at such odd hours."

Alison looked at Jenny anew. "When we got back from Richmond! That's what you were doing?"

"To be honest, I was sick with nerves, thinking you might have let the cat out of the bag."

Mention of cats and bags ignited a fresh flare of panic. "Jenny, you can't tell Andrew what I've just told you. I've had to agree to carry on as normal."

"Oh, you needn't worry. There's no love lost between the two of us, believe me."

"But I thought -"

"It's a job. There will be others. I'm just sorry they're using you to get to him."

"I - I don't know if I can face him again."

"*You* can't face him! But neither of us need worry. It won't be for long."

"Oh?"

"What I've told you so far is only half the story." Jenny's hair fell forwards and she frowned down at the contents of her cup. "My digging paid off. It's not only the auditor who's under an obligation to report his findings. Today, I'm going to do a very thorough whistle-blowing job." She lifted her chin and the corners of her mouth twitched. "On my boss."

"Oh, Jenny," Alison said.

"It's OK. But you see, if you're holding anything back out of some false sense of loyalty, there's no need. Andrew will never know where the information came from."

Kindness from the most unlikely quarters and where it was least deserved.

"Look at the pair of us!" Jenny removed one hand from her coffee cup and held it up for inspection. "I'm shaking like a leaf!"

And, whilst Alison was grateful, her mind was still racing. It was another pair it re-tuned to. The dual personality she had once adopted. Off-stage humility, on-stage audacity. What she needed to do for her survival - both hers and Belle's - was to resurrect Alicia Serafina. *Deafening applause erupted as she dropped a deep curtsey and waited for Jean-François to take her hand, so that she could look up and feign surprise as rosebuds fell about her feet.* Alicia would have to step into the limelight so that, when this bad dream was over, she could go back to being plain Alison Brabbage. A woman you'd happily pass on the street without a second glance. An ordinary mother, on her way to collect her daughter from school.

Jenny was looking around the library as if she had mislaid something. "You didn't say. Where *is* Belinda?"

Bring back my Bonnie to me. "On her way to school, I suspect. She stayed at Collette's last night."

"But -" Jenny shuffled in her chair but seemed disinclined to say more.

"The police asked me to concoct a story for Andrew. He seems to have fallen for it. So far." A shiver coursed down Alison's spine and her thoughts changed direction. "But you're absolutely right. I want to get Belle as far away from here as possible. I won't have her caught up in this."

"No. Of course not." Jenny nodded and pushed herself to standing. "How will you explain her absence to Andrew?"

"I don't have a plan myself yet. I wish I did. But if I don't make one pretty damned quickly, the decision will be taken out of my hands."

"You could say that she's going to stay with her father for Christmas."

The poor woman clearly thought that coming up with a believable excuse was the only issue. *The perfect Christmas she had been planning. Just the two of them.* "Yes," she said, gratefully. "That would make sense."

"I shall miss that little girl. Will you allow me to say goodbye?"

"Of course. Of course I will."

Jenny hesitated in the doorway and held onto the frame, almost as if to prevent herself from walking through it. She spoke without turning. "When you first came here, I was unforgivably rude. I thought Andrew had designs on you."

"So he said."

"You knew?" Jenny looked over her shoulder, her lips parting. "Why should I be surprised? Well that makes me feel like an even bigger fool!" She turned and walked back into the centre of the library. "I want you to know that I'm truly, truly sorry. I don't make friends easily. If the truth be known, I've always felt slightly intimidated by you."

"Me?" In other circumstances, Alison might have laughed.

"You're always so... poised."

"I never feel as if I belong anywhere!" She hesitated. "Would you do something for me, Jenny?"

"Of course."

What she had to say pained her and she chose her words with care. "Things are going to get very messy. You should distance yourself from here. From me, that is."

"I was about to ask if you needed somewhere to stay!"

She shook her head. "I couldn't do that to you. And anyway, I'm allergic to cats."

"Oh, gosh," said Jenny, her cheeks reddening. "I feel awful telling you this."

"What?"

"There are no cats."

"No cats?" Alison was stunned. This was the one fact she knew about Jenny's private life.

"Certain... assumptions are made when you're single and living on your own. I invented them as an excuse so that I didn't have to work late without good notice. Before I knew it, they became a bit of a talking point." Jenny looked sheepish. "I've even used vet's appointments as excuses to leave early occasionally!"

Alison did something she would have thought impossible a quarter of an hour earlier. She laughed. "You're wrong about not making friends. Belle loves you - and she's always been a very good judge of character."

"You're very kind to say so."

"No, I'm not. It's the truth. I should have paid more attention. I'm going to lose her, you know."

"In the short term, maybe."

"When she finds out what I've done, she won't want to know -"

Both women turned at the sound of the front door being opened. Alison swallowed and lifted her chin to the cold draft. Jenny's face reddened and she said, "Into the breach," before walking out into the hall. "Good morning," she added quickly, her head low.

"You're bright and early!" The man who had duped Alison was framed in the library doorway. She regarded Andrew with contempt as Jenny replied.

"I was awake. I thought I'd clear a few emails before the phone starts ringing."

He turned; saw Alison sitting in the armchair. "You're back! And how's your mother?"

"She's felt better." Alison prayed that her expression wasn't transparent; that tiredness would be interpreted as the reason for her remote manner. "I spent all night at the hospital. Belle wasn't too much trouble, I hope?"

"No trouble at all. She was a bit worried that she wouldn't have her fancy dress costume for the last day of term, so Collette found her some reindeer antlers."

"That was sweet of her. I must ring and say thank you."

"If you two don't mind, I'll crack on," Jenny said, bypassing Andrew as she leapt at the opportunity for escape.

"Thanks for the coffee," Alison called after her.

"You look as if you could do with something stronger," he said, and she hated him for his display of concern.

"Yes." It was time to take stock. "Now that you mention it, I'm absolutely shattered."

Andrew hesitated, waiting, Alison presumed, for Jenny to settle at her desk, then he softly closed the door. Trapped, a bright spark of panic flared in Alison's stomach.

"So, what happened exactly? I thought you'd stopped seeing your old clients."

The time had come to play a part. She shook her head and exhaled. "It was stupid really."

"What was?" He had unbuttoned his heavy coat and Alison could see that, underneath his striped scarf, he was wearing the yellow tie.

His eyes fixed on her, she looked at him directly. "I feel such an idiot." That at least was true. "I went to see if I could track down an old friend - Cat. I wanted to make sure she had somewhere to go over Christmas. I was talking to a group of prostitutes, asking if they'd seen her, when a police van pulled up." Watching for his reaction, Alison saw relief. "We were arrested. All of us."

"For soliciting?" Making a pantomime of looking astonished, Andrew put his laptop bag down on the seat of the chair that Jenny had been sitting on. He perched on its arm.

"Loitering, soliciting, whatever you want to call it. Apparently it was part of a pre-Christmas round-up. I tried to tell them why I was there but, believe it or not, *I* was the only one with a previous caution."

"Then it was nothing to do with any of my clients?"

She pretended to be taken aback. "Your clients? Unless there's something you're not telling me, there's nothing illegal about your business. But you should probably know that I now have an anti-social behaviour order to add to my CV. That nice safe desk job is looking less and less likely."

"So they won't be taking any further action?" Using a bookshelf for support, Andrew pushed himself to standing.

"It was a wrist-slapping exercise, no more. *Next* time, the police tell me, they won't be so lenient."

"Then we'll have to make sure there's not a next time." He picked up his bag.

"I won't make that mistake again, believe me! And now, to top it all, Belle's father - who's never taken the slightest interest in her - has decided he wants her to stay with him for Christmas." No acting, Alison's tears were real. The herringbone pattern of the parquet flooring blurred.

"Oh. Oh, I'm sorry. You could always say no."

"I could. But it's not for me to decide."

"You think she'll want to go."

It wasn't a question.

CHAPTER TWENTY-SIX

With no time to choose her words or worry what anyone thought of her, Alison tore around the flat doing what had to be done. She started with a call to Belle's school to reassure herself that her daughter had arrived safely.

"Would you like to speak to her?" the school secretary asked.

"No. No, there's no need to drag her out of class."

"And will it be you picking her up tonight?"

"Yes, I'll be there."

"I'll let her know."

She dialled again, asking, "Did I wake you?" when Collette answered sounding slightly dazed.

"What's the time? I must have nodded off while I was giving Ben his feed."

"I just called to say thank you. Especially for the reindeer antlers." Alison made sure her own voice sounded upbeat. "I hope Belle wasn't too much trouble."

"One more child really doesn't make very much difference. And, unlike the boys, at least yours doesn't answer back. Besides, Andrew took the morning shift. He did the breakfasts and dropped her off at school."

Collette didn't ask whether everything was OK, so there

was no need to resort to a white lie. Neither did she give any hint, not even in her tone of voice, as to what she knew.

"Well, I won't keep you," Alison said. "If I don't see you, have a very happy Christmas."

After making two further telephone calls, she rummaged through the sideboard to find a pad of airmail paper. The perforated edges of several discarded drafts were still evident. If anyone looked closely enough, they would be able to see the indentation of his first name. Her address and the date written, Alison's pen stalled on the flimsy blue sheet. *Come on, come on!* Her head throbbed. Describing how she had bought the pad seven years previously with the same intention - albeit that her circumstances were now altered - was as good a place to start as any. It also had the advantage of being true.

The words were down on paper. They were not perfect, but nothing would undo this damage. Turning on her laptop, Alison clicked through recent photographs of her and Belle - those taken after the Nativity play. She printed them out on her small colour Epson (setting aside extra copies for Jenny) and trimmed them carefully. She pitied Belle's father as she tore the sheets from the pad and read through what she'd written, imagining how she would react if she were on the receiving end. Denial wasn't a twenty-first century option, but he had every right to be angry. Alison was presenting him with a fully-formed child. He had been *denied*. Folding the photographs inside the letter, she wondered if he would see any similarity between his sons and Belle.

The envelope sealed, Alison retrieved her portfolio and the scrapbook of newspaper and magazine clippings she had been compiling from their hiding places. Positioning them on the coffee table in the living room, she stared at their closed covers for what seemed like an age. She'd kept the scrapbook a secret so long that she'd come to think of it as hers. Another of her father's old sayings that forced her back to practicalities.

"K.B.O.," she told herself. Her father's favourite expression. As it turned out, it wasn't Latin. *Keep buggering on* was what it stood for. She had found it in a book of Churchill's quotes while browsing in Waterstones. "Latin!" she had exclaimed out loud. And then she'd laughed, wondering if her mother, who didn't allow swearing (at least, not in front of her, not in the house) had also fallen for his explanation.

There was nothing private now. No need to be precious about things. Kneeling, Alison retrieved a cardboard box from the back of her wardrobe. Ballet shoes: relics from another life. She placed the box carefully on top of the books.

What else could she offer Belle? she asked herself as she wandered from room to room. What other proof did she have of her love?

Next, she stood on her bed to retrieve the large suitcase from the top of her wardrobe, and packed her daughter's things, not forgetting the discarded toys Belle had clung to as a younger child. The very things someone who went to boarding school understood that a child removed from home would need to surround herself with. Every so often Alison hesitated to ask herself why she had wasted so many opportunities. Why had she always said, "What are you?" when what she'd meant was, "I love you"? *"I love you, I love you, I love you: you wonderful, impossible child."* She caught herself sniffing. Teddy. The pig-shaped torch she had bought Belle so that she could zap the monsters in the shadows. Hugging Mr Cat to her chest, rocking it as she'd once rocked Belle, a haunting snatch of that old sea shanty Alison's father used to sing came to her again. *My Bonnie lies over the ocean, my Bonnie lies over the sea.* At his best when performing, his voice was the voice of a Welsh coalminer, deep, rich and pure. Perhaps he would sing for Belle, as her mother accompanied him on the piano. Imagining the alternative was almost unbearable. A separation of 10,571 miles.

This won't do, Alison. *Keep buggering on.*

Eventually, as emotionally and physically exhausted as she would have been at the end of a performance of *Giselle*, Alison fell into bed. She assumed a foetal position, hoping that sleep would claim her for a few hours, removing the need for her to think.

Waking on an intake of breath, the buzzer stifled Tchaikovsky's soothing score, the soundtrack to her dream. It was the entrance to the building. The sound had never grated on Alison's nerves before. Now that her arrest was an unchangeable fact, it turned her stomach to oil and dragged her from her bed. As the curve of her left hand smoothed the contours of her aching head, her parents' final harsh words came back to Alison.

"You don't own me!"

"Perhaps we don't owe you either."

"And what's that supposed to mean?"

At the White Lodge, students had been lectured that the difference between an average ballerina and a great ballerina wasn't talent or dedication, but the ability to harness adrenalin; a blank refusal to let it get the better of them. "This is no time for stage fright," Alison told her dishevelled reflection, revealed in the dressing-table mirror. Nor was it time for recriminations. Ironically, it was only since she'd had her hair layered expensively (at Collette's suggestion) that it failed to fall back into shape. Her eyes were tight. She felt nauseous. Not a single detail was how she'd planned this meeting one hundred times over in her mind. She was to have held the moral high ground. On any other day, Alison might have at least dragged a brush through her hair, but today was what it was. Perhaps a less than perfect appearance might draw a little sympathy.

She felt her way down the internal staircase (the small

stairs, as Belle insisted on calling them), one hand sliding down the smooth oak of the banister. Lifting the receiver, she spoke flatly into the intercom: "Come up. I'm on the first floor."

Alison traced her teeth with her tongue. Her mouth was dry. For a moment, she leaned the back of her head against the wall and found herself looking up at the coving of one of those desirable high ceilings. The ornate design incorporating grapes and feathers had drawn her gaze after the cramped conditions of Worlds End. Now it was nothing more than sand and cement.

At the sound of a light tapping she hauled her body towards the door and opened it.

"Mum," Alison said. After eight years of doing without a mother, with that one word, she was someone's daughter again. And yet they kept their distance. There was no 'hello'. No melting of expressions. Not even an awkward hug. A moment's pained stocktaking passed between them. A reappraisal. Feeling self-conscious, the daughter tucked stray hair behind her ears. Time had changed them both, but the most striking difference was that her mother usually came as one of a pair. That united parental front. Alison looked past her, out into the hallway. "You're on your own?" Perhaps her father had refused to come. That would make sense. In which case...

"I am on my own these days, yes. Your father and I are divorced."

Alison blinked. It was as if the foundations had been ripped out from under her. *Wasn't this something she should have been told?* If their splitting up wasn't reason enough for her parents to make contact - one of them at least - then what would it have taken? "When?" she heard herself asking stupidly.

"Oh, some time ago." Her mother was so matter of fact. As if the life-altering news she'd just sprung on her was barely worth expanding upon. "We couldn't agree on the crucial issues. In fact, we could hardly agree on anything at all."

"Do you still see each other?" Even dressed in jeans, Alison's mother looked as smart as ever, but she was smaller, somehow. Greyer. Neither the ferocious creature of her final memory nor Belle's elderly Grammy with the gammy leg.

"He hasn't moved far. Sometimes it's unavoidable."

There would be no *My Bonnie lies over the Ocean*. Mother and daughter stood looking at each other. Alison was unsure how to interpret what she found in her opposite's expression. She had anticipated criticism. Biting sarcasm, if the truth be known. Now, she felt entitled to explanations. None were to be volunteered, that much was apparent.

"Are you going to leave me standing out here in the hall or are you going to invite me in?" Her mother held the strap of her handbag in both hands. Two options: no choice.

"Of course," Alison said, stepping backwards, infuriated at herself for failing to ask the questions she wanted answers to. Necessity to conceal her emotions sometimes made her slow with words. Perhaps it was as well, she reflected. You cannot ask the greatest favour you have ever asked of anybody - from somebody who has made it blatantly clear that she thought her part in your life was over - and then hurl insults at her.

"I see you've packed." Her mother nodded at the upright hard-shelled suitcase standing in the hall. "It seems rather a lot. For a young girl. "

It was almost as tall as her daughter, Alison observed. "I'm not sure how long I'll be gone."

"You'll have to take it downstairs. I won't be able to manage."

"What about at your house?"

"I'm sure the cab driver will help if I ask him. Anything for a tip." Her mother looked around. Neither the fine grain of the walnut console, nor the modern art drew her comment.

She seemed to be waiting for direction.

"The living room's on the left. Why don't you take a seat and I'll put the kettle on - assuming you still take your tea how you used to?" It was as much of a dig as Alison would allow herself.

"I have my own sweeteners." She tightened her grip on her handbag. "No one seems to buy the ones I like."

When Alison returned carrying mugs, she experienced a ripple of irritation. The lid had been removed from the box containing her ballet shoes (those sacred relics), a satin ribbon set adrift. The scrapbook lay open in her mother's lap, the final cutting she hadn't yet fixed in place laid out on the table.

"For Belinda?" Mrs Brabbage asked, looking up.

Little point in protest. Soon all that anybody would need to do to pore over the intricate details of Alison's life was to open a newspaper. "She hasn't seen a picture of her father before." Her hand went to the place where her throat was tight. "It never seemed to be the right moment."

"No." With two efficient clicks, sweeteners were dispensed into the tea. "This is him?"

"Yes." Alison perched on the arm of the sofa, her eighty-year-old feet crossed at her twenty-eight-year-old ankles. A position she would never normally take, the scene - the tea, a mother and daughter, a scrapbook of clippings - might have appeared intimate to a stranger. To Alison, it felt slightly rebellious to peer over her mother's shoulder at the picture of a man who was both familiar and unfamiliar. All, save Belle, that linked her to another lifetime.

Her mother leaned closer to the page, the fingers of one hand holding the arm of her reading glasses. "I know him."

"Do you?" she asked and sipped her black coffee. One blessing stemmed from her mother's close-to-her-chest approach. Alison felt no obligation to divulge more than she was comfortable with. Her mother could have asked at any time, but had failed to do so. Besides, she was more than capable of reading the captions that accompanied the photographs for herself.

Her mother's hand - still wearing her engagement ring ("That? I chose it myself."), but minus her wedding band - turned the page. At the sight of the family group in front of the clean Sydney skyline, she stated the obvious: "He has other children."

"He does now." Alison noticed how her mother positioned her hands, obscuring the swimwear model wife and the blond-haired boys. But it was this ability to detach herself that Alison was relying on. "I've written to him."

"To tell him the latest?"

"To tell him that he has a daughter."

"He doesn't *know*?"

Holding her breath, Alison waited for the onslaught, knowing how she would respond. This conversation had taken place in her mind many times over. Instead, her mother's face paled. Had she assumed support had come from other quarters? But a mother shouldn't have made assumptions. She should have checked.

Angling her head away, clearing her throat, the older woman swiftly changed the subject. "She must be almost eight."

Couldn't she even find it in herself to use Belle's name? "Yes, it won't be long." Alison's focus shifted to the birthday celebrations she would miss. That banana split she had planned to buy Belle at Fortnum & Mason. "New Year's Day."

"Even younger than you were when I had to give you up."

She hadn't expected her mother to draw a parallel between their situations. "Was that how it felt?" Alison faltered. "That you were giving me up?"

Bowing her head, her mother said nothing for a few

moments. "You were gifted. We were told that you could accomplish great things - *if* we let go."

"They said that to you?" It was only possible to ask the question because they weren't looking each other in the eye. Both were facing outwards into the room, her mother on the seat of the sofa, she, perched on the arm.

"Did they ask me if I would be willing to give up my influence over you, hand you over to strangers? No, of course they didn't." Her mother extended a hand and straightened the satin ribbon attached to the ballet shoe. "Did they make me feel as if it would have been the ultimate selfishness had I not allowed you to take up your place at the White Lodge? Ah!"

Did her mother feel it was because Alison had spent her teenage years beyond the scope of her influence that she'd ended up where she was today? A single mum. Surroundings so lavish that they couldn't be commented on. Earning her living in an unmentionable way. And, if so, who did she blame? The school? The unthinking ten-year-old who, asked if she wanted to board, had answered "Yes!" without the slightest hesitation? Or herself, for allowing it to happen in the first place?

"If that was how you felt, why did you let me audition?" Alison felt her brow crease as the answer to the question arrived. "You thought I'd *fail!*"

"No. Not for one moment. The odds were stacked against you, but - don't ask me why - I was certain you would pass." For a moment, a hint of pride was detectable. "Even driving through Richmond Park on the way to the audition, I knew. But you're right. There seemed to be a sense of inevitability about it. It would have been very harsh to let you find out how good you actually were and then put my foot down."

Alison wanted to say that at least there'd been a choice. If only to act selflessly or selfishly. Making the right choice for her daughter was exactly what she now had to do. Removing

Belle from a damaging situation - of her own making - before someone else decided her daughter should be removed. The knowledge that she'd be better off elsewhere was agony. Alison had failed. At least Belle would get to know family. Some of her many questions about where she had come from would be answered. It was just that Alison had hoped for a small sign that her mother had mellowed.

"It was your father. He thought the discipline would be good for you."

In Alison's memory, her mother had been the disciplinarian of the household. But since her mother's tone was accusatory, and the news of her parents' separation was still raw, she bit her tongue.

"Anyway." Seeming to recover her emotions, the older woman turned and gave a stiff smile. Her first. "Shall I come to collect Belinda from school with you?"

Belle had always needed advance warning about what was going to happen. She only came round after every objection had been thoroughly explored and set aside. Today, there wouldn't be time. Alison would hear her own words in the objections Belle raised. Echoes of things she'd been telling her daughter her whole life, the thoughts she had planted in her mind. And she would have to contradict herself; to say she'd been mean to say those nasty things about her own mother.

"I'd prefer to speak to Belle on my own, if you don't mind."

"Whatever you think's best. But I do think you should shower and get changed before you go."

Despite herself, Alison smiled. There was comfort in being criticised for her slovenly appearance, in being told what to do. "I suppose I'd better get a move on." She bent down and placed a folded-over envelope secured with an elastic band on the coffee table. The rectangular bulk left little to the imagination. "That's virtually all the money I have."

Her mother's back visibly tensed.

"My bank account will be frozen. I don't know when I'll be able to let you have more. Please, Mum." She picked it up and held the package out. Instead of risking embarrassing her, Alison made use of her bartering techniques: "If you don't want it, the taxman will be more than happy to take it."

Her mother's chest rose and fell, then her hands closed around the package. Their eyes met, if only briefly. A flicker of doubt. Wariness. And was that *fear?* But she spoke with absolute certainty: "I think you should pack the scrapbook and these other bits and pieces. Belinda will have quite enough to cope with for one day."

CHAPTER TWENTY-SEVEN

Intoxicated at the sight of Belle hurtling towards her, reindeer antlers close to toppling, backpack bouncing on the off-beat, shouting "Mummy, Mummy, Mummy!" Alison inhaled deeply. She wished she could capture it all in slow motion.

Despite her daughter having grown in stature and confidence, Alison treasured the moments when the excitable little girl revealed herself, and the memory of this particular moment would need to be rationed out over a long time. Barely daring to blink for fear she might miss some miraculous detail of hair or cheek, of fallen leaf or flinty scent, Alison bent her knees and held out her arms. It was impossible to say, "I'm sorry I wasn't there to pick you up from school last night," when she wouldn't be there on so many future occasions. Resisting the urge to hug Belle to her chest for fear of crushing her, she said, "Hello, Rudolph. I don't suppose you've seen Belle?" Then, on impulse, Alison scooped her daughter up and, with Belle's legs hooked around her waist, swung her round, pretending to stagger. Belle shrieked and leant backwards. *So trusting.*

"I thought you'd been kidnapped!" she announced once she had whipped her head upwards, antlers askew. Her eyes shone bright and clear in the dusk.

"Kidnapped?" Alison deposited her daughter on the tarmac of the playground and knelt down to her level, straightening the Alice band that the padded brown felt was attached to. "I'm a little too old for that. Who'd want to kidnap me?"

Foot traffic passed them by on the way to the school gate: a scurry of Clarks shoes - T-bars and lace-ups - and the wheels of buggies. Shadowy children yelling goodbyes and Happy Christmases to classmates were instructed to keep up; to stop and wait when they reached the road.

"By the Russian ballet, of course!"

She would miss this; these conversations of theirs; trying to decipher sense from Belle's trains of thought, logical or otherwise. "What makes you say that?"

"Aunty Collette wouldn't tell me anything. It would have been rotten luck just before Christmas, but it was the only thing that made sense."

Alison swallowed painfully. "Tell me how it made sense."

"I only realised when we went to visit your old school. Everybody wanted you to dance but all you wanted to do was be my mummy."

Such simple confidence that Alison thought her heart would break. "That part is true. And always will be. Whatever you hear anyone say about me, all I ever wanted to be was your mummy."

"We girls stick together!"

Perhaps, Alison pondered, it had been cruel to make an appearance only to disappear again. She shivered. "Let's walk. You'll catch cold."

"Through Pelican Park?"

"If it's not too dark for you."

"Not with all the fairy lights, it won't be."

"Then, through Pelican Park it is."

Belle grabbed her smooth leather-gloved hand in her

mittened hand and giggled. "You know, I was almost going to ask you how Grammy is. I forgot she's only pretend." She tapped her own forehead with the palm of her free hand. "That's silly, isn't it?"

"No. It's not so silly at all -" About to say more, Alison found she was cut short.

"Hello, Mr Churchill," Belle addressed the stern-looking bronze statue with a walking stick in one hand and the other dug deep into the pocket of his greatcoat. Someone had given him a red tinsel scarf. Belle had become on good terms with Mr Churchill during their time at St James's. "It's a lovely evening for a walk."

"Belle," Alison began tentatively. "There's someone waiting at home to meet you."

"You're supposed to say *blood sweat and tears* when we get here," Belle protested using 'the voice', and tugging on her arm in encouragement.

But it wasn't blood and sweat that came to mind. Alison found herself unable to continue. They came to a halt in front of the zebra crossing. On the other side of the road lay the park. *Fancy cutting down those beautiful trees to make pulp for bloody newspapers.* That was one of Churchill's. The smaller trees were strung with fairy lights, a sight so magical, Alison wished she didn't have to do what had to be done. *K.B.O.*

"Who wants to meet me, Mummy?" Belle asked, eyes filled with trust as they looked up at her.

CHAPTER TWENTY-EIGHT

It was like walking into the doctor's surgery, knowing that you were there to have an injection. The first time, everybody said that it wasn't going to be so bad, but then it was. The second time, you had to go, even though you knew it was going to hurt.

In the downstairs hallway, even Aunty Jenny had looked nervous. She had pretended that she was watering the plants, but half of them were plastic. She seemed to be standing about with nothing very much to do. The trouble she had choosing ordinary words like 'hello' and 'goodbye' added to Belinda's sense that the things that weren't being said would tip the seesaw when balanced against what had.

Now Belinda stared at the suitcase that stood in the hallway and dropped her mother's hand. It was true, then. Despite what had been said about boarding school, despite the fact that she'd done nothing wrong, she was being sent away. "For a while." Fear pinched her insides. Lack of facts was the scariest thing of all. *A while* could mean many things, but this wasn't the suitcase they had used for their weekend away. This one was older and larger. Belinda had wanted to make a tremendous fuss. She had wanted to kick and scream but, seeing real tears glistening in her mother's eyes, she had promised to be brave. As brave as ten barrels full of bears. She swallowed. "Am I going to meet her now?"

"Yes. There's no need to be scared."

But it was difficult not to be scared when the hands steering her towards the living room door were trembling. It was difficult not to be scared when Belinda knew that once those trembling hands were removed, they wouldn't be replaced. Belinda's nose was running with the effort of being brave and her head hurt from all of the crying she had done. She approached the doorway, feeling dwarfed by its Wonderland-like proportions. One cautious baby-step after another hoping that, the slower she went, the greater the chance of some miracle.

It was a shame she didn't believe in God. Belinda had persevered for a week or so. Thinking she might sacrifice one of her precious notebooks to him, she was going to tear it up, but that would have been a waste. So she closed her eyes, threw it into the air and said, "Here you are, God!" She counted to one hundred before opening her eyes. The notebook was there, lying open on the bed. God hadn't taken it! And, secretly, Belinda had been rather pleased because it had lots of good words written in it. Of course, as a science experiment, it was open-ended. It was possible God existed and had rewarded her because she'd shown willing. If he did, he might come in rather useful right now. They were only a step away from the living room and there was nothing Belinda could think of doing to put off the moment everything would change.

"Ah!" The woman who was sitting on the sofa swivelled in her seat, turning to look. But that was all she appeared to be capable of saying. Her mouth became a cave and she seemed to be looking over the top of Belinda's head, waiting for Mummy to tell her she was allowed to speak.

"Go on," her mother coaxed, and, not sure who this instruction was aimed at, Belinda took two pigeon-steps forwards. "I'll make you both a nice drink."

It had been decided that, once Mummy had brought the drinks and the biscuits, she would walk out of the room, along the hallway, and down the big staircase. They had already said goodbye in private on a bench in Pelican Park, with Belinda sitting in her mother's lap, as it would be easier that way. Belinda twisted her head round and caught sight of Mummy's back.

"I won't bite," the old woman said in a wobbly voice. Although she had heard that one before, there was nothing for it: Belinda inched a little closer, keeping to the side of the leather sofa, thinking herself shielded by the armrest. But the woman reached for her face, hands as cold as frostbite - as if she'd been walking in the park with no gloves on.

Alison gripped the kitchen worktop, closed her eyes and bit her upper lip. Fighting to breathe normally, she recalled how she had plotted revenge on the mother who had played a cruel joke on her; sending her into a darkened room, instructing her to step, closer, closer. The cold sandpapery hands that came at her from out of the darkness, fingers like bones searching out and then settling, cupping the contours of her face, while she stood, feeling suffocated.

And the old woman's voice when it came at last, bewildered and afraid: "And *who* are you?"

"Alison," she had said, knowing exactly who she was and all that it meant.

"But I don't know an Alison."

It had been her first experience of doubt. Doubt in her mother; doubt in herself.

How could she go through with it? How could she just walk away? But it would be crueller still not to stick to the plan. Had her mother felt like this? As if her heart was being wrenched from her chest.

K.B.O.

With no choice, Alison arranged the tea-tray. Chastised herself that she had forgotten to buy more of Belle's favourite biscuits before they ran out. Now, even this small detail would be wrong.

"You look as if you could do with a tissue." The woman removed her hands from Belinda's face so that she could reach inside her small beige handbag, but the cold remained on the girl's cheeks. "Do you know who I am?"

"You're Mummy's Mummy." She wiped the end of her nose with the tissue she was given and tried to connect the woman on the sofa with the hints of dreadfulness she had been fed over the years. Despite what Mummy had said, Belinda knew she wasn't a mean person. She didn't say things unless there was some truth in them.

"That's right. And you're Belinda. Why don't you have a good old blow?"

Belinda blew but didn't feel any better.

"Do you know, you look very like your mummy did when she was your age."

"Do I?" Belinda's eyes widened, because, even though her mother didn't like her appearance being commented on (being kind or clever was much more important), she was very pretty (the prettiest person she knew), and Belinda wanted to be pretty when she grew up.

"Very like her. For a moment, when you walked in, I thought I was looking at my little Alison."

And although the situation was strange, the woman didn't seem particularly scary, so Belinda sat down next to her on the sofa and shuffled her bum backwards. "You look like Mummy when she's older," she ventured, and it was true: the woman did.

"I expect I probably do."

"So I might look like you when I'm old."

"It doesn't always work like that but, yes, it's possible."

"I've never seen any photograph of Mummy when she was a little girl." The woman's hands were more lined than her face was. She had ironed hard lines into the fronts of her jeans. They stuck up even when she was sitting down.

"Oh, I can help you out there. I have lots of photograph albums."

"Will I be allowed to look at them?"

"I should think so. Would you like that? Ah!"

Mummy came into the room with the drinks and Belinda's second-favourite biscuits on a tray. Belinda pretended that the old woman sitting next to her who had lots of photograph albums was fascinating. So fascinating in fact that she didn't look at Mummy, even though it might be her last chance. 'For a while'.

"Tell me, Belinda, what sort of things do you like doing?"

Belinda decided to keep talking. Saying things that were true, even though her lips were wobbling. "I like new words." The words wobbled too. "Words that fit. I write them all down. And I like to read. I'm good at reading. I can read to you if you want."

"That would be nice. Are you any good at crossword puzzles?"

"I don't know. I might be." She heard the door of the flat click shut. Her mother would be taking her things down to the hall. Mummy's Mummy seemed to have run out of words, so Belinda tried asking questions so that she didn't think about hurtling after her mother and burying her face in her nice soft coat. "Do you have a library where you live that we can go to?"

"Just around the corner."

"Will my library card work there?" Her mouth felt as if it was the wrong shape.

"I don't know, but if it doesn't, we can get you another one."

The woman took something out of her handbag and held it over her cup of tea. It made a clicking noise in her hand and something small and white fell into the drink.

"Is that your medicine?" Belinda asked, and then clunked herself on the forehead. "Oh no, I forgot. You're not really ill. We sometimes pretend."

The woman looked astonished. "You pretend I'm ill?"

Her mother would probably be sitting in the private garden in St James's Square by now. Even though Belinda wouldn't see her, because it was properly dark, Mummy would be watching out for them as they left. She would always be watching out for her.

"Don't sit out there on the bench for too long. Your bum will get cold," Belinda had told her.

"I won't. But don't say 'bum' to Grandma, will you?"

"What should I say?"

"Say 'bottom'. Or 'derriere'. Actually, forget that. Say 'bum'. Be yourself. Always be yourself."

Keep talking: "I've made you several Get Well Soon cards. In fact, I made you one today at school, if you'd like to see it." Belinda shrugged her Hello Kitty backpack off her shoulders and unzipped it. "Oh," she said, pulling it from the front pocket. The woman took it. "It's got a bit creased. I don't think it will stand up."

"Gammy?" the woman asked, reading the words.

Belinda angled her head so that she could look at what she had written. "I must have forgotten the 'r.' I used to call you Grammy when I couldn't say Granny. It kind of stuck. Like a nickname."

"I don't think anyone has ever given me a nickname before." Mummy's Mummy stared at the card for a long time and in such a way that Belinda thought she didn't like it. The drawing or the nickname. "You don't have to have it. I just thought -" That was when Belinda saw that the woman's shoulders were shaking. Looking closer, it was obvious *she was crying*.

"No, I'd like to keep it. And it's fine if you'd like to call me Grammy."

"Is it OK to stop pretending now?" Belinda asked, exhausted by the effort.

"Yes, it's high time we all stopped."

Without thinking, she lolled sideways against her grandmother. "Am I too old for a cuddle?"

"Never! At least I hope not."

Belinda's grandmother put her arm around her and it was a bit stiff and awkward but it was OK for a first go. "What are you?" asked her new grandmother, although she was still crying a bit herself, and Belinda had to stop herself from saying, "I'm not perfect, but I'll do," before the words almost came automatically. "How did you know?" she asked, wide-eyed.

"How did I know what?"

"How did you know that's what you say?" Unlike her hands, the rest of Grammy was nice and warm, especially the space underneath her arm.

"I know a thing or two. It's what my mother used to say to me, and I said it to my little Alison, and now, I suppose, she must say it to you."

Belinda didn't suppose Grammy could do rabbit noses, because that would be asking a bit too much. "Do you know how to make apple crumble?"

"I make a mean apple crumble, even if I do say it myself."

Hugged tighter, Belinda thought about this.

"I hate olives."

"So do I." Feeling her grandmother shudder, she decided she was telling the truth.

Alison had sat still for so long, she didn't realise how cold she was until she tried to stand and circle the private garden. A sensation almost like burning started at the top of her spine and spread down and outwards. A wall of darkness separated her from the Georgian terrace. Fingers and toes numbed, she moved like an elderly person, shoulders hunched and jaw clenched.

Belinda decided to test her new grandmother. "Mummy's bum will be getting cold by now."

"And having a numb bum isn't very nice."

A laugh tried to worm its way out of Belinda's throat, but she swallowed it. She wasn't ready for laughter. Not nearly. "We should probably go."

"We probably should. I'll call for the cab. Why don't you make sure you have everything you need?"

"Mummy said she packed for me. She's good at packing."

"Yes. She always was."

After they were sure the cab was on its way, they were both still a bit sniffy but they sat up straight and tried to be brave, although it was a little like pretending.

The flat felt strange without her mother in it. "We should probably wait downstairs," Belinda suggested.

"Yes, I think that's a good idea."

From the top of the big stairs, Belinda could see her suitcase standing by the front door. She took Grammy's hand to help her down, because the stairs were a bit tricky the first few times you did them. "Do you have a chimney?" she asked, catching sight of the beautiful tree she had helped decorate in the library's window. "Because it's Christmas Eve tomorrow."

"I believe it is. And, yes, I do."

"Do you think Father Christmas will know where to find me?"

"I should think so, don't you?"

"You know, some of the older children at school say he's not real." Belinda trod on the tile she had done her record-breaking *Geronimo!* slide to. Too bad, she thought: she'd hoped to better it. Now it would be her final record and there wasn't even a marker.

"Do they, now?"

She shrugged as if she wasn't that worried about it. "Not all of them. But some of them." Hesitating in the library doorway, her eyes skirted the lowest shelf and located the tatty green and white spine of Uncle Andrew's poetry book.

"And what do you think?"

"I thought he was." Having something on long-term loan probably didn't mean that you were allowed to take it with you if you moved house. "But now I'm not so sure."

If there was no Father Christmas, it didn't really matter whether you were good or not. No one was watching. "I'm just going to get something," she said.

"Quickly, then. I think that's our cab pulling up outside. I'll just need to ask the driver to fetch your case."

"I'll be very quick."

The man was holding the car door open for her.

She swallowed: there was no child seat in the back of the cab.

The poetry book stowed inside her backpack, she clambered inside.

PRIMA BALLERINA'S FALL FROM GRACE

A £1,000-a-night high-class escort who was jailed after making £300,000 without paying a penny in tax must pay back £174,243 or serve a further two and a half years in jail.

Alison Brabbage, 29, turned to prostitution to support herself and her young daughter after she was unable to find suitable employment offering flexible working hours, Southwark Crown Court heard.

But Alison Brabbage was no ordinary escort. The name by which the defendant is better known is Alicia Serafina, a prima ballerina who trained at the same prestigious school as Darcey Bussell. She enjoyed a rapid rise that brought her short-lived fame and then 'disappeared from sight'. Shockwaves have erupted in the close-knit ballet community, who claim to be devastated that one of their own should have had to resort to sex work.

Former dance partner, Jean-François Lambert, says that he saw Brabbage only recently when she brought her daughter to visit the White Lodge in Richmond Park, where he now teaches. Of Brabbage, he claimed, 'On the stage, she was absolutely peerless. But ballet is a cruel profession. It requires 24-hour a day commitment. For a ballerina who becomes a mother, options would have been very limited. Alison chose her own path. She chose motherhood and I respect that. But it destroys me to learn how she had to support herself. No one so beautiful, so talented, should have to sell herself,' he said. 'We should all feel ashamed.'

A spokesperson for the English Collective of Prostitutes argues that surprise is not an appropriate response. 'People must rid themselves of stereotypes, that sex workers are either poor victims or happy hookers. We are women like other women. Women looking to put food on the table for their families. Women looking to just get by.'

But in the case of Alison Brabbage, she did not 'just get by.' She entered into a lucrative arrangement with financial advisor, Andrew Simons, 45, who himself stands charged with seven counts of money laundering and of making financial gain through prostitution. This arrangement included the loan of a luxury apartment above Simons's office in London's exclusive St James's Square. Brabbage soon gained access to Simons's wealthy client-base, several of whom had direct connections with criminal and terrorist activities.

Asked if she knew about the identity of her clients, Brabbage protested: 'What escort asks questions about her clients' identities? As far as I was concerned, the fact that many of them were guests of so many high-profile businessmen and women - names that most people would recognise - validated their legitimacy.' When challenged further Brabbage contested, 'You've told me that some of my clients were terrorists. If that's the case I very much doubt they used their real names.' Whilst that may be true, the content of Brabbage's little black book has already led to several arrests.

Despite denying she was in Simons's employ, Brabbage admitted to receiving occasional payments from Mr Simons through an account set up in the name of a fake company, Lifestyle Support Ltd.

'I have never been in the habit of turning down money when it is offered. Gifts and bonuses are the norm in both of the professions I have worked in,' she explained in court. 'I wasn't privy to Mr Simons's accounting arrangements. I understood that he operated a franchise and I assumed that the cheques were written on behalf of the organisation that owned it.'

'And did you not think it strange that a financial institution would be paying you a bonus for your services?' prosecutor Robert Hunter asked.

'In my experience,' Brabbage replied, 'many companies budget for entertaining clients. When I received cash payments, as I almost always did, I made no enquiries whether that cash came from a company or from a private individual.'

Brabbage was so successful that she was able to save £110,000, money she intended to use as a deposit on a family home. 'That is money I have already paid tax on. There was no money left over to save during the period that I am accused of tax evasion.' By the time that she was receiving what most people would consider to be high-level earnings, Brabbage had registered as self-employed. 'If the message about sex work wasn't so conflicted, I might have sought professional advice earlier. But having previously been cautioned in relation to activities connected with my earnings, I never dreamed that my business would be described as 'legitimate'. I struggle with the concept that one aspect of my work is considered legitimate and another is illegal. It is difficult to reconcile the hypocrisy that the taxman is happy to receive a share of my earnings, but I am not allowed to advertise.'

Brabbage was sentenced to 8 months in May last year after admitting one count of cheating the public revenue. She denied five counts of money laundering. During that time, she wrote her autobiography, extracts of which have already been published.

She was heavily criticised by prosecutor, Robert Hunter for selling her story to the highest bidder. In her defence she said, 'I have a daughter, a family. Obviously for their sakes, I would have preferred that my private life remained my own. But since my accounts were frozen at the start of the investigation,

I was left with no option.' Prosecutor Robert Hunter instructed the jury not to be swayed by a wave of public sympathy. 'The defence will paint a picture of Brabbage as a tragic character, a victim, possibly even a feminist. But the truth is, between 2001 and 2007, she cheated the taxman out of £120,000.'

Asked to comment, she remained defiant, saying: 'I was brought up to work. I have never cost the taxpayer a penny in benefits. I wonder how much money another single mother in my position might have claimed over the same period. Does anyone know?'

This led to her supporters, who have kept a silent vigil outside the courts, displaying placards demanding that the amount owed be offset by the benefits that Brabbage would have received. A spokesperson for the group, which mainly consists of women, said, 'They cannot say on the one hand that she has swindled the taxman when in fact she has saved the taxpayer money.' Prior to this shift in direction, the group's focus has been to highlight the plight of children when single parents receive custodial sentences. Now, their placards pose the question: 'Who has cost the taxpayer more money: Sir Fred Goodwin or Alison Brabbage?'

Father of three, Simons, admitted embezzlement and six counts of money laundering involving an amount in excess of £3m. At a separate hearing in March 2009, the court heard how his scam had been picked up from irregular accounting transactions detected during a routine audit. Simons admitted to having discovered a way to relieve the financial pressure he was under. Asked about the nature of that pressure, Andrews said, 'My wife had unrealistic expectations of what a man in my position could earn. We both wanted the kids to be educated privately. I thought we had agreed that we needed to make sacrifices elsewhere, but she racked up huge credit card debts. As fast as I cut them up, she applied for more. To begin with, I was simply trying to clear the credit cards. But when I appeared to get away with it, I became greedy.' He was jailed for five years. A receiver has also been given permission to seize his family home, valued at over £950,000, with a view to paying off the debts he has accumulated. Mrs Simons was unavailable for comment.

ACKNOWLEDGMENTS

As always, a mounting debt of thanks is due to my team of beta readers, especially book blogger Cleo Bannister, Anne Clinton, Amanda Osborne, Sarah Marshall, Mary Fuller, Lynn Pearce, Karen Begg, Sue Darnell, Joe Thorpe, Kath Crowley and Sarah Diss. Special thanks to Helen Enefer, Louise Davis, Louise Voss and Liz Broomfield (www.libroediting.com) for editorial advice and assistance, and to my proofreader, 'Happy' Harry Matthews. IT guru, Jack Naisbett, has responded to my cries for help on many occasions. Payment will be made with coffee and cake.

Research took me in many directions. The wealth of information available on the Internet makes armchair experts of us all. Many of the personal accounts of the lives of prostitutes that I found there were brave, heartfelt and anonymous. Particularly helpful when searching for the mind-set of a ballerina was Meredith Daneman's candid biography of Margot Fonteyn. So, too, were accounts from ballerinas who have been forced into early retirement.

Grateful thanks to The English Collective of Prostitutes for granting permission for use of their name and for providing a quote for the newspaper article.

The Tale of Custard the Dragon is a poem by Ogden Nash.

ABOUT THE AUTHOR

Jane Davis is the author of six novels. Her debut, Half-truths and White Lies, won the Daily Mail First Novel Award and was described by Joanne Harris as 'A story of secrets, lies, grief and, ultimately, redemption, charmingly handled by this very promising new writer.' She was hailed by The Bookseller as 'One to Watch.' Of the following three novels she published, Compulsion Reads wrote, 'Davis is a phenomenal writer, whose ability to create well rounded characters that are easy to relate to feels effortless.' Jane's favourite description of fiction is that it is 'made-up truth.'

She lives in Carshalton, Surrey with her Formula 1 obsessed, star-gazing, beer-brewing partner, surrounded by growing piles of paperbacks, CDs and general chaos.

For further information, or to sign up for pre-launch specials and notifications about future projects, visit the author's website at www.jane-davis.co.uk.

A personal request from Jane: "Your opinion really matters to authors and to readers who are wondering which book to pick next. If you love a book, please tell your friends and post a review. Facebook, Amazon, Smashwords and Goodreads are all great places to start."

OTHER TITLES BY THE AUTHOR

Half-truths & White Lies

I Stopped Time

These Fragile Things

A Funeral for an Owl

An Unknown Woman